SURVIVAL

Over his small fire, sheltered by rocks and trees so that no glimmer escaped, he muttered the songs of his people, red and white, pausing only from time to time to listen.

The wind moaned in the stone pine thickets, rustling the leaves of the aspen just below. Old ghosts walked the night, peering as he did into the small dancing flame. The fire was scarcely enough to warm him, yet the flickering flames spoke to him in the poetry of his people.

Somewhere out in the darkness something moved, something other than the wind, something huge and ominous. "Old Bear," Joe Mack spoke aloud, "go back from where you came. I want your meat, your hide, and your fat, but not tonight.

"Go back, Old Bear, and tell your cubs that tonight you saw a Sioux warrior and he let you live because he had killed enough for the day."

"This book can't miss." —*Chicago Sun-Times*

"Sweeping adventure." —*Publishers Weekly*

A "large, robust novel."
—*The New York Times Book Review*

LOUIS L'AMOUR'S

LAST OF THE BREED

LAST OF THE BREED

Louis L'Amour

BANTAM BOOKS
TORONTO • NEW YORK • LONDON • SYDNEY • AUCKLAND

*This low-priced Bantam Book
has been completely reset in a type face
designed for easy reading, and was printed
from new plates. It contains the complete
text of the original hard-cover edition.*
NOT ONE WORD HAS BEEN OMITTED.

LAST OF THE BREED
A Bantam Book

*Bantam hardcover edition / July 1986
4 printings through September 1986
Bantam paperback edition / July 1987*

Maps by Alan McKnight

ISBN 0-553-26499-0

Published simultaneously in the United States and Canada

---

*Bantam Books are published by Bantam Books, Inc. Its
trademark, consisting of the words "Bantam Books" and the
portrayal of a rooster, is Registered in U.S. Patent and Trademark Office and in other countries. Marca Registrada. Bantam
Books, Inc., 666 Fifth Avenue, New York, New York 10103.*

PRINTED IN THE UNITED STATES OF AMERICA

O   0 9 8 7 6 5 4 3 2 1

**TO JOHN AND
CAROL LEE VEITCH**
Old Friends, Good Friends,
The Best Friends

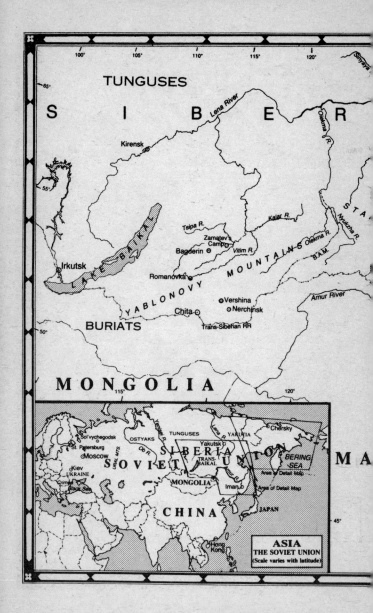

CENTRAL SIBERIA
--- Railways -------- Roadways
Scale of miles
0 25 50 75 100   150   200

CHUKCHI SEA

170° 175° 180° 175° 170°

Ust'-Chaun

ANADYR MOUNTAINS

CHUKCHIS

ALASKA

BERING STRAIT

65°

Arctic Circle

Anadyr R.

St. Lawrence I.

Penzhina R.

Main R.

U.S.S.R.
U.S.A.

KORIAKS

KORYAK MOUNTAINS

BERING

SEA

60°

55°

EASTERN SIBERIA

Railways   Roadways
Scale of miles
0 25 50 75 100   150   200

165° 170° 175°

Alan McKnight

The soldier placed the flat, skin-wrapped package on the table before Colonel Zamatev and stepped back, standing rigidly at attention. Before diverting his attention to the package, Zamatev studied the soldier.

Hunger, cold, and the exhaustion of long trails had sapped the man's strength and drained him of feeling. Gaunt and hollow eyed he awaited orders.

"You saw nothing of Alekhin?"

"Nothing, sir."

"And the American? You saw him? He spoke to you?"

"We were told to kill him. To shoot on sight. I glimpsed him through the trees and started forward. To kill him was my duty. He moved again and I saw an opening between two trees. I rushed forward."

"And then?"

"It was a trap. There was a rope of branches between the two trees, hidden by undergrowth. I tripped and fell." The soldier put a hand to his forehead where the remains of the bruise could still be seen. "My head hit very hard. When I awakened he was standing over me."

"He was armed?"

"He had my rifle, my knife. The muzzle of the rifle was at my throat. He looked at me for a long time and then he said, 'You are young to die. Lie there while you count to one

1

hundred. Then get up and take this package to Colonel Zamatev. To Zamatev and to no one else, you understand? No one else! Tell him to open it when he is alone.' "

"Nothing else?"

"Nothing."

"You counted?"

"There was nothing to be done. He had taken my rifle. He was gone."

Colonel Zamatev studied him with eyes that seemed to offer no mercy. "Nothing else? Nothing at all?"

The soldier's eyes were haunted. Hopelessly he glanced right and left.

"He said—"

"He said what?" Zamatev leaned forward. "He was heard to speak again. You were heard to reply. What was said?"

Miserably, the young soldier swallowed. Sweat stood out on his brow. "He—he said, 'You are two days from your unit. You will try to get there, but you cannot make it in less than two days, do you hear? If you reach your unit in less than two days I shall find and kill you.' "

"You believed him?"

"He is a devil! A fiend! I was afraid."

"How long did it take you to reach your unit?"

The soldier was utterly without hope. "Almost—almost two days."

Zamatev glanced at his aide Suvarov. "The Yakut who heard him speak? How far was he from your unit?"

"Less than a half day's travel, Colonel Zamatev."

Zamatev looked at the soldier. "Take him away, Lieutenant, and I do not wish to see him again."

When the soldier had been taken from the room a long silence followed. Lieutenant Suvarov waited, his heart beating heavily. Would Zamatev hold him responsible?

He backed up a step, wishing he dared sit down. The Colonel had walked to the window and was looking out at the compound. He was a big man, slightly stooped, wearing a simple uniform coat. It was a coat, Suvarov knew, that could have been covered with decorations, only Zamatev chose not to wear them.

Zamatev was like this room, a man who needed only the bare essentials. The room had only the table, a swivel chair behind it, two shelves, a wastebasket, a chair that faced the *desk, and a bench along the wall. Suvarov had been in the offices of other men of Zamatev's rank and they were never like this.*

Zamatev turned around. "So? He has eluded us again."

"Alekhin will find him," Suvarov said. "Alekhin will never stop until the American is dead. Alekhin never gives up, and this is a personal thing with him. He will never stop."

Zamatev looked around at him. "You may go, Lieutenant. I shall want to see you in the morning."

"In the morning, sir? But I just—"

Zamatev's eyes were icy. "In the morning, Suvarov."

When the Lieutenant had gone he walked around his table and sat down, staring at the skin-wrapped packet before him. It was the tanned hide of a small animal, of very little weight and tied with rawhide thongs. Something was inside. Something of light weight but stiff. A bit of bark, perhaps?

The sender of the packet could not have seen paper or string for many months, and the packet was just one more item in a pursuit that had seemed time and again to be nearing its end, only to have the American evade them once again.

Were there other Americans such as this one? Or was he one of a kind? For the first time in many months Colonel Arkady Arkadovich Zamatev was beginning to doubt the wisdom of his superiors.

He took up the packet and slowly, with careful fingers, he began to undo the knots, ignoring the knife that lay at hand.

ONE

Major Joe Makatozi stepped into the sunlight of a late afternoon. The first thing he must remember was the length of the days at this latitude. His eyes moved left and right.

About three hundred yards long, a hundred yards wide, three guard towers to a side, two men in each. A mounted machine gun in each tower. Each man armed with a submachine gun.

He walked behind Lieutenant Suvarov, and two armed guards followed him.

Five barracklike frame buildings, another under construction, prisoners in four of the five buildings but not all the cells occupied.

He had no illusions. He was a prisoner, and when they had extracted the information they knew he possessed, he would be killed. There was a cool freshness in the air like that from the sea, but he was far from any ocean. His first impression was, he believed, the right one. He was somewhere in the vicinity of Lake Baikal, in Siberia.

A white line six feet inside the barbed wire, the limit of approach for prisoners. The fence itself was ten feet high, twenty strands of tightly drawn, electrified wire. From the barbed wire to the edge of the forest, perhaps fifty yards.

4

No one knew he was alive but his captors. There would be no inquiries, no diplomatic feelers. Whatever happened now must be of his own doing. He had one asset. They had no idea what manner of man they had taken prisoner.

The office into which he was shown was much like a military orderly room. The man behind the table was tall and wide in the shoulder. He studied Joe Makatozi with appraising eyes.

For the first time Colonel Arkady Zamatev was seeing a man who had been the center of his thinking for more than a year. Up to this point his personally conceived plan had worked with a fine precision of which he could be proud.

When he had first proposed the capture of Major Makatozi his superiors thought he had lost his mind. Yet information was desperately needed on some of the experimental aircraft the Americans were designing, and Makatozi had test-flown most of them. Moreover, he had advised on the construction of some, had suggested innovations.

Only Zamatev knew there were three Soviet agents in the American division of military personnel assignment, no one of them aware of the others. All were Americans at whom no suspicion had been directed. The three had been carefully maneuvered into position for just such an emergency, and it was upon these three that he depended for the assignment of Major Makatozi to the Alaska command for a refresher course in Arctic flying before tests were made with a new aircraft.

It had not been difficult to arrange. A casual remark had been made about operating the new plane in sub-Arctic temperatures; a few days later the question of a refresher course had been raised, if Major Makatozi were to pilot the new plane. And the rest had been up to Zamatev.

The provision for the secret prison camp had been made four years before. The necessity for understanding the extent and ramifications of advances in American and British military and naval technology had given birth to the plan. The intelligence services of the combined armed forces had completed the arrangements.

The idea was simple enough. Locate and seize certain key personnel, bring them to this camp, a place known to only the most powerful figures in the Politburo, secure what information their prisoners had, and then get rid of them. The disappearances would be few, isolated, and seemingly unrelated. The possibility of suspicion being aroused was almost nonexistent.

Operations had begun two years before with the seizure of a warrant officer, a very minor figure who, in the normal progress of his duties, had come into possession of some key information. That had been a modest success. Then the chemist Pennington . . .

When Colonel Zamatev looked into the eyes of his newest prisoner he was angered. The blue-gray eyes were oddly disconcerting in the dark, strongly boned face, yet it was the prisoner's cool arrogance that aroused his ire. He was unaccustomed to find such arrogance in prisoners brought to him for interrogation. It was not arrogance alone, but a kind of bored contempt that irritated Zamatev.

Colonel Zamatev had a dossier before him that he believed told him all he needed to know about the man before him.

A university graduate, an athlete who had competed in various international tournaments, a decathlon star of almost Olympic caliber. He had scored Expert with a dozen weapons while in the Air Force and was reputed to be skilled in the martial arts. This was straightforward enough, and there were many other officers in the Army, Navy, and Air Force whose dossiers were little different, give or take a few skills.

As much as Zamatev knew about the American flyer, there was an essential fact he did not know. Beneath the veneer of education, culture, and training lay an unreconstructed savage.

When prisoners were brought before Colonel Zamatev they were frightened or wary. They had all heard the stories of brainwashings and torture, yet there was in this man no evidence of fear or of doubt in himself. Zamatev was irritated by a faint, uneasy feeling.

"You are Major Joseph Makatozi? Is that an American name?"

"If it is not there are no American names. I am an Indian, part Sioux, part Cheyenne."

"Ah? Then you are one of those from whom your country was taken?"

"As we had taken it from others."

"But they defeated you. You were beaten."

"We won the last battle." Joe Makatozi put into his tone a studied insolence. "As we always shall."

"You would defend a country that was taken from you?"

"It was our country then; it is our country now. Our battle records, in every war the United States has fought, have been surpassed by none."

Zamatev's irritation mounted. He prided himself on an unemotional detachment, and his manner of interrogation was based upon a casual, seemingly friendly attitude that disarmed the prisoner, who, before he realized it, was trying to reciprocate. The American's arrogance was making this approach difficult.

Zamatev also had an uneasy feeling that within seconds after entering the room Makatozi had assessed all it contained, including himself.

Zamatev had based much of his planning for the preliminary interrogation on the fact that Makatozi was of a badly treated minority.

In an effort to turn the interrogation into preferred channels, Zamatev indicated a thick-set, powerful man sitting quietly on the bench watching Makatozi through heavy-lidded eyes.

"As an American Indian you should be interested in meeting Alekhin. He is a Yakut, a Siberian counterpart of the American Indian. The Yakuts have a reputation in the Soviet. We call them the iron men of the north. They are among our greatest hunters and trackers."

Zamatev returned his gaze to the American. "It is the pride of Alekhin that no prisoner has ever escaped him."

Joe Mack, as he had been called since his days of athletic competition, glanced at the Siberian, and the Yakut stared back at him from flat, dull eyes of black. A small blaze of white where the hair had lost color over an old scar was his most distinguishing characteristic. He exuded the power of a gorilla and had the wrinkled, seamed face of a tired monkey until one looked a second time and recognized the lines for what they were, lines of cruelty and ruthlessness. Nor, despite his weathered features, was he much older than Joe Mack himself.

With deliberate contempt Joe Makatozi replied, "I don't believe he could track a muddy dog across a dry floor!"

Alekhin came off the bench, a single swift, fluid movement, feet apart, hands ready. Joe Mack turned easily, almost contemptuously, to meet him.

For an instant Zamatev had a queer feeling that a page of history had rolled back. Suddenly, in his small, bare office, two savages faced each other, each a paragon of his kind. A thrill of excitement went through him, and for a moment he was tempted to let them fight.

Zamatev's voice was a whip. "Alekhin! Sit down!"

His eyes went to Joe Mack. "Understand your position, Major. You are our prisoner. You are believed to be dead. So far as your country is concerned, you and your plane were lost at sea. No inquiries have been made, nor are any likely to be made.

"If you are to live it will be because I wish it, and your future, if any, depends on your replies to my questions. I will accept only complete cooperation, including a complete account of your operations as pilot of several varieties of experimental aircraft.

"You are an intelligent man, and I shall allow you twenty-four hours in which to consider your position. If you are reasonable you may find a place of honor among us. You will be permitted to retain your rank and the privileges pertaining to it. You can serve us, or you can die."

"When was a traitor honored anywhere, even among those who profit from his betrayal? You waste your time, Colonel Zamatev."

The Russian was startled. "You know me, then?"

"We also have our dossiers, Colonel."

Zamatev was shaken by cold fury, but he forced himself to remain calm. "You are married, Major?"

"No."

"Your parents are living?"

"No."

"How old are you?"

"Thirty-one."

Colonel Zamatev shuffled papers on his desk. "To your country, Major, you are already dead. To us you may yet be useful. A man of your talents can do well here, and you do not appear to be a man who would willingly choose death. At home you have no ties."

"You forget the most important one, Colonel. There is my country."

Zamatev spoke to Suvarov. "Return this man to his quarters, Lieutenant. I shall speak to him again after he has had time to consider his position."

When they had gone Zamatev leaned back in his chair. He prided himself on his detachment, yet there was something about this particular American that irritated him. Perhaps it was the man's total lack of fear, even of uncertainty. Yet was that normal? Was it not natural to fear in such a situation? To be wary? Uncertain? Worried? Major Makatozi showed no signs of apprehension, and at the brief meeting in this office he had seemed completely at ease. What was it about this man?

He was an Indian. What did that mean? Zamatev made a mental note to learn something about Indians. He was part Sioux and part Cheyenne. He made a note of the names. Yet he had blue eyes. Some white blood, too?

He took Makatozi's dossier from his file and glanced through it. The man was a daring flyer, a superb pilot. He had both skill and judgment. He had gone to college on an athletic scholarship, one means of paying an athlete without appearing to do so. They had such situations in Russia as well, but in Russia they played for the country rather than for a college.

The Makatozi Project had been his most daring, and his superiors would expect results. So far they had given him much freedom of action but there were those who wished to take over the entire operation. Success was imperative in both the Pennington and the Makatozi operations, and his plans had been carefully laid. His earlier ventures, in which he had been tentative, testing, feeling his way, had been uniformly successful. Pennington, his first venture into deeper waters, had not been a well-known man. Indeed, few outside of a limited circle had any idea what he was doing. Something in chemistry, they believed. He had always had a bent in that direction. Only three men in England knew that one of his projects had achieved a startling breakthrough, and that one aspect of the breakthrough could revolutionize chemical warfare.

Only three men in England, but one of them had a talkative wife. "Something very hush-hush," she said, "so the Admiral won't be coming." And the Admiral *always* came, so it was something very important, indeed. The Baroness, who had a way of life to maintain, commented, "Surely he will be here for the Finals?"

"Not likely," the talkative woman replied. "He's gone off to some place outside Glasgow. Oh, he'll miss it! He'll miss it frightfully!"

A few hours later the Baroness was on the telephone. "Yes, *the* Admiral." A pause. "Nothing but the Second Coming would keep him away."

The man on the other end of the line knew enough about the Admiral to know she was right. And the Admiral was a top authority in chemical warfare. Outside Glasgow was a small chemical plant engaged in insecticide research, a plant with no military significance.

Within the hour The Man On The Other End was on a train for Glasgow, and the morning after he arrived he knew where the Admiral was staying and was himself having a drink in a pub near the chemical plant, a pub where workers at the plant dropped in for an evening libation before going home.

"Lots of bustle," he heard a man say, "like somebody kicked over a hive of bees."

"It's the new contract," another was saying, "the one with Commonwealth. Keep us busy for months, they say."

"Who was the white-haired gent? The way they was treatin' him he must *own* Commonwealth."

"Nah," the first man replied, " 'e was in to see Pennington. Not likely Pennington would have aught to do with Commonwealth. 'E's pure research."

"There was two others come in, too. Nobody I've seen around before, an' it's Parkins 'o handles Commonwealth."

The Man On The Other End needed little more, although he finished his bitter and ordered another. The white-haired man would be the Admiral. He and two others had come to see this man Pennington, in "pure research."

That was how it began, and the Baroness received a neat packet of bank notes, dropped in her mailbox in a candy box: something to help her maintain her position, as it might be put. It helped to have a listening post where the mighty gathered, and it was so expensive to live, these days.

He was in the pub at the inn where the Admiral had put up when the Admiral came in. Two men were with him, and The Man On The Other End recognized one of them—another bigwig in chemical warfare. So it was something. Trust the Baroness. Her intuition was good.

Three weeks later, Pennington disappeared.

TWO

Inside the prison barracks a row of eight cell doors faced a blank wall. In the door of each cell was a window four inches square crossed by two upright bars. The window remained open at all times.

Inside each cell there was a narrow cot, a small table, a chair, and toilet facilities. Another type of cell awaited him, no doubt, if he failed to cooperate.

The walls were of logs, squared and perfectly fitted. The lock on the outer door was a simple one. Those on the cells were only slightly more complicated. Obviously they depended on the electrified barbed wire and the guard towers. Also, beyond the wire lay the enormous length and breadth of a friendless land.

He had never lived on a reservation. His one white grandparent had left considerable property to the Makatozi family in the Snake River country of Idaho, most of it high country in the mountains, a land of rushing rivers, of small meadows and forest. Most of the land lay far from any highway, completely cut off in winter, isolated even in summer. It was land nobody wanted, a land without visitors. Occasionally, trappers had come through the land, but had been warned off. A friendly prospector had assured Joe's family that there was both gold and silver on the land, but was ignored. Lumber interests had offered modest prices that were refused, and they did not persist. Access was too difficult, building roads too expensive, and Joe Makatozi's father had been just as pleased. He loved the lonely mountains, loved the isolation. Yet when Joe became five his father took him away to send him to school.

There had always been books in the house. The white grandparent had been a Scotsman of good family, and he had had several hundred books packed into his lonely hideout. Later, when a Hudson's Bay post was being abandoned he had appropriated its extensive library. He had taught his family to read, and he was continually reading aloud himself. It became a way of life for them all, and Joe had grown up on stories of his Indian ancestors and those of the Scottish Highlands as well.

The old man had died after a fall at the age of one hundred and one. During his last year on earth he had taught young Joe to read and had read to him from Scott's *Tales of a Grandfather*, as well as many of the Waverly novels.

Joe's thoughts returned to his present situation. The approximate position of his prison he could guess, but its exact position he did not know. He was, he was sure, in the vicinity of Lake Baikal, and to the north, east, and south stretched forest, swamp, and tundra. He knew nothing of the lands to the west.

The taiga, as it was called, was one of the finest stands of timber on earth, hundreds of miles wide and just as long. Or so he had heard.

From the moment of his capture his one thought had been to escape, and to escape at the earliest possible moment.

Lying on his back on the cot, he considered the possibilities. He must expect to be fired upon. He might be hit. Once beyond the wire he could cover the distance to the woods in five or six seconds. With guns behind him to lend impetus he might do even better. If the attention of the guards could be diverted he might be under fire for no more than three seconds.

He might be killed, he might be severely wounded, but

those were things he could not consider now. If either of these things happened he would be either buried or a helpless prisoner. All his attention must be devoted to escape.

All right, then. Suppose he got into the trees? He must run as he had never run before. He must put so much distance between himself and the compound that efforts to recapture him would be well behind him.

If he could run farther, faster than they expected that just might happen. So his first efforts must be for distance and then to mislead his pursuers concerning the direction he was taking.

The nearest border was with Mongolia, and beyond that, China. Of Mongolia he knew virtually nothing except that it was somehow affiliated with the Soviets. He also believed it to be a land of rolling hills, grassland, and desert, and its border with China would be patrolled with great care. It was that border, the nearest one, which he would be expected to attempt.

To the north lay the Arctic, to the east and northeast a vast stretch of taiga, tundra, and extremes of weather. Beyond it was the Bering Sea and Alaska. If the anthropologists were correct, his own people had once followed that migration route, pursuing the game that led them across the then-existing land bridge to America. If they had done it, he could do it.

At night the compound would be a glare of light, but suppose the lights could be shorted out? Undoubtedly there was a backup system. But might there not be a time lapse?

If he remained where he was they would find means to break him and extract the information they wanted, as one would remove the meat from a cracked nut.

He was not afraid of pain. He had endured pain and could do so again.

Morning came and with it a crust of black bread and some thin gruel. He was informed there would be a fifteen-minute exercise period in which he must keep walking. If he stopped he would be shot. No prisoner was to approach to within six feet of the wire. A white line was drawn on the ground so there would be no mistake. There was no restriction on speech, but they must keep moving.

He had taken no more than a dozen steps when a man
fell in beside him, a slender man with a thin face and gray
eyes. "Keep walking," the other prisoner said. "I'm Pennington,
a chemist, from England."

As they reached the corner of a building Pennington
said, "They listen. We have three steps now where they
cannot hear, but only three steps."

As they passed beyond the corner Pennington said, "Sleep
well?"

"Well enough."

"This time of year the days are long."

He made no reply. Then the Englishman asked, "What
do they call you?"

"Joe Mack. Officially, Major Joseph Makatozi, United
States Army Air Force."

"You're dark for an American."

"I'm an Indian. Sioux."

"Well, I'll be damned! A Red Indian? I never met one
before."

The man could be a stool pigeon, and this could be a
trap. When they reached the blind corner, Pennington spoke
swiftly. "If you've any idea of escaping, do it now! At once!
The food is lacking in vitamins. Your strength will be de-
pleted and your courage as well."

As they came within range of the listening devices
Pennington said, "If a man cooperates, they say, things get
better. There's more food, more freedom. It's summer now,
but not far from here is the coldest spot on the planet.
Registered ninety-four degrees below zero."

"The coldest I've seen it was fifty below."

"Man! That's cold! Where was it?"

"Montana."

When they reached the corner again, Pennington said,
"There are roads encircling the compound, and they are
patrolled. One is two hundred yards out, the next is a mile,
and then two miles."

There were five buildings, with another beginning construction. The new building was to be of frame construction.
The planks and timbers were laid out ready for work, along
with slender pipes for water, kegs of nails, and what looked
like sacks of cement.

"If I can help . . . ?" Pennington suggested.

It was a crazy idea, yet what choice did he have? And crazy ideas had a way of succeeding, because they were unexpected.

He might be a fool, but he decided to trust the Englishman; yet he could not take him along. There was no way it could be done.

They were in the blind spot for the last time on that walk. "I could use help. I need a few minutes of darkness. Can you get out of your cell?"

Back on the cot again he turned it over in his mind. The situation that existed might never occur again. Somebody had not been thinking. Somebody had been careless. The connection for the new building might have no tie-in with the compound lights, yet it was there, on the end of the nearest building.

After he was free he would need weapons, food, and clothing.

He slept, he ate the food, he waited. Distance first, then a place to hide, then more distance. Manchuria was a part of China and it was fairly close. He would start toward it.

When the exercise period came, he was ready. "No one knows of this place," Pennington told him. "They do not know, but I understand some Russian. I have heard them speaking. If you make it, tell them where I am. Try to get me out." He paused. "It will take strength and endurance I do not have."

Zamatev, or whoever supervised the construction, depended too much on the camp's isolation, the barbed wire, and the guards.

There were three other prisoners, but they kept to themselves. One was a West German, Pennington said. Or so the man told him. Pennington, suspicious, had avoided him after the man had asked too many questions. "I do not believe he is German," Pennington said.

The others were a Swedish naval officer and a French diplomat, a very minor one apparently, who happened to have some information that was anything but minor.

"There was another," Pennington said, and pointed. "They buried him over there."

Joe Mack was not surprised. Whatever else Zamatev might be, he was efficient, and he was no time waster. He would get what he wanted or he would be rid of anyone who did not cooperate. The man was cool and tough, and he knew his business.

Pennington talked quite freely while they were being observed and listened to. His home had been in Weymouth before he was transferred to Scotland. He had a brother, two sisters, and a wife.

"No children?"

"One was on the way. Should be three months old by now." He glanced around at Joe Mack. "I've been here nearly six months."

"So long?"

"They are patient with me. You see, Yakutia is booming now. They need scientists in every field. I had been working in insecticides, and all of eastern Siberia is beset with vicious flies and mosquitoes. They've been trying, but there is much to be done." He paused again. "They've even offered to bring over my wife and child."

They walked in silence, and then Joe Mack said, "It may take time."

Pennington nodded. "You're my one chance."

"Nobody likes those flies," Joe Mack said. "I've had experience with their like while hunting."

"It will be bitter cold. Think of that."

"I have."

"The nights here are short. In summer there is no night if you go above the Arctic Circle."

When they were around the corner Joe Mack said, "Tonight, then?"

"Tonight."

The time was settled, and they walked on into the clear and back to their cells. Tonight, and God help them both!

There were no preparations to make. There was simply nothing to be done.

The light flashed in his face as the guard checked his presence from the small window.

Less than two hours of darkness would remain. He tightened his shoelaces, went over in his mind the position of the pipe.

He could hear the footsteps of the guard, heard him pause at a cell door and then another. His would be next. He huddled under his blanket.

Light flashed into his cell. The guard passed. Joe Mack swung his feet to the floor.

THREE

The prison did not rely upon locks. Anyone seen in the compound would be shot. It was as simple as that. Only during the exercise periods or when being moved by the guards themselves was movement permitted.

In the Idaho mountains where he had grown up, and where he had returned many times, all repairs were made by the family. There was no telephone to call a repairman. You simply did it yourself. The locks were simple, and Joe Mack had known what to do the minute he saw them.

One minute after his feet touched the floor his cell door was open. He took six steps to the outer door on cat feet, then waited, listening.

Pennington was listening too and now he spoke softly. "Just let my wife know I did not run out on her. Tell her I miss her."

"You can be sure."

You haven't a chance, he told himself. *This thing is crazy! If there had only been time to plan!* He was outside, and something moved behind him. It was Pennington.

Joe Mack flattened against the wall, listening, waiting, judging the time to the slender pipe he wanted. He already knew how many steps he must take and how many to the wire.

The lights went out. There were shouts from the guard

towers, running feet, and he was moving. There was dampness on his face, and for the first time he realized there was fog.

Lightly he ran to the pile of building material, grasped the pipe, lifted it, and ran. Any time now the emergency lights would come on.

A guard tower loomed through the mist. There was a questioning shout. The end of the pipe touched the ground and his body lifted. He had often vaulted over sixteen feet, but that had been with a resilient pole, and when he was dressed lightly.

His body lifted, soared. High, higher . . . he released the pole as his body shot over and down.

For one brief, awful moment he was above the wire and fear flashed through him. If he fell into it . . . !

He landed on the balls of his feet, knees slightly bent. He fell forward, his fingers touched the ground, and then he was running. As his pole hit the ground there was a burst of fire, and then the lights flashed on. The edge of the forest was just feet away.

Wet branches slapped his face, tore at his clothing. He pivoted away, saw a dip in the ground, and ran down a small declivity as bullets tore the leaves above his head. In his track days he had done the mile in four minutes and fifteen seconds. Not good enough to put him up where the winners were, but how fast could he do a mile now over strange ground and through brush and trees?

When he had covered what he believed was a half mile he slowed to a fast walk. Distance was essential, but he must conserve his energy, also. He walked a hundred fast steps, then ran again.

A road, scarcely more than a dim trail. He looked, then crossed swiftly, and ran through a small water course. His lungs sucked at the fresh, tangy air. He could smell the pines.

It would take them five minutes to discover that he had escaped. They would find the pipe, but would they guess at once that he had pole-vaulted over the wire? Say another five minutes to get a search organized and moving. In the night and fog they would be handicapped in following his trail and would trust to a hurried search and patrols on all existing roads.

Through a momentary rift in the fog he glimpsed the stars. He was not far off the route he intended to follow.

Off to his right he heard the roar of a stream. He felt his way to the bottom of a small gorge where he stepped into the water and walked upstream. Several times he paused to listen, but the rush of the water drowned all other sounds.

Coming up to a stone shelf, he left the water without leaving a trace. He stepped from that rocky ledge to another, leaving no tracks. He swung from one low-hanging limb to another, then came upon a path where he ran, following it for some fifty yards. He crossed another road, dipped into the forest, and ran through the trees. Behind him he heard the roar of a motor.

A car was passing along the road he had just crossed. He stood, not moving, until it had raced away.

Before and around him was the taiga, the Siberian forest. One of the guards had mentioned Malovsky, obviously a village or town, but one of which he knew nothing. He knew the prison was in an area of the Trans-Baikal, in Siberia, and he had read enough to know that the region was changing. An almost unbroken wilderness not too many years ago, the Russians had discovered that the area was a treasure house of mineral wealth. Consequently, new roads were being built and lumbering and mining were increasing; at any time, he might come upon such operations. He must move with caution.

The prison compound had been in a basin some six or seven miles across, and except for the area around the prison, it was thickly forested. His escape had been to the west, but he had swung around to the east and was now climbing into a rocky, mountainous area scattered with pine forest. He kept under cover, for it was growing light and searchers would be sweeping the country around with binoculars. Keeping to a slope, he found his way to a small stream that ran down from the mountains toward the east.

He saw no signs of life—no wood cutting, no mining. Walking on rocks, he left few tracks, although at this stage he doubted if they would be looking for them. At first there would simply be a wide, sweeping search, and not until they failed to find him would they begin looking for tracks or a trail.

He no longer ran, but walked as steadily as the terrain would permit. The stream turned north and he followed it.

From a slight elevation he glimpsed a river into which this emptied. It offered the easiest way, but one that would grow increasingly dangerous, as rivers were likely to be used or lived along. He took the chance and followed the stream down. The river ran east and west, and when he reached it he found the flow was toward the east.

The banks were heavily forested, and at one point he discovered a large drift log with many branches clinging to it that had hung up in the sand on a small point. He squatted among the branches, got onto the log, and pushed off, crouching low and hoping not to be seen.

Several times he saw deer, and once he glimpsed a brown bear. The animal looked toward him incuriously; then seeming to catch his scent it lumbered off into the trees. It was a large bear, fully as big as some grizzlies he had seen.

The sun was high and the sky cloudless. With a broken branch still retaining some foliage, he tried steering the drift log, moving in toward the shore.

He judged the drift to have been about two miles an hour, and when he finally edged the tree to shore at least eight hours had passed. He beached the tree with several of its kind and staggered ashore, his legs stiff from holding virtually a single position. He was hungry, but he had been hungry before. Working his way back into the woods he made a bed in the moss and leaves and lay down to sleep.

Hours later he awakened, drank from a nearby stream, and sat down again to study his situation.

He did not know where he was except in a very general sense. He was east or northeast of Lake Baikal, possibly in an area known as Yakutia, which was now undergoing rapid development. Hence he might come upon people at any time. These he must avoid.

He must travel with extreme care not to be seen or to leave any vestige behind that might arouse the curiosity of dwellers in the country.

He would need food, warmer clothing, a weapon, and if he could find it, a blanket. Somewhere, somehow, he must learn his location. At present what he needed was distance. Travel on the river had been slow and very risky, but also it meant no trail was left behind. Following the river was an easy way, but one that would grow ever more perilous.

Food could wait. At times he had gone several days without eating, and he could do so again.

Among the fallen timber and broken limbs he found a staff that suited his purpose. It would help in walking and would be a weapon if he needed it. And he knew how to fight with a stick.

He started walking, moving away from the river. He had gone but a few hundred yards when he came upon a trail, evidently a game trail but perhaps used by hunters as well. He walked along at a steady pace, ears alert for any sound, eyes constantly seeking, searching.

Long ago he had attended a lecture given by an Army Intelligence officer on Siberia and its terrain. His memory was geared to such things, and he tried now to recall what had been said and what had been pointed out on the blown-up map. There were low mountains, much swamp, and an involved river system. Despite the cold, much of the country in the Trans-Baikal received little snowfall.

Lake Baikal he remembered well, as it is one of the most interesting bodies of water on the planet. Some four hundred miles long, in places more than fifty miles wide, and over five thousand feet deep, it holds a large part of the fresh water on earth. Visited often by Russian tourists, it was also a haven for the Japanese who were playing a major role in the development of Siberian industry. The Japanese were relying on the Trans-Baikal for much of their raw material.

Since his capture he had been trying to reconstruct mentally that map he had seen and to recall what he had heard. Fortunately he had always liked to read, and the books his grandfather had brought from the Hudson's Bay post had included many on Canada, the Bering Strait, and the coasts opposite.

Four of the largest rivers on earth flowed out of Siberia. If he was where he believed, the nearest river was the Lena, and the Amur would be off to the south, some of it along the Manchurian border.

Several times he paused to listen, but heard nothing but a soft wind blowing through the trees. Occasionally he saw birds. Grouse seemed common and a kind of lark that was unfamiliar to him.

Squatting near a piece of bare earth he tried to redraw from memory the map he had studied. South was the Amur

and north the Lena. He was now east of Lake Baikal and
moving toward the faraway coast, toward the Bering Strait
and the Sea of Okhotsk. Between the Bering Strait and his
present position lay several low ranges of mountains, much
forest, swamp, and tundra lying just below or within the
Arctic Circle.

The Yablonovyi, the Stanovoy, and the Verkhoyansk mountains lay between him and his objective, and some of the
coldest land on earth.

Moving as he must, with great care, and traveling on
foot, there was no way he could escape Siberia before winter.
Nor was there any way in which he could last out the winter.

He had not the clothing, the shelter, or the supply of
food necessary.

At more than fifty below, rubber tires crack and metal
becomes fragile. If a car survives two to three years the
owner is fortunate.

And winter was coming, with temperatures that would
hover between fifty and eighty degrees below zero.

He stood up and with his boot he rubbed out his crude
map. He started on, and just over the mountains the cold
awaited.

Icy, bitter, deathly cold . . .

FOUR

Colonel Zamatev was sitting behind his table when Pennington entered the room. On the bench at one side sat Lieutenant Suvarov and the Yakut, Alekhin. There was a chair placed near the table that faced all three.

Zamatev gestured to the chair. "Sit down, please." The Colonel had been an attaché in both London and Paris. He spoke English and French with equal fluency.

Pennington seated himself warily. What lay before him he did not know. Did they know he had helped the American?

"Major Makatozi has escaped, and you talked with him."

"A few words during the exercise period."

"Nevertheless, you did speak. Did he tell you he planned to escape?"

"Would it be likely? He would not have trusted someone he did not know. He is an Indian. I do not believe they talk very much. Not, at least, to a strange white man."

Makatozi was gone, and what harm could speaking do now? "As a matter of fact," he added, "he did say something about leaving. I believe he disliked the accommodations." Pennington smiled. "Even Indians expect better."

Zamatev ignored the comment. He seemed disposed to be affable. What he wanted was information. Pennington considered that while he waited for the next question. He knew of nothing he could say that would affect the American's chances, and he wished to apply the needle.

"Anything you can tell us might help him," Zamatev suggested. "I am sure the Major had no idea what he was escaping to. You see, we had plans for the Major as we do for you. Both of you can be employed here, can live in comfort and security and have a better life than in your own countries.

"Escape from Siberia is impossible! Soon it will be winter. Without clothing, food, and shelter a man cannot exist.

"If he is unfortunate enough to elude pursuit, the land will kill him. I have seen men frozen, but we rarely find them before the wild animals have been at them. If you could help us—?"

Pennington had no intention of helping, nor did he know anything of the American, who had made no mention of his plans once he was over the wire. However, he had once done a paper on the Sioux. At the time he had been wavering between chemistry, his first love, and a developing interest in anthropology.

"Major Makatozi," he commented, "is a Sioux. They were a warrior people, noted for their courage and their ability to bear great pain without flinching. A Sioux warrior was conditioned to endure long periods of hunger and exposure. It was their belief that it was better to die in battle than to live to an old age."

Pennington smiled again. "You have chosen a formidable antagonist, Colonel Zamatev."

"I had hoped you would help us, and him." Zamatev was curt. "If you can, you are a fool not to do so. We have use for him; otherwise we would just let him go. Siberia would provide its own solution."

He stood erect. "Lieutenant! Take the prisoner to his cell." Then he added, "I do not believe Mr. Pennington has much of an appetite. Two days without food may enable him to understand the Major's situation."

When Pennington had gone, Zamatev seated himself. He had expected no more than he had gotten, but there was always a chance that Makatozi had dropped a hint or even confided in Pennington.

Zamatev's position had been secure. He was a known man of known abilities. That he had been permitted this project was evidence of it. Zamatev was also an ambitious man, although his ambitions were carefully hidden. He was a good Party man as well as an efficient officer, and so far he had made no mistakes. He had begun this particular task with a few small successes, and now, suddenly, he was caught in a situation that could ruin his career.

Zamatev dismissed Alekhin and leaned back in his chair. He needed to think.

The American had pole-vaulted over the wire. There was no other explanation, but who could have dreamt of such an act? There had been a blackout, which needed no investigation. How the momentary shorting of the lights had been accomplished was obvious enough. Carelessness, pure carelessness!

The American had escaped. A thorough search of the area had turned up nothing. The search had been mounted within four minutes, yet the American had vanished.

Had he gotten help from outside the prison? No one knew he was a prisoner and no such arrangements could have been made in the time available.

The usual quick sweep of the area had been carried out, a search that moved in steadily widening circles. They had seen nothing, found nothing.

The obvious escape route toward China had been covered. Border troops, already on the alert, had been ordered to watch for an escaped prisoner. That border was protected in depth, and the soldiers were prepared for invasion or raids by the Chinese.

To the Trans-Siberian Railway? It was not far away and offered the quickest escape from the country. A man would need a ticket and a passport or a visa. The American would have neither, yet people had used that method of escape, and it could not be dismissed.

Colonel Zamatev had ambitions. He also had enemies who would be quick to discredit him, so he had no wish to broadcast the escape. As the existence of his prison was known to only a handful of officials this was easily arranged, but much depended on the immediate recapture of the American.

For a moment his thoughts turned eastward. Hardly to be considered. It was too far, too rugged, too cold. The American had no weapons, he lacked proper clothing for even this time of year, and he did not know the country. Yet he would alert people to the eastward, too.

That he would recapture Makatozi he had no doubt. Escape was impossible, and summer was more than half gone. If the man was not taken he would surely surrender or die in the intense cold.

Nothing positive had so far resulted from the search. A few tracks had been found in the woods where he had first fled but they gave no indication of anything except an urge to get away. Obviously the man had escaped the immediate search area before the searchers arrived.

Although Colonel Zamatev had himself been born in Siberia, he came of an old Ukrainian family, and his father and grandfather had both been generals. His father had been closely associated with Marshal Vasily Blucher, perhaps the greatest military genius the Soviet Union had produced. But Blucher had become too well known and too popular, and as a result he disappeared in one of the Stalinist purges of the 1930s.

Blucher had served in China under the name of Galin and had helped to train the Nationalist Chinese army at a time when the Nationalist Chinese were inviting help from Russia. Along with Michael Borodin he was thrown out of China, but later, in an undeclared war against the Japanese, he defeated them in one of the greatest tank battles ever fought.

General Zamatev, hoping to stay as far from Stalin's attention as possible, had volunteered to serve in Siberia and remained there. He had, however, kept many old friendships, and not a few of them had aided the rise of Arkady Zamatev.

Colonel Zamatev was under no delusion. He knew peace was an illusory thing, something that hovered on a distant horizon, for which all men wished but which had only a small chance of realization as long as men remained what they were. There was now no declared war between the Soviet Union and anyone else, but there was war nonetheless, a bitter, ruthless war for military and communication advantages, and he was in the front line of that war and planned to remain there.

That he had already been considered for promotion, he knew. If he failed with Pennington and Makatozi, that promotion would never come about, or not for many years. He was thirty-five and hoped to be a field marshal by the time he was fifty. What else remained to be seen.

Pennington might never come over to the Soviets. That whatever he knew about chemical warfare would be his, Zamatev was sure. Pennington could not be forced to join the Soviets, but he could be made to talk. There were drugs that would take care of that, as well as a few time-worn and less gentle methods.

Pennington, however, was of much less importance than the American. Makatozi could not be allowed to escape.

Zamatev reviewed what had been done. The troops along the border had been alerted, as had police officials throughout the Trans-Baikal, especially in Chita, Nerchinsk, and such villages as Romanovka, Bagdarin, Vitimkon, and Vershina.

Airfields had been alerted as well, for the escaped prisoner was a flyer who might attempt to steal a plane.

Now he could do little but await the American's capture.

Zamatev walked outside. It was one of those bright, clear days so common in the Trans-Baikal. He looked eastward toward the mountains, where one peak was almost a mile high. That was rough country, not an easy way to travel, and so far as he was aware no paths crossed those mountains, but he had never explored widely outside the compound. He scowled impatiently, irritably. He should know the country better.

The telephone sounded and he turned quickly. Maybe they had him! Maybe—

It was Shepilov. KGB. "Is it true? There has been an escape?"

"From Siberia? That's a joke."

"But I heard—?"

So, already the word was out! Were there no secrets in this land?

"It is nothing," he said, keeping his tone casual. "A minor difficulty, no more."

Shepilov was in a sense his superior, but in another department. And Shepilov did not like him. He resented Zamatev's friendships in Moscow, his influence in the higher reaches of command.

"If you need help—?"

"Thank you, but we will manage nicely." He hung up

the phone and sat back in his chair. He swore then, softly, bitterly. To have this happen now! Now, when all was going so well!

Who would dream that a man could go *over* the wire?

Tomorrow they would have him, tomorrow without fail.

For a moment he sat thinking, and then he lifted the phone again. He made three calls, mobilizing still stronger searching parties.

The bastard! Where *had* he gotten to? Why was he not already caught?

Tomorrow night there was a meeting he must attend, and surely he would be questioned, if only casually. His activities were little known, and talk about them was not welcomed, but there was a lively curiosity, and some, such as Shepilov, knew a little. Such a search as he had now instituted was sure to excite comment.

Irritably, Zamatev walked to the window, staring out at the low mountains. Despite his ambitions, which if realized would take him to Moscow, Zamatev loved Siberia, although sometimes it worried him that the manners were more casual here, that there was, or seemed to be, less respect. To get the technical people to come out here and stay they had to be accorded privileges as well as much higher pay, and this had brought innovators and thinkers, men and women whose ideas did not always agree with those expressed in Moscow. As yet there had been no trouble, nor did Zamatev believe such people would go too far, yet a bridle must be put upon some of the free thinking.

His thoughts returned to the American. Where could he go? What would he do? He must have food. He would need warmer clothing.

He would steal. But from whom? Some isolated miner, trapper, or scientific station? A theft would draw an immediate report, and then they could concentrate their search.

Zamatev walked back to his table and sat down heavily. *Soon*, they must have him soon. It was impossible for him to remain unseen.

Why did the telephone not ring?

Some fifty miles away, not far from where the Tsipa River flowed into the Kalar, Joe Mack was huddled in a thick grove of mixed Japanese stone pine and larch watching a shack built against a cliff. Two men lived there, and one of them had just started off with an empty backpack. He had taken a path to the south, and from the way he had waved good-bye he had expected to be gone for more than a few hours. He was probably going to town.

The other man watched him go; then, taking some tools, he went into the portal of a mine tunnel.

Joe Mack waited an instant longer, and then using a carefully plotted route he went down the slope, keeping under cover until within fifty feet of the house.

He waited, trying to breathe evenly. He must make the attempt, even at the risk of discovery. An instant he poised, then he was across the open space and into the house.

A quick glance around. Warm clothing on hooks. He reached under one coat and took a thick sweatshirt. Quickly to the shelves. Rows of canned goods. He selected a dozen cans, taking them from the front row and moving others into their place so their loss would not be detected. He made a sack out of the shirt and put the cans in it.

There was much here he could use, but he wasted no time. Another quick glance around.

A hunting knife! It was under a table, lying upon some chunks of firewood.

He caught it up, took a quick look, and was out of the door and across the open space. There he paused and glanced back. No one in sight. The earth was packed hard, and he believed he had left no tracks. Carrying his sack, he climbed higher. When he had reached a point from which he could watch, he squatted on his heels and opened the first can.

Fish, of a kind he did not know. He had not eaten in two days so he ate with care. A bit, a nibble, then a bite. He drank a little of the oil in the can. Then he waited, but his stomach did not react. After a while he ate a little more, then drank from a trickle of water running from a crack in the rock. Crawling under some fallen boughs, he slept.

In the first light of morning, he finished the fish, then began to study the river. From where he sat he could see that the river he had been following flowed into a larger stream that flowed off to the northeast.

Putting the remaining cans in his pockets and inside his shirt, he donned the heavy sweatshirt. Then keeping under cover he went down the mountain to the river.

It was the Tsipa, but this he did not know. It was a river, and he crouched in the willows along the bank and watched it.

No boats, no travel, nothing.

For a half hour he waited, picking out the log he would use to cross.

When enough time had passed he went into the water and pushed off. The stream was not wide, but crossing was slow. Then, suddenly, he heard the put-put of a small motor!

A boat was coming up the river.

FIVE

To go back was impossible. He could only go across and downstream, and the log offered scant cover. He slid into the water, and grasping the stub of a branch, he clung to the log, keeping his nose and mouth barely above water.

The steady put-put of the motor continued. He dared not raise his head to look, and he tried not to guide the log too much. Steadily the motorboat drew closer. By the sound it was an outboard motor.

His heart began to pound with slow, heavy beats. He breathed deeply, prepared to submerge if need be. Up to this point he was sure he had not been seen, nor had he left any evidence of his passing since the first hour or so of his escape. Consequently, any search for him must cover a wide area and could not be concentrated. If he were seen by someone who could report him, all that would be ended.

If the unknown man in the boat so much as glimpsed him, that man must be destroyed. That the man might be armed and might shoot on sight, he understood.

Was this someone searching for him? A hunter? A fisherman? Or some traveler returning to his home?

The log was between himself and the boat, yet the top of it cleared the water by no more than six inches. Suddenly the sound of the motor seemed to change. The boat was coming nearer, nearer.

He took a deep breath and went under the water. The boat came nearer, then passed so close he felt the surge of water from the propeller. Carefully, he let his head rise above water. The boat was going on upstream, and he steered the log more crosswise of the slight current to give him cover until he could get to shore.

It was a low shore of willows, and he crawled up on the bank, shivering, glad to have the sun's warmth. He lay there for a few minutes, letting the sun dry away some of the water that soaked his clothes.

He had lost his staff but found another, a stout stick that he improved a little with the stolen knife.

Restless and eager to be moving on, he walked away from the river, heading east. He left the willows and poplar of the river bottom and worked his way through a larch forest, mingled with some fir and pine of an unfamiliar kind. There were thickets of chokecherry, which he remembered from boyhood days, and groves of aspen.

He took his time, speed being no longer an essential. Now he must prevent discovery and think of survival. At noon, in a tight grove of fir, he ate his second can. It was also fish.

Here and there he found a few chokecherries, but the fruit was so thin around the pits that it offered little except the tart sweetness of the taste.

Slowly, his clothes dried out.

He moved carefully, for at any time he might come upon a hunter or a prospecting party. Hunters he hoped to avoid, but a party of prospectors might provide what he wanted most, a map.

A prospector in Siberia was unlikely to be alone. He would probably be one of a party sent out by the government, and he would be well provided with maps of the terrain over which he was working.

When he had walked for two hours and covered what he believed was about five miles, he sighted the larger river, flowing toward him. He walked on, keeping under cover. He found animal tracks but nothing human. The river lay between two mountain ridges, and when the shadows began to grow long he turned and climbed higher on the flank of the nearest ridge. Warm air rises, and it would be warmer halfway up the ridge than at the bottom.

On the slope where he found his bed he also found some
ptarmigan berry, or what the Indians knew as kinnikinic. He
ate some of the berries, which were nourishing but rather
tasteless. From under the bushes he gathered some of the
dried leaves, to make a tea.

From birchbark he prepared a dish, and kindling a small
fire he boiled water for his tea, making sure the flames did
not touch the bark above the water level. The tea was bitter
but tasted good.

He had built his fire of dried sticks that gave off almost
no smoke, and he had built it under a fir tree where the
rising smoke, little though it was, was thinned by passage
through the thick boughs.

Keeping his fire small and using a rock for a reflector, he
huddled close and began to examine his situation more closely.

He was a hunted man in the largest country on earth.
Most of the area where he now moved was a wilderness. His
travel would be on foot, hence slow. Winter was going to
overtake him, and travel in winter, in his condition, was
unthinkable.

His situation had been improved by his stealing the knife
and the sweatshirt, but only a little. He needed a weapon
that could kill game at a distance and was silent. Well, his
people had solved that question long ago with the bow and
arrow.

He had often made bows and was skilled in their use.
Often he had lived in the wilds of the mountains of Montana
or Idaho and on up into British Columbia with no other
weapon. To make a good bow needed time, so he must find a
secure place in which to hide out.

He would need meat. More than that, he would need
fat, always the most difficult thing for a man to obtain in the
wilds. So far he had thought only of putting distance between
himself and his pursuers, but by now the chase would have
widened and they would be everywhere. He must move on,
more slowly, seeking out a place to hide and wait, a place
where he could kill some of the game he had glimpsed or
whose tracks he had seen.

He must take some skins. Above all he must get some
furs. He would need warm clothing.

Yet he must face reality. Acquiring a supply of food to

last a winter through was virtually impossible, starting at this
late date.

He considered himself. From boyhood he had at every
opportunity gone back to the woods. He had lived and survived under some of the bitterest conditions. He had killed
or gathered his own food; he knew how to make clothing; he
had often made moccasins, something not every Indian knew
how to do anymore. Joe Mack banked his small fire and
bedded down in a mound of leaves with fir boughs over him.
It was cold and it was drafty, but Joe Mack had lived so
before this.

Suddenly his eyes opened wide.

Alekhin! Alekhin had never failed to track down an escaped prisoner. Alekhin was a Yakut, a counterpart of the
American Indian. He would know the wilderness and he
would know how to think about it. He would know how Joe
Mack would try to survive, and he would know what he
needed.

It was Alekhin, not Zamatev, who was his first and worst
enemy. Zamatev might direct. He might order. He might
muster all the forces in Soviet Siberia to find one man, but it
was Alekhin of whom he must beware, for Alekhin would
think like an Indian. He would understand survival, and
sooner or later somebody would see him and report his
presence.

Alekhin was a master tracker, and Joe Mack knew that
no man could long deceive such as Alekhin. The Yakut would
find his trail and follow him. He might even surmise where
he was going and be there waiting when Joe Mack arrived.

He, Joe Mack, had no friends in Siberia. Or none that he
knew of. He supposed there were dissidents. In fact, he had
heard of them. There were also many people in Siberia who
longed for freer and less stringent ways, but that did not
mean they would be disloyal to their government. Mother
Russia they had called it under the Tsars and many still
thought of it so. They might not entirely approve of their
government but it was *their* government, and they had but
little good news about America.

If he was seen he would be reported, captured, or shot.
Although there might be people sympathetic or friendly, he
knew none of them nor where to find them. He must consider every man and every woman his enemy.

Most of all he must think of Alekhin.

On the thirty-second day of the search Alekhin arrived at the remote cabin of Alexei Vanyushin. Alexei, whose partner had gone back to Chita, was alone, and he was glad of the visitor even if it was a Yakut.

Alekhin was a man of patience. The search for the escaped American had covered Siberia for three weeks before he had been ordered to participate, yet he had watched and listened for all that time. It had amused him that the American should disappear so completely and that he alone knew how and why.

The search had centered around towns, along the borders, along the Trans-Siberian, everywhere but where it should have been. Alekhin respected Zamatev even though he did not like him. The Russian was unbelievably thorough. He was also cruel and completely ruthless, something the Yakut understood and admired. Zamatev's trouble was that he was Zamatev and a Russian.

A Russian did not think like a Yakut. Moreover, he did not think like a Sioux. Zamatev did all the right things, but in this case they were wrong, for he did not understand the manner of man he was pursuing.

When the Yakut was ordered to take up the search he knew every vestige of a track had been wiped out by tramping feet, racing automobiles, and the generally wasted efforts.

To capture an escaped prisoner one has to think like an escaped prisoner. And if that prisoner is an Indian, one has to think like one.

Alekhin was in no hurry. The American was not going to get out of Siberia before winter, and the winter would probably kill him. It was no use rushing off in all directions. First, one had to decide what the American had done.

The initial search had been quick and thorough, yet the American had not been found. Hence, he was beyond the limits of their search before it began. The American had been an athlete, hence he could run, and so he had.

The first search had failed, the further search had employed larger numbers of soldiers but with a total misunderstanding of the man whom they sought.

Slowly, day after day and with meticulous care, Alekhin prowled the country around. He visited every prospector's camp, talked with hunters and fishermen, with bargemen and surveyors, and he heard nothing of significance until the day he visited Vanyushin's remote camp.

Vanyushin made tea. He was a young geologist and mining engineer who had found an important prospect and was developing it himself. At least, to the point where he could turn it over to a competent developing engineer and miners. He enjoyed working in wild country, and once this prospect was launched he would be off to discover another.

"Oh, I remember the day, all right! It was either that day or the day after when Paul went to town. Left me alone for two weeks and almost out of supplies."

He frowned. "We thought we had more than we did, but we came up short. At least, I did."

"You mean you missed some supplies?"

"Oh, no! Not really." He gestured toward the shelves with their neat rows of cans. "I thought we had more than we did. I thought the cans were stacked three deep, but they were not."

Alekhin stared out the window. He looked sleepy. "Paul went to town that day? And what did you do?"

"Went to work, of course. I was drilling at the face of the tunnel. We have no power here, so it was hand work all the way."

Alekhin pushed his empty teacup toward Vanyushin. "Then nobody was at the cabin?"

Vanyushin shrugged. "No reason why there should be. Often we were both working, but there was nobody around to steal anything."

"But you did miss some canned goods."

"Oh, that was just a miscount! Paul probably put them on the shelves. We had a dozen cans of fish. It was fish from Baikal, my favorite." He shrugged. "Maybe he ate them himself."

"Some men will do that. I have known soldiers to hoard food." Alekhin sipped his tea. It was warm out there in the sunshine, another of those amazingly clear days for which the area near Yakutia was noted. "Lose anything else?"

"No, not really." Vanyushin frowned. "Come to think of it, yes. I lost my knife. My favorite knife. But that was Paul! Always using things and not putting them back where they belong."

Vanyushin made an excellent tea, Alekhin reflected. An excellent tea. His eyes scanned the tree-clad slopes, then returned to the cabin. He finished his tea and then stood up.

Vanyushin looked up at him. God, but the man was big! Not tall, just big. He was broad and thick and not with fat. Yet he moved as smoothly as a skilled ballet dancer. Vanyushin had known such men before, but not often. What they had was power.

Alekhin's eyes swept the cabin again. "Snug," he said, "but no place to spend the winter."

"No, I'll come down to Chita for that. I might even go to Irkutsk." Vanyushin stood up, too. "Sorry I couldn't help you."

Alekhin's eyes swept over the old clothing hanging from nails in the log wall. Some of the pieces were quite dusty. If something was taken from there, how long before it would be noticed?

"You have helped," Alekhin said. "And thank you for the tea."

He went outside and looked up at the hills and smiled. Now he knew.

Alekhin did not often smile, but now he knew not only the American's direction but something of the kind of man he was. He had stolen food so cleverly that Vanyushin had not realized, and very likely some article of warm clothing. The knife had been his only false move, but that was necessity. A man can survive with a knife. A really good man needs nothing else. Of course, he might be wrong, but Alekhin was sure. His every instinct told him Makatozi had come this way.

A few hours later he was seated in Colonel Zamatev's office.

"East? The man's insane! It's too far! It will be too cold! Why not to China? That's the logical way, the easy way."

Alekhin stared at Zamatev from heavy-lidded eyes, eyes that seemed without expression, without emotion. "He is a man of the woods, a wilderness man. You would never catch him."

Zamatev felt a flash of anger. Alekhin presumed too much on their years of working together. How dare the Yakut say that to *him*? What had come over him?

"He is an Indian. To catch an Indian you must think like an Indian."

"Bah! He is a civilized man! An officer in his country's air force! He is a graduate of a university!"

"He is an Indian." The Yakut put his hand on his heart. "I feel it here. Whatever else he has become, he is still an Indian."

"So? You understand him then? What will he do now?"

"He will try to escape. He will live like an Indian. If trouble comes he will die like an Indian, but first he will try one more thing."

"What thing?"

The Yakut looked at Colonel Zamatev, and not without satisfaction. "He will kill you," he said.

SIX

On the day Alekhin drank tea in Vanyushin's cabin Joe Mack was squatting under a stone pine some fifty miles away. The stone pine was one of a considerable grove on a ridge over-looking the Kalar River.

The last of the stolen cans of fish had been eaten, and he had several snares set under the brush not far away. Now he was watching the river.

As a possible escape route it did not seem a likely choice: the current was strong and he would be going upstream against it. His best chance was to follow along the mountain-side, letting it guide him without the danger of encountering anyone on the river or its banks.

Thus far he had been lucky, but that could not last. The food had not been enough, but he was used to hunger. Many times as a boy in the mountains he had lived upon what he had hunted, trapped, or gathered from the forest. He must prepare to do so again.

Progress along the mountainside would be slow, but he could keep under cover, and he doubted he would encounter anyone up in the forest.

Animal tracks were everywhere, mostly those of deer or elk, but wolf tracks were common as well, and twice he came upon the tracks of large bear.

His improvised snares yielded nothing in the time he

could allow, so he retrieved his shoelaces and went on along
the mountain. From time to time he found partridge berries,
picking a few as he went along. They did little to appease his
hunger but were pleasant to taste and gave him the illusion of
eating something worthwhile.

From an aspen he cut a strip of bark, scraping off the soft
tissues between the bark and the wood. He ate the moist,
pulpy flesh, as he had often done as a boy, and continued on.

He had no illusions. Zamatev would never give up the
search, and he had behind him all the power of the Soviet
Union, and all they could muster in men, planes, cars, and
helicopters, all linked by radio. The Armed Services would
be alerted and civilian agencies mustered, and his description
would be broadcast. And winter with its terrible cold would
be coming.

His one advantage was that they did not know where he
was and hence could not concentrate their search. Once they
did know, his chances would be cut in half at the very least.

The air was clear and cool. The sun was bright. Siberia had
very little rain and less snow, and in this area at least, clouds
were rare. Yet in a mountain range somewhere before him the
coldest temperatures outside Antarctica had been recorded.

So far he had traveled slowly, hiding out when he sensed
any movement, avoiding all signs left by men. He slept in
snatches when the sun was warm, but the weather grew
colder. He had to stop soon, as he must trap some animals for
their skins. He would need clothing.

The valley of the Kalar narrowed into a canyon, and Joe
Mack, staggering and ready to drop from exhaustion, leaned
against the trunk of a dead tree and stared down at the river,
several miles away. He could occasionally catch a gleam of
water, no more.

He should not be tired, but lack of food was sapping
even his great strength. He had traveled, he estimated, at
least one hundred and fifty miles since breaking out. Most of
that time he had been cold and hungry, barely subsisting on
the food he could find. He had to stop. He had to recoup his
strength. He had to prepare for the winter.

In the past several days he had survived on berries,
scrapings from aspen bark, several ptarmigan he had killed, a
number of squirrels, a marmot, and fish he had speared.

For a long time he stared wearily down toward the river;

then slowly he turned his head to scan his immediate surroundings.

The face of the cliff behind him was obscured by a thick, almost impenetrable thicket of stone pine. Below him, stands of birch and aspen covered the slope, and a trickle of water ran down through the rocks toward the river, far below. He was turning his head away when something caught his attention. Under the stone pine the shadows seemed unusually black. He looked again, then went closer and dropped to his knees. Behind the thicket of stone pine there appeared to be a cave.

Crawling under the lowest branches he found himself in an overhang perhaps ten feet deep and as many wide. Here, for a little while, he would rest.

Outside, several times in the past few hours, he had seen the droppings of either mountain sheep or deer. They looked much the same.

If he could kill a mountain sheep he would have both meat and the hide.

The spear he had fashioned was adequate, but no more. What he needed was a bow and some arrows. Even if he had a rifle it would do him more harm than good to fire it, as the sound would be sure to attract attention. He also could make a sling. Many Indians had used the sling, and he had been expert in its use since childhood.

His grandfather had been both a harsh and a kindly man. "Learn to live off the land," he had said. "Your ancestors did it, and you can. Learn the roots, the leaves, the nuts, and the seeds. Now you do not have to live so, but who knows what the future may hold?"

The great men of his boyhood days had not been George Washington or Abraham Lincoln, not Jim Thorpe or Babe Ruth, but Red Cloud, Crazy Horse, Gall, and a dozen others. From his grandmother he heard the stories of Indian war parties, of raids against the Arikara, the Kiowa, the Crow, and the Shoshone. Throughout his boyhood he had been enchanted by tales of the great warriors of the Sioux nation, of scalps taken, of coups, of men who would die rather than yield.

Each summer when school was over he went into the woods with several companions, where they lived as Indians once had, where they hunted, trapped, and lived off the country as they had been taught.

He slept, shivering and cold, beside a small fire in his cave, and when dawn broke he knew he must remain here until he had killed animals to provide him with food and clothing. He must make a bow and arrows. In the meanwhile, he made a sling and gathered stones with which to arm it.

He teased his fire to life with bits of bark and then added larger sticks. Then, armed with spear and sling, he went out on the mountainside.

First he listened long and carefully for any sounds other than those of the taiga, as the forest was called in Siberia. He went to a vantage point and watched the river, but saw nothing. He sat very still, every sense alert. He needed meat and he needed clothing. He also needed sinews to make a bowstring. In the old days these had been made from sinews taken from a buffalo's shoulder or just below it. Now he must make do. There were wild reindeer in the valleys and along the slopes. So far he had seen two, but had been without a weapon to kill them. The spear would do if he could get close enough, or even the sling if the distance were right and if he could throw with sufficient accuracy.

Slowly the minutes passed, and he waited, watching. A glutton passed, but he had no wish to attack so formidable and useless a creature. Yet the fur might be used, and on another occasion—

A huge bear lumbered along the mountain, keeping under cover of the aspen well below where he sat. Again he had no adequate weapon with which to face such a beast. Yet it was fat he needed, and the bear was rolling with it.

Joe Mack shivered in the chill morning air. It was now August, The Moon of the Ripe Plums, but most of the month had already gone, and the time of Yellow Leaves was approaching.

Shortly before the sun was high he killed a blue fox, skinned it, and roasted the meat over his fire. He stretched the skin and scraped it. Then he left it stretched in the cave and returned to watch the trail again.

The next day he went down to the river and speared three fish. Carrying them back, he came into a small hollow where the air was warmer, and there was even a slight change in the vegetation. Tiny microclimates like these occurred in the mountains from time to time, places that through some chance were warmer or colder than elsewhere. Hunting through the woods, he came upon several plants more typical of Manchuria or Japan than Siberia. Suddenly alerted, he searched carefully and found a half dozen ash trees. From the hidden side of one of them he cut a limb he believed might make a good bow, then worked his way by a devious route to his cave.

All the next day he worked on his bow, shaving it with edges of stone and trimming it with care. At times he tried bending it. He made two notches in the bottom, one in the top.

Yet he was worried. He was staying too long in one place, and he could not avoid leaving some sign of his presence.

On his fifth day he killed a mountain sheep, skinned it, dined well, and went to work curing the hide. At noon, tired of his work, he went out into the air and sat on his rock, watching the river.

He heard the sound before he realized its meaning. He listened, watching the river, and at last a motorcraft of some sort came within sight. Although he was too far off to make out its cargo, it seemed to be loaded with men. Then as the boat passed he caught the gleam of sunlight on rifle barrels.

Soldiers! At least a squad of them!

Worried, he returned to his cave. Had they, then, discovered where he was? Had he somehow given himself away? Was this a search party or just some natural movement of troops?

The latter he could not believe. There was no border here to be protected, no fortress, no camp. Such a small group would not be on a maneuver, so where were they bound?

Cutting the meat from the mountain sheep into thin strips, he smoked and dried it, meanwhile cleaning some of the sinews and rolling three strands together to make a bowstring. Then he took his bow, his bowstring not ready for use, and his small packet of meat wrapped in the skin, and he went up the mountain.

Leaving the bank of the Kalar he went off to the north following a ridge above a smaller stream, traveling northeast. He did not pause to hunt or to rest, but continued to move, keeping under cover of the forest and among the rocky crags. By nightfall he was sure he had covered twenty miles, and he camped that night beside a huge fallen tree, in the open and without a fire. In the morning he carefully removed all sign of his presence, and lifting handfuls of leaves he let the soft wind scatter them where he had slept.

Crossing a saddle between the highest peak and a long ridge, he started cautiously to descend toward the valley.

Finding a shelter in a thick stand of stone pine, he went to work on the sheep's hide to make it into a vest, using rawhide for a lacing. It was slow, painstaking work, but from where he sat he had a good view of the mountainside, and he could work and keep a good lookout, too.

He did not want heavy clothing but several layers of light clothing that would conserve his body heat and still allow free movement of all his limbs.

Before darkness came he moved off along the slope of the mountain, working his way down into the aspen, where he found a thicket where many leaves had fallen. There he bedded down, a dry camp with no fire.

When he awakened he saw not far below him several towers of a relay station or something of the kind, and a small village. He was close enough to distinguish people moving about but not to judge who or what they were. He turned back to the thicker forest, working along a steep ridge where he camped again. There, hidden among rocks and trees, he continued his work on the sheepskin vest and on his bow. Now he began to look for the proper sort of wood for arrows. He did not like the bowstring he had, but it would do until he found better.

Watching the scene below he glimpsed people moving along what seemed to be a road, and far in the distance to the south he saw a thin trail of smoke from what might be a village. Where there was a village there would be dogs. From where he sat he could see that the Kalar took a bend toward the south and then back to the north again. Without doubt he must cross the river again, and he did not look forward to it. Crossing a river meant exposing himself to possible observation, aside from the discomfort of getting wet in what was increasingly chilly weather.

Rising, he worked his way along the mountain under the shadow of the ridge and walked east, trying to keep under cover. Here, however, the trees were scattered and much of the mountainside was exposed.

The nights were growing longer now. He walked on, stumbling occasionally and very tired.

At last he sat down, unable to go further without resting.

He sat leaning against a rock, half concealed by a bush and tree that grew nearby. The sun was rising and even that slight warmth felt good. He leaned back against the rock. His eyes closed.

Had he gone fifty feet further he would have found a path, a very dim path, but nonetheless a path.

About two miles from where he sat, the Kalar River flowed down from the north, the river he dreaded to cross. And some miles beyond was another river, still larger and much more dangerous.

Days of constant moving with too little food and little rest had drugged him with weariness. Slowly, his muscles relaxed, once his eyes almost half opened, and then he slept.

A cold wind moaned in the stone pines; a dried leaf skittered along the path and came to rest. A rock thrush poised on a twig and then flew off a few yards.

On the path there was a faint scuffling, and a man came into sight. He was a short, stocky man, as wide as he was deep, a man in a ragged fur cap, a motheaten fur coat, and thick pants stuffed into clumsy-looking boots. He had started around a small bend in the path when he saw a foot.

He stopped, looking carefully around. Nobody else. Nobody near, at least. He listened again and heard a faint snore. From under his coat he took an AK-47, and the gun gleamed brightly. His clothing was ragged, but there was nothing wrong about the gun.

Stepping around the tree, he saw a man asleep against a rock, a man emaciated and worn. He saw the pack of smoked meat, the spear, the sling, and the bow without a string and without arrows.

Yakov moved quietly to a seat on a rock facing the sleeping man. Then he picked up a pebble and tossed it against the man's face.

Joe Mack awakened with a start, but with every sense alert. His opening eyes looked into the muzzle of the AK-47.

SEVEN

The man's cheeks were chubby and he looked fat, but Joe Mack was not deceived. He had seen such men before and knew that what looked like fat was the natural muscle of an extremely powerful man, one naturally strong, born to the strength he had.

For a moment each measured the other, and then the man spoke in what Joe Mack knew was Russian, although he knew no more than a few words of the language.

"I do not speak your language," he replied.

To his surprise the man's face lit up with humor. "Engless!" he said, astonished. "Spik Engless!"

The AK-47 did not waver. "Who you are?"

"I am an American"—he spoke slowly—"traveling in your country."

The man's eyes made a point of looking him over. "This clothes? It is tourist fashion?"

Joe Mack grinned suddenly, and the man's face lit up again. "Tourist the hard way," he said.

For a moment the man puzzled over that, and then he smiled again. "Why you here? This is far-off place."

Joe Mack was puzzled. The man was no soldier, yet he carried an AK-47 and gave every evidence of being ready to use it. His clothes were nondescript, his manner as guarded as his own. Was this man also a fugitive?

48

"It is better I travel in far-off places," he spoke slowly again. "I eat what the land provides."

The man's eyes searched his. "I am Yakov," he said.

"I am Joe Mack," he replied.

"Where you live?"

"In America. Until I return there I live as I can, where I can. Soon winter comes. I have no home for winter."

"Ah?"

Yakov was ten feet away, and the AK-47 did not waver. There was no way he was going to cover that ten feet and lay a hand on that gun without catching four or five slugs, and the man was no fool.

"Why you not go down there?" Yakov waved toward the distant village.

Joe Mack took a chance. After all, what was Yakov doing up in the mountains with an AK-47? "They would put me in a house with bars."

"Ah! An American? A prisoner? In Siberia? Russia is not at war with America!"

"No?" Joe Mack lifted an eyebrow. "Tell that to Colonel Zamatev."

Instantly, the man's manner changed. "Zamatev? You spik Zamatev?"

For the first time the muzzle of the gun lowered. "Where you spik Zamatev?"

"West of here, many miles. I was his prisoner."

"You escape? He look for you?"

"He looks."

Yakov was silent, obviously thinking. He pointed to the crude sheepskin vest. "You make?"

"I did."

Yakov indicated the bow staff. "What that?"

"A bow. I am making a bow. Then I shall make arrows. I need to hunt." Joe Mack lifted the sling, and the AK-47 covered him again. "The bow will be better than this."

"How you kill sheep?"

Joe Mack indicated the sling. He took from his pack a piece of the smoked and dried mutton. He extended it to Yakov. "You like? It is sheep."

Yakov accepted it, and Joe Mack went to the pack for another piece. They chewed in silence.

"You no look American."

"I am an Indian, a Red Indian."

"Ah! I see Indian in film. Cinema."

"I'm no cinema Indian," Joe Mack replied irritably.

Yakov looked around at him. "Soon cold, very cold." He hesitated. "I am escape also. I escape three years past."

"Three years?" Joe Mack studied him with quickened interest. "How do you live?"

"I live."

He hesitated, as if thinking. "My father," he said, "was Lithuanian. He is exile to Siberia. My mother is Tungus woman." Yakov looked at him. "Tungus are reindeer people."

He got up. "I think better we go."

Joe Mack got up. "I travel alone."

Yakov spoke over his shoulder. "Cold come, you die. It needs much food to last the cold. Better you come with me."

Reluctantly, warily, Joe Mack followed. Yakov led off at a fast pace, turning back along the path he had come. After a moment he broke into a trot, glancing back once to see if Joe Mack followed.

For an hour they ran, and then Yakov slowed and began to walk. "The Kalar," he pointed.

The river crossed in front of them, about a quarter of a mile away. Now Yakov moved with a caution that equaled his own as they worked their way through the trees to the riverbank. There, artfully concealed, Yakov had a canoe.

In a small cove, hidden among reeds, they waited, listening. At a word, Yakov dipped his paddle deep and Joe Mack followed suit. In less than twenty minutes they were across and hiding the canoe at a place known to Yakov; then he led off through the brush.

At a clearing, he stopped. "East is Olekma. Big river. Very dangerous for cross. Too many peoples, boats. Sometimes nobody, so better you wait."

He drew a diagram in the clay, a diagram of a route and landmarks still further east. "Here"—he put a finger on the map—"is people like me, like you. If they like you, you stay the cold. If they do not like, you go."

He got to his feet. "I go back now. It is far to go. You spik my name." He shrugged. "I do not know. It is a woman who spik yes or no." He waved a hand. "You go."

Joe Mack stood and watched him go, but Yakov did not

look back. Again he looked at the crude map drawn in the clay; then he rubbed it out.

Yakov, a strange one. He had ferried Joe Mack across the river, set him on his path and then returned to doing whatever had been on his mind. Whatever it was required an AK-47.

A woman who says yes or no? What manner of woman? He had read of beautiful Russian women, but that was in Tsarist days. The only Soviet women he had encountered had been Russian athletes whose femininity was doubtful, to say the least. He had seen others in photographs, but with the clothes they wore it was hard to say if they were attractive.

In any event, that was a bridge he did not propose to cross. Somewhere to the eastward he would find shelter and somehow endure the winter.

Yakov had taken him across the river, and for that he was grateful. Now he must survive, and that night by the campfire he worked at his bow, tapering it slightly, testing it from time to time by bending it over his knee. And that night it was cold, so very, very cold. Merely a taste of what was to come.

In the morning he made arrows, choosing the light wood with care, straightening and smoothing them. After two days he started on, his arrow shafts carried in a crude quiver until such a time as he could make better.

Ahead somewhere was the Olekma River, and he knew the name. Often he had sat with flyers who knew or had studied Siberia.

He knew that four of the greatest rivers in the world poured out of Siberia—the Ob, the Yenisei, the Lena, and the Amur. He knew that the United States was more than 3,000,000 square miles, but that Siberia was more than 5,000,000, and there were vast areas still almost unknown except to native peoples.

From obsidian, found the second night after leaving Yakov, he chipped out arrowheads that were masterpieces of the art. As he worked he studied the country. No matter where he stopped he must ever be alert, watching the country, noting every subtle change of air or wind.

Yet now, for the first time since leaving home as a small child to attend school, he was lonely. Not for people, but for

something else, he felt some indescribable yearning, some
reaching out from within him, some strange wanting.

He looked now across the vastness that lay before him,
from the bare and icy mountains that arose around him,
across the forest to the bare knife ridges that hacked the sky,
and he felt that longing again.

If tonight he should die, who would remember? Who
would inter his body? Burn his flesh? He would be left to the
wolves and the gluttons, to the vultures and the ants. He
would have come and gone and left nothing behind by which
he could be remembered. He had no wife, no son, no daughter.

He was what a Sioux had been bred to be, a warrior. Of
the four virtues expected of a warrior, he had two, bravery
and fortitude. Did he have generosity? And wisdom?

When he was a boy and killed meat, there were no
others with whom to share it. Yet when he had left for school
he had given his favorite horse to a friend. At the university,
except for those with whom he played football or went out for
track, he walked alone. He was, because of his extensive
reading and his grandfather's guidance, an apt and ready
pupil. He learned quickly and was diligent as well. He knew
women were attracted to him, and he danced well, but he
was not drawn to any particular girl. He kept much to himself, and with each vacation he vanished into the mountains.
He felt no enmity toward the white man. They had superior
weapons and better strategy, and he recognized that fact. The
white man occupied the land, but the Sioux had taken the
Black Hills from the Kiowa, and they in turn had taken it
from others.

He was fiercely proud and walked tall, proud of being an
Indian and proud of his place in the white man's world. He
had known from childhood that he would be a soldier; the
flying came later. He found he had an immediate grasp of the
necessities of flying and an instinctive appreciation for a finely
tuned machine. He liked flying and he liked testing. He liked
taking a machine to its utmost and just a little beyond, and
his skills and his ear enabled him to detect the slightest
weakness or tendency toward weakness.

He had known at once why the Russians had seized him,
and he was determined to give them nothing. Escape had
been the first thing in his mind, and he had been alert for any
chance. His eye had measured the wire, the distance to the

forest, the time needed. He had noted the slender pipe and remembered using it as a young boy. It lacked the resilience of contemporary poles but was not unlike those used in earlier competition.

He had known at once what he must do and how to do it. The Englishman's aid had been an unexpected plus that had made all the difference. To escape was one thing, to remain alive another. If he died or was killed before returning to America, his victory would be only half won. If he escaped Russia and survived he would count it a complete victory and a real coup.

A little mutton was left, but he needed another kill. Now, however, he had a bow and arrows.

When morning came again, he arose and walked upon the mountain, and the ghosts of Red Cloud and Gall walked beside him. Perhaps the ghosts of even older Indians were there also, those who first followed this same trail to America, following the game out of Asia and into what we foolishly call the New World.

New it was to the first Europeans, but an old, old world to others who had come before, and the trails they had followed were ancient trails, worn deep in the forest, deep in the tundra.

Joe Mack, an officer and a gentleman, was once more the savage his ancestors had been, including that noble Scotsman whose ancestors had bloodied their claymores in the flesh of enemy clansmen.

When the evening came he descended to a small stream and slew a reindeer that had come to drink. In the chill of evening he skinned out the beast, chose the cuts of meat, and roasted them over a fire. Other meat he cut into strips as his family had done and dried them over a small fire, while far into the cold night he scraped the staked-out hide and cut the sinews from the reindeer's shoulders to make yet another, and better, bowstring.

Over his small fire, sheltered by rocks and trees so that no glimmer escaped, he muttered the songs of his people, red and white, pausing only from time to time to listen.

The wind was rising, the wind was cold. The stars were very bright, and in the north there was a hint of the northern lights high in the sky. The wind moaned in the stone pine thickets, rustling the leaves of the aspen just below. Old

ghosts walked the night, peering as he did into the small
dancing flame. The fire was scarcely enough to warm him,
yet the flickering flames spoke to him in the poetry of his
people.

Somewhere out in the darkness something moved, something other than the wind, something huge and ominous.
"Old Bear," Joe Mack spoke aloud, "go back from where you
came. I want your meat, your hide, and your fat, but not
tonight.

"Go back, Old Bear, and tell your cubs that tonight you
saw a Sioux warrior and he let you live because he had killed
enough for the day."

He awakened to a cold gray morning and stirred his dull
ashes to life, rubbing his muscles to restore circulation. The
wind that had moaned the long night through moaned still,
and southward ran the streams, hurrying their waters away to
a warmer land.

"Be warm, my body," Joe Mack said, "you will suffer
worse than this!"

He folded his reindeer hide and gathered his bow and
arrows.

The shoes on his feet were worn and torn by the rocks of
the trail. "Tonight," he told himself, "I will make moccasins."

EIGHT

That evening, spreading out the reindeer hide, he drew a tracing of each foot. Allowing for the sides, he carefully cut out the selected sections. Bringing up the two sides, he used thin strips to stitch them together at the heel and then at the toe. After trying them on, he made holes for the laces of rawhide.

A hide such as he had before him would easily make nine pair of moccasins. He made only four pair, knowing they would quickly wear out but needing the remainder of the hide for rawhide strings.

For cold weather he would need much better footwear, but there would be time for that later. Moccasins such as these, made from poorly treated skins, would not last long, but for the present they must do. The hide he had used had not been well-prepared because of the lack of time and the necessity for travel. Made from a properly treated hide, the moccasins would last much longer.

In the morning, the air was clear and cold. From where he sat his eyes could sweep a broad section of the country. It was forest land, broken by low, raw-backed mountains and wide stretches of marsh. Because of the marsh, travel would be channeled to some degree, so he must move with even greater care.

Joe Mack had discarded his spear, keeping the bow and

his quiver of arrows, as well as his sling and a small pouch of stones of a proper size. The knife he had stolen was a good one.

Deliberately, he had kept to the high country, holding to the forest's edge at timberline. Rarely did he find tracks of humans, yet as he moved he had grown increasingly aware that if he hoped to survive the winter he might have to work his way further south, as well as east. To the south lay the Amur region, where there would be more game but also a greater risk of discovery.

It was midday before he moved, but first he buried the worn-out soles of his boots and their heels. Their discovery might indicate his presence.

To the east was the Olekma, a wide river. Yakov had said crossing might be dangerous, but cross he must.

According to the map Yakov had drawn in the clay the river, flowing at this point from south to north, lay directly before him. Somewhere further south the Olekma took a decided bend toward the west, gaining in width.

Yakov puzzled him. Where was he going, armed as he was? Was there armed anti-Soviet resistance in Siberia? He doubted it. Or was he a thief, associated with a gang of thieves? There had been robberies in the Soviet Union, some of them quite dramatic, but beyond an occasional article printed in their papers and copied in American or European papers, or information gleaned from reports of trials, he knew nothing.

He kept to the cover of the trees. The earth was covered with needles from the pines and was soft underfoot. When he came within sight of the Olekma, from a high point among the trees he studied what he could see of the stream.

Almost at once he heard the distant mutter of an engine, and then a steam launch came within sight. It was headed upstream, and it carried at least a dozen soldiers.

Searching for him? But how could they know where he was? Had he somehow failed to conceal his presence? Or was this a blanket search across a wide area? Even as he watched, the boat veered in toward the shore. He waited, then watched the soldiers disembark. At once they began making camp.

It was warm in the sunshine, and Joe Mack sat watching the movements in the growing camp. A dozen soldiers—he counted them again—and an officer, perhaps a noncommissioned officer. He could see the sun glint from their weapons. If they were not hunting him, they were certainly hunting somebody or something.

The steamboat, not over forty feet long, had tied up at the bank. It was too far away for him to make out details, but he had the impression that it was old, probably a boat long in use on the river. He should be moving on, but he hoped to get some idea of their direction. Yet once they were under cover of the forest, he would be unable to follow their progress.

Rising and keeping under the trees, he started north along the face of the mountain. Below him and not far from where the soldiers had camped, two streams entered the Olekma, one from either side. The wind was cold and he was glad when he dipped deeper into the forest and away from it. He weaved among the trees, careful to break no branches and leave no obvious sign. His soft moccasins made almost no impression on the needles underfoot.

What awaited him beyond the Olekma he did not know, yet slowly things forgotten were returning to mind—from books he had read long ago and Army orientation lectures.

How to cross the Olekma?

Finding a game trail, he followed it along the mountainside, pausing from time to time to listen. He heard nothing.

When he had walked for what he believed was over two miles he paused to rest and to listen. As he waited, he chewed on some of the dried mutton from the mountain sheep.

If that group of soldiers was hunting him there would be others. Somehow he had given away his presence here, or he had been seen.

The river would be watched. Crossing the Olekma would not be as easy as crossing the Kalar.

Would they try to take him alive? It did not matter. He would be better dead than a prisoner again. But what if he could cross the river in darkness? The nights were growing longer. Could he find some means, some way?

He turned down the slope among the stone pines, taking a diagonal route along the mountainside. Ahead of him was a small stream. He paused before approaching to listen again. Then he went down to the water and followed the stream down toward the main river, pausing often to listen.

He was one man alone in a hostile country, where no man was his friend. He must be prepared to kill or be killed.

Above all, he must remain alert. Although the land before him was virtually uninhabited, there was always the chance of coming up to a hunter or prospector. If he remembered correctly, the Russians were building a new railroad across the country before him. Their Trans-Siberian line ran along the Amur, too close to China for comfort.

Finding a rock under larch trees, closely screened from behind by thick brush, he seated himself. From the flat rock he could look down upon and across the Olekma to study its traffic. This high up, the stream was moving little. For a half hour he scanned the stream, as much as he could see of its shores, and the country around. Across the river there was a narrow belt of what seemed to be low-growing trees and brush, and beyond that the bare mountainside. He watched the shadows gather in the canyons opposite, and he thought he saw a way over the ridge that might offer concealment. Apparently there was a small river that headed up in the mountains opposite, flowing off to the northwest. If he could follow it up to its source near the rim he would be hidden until he had to cross the divide.

Going back into the trees he lay down to rest, staring up into the dark green latticework of evergreen boughs. Slowly, his muscles relaxed and he rested easier. Tonight he must cross the Olekma, strike through the low trees to reach the streambed, and then turn southeast following the stream toward the rim.

To think that only a few weeks ago he had driven in from Edwards Air Force Base to lunch with some friends in Beverly Hills, looking forward to his few days in Alaska. Now he was a fugitive, fleeing for his life in the interior of Siberia.

He was six feet two inches, and when he had left for Alaska he had weighed one ninety. He smiled wryly up into the branches overhead. He doubted if he would weigh more than one seventy-five now, and he would probably be leaner than that before this ordeal was over.

The nights were growing longer and colder. He would need warmer clothing, and he would need, most of all, a place to hole up and wait out the winter.

But where? How?

He slept then, and awakened to a faint stirring in the brush nearby. He sat up, reaching for his weapons.

The stirring stopped. Something was there, watching him. He got to his feet and took up his bow and notched an arrow, waiting. Nothing happened.

The day was gone. Now it would soon be dark. Ignoring whatever was in the brush, he started away, following the stream down toward the Olekma. An animal, he thought, perhaps a wolf prowling in search of prey. But not in search of him.

The river lay suddenly before him, its dark waters glistening in the dim light. There were many willows along the shore and some larger trees he could not make out in the semidarkness. He looked across. He was a good swimmer but not a great one. He had never spent much time in the water. The mountain streams of his homeland had been narrow, rushing streams, rarely deep. He looked around for a drift log but found none. There was driftwood everywhere, but most of it too light to be of use, except for a few gigantic old floaters that had buried themselves in the mud, their roots splayed out like immense black spiders.

Then he found what he wanted. This time it was a plank, a three-by-twelve fully eight feet long washed down from some lumber mill or construction project. He pushed the plank into the water, sliding it over a log. When the end dropped off the log, it splashed.

Instantly the quiet of the night was ripped apart by the vicious barking of a big dog, and not far away.

A dwelling nearby? He had seen no signs of it. Yet suddenly, not fifty yards off, there was a rectangle of light as a door opened. A gruff voice demanded the dog be still.

The man stood listening; then he admonished the dog in a softer tone and went back inside.

Joe Mack waited until the dog walked back and lay down at the door. Carefully, then, he removed his vest and sweatshirt, wrapped his bow, arrows, and sling, and waded into the water, trying to make no sound.

The water was icy cold, and the night was still. Despite his efforts, the water splashed and the dog came to its feet growling. He pushed off, and the dog rushed down to the water, barking furiously. The door slammed open and the man shouted angrily; then, flashlight in hand, he walked down to the water's edge.

He was downstream of Joe Mack, and when he flashed the light out upon the water it swept fifty feet away from him. One hand on the heavy plank, Joe Mack swam across the current, but inexorably he was moved down toward the spying, examining light.

Joe Mack, his heart pounding, turned the plank downstream and tried to swim more strongly, going with the current but across the stream. The light swept above him, hesitated, and swung back, as if the man had glimpsed something to arouse his suspicion. Joe Mack let himself sink under the water but kept the plank and its small burden between himself and the light.

The light's rays reached them, but feebly. Slowly, Mack had been working his way across and downstream, carried by the current at a swifter pace than his swimming could have done. The flashlight touched his burden, but he knew he was by now so far out that the light would reveal nothing but some floating debris.

The light veered away and he heard the man calling to the dog, his light bobbing as he walked back to the house.

It seemed a long time before he reached the opposite bank, and when he at last scrambled ashore on a muddy bank and retrieved his small bundle, he was at least a mile further downstream than he wished to be.

Shivering, he tried to wipe himself dry with a handful of grass. Then he donned his clothes again. They were only partly dry, but brought almost immediate warmth.

Going back on the mudbank, he shoved the plank back into the stream. There was no time to erase the footprints he had made.

Walking swiftly, he pushed his way through the willows into a thick stand of birch. Weaving among the slim white trunks, he climbed steadily, getting away from the river. He entered a forest of mingled birch, mountain ash, bird cherry, and a kind of poplar. When he had a good mile between himself and the river, he slowed his pace. Soon he was going to have to stop, rest, and prepare food. Better still, he would make a hot drink of some sort.

He was tired but he struggled on, holding to the edge of the forest and working his way back north until he reached the stream he had glimpsed coming down from the ridge above him. The streambed was cut into the mountain, offering him cover for his climb up the bare rock.

Only a few shrubs appeared, but considerable moss. It was hard climbing now, all uphill, and morning had come. He would either have to remain hiding in the streambed or cross the ridge in daylight and hope he would not be seen.

If he were to remain in the streambed, there was no chance of being seen unless somebody flew along the ridge or some chance hunter or prospector came upon him. Nor did he know what awaited him on the other side of the ridge.

Finding a mossy bank sheltered from the wind he lay down to let the sun's warmth take the chill from his flesh. Long ago he had learned to relax completely, to simply rest. He did so now.

The sky was an impossible blue, the soft wind was chill but fresh and pleasant. There, under the open sky, he rested and then slept for a few minutes, awakening refreshed.

He restrung his bow, hung his quiver in place behind his shoulder, and slowly began to work his way up the streambed toward where the stream began, flowing from under the sliderock near the top of the ridge. He mounted slowly, working his way through a vast tumble of broken granite slabs that offered some concealment.

He was behind the slabs when he heard a sudden rumble of heavy machinery, then a shout, and again a rumble. His heart pounding, he squatted behind a slab, waiting and listening. Again he heard it.

In the valley below him some kind of heavy work was under way. He heard the rumble of what had to be a Caterpillar tractor. Easing himself forward he found a place to peer around a boulder and look down into the valley.

Another river! He swore under his breath. But between where he crouched and the river, there was work going on. He could see for more than a mile in either direction, and at least three pieces of heavy equipment were working. A bulldozer, a backhoe, and a third piece that he could not make out. Fifty or sixty men and women with shovels were working down there preparing the roadbed for a railroad.

He swore again, looking at the mountains beyond. Somehow, he would have to cross to the mountains. He would have to get past the railroad bed they were preparing, cross the river, and get into the mountains beyond.

Somehow, but *how*?

From his pack he took another bit of the dried mutton. It was stiff, hard, and cold, but he bit off a piece and began to chew, studying the situation.

At night, they would surely stop at night. He had heard of this railroad, had known it would be somewhere ahead of him, but just where he had not known.

Something moved! He turned sharply, half rising. He was looking into the business end of a pistol. The man holding the pistol was thirty feet away, standing with his feet apart, staring at him. It was a narrow, scholarly sort of face, and the man had sandy red hair and cool, blue-gray eyes.

Joe Mack looked at the gun and considered the distance. His muscles tensed. He leaned slightly forward.

NINE

Colonel Arkady Zamatev was shaving. He looked at himself in the mirror, but without approval. There was still power in the heavy muscles of shoulders and chest, but there was a hint of softness, too, and he did not like it. He finished shaving and cleaned his razor. Looking in the mirror he could see the girl. She was sitting up in bed, watching him.

Kyra was, he reflected, the best of them. This one had brains. She would make a good wife. The trouble was there was no place for her in his plans, though marriage was an important part of them. To marry the right woman, that was important. Deliberately he had avoided entanglements, avoided anything that hinted at permanence. When he married it would be the daughter or sister of an important man.

Arkady Zamatev knew where he was going, and he knew how to get there. So far, he had made no mistakes. So far, all the pieces had been falling into place, all but this damned American. His escape could ruin everything.

"You're a handsome man, Arkady."

He glanced at her, making a slight bow. "I thank you."

She was beautiful, and there was something special about her, something different. Or was that his glands speaking? He looked at himself wryly in the mirror and said in his mind, *Don't be a fool*.

"I think," she was lighting a cigarette, and for a moment

a flicker of irritation went through him, "you will go far, just as far as you wish." She paused. "*If* you catch the American."

"You know about him?"

"Everybody does. When the Army is alerted, word gets around. You will catch him, I think. How could he get away?"

Zamatev did not like talking about it. This one was closemouthed; he had already made sure of that. Nevertheless—

"He may already be dead. How could he survive? Without food? And it is growing cold."

Arkady Zamatev said something that had been in his mind but unspoken until now. "This one is different," he admitted, "but we will get him."

"Shepilov wants him, too."

"What do you know about Shepilov?" Zamatev's eyes were cold. "I did not know you knew him."

"I worked in his bureau."

"I knew that, but—"

She smiled teasingly. "No, I didn't, if that is what you're wondering. Anyway, Shepilov does not encourage the girls. He is too afraid of his wife. She's a terror. Or so I hear."

Zamatev knew all about Masha. People avoided her, and Shepilov had been passed over for promotion at least once because of her. Associate with a man and you associate with his wife, and she was not liked. It was a mistake Zamatev did not intend to make. He told himself that again.

"Shepilov"—she brushed ash from her cigarette—"wants him. He wants to say you lost the prisoner and it took Shepilov to catch him."

"I will get him."

"I am sure you will. I hope you will. You are a good man, Arkady, good for Russia, but you have enemies. You stand in the way of too many people. Shepilov, for one. Until now there has been nothing they could say; now they are saying it, quietly and among themselves. Tomorrow, if Shepilov should catch him—"

"I know," he admitted.

He put away his razor and picked up his shirt. She was getting out of bed and he averted his eyes. Somehow it always embarrassed him to see a woman dressing. It was stupid of him, after all that had passed between them, but still the feeling was there.

"What is he like, this American?"

Zamatev paused, buttoning his shirt. He stared at the mirror but remembered the American. "Tall," he said, "strong-looking. Arrogant." He paused, buttoned another button, and added, "He was not afraid. All of the others, all of them, were afraid, but not him."

"I heard he is an Indian?"

"He is."

"But they were savages! Primitive!"

He shrugged. "Once. Now I hear they are heads of oil companies. Suvarov tells me one of them was Vice President of the United States."

"But he is an Indian? Shepilov is wrong, then. He is looking in the cities. He is looking along the Amur."

"Where do you think we should look?"

"In the taiga. If he is an Indian—"

"That's what Alekhin believes."

"Alekhin is looking for him?" She shuddered a little. "He frightens me, Alekhin does. There's something about him, something ugly."

Zamatev knew what she meant, but he shrugged. "He is a Yakut."

"I've known many Yakuts. Two of my closest girlfriends are Yakuts. They are afraid of him, too."

Zamatev finished dressing and reached for his coat. Alekhin always got his man. The trouble was that by the time the GRU got to them they were dead. It happened too often, much too often. Often one killed from necessity but Alekhin seemed to like killing. Well, he must speak to him. This American he wanted alive, if possible. The American was no good to him dead.

Strange, that in all this time he had not been seen or heard from. Alekhin believed he had a clue. The Yakut was sure he knew where he was but as yet had not caught him. Arkady Zamatev did not like leaving for the taiga himself. It gave his enemies too much of an opportunity. While he was around they were afraid of him, and he wanted them to remain so.

She was buttoning her blouse. "Arkady? Do you want me to help?"

Astonished, he glanced at her. "You? How could you help?"

She smiled at him. "I can help. I worked in the bureau for three years."

"You believe that taught you enough?" he scoffed gently.

"It taught me that most of them are time wasters. Most of them are stupid plodders. They have no insight, no intuition. If he has evaded you this long, something new is needed."

Zamatev could not have agreed more. Yet how could she help?

"Perhaps a new viewpoint," she suggested. "Let me work with you."

He shook his head. "No. This"—he gestured at the room and the bed—"is one thing. Work is another."

"I want no favors," she replied coolly, "and would expect to be treated as the others." Her eyes met his directly. "I, too, am ambitious. For you as well as for me. There will be times when you must be gone, and I can be there. Also, I know Comrade Shepilov."

Zamatev shook his head, but not as decisively. "Think about it," she added, and went into the bathroom.

He stood for a minute, undecided. It went against everything he believed, every resolution he had made, yet it was tempting to have an ally in the bureau. Or was she a plant from Shepilov himself? She had worked in his office.

It was cold in the street. He stood for a moment looking along the avenue, noting the cars that were there. It was an old practice from his days as a military attaché in London and Paris, where one could almost expect to be followed. He seemed to be merely buttoning his heavy coat and turning up the collar against the wind, but his eyes were busy. The little car was there again today. He waved his driver aside and started walking briskly along the street.

As he turned the first corner he stopped abruptly, tugging on his gloves. A moment later the little car swept by. He chuckled, and crossing the street, he went on to the office.

On his desk the usual work awaited: papers to be read and initialed, others to be read and discarded. He went through the stack methodically until he came to the reports on the search for Major Makatozi. They were arranged in four neat stacks. Nothing . . . nothing . . . at Albazino near the Amur border, guards had shot and killed a Buriat attempting to escape into China . . . a Yakut tracker had followed tracks for some distance only to have the trail vanish under his eyes.

The American's boots had left a distinct impression when the tracks could be found at all. Now they were gone, as if the man had been whisked away by what the Americans called a flying saucer.

Zamatev swore. Maybe he did need Kyra. Certainly, he needed somebody with brains. By this time they should have captured any number of escapees. Always before it had been a matter of hours only, occasionally of days.

Yet what could Kyra do that was not being done? What could *he* do? Carefully, he went over in detail what had been done.

The quick, immediate search that caught eight out of ten who escaped from anywhere. Then the wider, more complete search, the issuing of orders to the Amur troops, search parties sent out from various centers, people everywhere alerted. Nobody had seen anything.

Alekhin claimed to have a lead, flimsy at best. The possible theft of a knife, unproved; the possible theft of canned supplies, also unproved. The remains of a sheep Alekhin said had been butchered by a hunter before wild animals reached the carcass. That was at least questionable.

The truth was they had nothing. They had seen nothing, and they knew nothing. The man might be dead. He might have drowned crossing a river, been killed by wild animals, or be dying of starvation.

It was a vast, barren land out there, and few could survive. The man had no weapons, no means of obtaining food. He did not know the country. He would have no allies among the people. Any loyal Russian might turn him in. But, he paused in his thinking, this was not Russia. This was Siberia. There were people here who did not love the government no matter how much they might love Mother Russia.

Zamatev dismissed the idea. The chances of his coming upon such a one was limited, indeed.

No, if the man still lived he was out there now, cold, hungry, and in fear of capture.

Zamatev got to his feet and walked to the window. The little car was down there. He chuckled. Shepilov was so obvious! Yet, he frowned, did they know about Kyra? If they

did, and she was not already a plant, they would find the
means to make her so. Or they would try.

Colonel Zamatev drew a sheet of paper from the drawer
in his desk and wrote down the name Makatozi. After it he
listed *Alternatives*: north, south, east, west.

North was impossible: cold, an icy sea, no chance of
escape. West, all of Russia: very doubtful. South, to the
Amur and China: probable. East, toward the Bering Strait or
the Sea of Okhotsk: possible but unlikely.

Best area for concentrated search: the Amur region.
Troops were alerted there, the Party was conducting a quiet
but thorough search, and all officials had been notified. The
man would need food, so he could not remain long in the
wilderness. But what if, as Alekhin suggested, the man could
hunt? What if he had actually killed that sheep whose carcass
they had found?

All right, he would take that into consideration. Suppose
he was, as Zamatev believed, still alive? Any man of sense
must understand he could not live out the winter in the area
where he now was. Much of the game would move south into
warmer lands; the rest would be hard to track down. Game
would move much less in the cold. The rivers would be
frozen with ice too thick to cut through for fishing, unless the
fugitive remained in one place to keep the ice out of the hole
he would cut.

So then, the fugitive would move south into the Amur
region. He might even attempt the Sikhote Alin Mountains
along the coast of the Sea of Japan. There was good hunting
there or had been the last he had heard.

The border was taken care of. The Army could be relied
upon. Now he needed a careful sweep of the country north
and east of the Olekma, largely from the Amur to the Stanovoy
Range.

He went to the door and opened it into the outer office.
"Yavorsky? I will speak to Comrade Lebedev."

Emma Yavorsky arose. She was a stocky, untidy woman,
but she was efficient. "The new one? She is attractive."

His eyes were cold. "Perhaps. She is also astute. I have
work for her."

Yavorsky was well connected. She was also inclined to
speak her mind. Her disapproval was obvious. "Of course."
Her smile was almost insulting.

Coolly he said, "I am sending her to Aldan."

Yavorsky was astonished, her imaginings dashed. "To *Aldan?*"

"She is an intelligent woman. I need someone there who can supervise the search." He paused and stared at her. "Did you wish to go in her place, comrade? Is that what I am to understand?"

"To Aldan? No, no, of course not. I just thought—"

"It is a focal point," Zamatev replied. "I need someone there to be sure the cold weather does not make them laggard." He could see this had been the right move. No man would send to Aldan a woman in whom he had interest. "Send her in to me as soon as she arrives."

He went back into the office and stood before the map of Siberia. Aldan was probably too far now, but he must shake them up, get them out looking. His eyes scanned the rivers, checking the towns to the south of Aldan.

He heard a knock and turned around. Her brown hair was drawn back from her forehead. She was dressed neatly but plainly. Trust Kyra Lebedev to do the correct thing. Briefly, he explained. He half expected a protest, but there was none.

Using the map he explained his thinking. "It is a vast area, and I cannot be everywhere. Get out there. Make sure they are conducting an active search. Demand reports, detailed reports. Be sure they speak to all the hunters and prospectors, the engineers on the BAM project, and the workmen. Check for anything suspicious, even remotely so."

"Do you want me to go out myself?"

"No, no, of course not! If he's out there we've got to find him! We've got to get him back!" He glanced at her. "When can you leave?"

She glanced out the window. "It is too late now. I can leave in the morning."

"Take Stegman. He is a good driver and knows how to care for a car in cold weather. He is also a strong man if you need him, and he's no fool."

There was a moment of silence, and then he said, "I shall miss you."

"And I, you. But I asked to help. I wanted this."

"Fly to Aldan. You can get a car there."

He took her to the map and discussed the possibilities.
Her questions were few and intelligent. "And if I find him?"

"Bring him back in chains. And I mean, in *chains*. If you
cannot bring him back alive, kill him. I trust your judgment."

He paused again. "Stegman can do it."

Her expression was cool. "I do not need Stegman for
that. I can do it."

TEN

The pistol was steady, but the eyes behind it were not those of a killer. They were cool, appraising, interested eyes. The man spoke, but the words were Russian. There was a question in them, and Joe Mack supposed he was asking who he was or what he was doing.

"I am a man who wishes to be left alone."

Surprisingly, the man replied in English. "Who are you? What do you do here?"

"I am hiking," Joe Mack lied smoothly. "I am walking around the world. It was a wager," he said, "a bet, a sporting thing. I must succeed by next June. I have only to reach Los Angeles."

Whether the man believed him or not, Joe Mack had no idea. In any event he was stalling for time, trying to see a way out, a way that would take him away from the gun.

"This was permitted?" The man was skeptical, and the pistol did not waver.

"No, it was not. I have no business to be here. I bother no one; I live off the country."

"If you plan to walk, you have far to go. Winter comes. You had better come with me. I will find you shelter."

"No," Joe Mack said.

"No?" The pistol gestured. "I do not wish to shoot."

"Then do not." Joe Mack was poised, waiting. "Just walk

71

away and forget me. After all," he added, "if you take me down there, you will have to answer many questions. One question will be what you were doing up here at this hour."

The man's eyes were suddenly wary. "I have come to see the railroad route." He gestured with the pistol. "I am an engineer. I wished to stand off to see it properly."

"They will believe that? They will not assume you came to meet me?"

"To meet with you? What is this? How do I know you are here?"

"How, indeed? Of all the places you could go you come right to me. I shall not say the meeting was arranged, but I shall not deny it, either."

He was considering that, and he did not like it. The KGB would be asking the questions, and they rarely accepted simple explanations.

"You speak well. You lived in America?" Joe Mack said.

"In Canada. I study there."

"Sit down. Relax. Canada is a good place. I have many friends there."

He did not sit down. "I must get back. You will come with me."

Joe Mack shook his head. "Not if you are intelligent. You can take me in, but the KGB is suspicious. They will ask questions. They will want to know how I happened to come here. They will wonder if I did not come because I had a friend. Why, in all Siberia, did I come here? I will deny I ever knew you before. I will deny I came to meet you because you would help me." Joe Mack smiled. "They will not believe me. It is best for you if you simply walk away, having seen nothing."

"But if I take you in? A prisoner? They will believe me."

"I shall hint we were seen together. That you became frightened. I will not say that, exactly, but they will understand. In Russia is it ever wise to know too much? You are an engineer. You have seen the route from here. Walk away as you would have, as if nothing had happened."

"And when they do catch you? And catch you they will."

"Perhaps. If they do I shall say nothing, and they will have no reason to ask questions about this meeting. They will not suspect it to have happened."

Slowly the pistol lowered, but Joe Mack did not move. A pistol shot now, accidental or otherwise, would ruin everything.

"Walk back, take your time, be seen studying the route from here. I shall be gone with no sign of my presence."

"But I will be a traitor."

"How? What can I, one man, do to your country? All I wish is to be home, with my family," he added.

The engineer looked at him. Then he put the pistol away and walked away. Sweat beaded Joe Mack's forehead despite the chill of the wind. Swiftly, he was on his feet and walking away, moving very rapidly down into the larch forest. When he found a game trail he began to run. He ran smoothly, steadily, for several minutes and then slowed to a walk. When the shadows grew long, he went over the ridge again and down toward the construction line.

Far away he could see a cluster of shacks and lights. Here all was quiet. He crossed the line without trouble and went on to the riverbank. Downstream there was a bridge, obviously a bridge for the transport of construction equipment and materials. It might be guarded, but he doubted it. Here, in the middle of Siberia, there would be no reason for it. Yet he would be cautious.

The wind was cold. He shivered, seeking to get down where the wind would not strike him. He found a place behind a construction shack and crouched there, watching the bridge. It was starkly outlined against the sky, but he could see no movement, no sign of life. He waited, still watching.

What about the shack where he waited? There was no light, no sound of movement. Storage for equipment no doubt, yet might it not be the office for the engineer? He listened and watched. About a hundred yards off was what was probably a mess hall and beyond it a square long building he had noticed earlier. There were lights in both places and a sound of music from the square building.

Cautiously, he eased around the corner of the building and tried the door. It opened easily under his hand. He waited an instant and then stepped in. There was a faint reddish glow from the stove.

Waiting, listening, he looked all around. His eyes grew accustomed to the vague light from the stove.

He saw a flat table on which there were maps, blue-

prints, a square, a compass, pens. A sort of haversack with
many pockets hung from a nail on the end of the table. It was
stuffed with maps and papers. Opening the door of the stove
to get more light, he leafed through the maps and papers.
One was a map of the Trans-Baikal that covered the region
where he now was. He put it inside his shirt, went back to
the door, waited an instant, and then slipped out. He had
taken time to close the stove door; now he closed the outer
door behind him and stood very still, watching and listening.
Nothing moved.

Cold wind whispered around the eaves of the shack. He
heard a shout of laughter from the building he had taken for a
mess hall; then he walked toward the bridge. If anyone
looked out they would simply see a man going about his
business.

The nearest end of the bridge was not guarded. He
started across, carrying his bow ready for use as a thrusting
weapon if need be. There was no need. The bridge was not
guarded at all.

Two parallel ridges came down to the river at this point
and a stream flowed between them. He went up the stream,
finding a narrow path, and walked northeast.

There was a vague, pale light in the sky, and he walked
steadily, not pausing to rest. When dawn came he turned
into the deeper forest, a close stand of birch and larch, and
finding a small hollow partly protected from the wind by
deadfalls, he bedded down for rest. Before he slept he took
out the map and studied it.

He was, he decided, somewhere on a southern slope of
what was called the Stanovoy Range. There was no chance he
could escape Siberia now. It was as he had surmised. He
would need to find a place to hide out during the long winter,
and the best chance of that lay further south. He had known
this, but had been without a map to clarify the situation.

All about him were enemies. He had been unbelievably
lucky in his two brief contacts. He could not expect that to
happen again.

The map he had stolen was much too general to be of
use to an engineer in his work, so there was a good chance it
would not be missed. If the man he had met on the ridge was
that engineer, he would say nothing, yet Joe Mack knew he
needed to put distance behind him.

Now, curled up in his shaded, hidden retreat, he slept. Hours later, he awakened, chilled and shaking. He got to his feet and warmed himself by swinging his arms in what had once been known as a teamster's warming to get his blood circulating. His small supply of mutton was gone, and now he needed to hunt again. He needed food and warmer clothing.

Only when he moved out of his small hollow did he see what he had done. His northeastward march had taken him into a cul-de-sac rimmed with high mountains. To escape he must scale those icy ridges. They rose steeply up to at least a half mile higher than he now was, and climbing on the slippery rocks would not be easy.

Suddenly his eye caught a glimpse of something in the trees not far off. It was the corner of a roof—a building of some sort! He looked, looked away, and then looked back. It was still there, but there was no sign of smoke. He went closer through the trees. It was a good-sized structure, almost square, built of logs. No smoke came from the chimney. He went down through the trees to the path that led to it. He saw no tracks or any sign of travel in a long time. With the coming onset of winter, it was doubtful if there would be anyone traveling this way. Avoiding the path, he kept under cover of the trees.

Bit by bit he worked his way around the structure. There were four windows and a back door. That door showed no signs of recent use.

He waited for a while, watching the house. There was a trough behind it into which water ran, water from a spring. He could see and hear the water falling from the pipe into the trough. As he watched, a deer came down from the trees opposite and drank at the trough. Waiting for the right shot, he killed the deer with an arrow and went forward to skin it. He was expert, and it took him but little time to skin out the deer and save the best cuts of meat, yet ever and anon he straightened up to listen and to look all about him.

Aside from the structure beside him the place reminded him of a corner of the Seven Devils country in Idaho. His father had sometimes hunted there with old Cougar Dave, crossing the mountains to get together.

He went up to the back door and tried it, but it was locked. He walked around the building and tried the front door, and it opened easily under his hand. He stood in the doorway, making a careful survey of the inside.

Along one side was a row of bunks, enough for a dozen men. There was a stove and a much older fireplace. A few utensils lay about, and old clothes hung on nails along the wall. There was much dust and no evidence the place had been occupied for years.

The clothing was ragged and old, most of it filthy. He guessed convicts had been working here, probably at a mine, for he had discovered a few tools and a miner's lamp. There was nothing else of use. He backed out and closed the door behind him. Surrounded by mountains as it was, he took a chance and built fires to smoke his meat and dry it. For three days he remained where he was, cleaning the deer hide and resting. On the fourth day he buried what remained of the carcass, hid the sticks on which he had dried his meat, and wiped out what tracks he had left, sifting leaves and dust over the area. Only then did he strike out upstream.

Following the stream he came to its source and found himself facing a low saddle in the mountains. He slept there, and on the following morning started across the pass over the saddle.

The morning was cold, and there was ice along the shores of the stream he followed. Plodding on steadily, he saw no game. He had walked several miles when he became aware of a faint drone. Pausing to listen, he heard it again, the faint but unmistakable sound of a helicopter!

Hastily, he glanced around. Some low-growing spruce mingled with larch grew along the stream; running, he took a dive under the nearest spruce, pulling himself in tight beside its trunk. The spruce branches swept the ground, making perfect cover.

Had he been seen? He had not seen the helicopter, not taking time to look around for it. But had they seen *him*?

It was overhead now, circling. Then it rose, flying higher, took a half turn around the basin, and then went off downstream. Watching through parted branches he saw the copter dip down; it seemed to be landing near the structure.

Suppose they came upstream, looking? It was all of five miles of uphill walking, but they could hop it and land close beside him. He had to get away, but once out from under the spruce he would be in plain sight if they flew this way again, and cover was scarce.

To go or not to go? He waited, listening, thinking.

Peering through the spruce branches, he studied the terrain before him. Some two hundred yards away was a cluster of granite slabs, apparently pieces broken off by frost that had slid down the mountain. Once among them he should have cover, and his clothing blended well with the surroundings. He left the spruce at a run and then slowed to look and listen. He saw and heard nothing.

Were they still at the log house? Had they discovered some sign of his presence that he had failed to eradicate? He trotted on, weaving his way among the rocky debris, and reached the small forest of slabs and took shelter among them. No sound, nothing.

He was about to leave his shelter for another run when he heard the helicopter. It was coming in low through the very pass he had chosen. The slabs of granite had fallen in several places, so they provided crude shelters. He crawled well back under one slab and waited.

The copter came in so low he could feel the wind from the beat of the rotor blades, but it continued on through the pass and turned north to avoid the peak that faced the end of the pass, lying a few miles further east.

Rising, he followed on through the pass. There was little cover, but he knew he must accept the risk. Often, he saw the tracks of animals, and several times, of wolves. He was carrying meat, and even though it had been smoked and dried the wolves would smell it. He camped that night among a patch of stunted birch trees and slept, shivering and cold with no fire and only flimsy cover. Morning was a relief and he started again, his body stiff with cold. It was a long time before he warmed up, and fear rode his shoulders like some monster he could not cast off. He crossed the saddle and by midday had turned south again, leaving the towering peak behind him. His feet were numb and moved awkwardly. There was no shelter from the wind or any place to hide. He stumbled on, cold and tired, for he had slept badly, fighting the cold through the long night.

Desperately, he needed to find some animal that could provide him with a warmer coat or something to wrap around himself when he slept.

Day after day he worked his way southward. Several times he saw planes, and twice there were helicopters. Were they searching for him or involved somehow with the railroad? He had no way of knowing, but it mattered little, for by now all Siberia must be aware of his escape.

He was always cold. He needed better food, and he needed fat, always the hardest thing to find in the wilderness. He had worn out another pair of moccasins, and his feet were sore from walking over rocky terrain. More and more often he was stopping to rest. From time to time he killed a ptarmigan or grouse. Once he caught some fish. Time had ceased to exist; all he thought of now was to move on.

And then he saw the bear.

ELEVEN

It was a large brown bear, rolling in fat. Joe Mack squatted down beside a fallen tree and studied the situation. He needed that bear, needed it badly, but could he kill a bear of that size with an arrow? It had been done and no doubt might be done again, but he had never done it.

He glanced around for a tree with low branches. He might need to climb very fast, and it was unlikely a bear of that size would attempt a tree. The larger bears rarely climbed trees, instinctively knowing what their weight could do.

He glanced again at the tree, decided what branches he would take, and looked again at the bear. There was almost no wind. Joe Mack took an arrow from his quiver, put it in position, and then waited an instant. Then, reaching back, he withdrew two more arrows. Once more he lifted the bow, waiting and watching. The distance was about right; the bear was facing away from him, its left side clearly visible. He drew back the bowstring and let the arrow go.

It went true, into the bear's side right behind his left foreleg.

The bear let out a grunting roar and half raised itself to a standing position; then it fell back, trying to grab at the arrow or to bite it. Joe Mack stood up and too eager, missed his second shot. The arrow barely grazed the bear, which wheeled about and saw Joe Mack. With a roar, it started for him. He let go his third arrow as the bear leaped over a log. For an instant the bear's throat had been clearly visible, and this time his aim was good, but the bear kept coming.

Wheeling, he grabbed a limb and hoisted himself up. The bear lunged against the tree, his long claws raking Joe Mack's leg, ripping his pants and pulling the moccasin from his foot.

Joe Mack climbed higher and then looked down. The bear was clawing at the tree, breaking the lower dead branches in a fury to reach him. Joe Mack notched another arrow, and as the bear started to climb, he shot the arrow down the wide red maw into the bear's throat.

Its shoulders were already covered with blood from the previous wound, but it clawed after him, shaking the tree until Joe Mack was hanging on desperately. Choking, the bear tried to climb. Joe Mack prepared another arrow but lost it when he had to grab wildly at the tree to keep from being shaken loose.

He clung to the tree, getting a good grip on a higher branch and pulling himself up.

The bear's efforts seemed to weaken. It dropped back on its haunches and then reared again as Joe Mack moved.

Then it fell back, struggled to rise, and finally lay still. Joe Mack waited, watching. At last, very carefully, he crawled down the tree. He poked at the bear with the end of his bow. There was no reaction.

First he retrieved the dropped arrow and then the one buried in the bear's side. Arrows were hard to come by and would be needed. Then he looked carefully around.

The land about was bleak and harsh. A small stream raced among the rocks nearby, a little ice along its fringes. The pines were ragged and storm torn, growing sometimes from the naked rock.

From under straggling birches he gathered dry sticks and built a small fire, concealed by the trees around. Then he went to work on the carcass of the bear.

It was a long, tiresome job, and his strength was not what it had been. He peeled back the hide and began gathering the fat, taking the best cuts of meat. Over the fire he roasted some, eating it as he worked.

What he would have given for a good cup of coffee!

A cold sun was disappearing behind an icy ridge. The

wind crept down the canyon and prowled among the trees, finding leaves to rustle and branches to rattle in the cold. Joe Mack worked on into the night, warming his cold hands by the fire, building a rack on which to dry meat and smoke it. Clearing a flat place he staked out the great hide and began to scrape it clean of fat and fragments of meat.

Out in the night, a wolf howled. From somewhere further off, another replied. They smelled the bear's fresh blood, and they would be coming. He stood his bow and his arrows close at hand. Firelight flickered on the pines and the stark, bare branches of the birch. He warmed his cold fingers. Would he ever be warm again?

He built his fire up, and when it had burned down he moved the ashes and lay down upon the warm earth. Then he slept a little, awakening in an icy dawn. The water of the creek was so cold it made his teeth ache, but he drank and drank again.

The wolves were not gone. He glimpsed them from time to time, swift gray shadows among the trees, waiting for what they knew would be theirs. "I will leave some," he said.

Later, standing beside the bear's skull, he rested a hand upon it. "I beg your pardon, Bear. It was with no anger that I killed you. I needed your meat. I needed the fat from your ribs."

He roasted more meat and ate it, and ate great pieces of the fat. This he would need to survive.

At last he began gathering what he could carry of the meat, packing away what he had smoked and dried. He worked on the hide and finally gathered it up to carry along. It would be heavy, but now he could be warm, warm.

On the third day he went away, leaving the bear's head in a fork on the tree, and the carcass for the wolves. He walked away between the raw-backed ridges that gnawed the gray sky, away from the ragged pines where his bear skull rested, and downstream toward a warmer land.

Two days later, gaining in strength, he found a landmark—a gash upon a tree, a thin gash only, with a smaller above it—and he hesitated. He was close then, close to the people of whom Yakov had spoken. Beside a stream he sat to wash the wounds left by the bear's claws. They seemed to be healing nicely. In a still pool he saw himself in the water. His hair was ragged and wild, and his clothes were soiled from travel. The day was warm, so he took time to wash and dry his shirt, to brush out his hair and shake his sheepskin vest clear of the leaves and twigs it had picked up in passing through the woods. As was the case with most Indians, he had little facial hair, so shaving was rarely a problem. The few hairs growing on his chin he could pull out if they bothered him.

He washed his face and hands, then checked his gear. Yet he did not move on. Should he, or should he not try to find the people of whom Yakov had spoken? He knew no one here, could trust no one. Whenever such a group got together there was always one who was an informer or who would sell out for a privilege or some benefit to himself or herself. Yet he needed shelter, and they would have shelter. Obviously they were surviving the cold, and with them he might have a better chance.

He had lost count of the days since escaping from the prison.

There was no more time. He must find a place in which to last out the winter, and certainly in this vast land, with its miles of forest and tundra, with its bleak mountains and rocky gorges, there had to be a place.

Still he shied from the refugees of whom he had heard. How could they exist free of the law? How support themselves? How remain undiscovered? Was there official connivance? Would he, a much sought man, be welcomed?

A pale sun hung in a gray sky, a faraway sun, dimmed by distance. The forest was dense, the mountains visible only through occasional breaks. He saw deer, and once he saw the track of a large cat.

A tiger? There were many of them south of here in the Ussuri River country and in the mountains along the sea. How far south was he? The growth had changed a little. Again he saw the faint scars on a tree, but he saw no human tracks. This path was rarely used.

His moccasins made no sound on the pine needles that covered the path. Here and there leaves had fallen from other trees, but he avoided them. They rustled when one walked through them, crackled when dry. This was not the forest of Idaho, Oregon, or Washington, but it was a forest, and now he was at home. He had meat and a warm robe he would trim to the size he wished, and he would find a place in which to await the spring with its bright and running waters.

He smelled the smoke first, just the faintest, most intangible of odors, and he paused in midstride, moved under the trees, and waited, listening, scenting the wind.

It was a moment before he caught it again, and then he moved away, more slowly now. He was dipping down into a grove of aspen now, aspen most of whose golden leaves had fallen, littering the forest floor on which he walked, paving it with a scattering of leaves like gold coins.

Somewhere before him there was a fire, wood smoke from that fire was what he had smelled. A fire meant people, life, something dangerous to him.

Ghostlike he moved among the trees, stepping over deadfalls, avoiding the path. From time to time he hesitated, waiting for his senses to pick up some scent, some sound. He heard nothing.

It was there quite suddenly, an odd-looking shelter among the trees, smoke coming from a squat chimney, a door open and a woman's voice, her tone cold, level. It was a tone of dismissal, and he needed no language to understand.

A man appeared in the doorway, a bulky man, big and dressed as roughly as Joe himself. The man was arguing in a threatening tone, but he was backing away. Then a woman appeared in the door, blond hair under a fur hat. In her hand she held a pistol.

She was not frightened. She was coldly angry. The words he did not understand, but their tone was commanding. She gestured with the gun, and the man backed away, muttering. Then he turned and went down the path and away from the shelter. Once he turned to look back; pausing, he spat into the dirt.

Were these the people he sought? Yakov had spoken of a woman who said yes or no, and this one appeared capable of it. He chuckled, amused, and the woman, who had started back inside, must have heard, because she paused suddenly, looking carefully about.

From where she stood she could see her antagonist, if such he might be called, walking away and some distance off. She looked after him, then looked carefully around. She spoke a question, as if to ask if anyone were there.

Suddenly he smelled something else.

Coffee!

He stood up, and her eyes were quick. They found him at once, and she spoke, questioning.

"I would like a cup of coffee." He spoke quietly, just loud enough.

Surprisingly, her reply was in English. "Then come and get it."

Her pistol was still in her hand when he stepped from the trees. He crossed the narrow path and went up through the scattered trees to where she stood on the step of the shelter. She was tall; her eyes measured him. "Who are you?"

"My friends call me Joe Mack."

She was startled but not afraid. She knew at once who he was, who he had to be. And she knew trouble when she saw it. If they came looking for him, they would find them, they would be exposed, ruined, destroyed. All they had built would be lost.

First, the promised coffee, and then to be rid of him. She hoped it would be that simple.

He was tall and very straight. He walked easily, and his eyes swept the room as he entered. He stopped just inside the door where a sawed-off end of a log offered itself as a seat. He unslung his pack, placing it down beside him. "I have meat," he said.

Her look was a question. "Bear meat," he said. "If you like it."

"I have eaten it but once." She accepted a chunk of the meat and turned toward the stove, getting out some pans. When the meat was on the fire she brought him coffee. He tasted it carefully, then smiled. His teeth were very white. "That's good! I've missed it."

"Where are you going?"

He glanced at her. "You know who I am?"

"No, only that there is a search, a very serious search. They want you badly."

He sipped the coffee. "I can't get out of the country until spring," he said. "I must find a place to live until then."

"How did you come here?"

He shrugged. "Partly by chance. But I met a man, a man who said his name was Yakov. He spoke of people who live in the forest."

"Live? Hide is the correct word. They have not come for us because they do not care. We are nothing, or less than nothing, and sometimes we are valuable."

He glanced at her quickly. "Valuable? How?"

"Wulff—he is the man in power here—makes something from our trapping. Each year he receives furs, the best of them, and he looks the other way."

"Are there many of you?"

"Twenty-nine now." She looked at him with cool, measuring eyes. "Some of us are descendants of old exiles, from the time of the Tsar. Others served out their terms and had nowhere else to go. Some of us simply knew the wrong people. Nobody among us is looked for."

"I see." He looked up. "When I have eaten I shall move on. I will not endanger you."

He sipped his coffee. She stole a quick look at him from under her brows. "I am Natalya," she said. "Here they simply call me Talya."

"It is a pretty name."

She said nothing. He finished the coffee, and she went to the stove to turn the meat again.

"That man who left? He was angry with you."

She shrugged. "He is a fool, but a dangerous fool. He will ruin us all. He is Peshkov. He was a soldier, a butcher by trade." She paused. "He says his name is Peshkov. I think he lies. I do not trust him."

He watched her as she prepared the meat. She was slim and graceful, a truly lovely woman. He was no good at women's ages, never had been. She was probably in her twenties. She was poised, assured.

"What did Yakov tell you?"

"Nothing, except that you were here, a few of you."

"Why did he tell you?"

"Winter was coming. He knew I would need a place to live out the winter, but do not worry. I shall not stay."

She looked at his pack. "What is there?"

"Meat, nearly three hundred pounds of it, and a bear hide."

"You carried all that?"

"It is nothing. I have carried such packs since I was a boy." He smiled a little. "If you lived in America you might have heard of the Alaskan Indian who carried a piano over Chilkoot Pass during the gold rush days."

"We have our packers, too. The Yakuts carry enormous packs."

She brought a plate of sliced meat to him and refilled his cup. "You can hunt, then? Can you trap?"

"There's a blue fox skin in there, too. It was not well treated. I hadn't the time."

"Will you share what you kill?"

"I am an Indian, a Sioux. The hunters among us always shared. But I shall not worry you. I shall move on, further away, and when spring comes I shall go back to America."

She lifted a cynical eyebrow. "Is that so easy?"

He shrugged again. "I do not say it will be easy. I say I will do it."

He ate in silence. The meat had not only been cooked, but seasoned. Nothing he had ever tasted had seemed so good. And with the coffee it was a dream time.

She stood up. "Ssh! Someone is coming!"

TWELVE

The footsteps drew nearer. Joe Mack continued to eat, taking his time, enjoying every bite. Only one person was coming, probably a man by the sound of the steps, and Joe Mack knew what he could do.

The door stood open. Natalya stepped back, but she said, "It is all right. I know the footstep. It is my father."

He appeared in the doorway, a slender man who appeared taller than he was. He had a thin, scholar's face, clean shaven. He stopped abruptly when he saw Joe Mack.

Natalya spoke to him and he listened; then haltingly, but in English, he said, "You are welcome here. We do not often have visitors."

Joe Mack smiled. He liked this man. "I should imagine not, but this one will not be with you long. I do not wish to create problems."

"Talya says you are a hunter."

"I can hunt," and then he added, "and trap."

"It is an advantage. Our only income is from trapping. And our best hunter is gone. We need meat."

Joe Mack indicated his pack. "It is yours, a fat bear."

"Ah? I understood your people do not kill bears." He flushed a little. "I mean the Indian people."

"Only when there is need. We explain it to the bear."

"I see." He turned to his daughter. "We must instruct

87

him in our procedure." He turned back to Joe Mack. "We are
left alone, but in the event a search should be made we have
places to hide. So far Wulff does not know there are so many
of us. And we make ourselves useful. Every two months a
bundle of furs is left behind his dwelling. He wants only the
best."

Joe Mack glanced over at Natalya. "If you wish? I would
share the meat with you and your father."

He looked at her father. "Your home is here?"

The older man smiled. "For the present. One day we
hope to return to our own country. We are from Lithuania, a
country the Russians absorbed after World War II. You know
of us?"

"A little. There were Lithuanian miners who lived in the
town where I first went to school. Often I visited in the home
of one of my friends at school. His father was forever reciting
the poetry of Martin Lap."

"Of course. He was one of our best-known poets." He
shook his head. "Amazing! To hear his name from an American!" He paused. "I was a teacher, you know. A professor in a
university, but the Russians only remembered that I was one
of those who went to the forest to live as a guerrilla."

"You fought the Germans?"

"I did, but the Russians only remember that I fought,
that I resisted. All such are suspect for fear we might do so
again, against the Russians. I fear I am past all that. Now all I
wish is peace and to return to my home."

"Will it be there? Will anything be the same?"

The older man shook his head. "Very little, I am afraid.
It would be home, however, our own country. I wish Talya to
know it."

"This," Joe Mack gestured, "is your home? Your home
now?"

"Oh, no!" he smiled. "This is an old stable that was fixed
up as a place to sleep for workmen. We use it from time to
time when traveling. Nobody lives here."

He tasted the meat Talya served and then ate with
relish. "It is good." He glanced up again. "You killed a *bear*?
With that?" He indicated the bow.

"Why not? My people knew nothing else until the white
man came. We killed even larger beasts with it, although,"
he added, "this *was* a large bear."

The wind blew down the narrow valley, whining around the eaves and rustling the branches of the evergreens. They told him of their life and of the risks they ran and that despite the various prisons of one kind or another, all Siberia was considered a prison. "Many of those sent here in exile did not wish to leave, even when they could. They stayed on, and many have raised familes here.

"Many of us prefer the deep woods. We are not bothered here. As I have said, some know we are here, but not exactly where, and we bother no one. Out of sight, out of mind, as the saying is."

He got to his feet. "Come! It is time to go. We will share your burdens."

It was cold in the outer air. Joe Mack shivered and looked along the icy gorge. Then he followed Natalya and her father. His name, he had said, was Stephan Baronas. Leaving the canyon, they took a dim trail up through the trees. It was sheltered from the wind, so though it was cold, there was less wind chill.

The village, when they came to it, was a mere cluster of huts in the deep forest. No effort having been made to establish a clearing, there were just the huts, some of them mere dugouts faced with logs, scarcely to be seen until within a few feet, for trees and brush masked their faces.

"This Wulff you spoke of, is he a district official of some kind? Is he close by?"

"He is miles from here, in Aldan. One of us was caught selling furs. Now if we deliver furs to him he says nothing. It is a trouble to meet his demands."

The place they stopped at was a dugout faced with logs. It was tight, warm, and almost impossible to see. They had hidden themselves well.

"But how do you live?"

"We hunt and gather. Here and there in the woods we have patches of corn. We grow vegetables and barley, always far from here. It is very difficult, but we manage. Actually," he added, "we live better than many of the people in the villages."

"Share meat with the others," Joe Mack suggested. "In the morning I will hunt again."

"That is good of you. Will you spend the night with us?"

"The night, but then I must find my own place. I would not intrude," he added.

The night was very still, yet he slept badly. He had become accustomed to the open air and the sounds of the trees, of animals moving. Here it was too still, too comfortable.

Did they have another way out? He knew better than to ask, but was restless at not knowing. To be caught in such a place . . . it was a trap. Or could be.

He found that he liked Stephan Baronas. He was a quiet, pleasant man, yet he seemed to have strength of character. As for Talya, she was quietly beautiful.

Both moved well in the forest. They were learning to live with it, he decided, learning to move with the wind, to accept the wilderness and not fight it. And that was the key to survival.

At last he slept, and when dawn came Talya's moving about awakened him. He sat up quickly. "I was tired," he said. "I did not realize how tired."

Coffee was on, and it tasted good. He sipped the coffee and tried not to watch Talya as she moved about. Her father joined them.

"I shall find a place," Joe Mack said, "but first I will set out a line of traps. Snares and deadfalls," he added, at their questioning looks. "I trapped to pay my way at school," he explained. "In the mountains of America there are many wild animals."

It was pleasant not to have to think about moving on, and for the moment not to worry about being discovered. Baronas talked well, and as he talked his English returned to him. He spoke, he said, Polish, French, and German, as well as Russian. "The language of the Lithuanians is closer to Sanskrit than to any other, and we were an Indo-European people. Most of us were Protestants, Lutherans, or Calvinists."

"It would help," Joe Mack suggested, "if I could speak Russian."

"We will teach you," Baronas replied, "if there is time."

Joe Mack found his own place in a thick stand of birch mingled with aspen. Here and there were clusters of larch and pine. As usual in aspen forests the deadfalls were many, but as he worked his way deeper into the forest, planning to build a shelter from the dead timber, he found a crack in the rock of the cliff that lay behind the aspen. It was scarcely wide enough to edge through, but he had long since learned never to trust first appearances. He had edged back about eight feet when he stopped in midstep. Before him there was an ominous black hole that seemed to extend on into the mountain. Tossing a piece of rock, he heard it bound from side to side and finally end, far below, in a splash. He was starting to edge back when he noticed a shelf of rock going off to his left. It was all of four feet wide and ended in a much wider shelf.

Preparing a torch, he edged back into the crack, and lighting the torch he saw a wide area of bare flat rock under an overhang higher than a man's head. It was a cave-shelter, opening on that crevasse in which he had heard water, but the cave was partly sheltered by the rock wall and partly by a thick stand of larch. It was a fine hiding place, an excellent shelter, and it needed exploration.

He spent the afternoon setting snares along some small creeks where he saw the tracks of small animals. The weather was cold and the water was icy. He worked along several small streams that flowed toward the river in an area where he saw no tracks or evidence of trapping by others.

No matter how friendly Baronas and his daughter might be, Joe Mack knew there would be opposition from some of the community to his being included, even for a short time. Hence, he must prove his value to the group so they would accept him, no matter how reluctantly. He could live out the winter anywhere in this area, with or without them, but to finally escape he needed to know some Russian and he needed to get some rubles.

Returning at night to the Baronas's, he secured his bear-skin and the rest of his gear.

"You needn't go," Baronas said. "We enjoy your company. It isn't often we have visitors, and I haven't talked to an American for nearly forty years. Not since the War."

"Tomorrow night," he promised. "Tonight I have work."

Several people came to the doors of their lodges to watch him pass. He merely nodded and went on about his business. He knew that during his absence his presence would be discussed, and he did not wish to interfere by being anywhere about during the discussions.

Returning to his cave, he packed firewood and stored it, working hard, clearing some of the deadfalls from near the

trail he would use. In the process he found another entry to
the cave, well hidden behind the trunk of a huge old tree. He
carried in spruce boughs for a bed and found a place for his
fire where the smoke would be dissipated by the foliage.

His cave was a mere overhang of rock, with the deep
crevasse in front of it, half the front covered by the upthrust
of rock through a crack of which he had first entered. The
rest of the cave was hidden by the thick stand of tangled larch
across the crevasse.

He had shelter from overhead, shelter from the wind,
and a hidden corner of the cave that a fire would heat. As
time went on he could make it more secure against cold.
Sooner or later his neighbors would know where he was
living, but he did not intend to show them, except, perhaps,
Stephan Baronas and Talya.

Perhaps he could hide out the winter here, and in the
spring, when the search for him had run its course, he might
escape. On the third day he hunted.

The vegetation here was a mixture of the Trans-Baikal
through which he had traveled and the Far Eastern region,
similar, he supposed, to what grew in Manchuria. Working
his way up the low mountains, he sighted and stalked a goral,
a small curly-haired antelope. Later, coming back into the
larch, he killed three large grouse. In each case he made his
kills with the sling, and the grouse, after he struck one down,
seemed in no way frightened. He was able to kill two more
before they flew away.

He returned to the community under the trees and hung
up the goral, keeping its hide. The grouse he took to the
Baronas's and ate with them.

When he ran his trap line, he discovered that eleven of
the more than thirty snares had paid off. He had taken two
ermine, five squirrels, and four blue foxes. It was a good
catch, but he reset the snares and deadfalls and then returned to his hideout, where he skinned out the hides and
kept some of the flesh to bait his traps. That night he began
his lessons in speaking Russian, learning the simplest things
first, greetings and replies, and a number of terms: hot and
cold, near and far, and high and low, and the terms for forest,
swamp, river, lake, pool, house, and town.

"Tomorrow," Baronas commented, "I start for Aldan. I
shall be gone several days. We are taking a bundle of furs for

Wulff, and there is a man there who buys furs and does not ask questions."

"I have furs to contribute to Wulff and some to sell."

"Good! I thought as much. Bring them over very early, and we will see what we can do."

Next morning before dawn he brought the furs to Baronas. Handing them to him, he said, "Hurry back. I have much to learn."

Two others were going with Baronas, a short, heavyset man named Botev and his partner, Borowsky. When they had disappeared from sight, Talya said, "I've coffee on. Will you come in?"

When he was seated with a cup in his hand, she said, "You have done well with the trapping."

"As a boy I knew little else. It was a way of my people."

"I do not know your people."

"We were a nation of warriors," he said simply. "We had conquered more territory than Charlemagne. Perhaps, had the white man not come, we could have conquered it all." He paused. "There were, of course, the Blackfeet. They were warriors, also."

"You were defeated by the white man?"

"By our own ignorance and by our customs. The Indian thought of a battle as a war. He did not think in terms of campaigns. It was a handicap. Also, there was the matter of supplies. We had no extended plan. The white man thought in campaigns, of a series of battles until an enemy was defeated. He did not fight for glory, but for victory. The Indian could not adjust, not in time.

"Nor was he accustomed to fight in winter. When the white man attacked his winter camps he was not prepared and was driven into the snow."

They were silent, and then she said, "And when spring comes, what will you do?"

"Return to my country."

"It must be beautiful, your country. We hear much of it, and I would like to see it, but I would be afraid of the gangsters."

He chuckled. "I lived there many years and I never saw one. There are thieves, dope smugglers, the rats that always live on the fringes of what we wish to be a civilization. They are something that exists and must be coped with, just as you do here in Soviet Russia."

He paused. "My country is beautiful, much of it. We have our sore spots, as do all countries, but that is where I belong."

"Maybe I can go there sometime. I would like that."

He looked at her. "You could go. If you could leave Russia they would welcome you. Maybe Russians will be free to travel someday, too. All things change. We would welcome Russians as visitors. In the old days many Russians settled in America and became good farmers, good citizens."

He got up. "I have much to do. May I come for coffee again?"

"When you wish."

At the door he paused. "It is better, I believe, if no one knows exactly where I live, except for you and your father, if you wish to know."

"Perhaps."

A rough voice interrupted. "So? You have a visitor!"

It was the man Peshkov.

"Yes," Joe Mack said.

Peshkov scowled. "I do not know you."

Joe Mack suddenly felt good. "Oh, but you will! You will!"

THIRTEEN

Peshkov stared at Joe as he muttered a few words to Talya. He was a powerfully built man with thick eyebrows and rather protuberant eyes. He had a way of lowering his head and glaring from under his brows.

Joe Mack understood the sense of the words and suddenly realized why the language had a familiar sound. Had those Lithuanian miners' children he had known been speaking Russian? If so, he might recall a few words.

Peshkov spoke to Talya, speaking rapidly, irritably. Her reply was quiet but firm. Of this exchange he understood nothing, but he knew trouble when he saw it, and he stood where he was, making no move to leave.

Finally, obviously angry, Peshkov strode away, muttering.

"Trouble?" Joe Mack asked.

"He's a disagreeable beast," she said, "but we need him. He is one of our best hunters."

"He does not like me."

"He likes nobody. He would like to take command, but it is my father to whom the people look."

"And to you, I think."

She shrugged. "Peshkov wants to give the orders. He also wants me."

"I suspected as much." Joe Mack turned to go. "If you have trouble I will handle it."

During the week that followed he saw nothing of Peshkov, but nothing of Talya, either. He killed a wapiti and brought in more than three hundred pounds of meat. His traps yielded well, and in his cave he made two packs, one for Wulff and the other to be sold for whatever the furs would bring. There was, he understood, a black market in furs.

Now, with time in which to do so, he prepared his skins carefully, as he had been taught to do. Each time he met any of the people of the commune he tried his Russian upon them. It was true, as he soon became aware, that the miners' children had been speaking Russian, and a few words came back to him now. Occasionally he would hear a word spoken by one of the village people that he recognized. In school the children had talked English, but among themselves they reverted to the tongue spoken at home.

In the third week he left the stream where he had been trapping and went up the mountain to the north and set his snares in the headwaters of several small streams there. It was an area that did not seem to have been trapped, far from the village and where he found no tracks of men or any sign that anyone had ever been there before.

His take was rich. From the first setting of the snares he had success. Squirrels, Baronas had told him, were much in demand, and he found them in numbers. He also caught ermine, blue fox, and marmot, whose fur was much sought after. Several times he saw tracks of large bear; from their paw prints it was obvious they were some type of grizzly.

Squatting beside a stream one late afternoon, he considered his position. If he could sell furs he might accumulate a little money to pay his way, if need be. He was progressing with his learning of Russian. Meanwhile he had learned that many of the aborigine population, and he might pass as one, spoke little if any Russian. The Koriak, Yakut, and Lamut peoples had only a smattering of the language. Before spring he must concoct a story he could tell, a cover story that would be plausible enough to be accepted. At least until they had time to think, and by that time he could be gone.

Kyra Lebedev was a beautiful woman who made every effort to appear plain. She had discovered long ago that beautiful women did not advance as rapidly as the less beautiful. Good looks were an asset in a man's march to success, but not so with a woman. Men suspected you had no brains, and other women were jealous. Success was important to her, and she had quickly taken the measure of Comrade Shepilov. He was an intelligent man, but he was lacking in energy. He wanted success and expected it to come to him. He advanced steadily until suddenly he found himself moving forward alongside Arkady Zamatev.

From the first he recognized the threat. Shepilov was lazy, sometimes careless, an undeviating Party man but one who liked good living and made sure that it came his way.

Zamatev ignored the trappings and the benefits. He did each job thoroughly and efficiently. His bureau functioned with fewer helpers than any other. Every job given to him was done with speed and finesse. There was less waste in his department than in any other in central Siberia, and he had carefully weeded out the alcoholics and the timeservers. Kyra Lebedev saw that Zamatev was going somewhere, and she determined to go along with him.

Was she in love with him? Looking into the small mirror in her hotel room she smiled at that. She was not. Did she believe in love at all? She shrugged. She respected Zamatev, and she admired his cool, intelligent way of doing things. One always knew where one stood with Zamatev. Everything fitted; everything fell into place. He made no promises, and she knew she did not fit into his plans for the future. He did fit into hers.

She quite understood what was in his mind, but she also knew that if she wished to reach the higher echelons of government he was her ticket. So, never to demand anything, never to expect anything, never to get in the way, but always to understand, to be helpful and as efficient as he was himself.

She did not know whether Zamatev would achieve his ambitions or not. In fact, she did not believe he would. Such men made their superiors uneasy. Not that they might fear his success, but that his very efficiency and drive might force them to move faster than they wanted. The men in staff positions in any army were rarely there for their skills, but because they were easy to get along with. Men in command did not want abrasive types. They had come to the top, and now they wished to relax. They wanted men who were socially acceptable and just reasonably efficient.

Zamatev might get somewhere. Occasionally such men did. Gorbachev had done it; others almost had, but they failed by being a little too sure of themselves.

Nevertheless, Arkady Zamatev was on his way and he would go far, and Kyra intended to go with him until such a time as she should cut loose and be on her own. If Zamatev recaptured the American, it was positive that he would go on to Moscow. So the American must be retaken.

Wulff was the man in charge here. She knew very little about him that was good. His department was administered but poorly; nonetheless, he was well connected and seemed solidly in control. It was not the first such situation she had seen. His department created no problems for his superiors. The results might not be the best but whatever happened in his area was confined to that area, and no one wished to create problems where none seemed to exist. Discipline was harsh, according to rumor, and there were other rumors that his superiors profited nicely from the situation. Whatever else might be said of him, Wulff was in control, and if she was to get cooperation she must move with care.

Wulff knew Arkady Zamatev and would be wary of crossing him. What she sought was cooperation and a hands-off attitude from Wulff. He was not, she had gathered, an ambitious man. He had what he wanted and wished it to remain as it was. He would not, she was sure, want anybody rocking the boat when it was moving so smoothly.

He received her sitting behind a table. He was a fat but solid-looking man, partially bald, with round, wary eyes. His lips smiled, but his eyes measured her for problems.

"I have heard nothing," he assured her, after she had explained, "and I would have heard. Of course, it is a large area, and if you are right and he has come this way, we must find him."

"I would prefer not to disturb you or your department," she suggested. "I want to be free to move about. I believe I know what must be done."

"Of course, but you must be prepared. It is very wild out there. It would be best, I believe, if you remained here in the city. We are remote, but it can be very pleasant, and we would enjoy entertaining you." He smiled. "My wife would be particularly happy, as we have too few visitors."

"I should like to meet her, but there is much to do, and I wish to be," she smiled, "where the action is."

She was, Wulff thought, a striking woman. She worked for Zamatev? Was there anything going on there, he wondered? Well, why not? Arkady was a single man. But hard, he thought, very hard.

"Is there any word from hunters? Prospectors? Engineers? I mean, of anything unusual? Any strangers? Any thefts?"

He smiled, shaking his heavy head. "Nothing. We have thought of all that, and we've been out around the country." He smiled again. "As you have."

Her smile was a little tight. "Flying over the country we saw a place—"

"I know," he said, "my men were there some time ago." He did not want strangers nosing about, and the sooner he got rid of this one the better.

She was no fool. This one was sharp, unusually intelligent. The sooner he was rid of her the better.

"Who is this man you seek? An American, I hear?"

"I have heard that, too," she replied. She had detected some uneasiness and decided Wulff did not want strangers looking about. Well, that was his business. Her business was to find and recapture Major Makatozi. Yet he was no fool, and he must already have the basic facts. "He is a flyer who has information we wish to have. It is as simple as that. It is very important that we capture him at once."

"It has been a long time now," Wulff said. "He is probably dead." He paused. "The watch along the border has been very careful. My men have gone into every town, every village, every camp all along the Amur. The army is uncommonly alert. If he is alive, we will find him."

"It would help," she said, "if I found him. Or if he was turned over to me. I can assure you Colonel Zamatev would be most grateful."

"Of course. I am an admirer of the Colonel. I wish him every success." He hitched around in his chair. "His capture might mean a lot to the Colonel. It might even take him to Moscow."

A move, Wulff thought, that would please a lot of people. Zamatev was too sharp, too hard to deal with. Or perhaps the trouble was that he would not deal at all. If he failed to recapture this American, he might be with them always. That in itself was incentive enough. Colonel Zamatev had many admirers, but it would be easier to admire him if he were in Moscow.

"How he ever got such a man is beyond me. The GRU—"

"It was Colonel Zamatev who arranged it"—she smiled—"as he arranges many things."

Wulff stood up. The interview was over. "If I can help, call on me, but I believe your American is dead."

"Where would he go? How could he live? Winter is here, and that is a vast wilderness out there. Believe me, comrade, I have traveled it. When I was younger—"

"This man is different. He is a Red Indian."

Wulff was astonished. An Indian? He had believed they were all dead. He had not heard of any Indians since he was a boy and saw those American movies. Exciting stuff, too.

"How could that be? I understood he was an officer in the American air force?"

"He's that, too." Kyra turned toward the door. "What you must understand is that he is a man who knows how to live in the taiga."

Outside, Kyra was irritated. Nothing had come of that. What would Wulff do? Would he cooperate? Or try to take the American himself? Or would he work with Shepilov? She drew her belt tight against the wind. He would do what was expedient for Wulff.

Stegman was waiting with a car. He was a lean but powerful man of some forty years who carried himself like a man ten years younger. He was one of Zamatev's best men.

"Nothing definite," she told him. "Whatever is done we must do ourselves." She paused. "Does he know you?"

"I do not believe so."

"I will walk. But what I want is to find out what Comrade Wulff does next. It could be very helpful."

Stegman got in the car and drove away around the block; then he parked some distance off where he could watch the door. Kyra Lebedev went back to the hotel and getting out the maps she had brought, spread them out on the bed. She was dismayed. Even she, who had lived and worked in Siberia, was amazed at its sheer size. Now, thinking of finding one man in all that vastness, she was appalled.

So many rivers! So much forest! Yet if he was an Indian

he must be a hunter, and he would try to live off the land. In the dead of winter that would be almost impossible. Wulff was probably right. The man was dead or soon would be.

They had to be sure. Studying the map, she started to think, trying to imagine what the escaped prisoner must have done.

First he had to get away from the prison area, and he dare not be seen. Yet he might have gone in any direction, and they had no leads, nothing except Alekhin's belief that he had gone east, a belief based on something so flimsy—

A missing knife that might have simply been lost. The chance of some missing food. The food might never have been there at all, or it might have been eaten by some hungry workman who came to the place, saw the food, and simply took it.

Yet she had heard much of Alekhin from Arkady and from two Yakut friends. They did not like him. He was a surly brute who kept much to himself and was notoriously cruel. Nonetheless, all agreed nobody was better at capturing escapees. She must talk to him. But where *was* he?

The helicopter again—that was the fastest way of searching, and Stegman was a superb pilot.

Earlier they had tried to check every abandoned building of which there was record, and they had followed streams and roads and landed to make inquiries . . . nothing. Simply nothing.

There was a tap on the door. It was Stegman.

"He left immediately after you did, and he walked to a small building on a side street." Stegman looked up at her. "The man within deals in furs."

"Ah? In furs. A man, then, who might know trappers and hunters. And Wulff did not send somebody? He went himself? That's interesting."

"Yes."

She thought about that while Stegman waited. Aloud, she said, "It might be some personal affair, but if not, why would he go himself and not have somebody else go?"

"A source?" Stegman suggested.

"Just what I was thinking. A *private* source." She glanced at Stegman. "Did you notice the fur coat hanging in his office? Excellent fur."

"Yes."

"I believe I will have a talk with this furrier. Did you get
his name?"

"Zhikarev, Evgeny Zhikarev, in business in the same
location for fifty years."

"Ah? A survivor. Well, we shall see."

Her heart was beating faster. Maybe Wulff knew something, maybe he was just fishing, but a furrier?

Maybe this was it, the break she had been hoping for. If
it was—

To move swiftly, that was the thing. If this was the lead
she needed, she might have Makatozi before the week was
out. Maybe even today!

She was almost running when she reached the car.

FOURTEEN

Evgeny Zhikarev was disturbed. He was a small man with rumpled gray hair and a thick black mustache. He wore steel-rimmed glasses that were perpetually resting near the end of his nose and seemed in acute danger of falling off. He wore this morning a gray shirt with a vest of worn velvet on which arabesques were embroidered in red, gold, and green thread.

Around the shop he wore slippers. Several times during his earlier years he had undergone torture by the Cheka, and as a result his feet were crippled. He wore shoes only when it was necessary to leave the shop. As his living quarters were in the rear alongside his storeroom, his absences were rare.

His father had been substantially well off under the Tsar, operating a highly successful fur business in what was then called St. Petersburg. The Revolution had ended all that, and having lost everything in Russia, the elder Zhikarev had fled to Siberia, where a source of his furs was still operating. There, far from the seat of power, the Zhikarevs had carried on. There was always a market for furs in Russia, as there was in Manchuria and China. The Zhikarevs, father and son, had done well, maintaining a low profile in rather shabby quarters, outwardly conforming to all the rules, but operating with a comfortable margin of profit.

It was understood that officials such as Wulff could always secure furs from him at a modest price; in Wulff's case this meant fur coats for himself, his wife, and at least two other ladies at no cost at all. Moreover, on occasion fur coats had been made for people Wulff wished to impress, and Wulff himself looked the other way as to some of Zhikarev's other dealings. He took what was given, made occasional discreet suggestions, and maintained a nice relationship with Zhikarev without saying anything at all.

Wulff promised nothing, offered nothing. His comments were few but understood. He would simply say, "Comrade Thus-and-such is looking for a fur coat. You know, something very fine. He asked if I could recommend a furrier." That was the way such matters were handled.

The shop smelled faintly of the cooking Zhikarev did in his own rooms. It also smelled of fresh leather, in which he also dealt in a modest way.

The walls of the shop and of the rooms behind it were thick. It was never actually warm, however, as Zhikarev kept the temperature down because of the furs on display. Usually, there were stacks of hides and furs about, single furs or in bales.

Unknown to Wulff or to anyone else, Evgeny Zhikarev maintained a private account in a Hong Kong bank, a procedure he handled as he did other things, quietly, efficiently, and with skill.

Evgeny Zhikarev thought of himself as a loyal Russian. He loved his country. He did not love some of its officials. He had survived a revolution, several purges, and a number of inquiries. These last had left him somewhat crippled in body but not in mind.

For the past dozen years events had moved quietly along, and now he was thinking more and more of retirement. This would mean leaving Russia, but it would also mean freedom from inquiries and a time to relax and read. Somehow he never had found time to read all the books he wished, many of them books difficult to obtain in Russia.

Lately he had been thinking more and more of an apartment in Hong Kong, in Japan, or even in California. His feet had been hurting more of late, and it worried him. Was it a warning?

He went back into his shabby living quarters and put cabbage on the chopping board. He would have cabbage soup again. The smell of it was always reassuring to officials, for it had the odor of innocence.

Ever since opening the new bale of furs he had been disturbed. It was an especially fine collection, especially the blue fox and ermine. Squirrel skins were there in plenty, but those ermine and blue fox skins—

He added water and dropped cabbage into the pot, adding a few slices of carrot. As he stirred and thought, he was mulling over Wulff's visit.

The bale of furs had been there on the table, but Wulff had merely glanced at them. He had come right to the point.

"Comrade, there is an American at large. He is a Red Indian, and he must be taken. You know more hunters and trappers than anyone. Put the word out. We want him. *I* want him! I want him, and I want him alive. If we do not find him, there will be soldiers all over the country. There will be rest for nobody until we do find him!

"If you hear anything, see anything, suspect anything, you are to come to me at once. *At once!* Do you hear?"

He paused and said, more gently, "I would not want anything to happen to you. I would not want anybody asking you questions. Do you understand?

"Find him! Find him at once! Put the word out. The man is an enemy of the Soviet."

Wulff had strode out, and Zhikarev had turned to making his cabbage soup, but he was worried. Comrade Wulff rarely spoke so forcefully. He had no need of it. Everyone knew what he could and would do, if necessary.

Zhikarev brushed a lock of gray hair away from his brow. He peered at the soup. He liked it a little thicker. He hesitated, hearing the outer door open. Turning, he looked toward the front of the shop.

A young woman was standing there, a very attractive young woman, but one of those sharp ones. He knew their kind. They were quick, crisp, and demanding and almost impossible to please. He wiped his hands on a cloth, put it down, and went toward the front of the shop.

She was looking at the furs.

He ran his fingers through the gray hair. She had turned to look at him. He hoped he had spilled nothing on his vest.

Looking past her out the window, he could see a car

standing in the street; a big, strong-looking man stood beside it. That could be trouble.

"I am Comrade Lebedev. You are Evgeny Zhikarev?"

"I am."

"You have heard of the escaped prisoner? Of the American?"

He shrugged. "There has been talk, but I meet so few people. You see, I am busy with the furs—"

"I know. You do business with trappers?"

He shrugged again, letting his eyes blink vaguely. "If they have furs to sell. Often it is with someone who has been out in the taiga who buys furs. I don't see many men who trap. They do not come to the towns."

"I work with Colonel Zamatev. We are looking for the American." She gestured toward the just-opened bale. "Have you just bought these?"

"Yes. They come from far away."

"Who sold them to you?"

A direct question and hard to evade. He shrugged again. "A trapper, I—"

"I want his name. His location." Her eyes were cold. "I want it now!"

Zhikarev blinked. "He is only an occasional trapper. I do business with so many. This one," he scowled, shaking his head, "I believe it was Comrade Borowsky."

"Tell me about him."

Zhikarev was wary. This was a very bright young woman, and if Colonel Zamatev was involved—

"One knows so little. No doubt Comrade Wulff has a dossier on him. There is gossip, of course. One hears he was a soldier who fought bravely against the Germans, but his father was a Jew, and he wished to leave the country. He was sent out here and his family with him. Borowsky was not wanted anywhere, so took to trapping. I do not know if this is true."

"Does he come often?"

"Once, twice a year."

"Where does he live?"

Zhikarev shrugged. "They do not talk, these trappers. They are afraid others will come where they are. I believe," he lied, "he traps branches of the Sinyaya, north of here. I suspect," he added, "he sells most of his furs in Yakutsk."

"Open the bale."

Evgeny Zhikarev picked up a knife and cut the strings, partly opening the bale. Did she know anything about furs? He spread the furs and stepped back from the table. His heart was pounding heavily.

She turned the skins rapidly, glancing at this one and that. He watched her, and fear mounted. She did know something. She did. He could see it.

Suddenly she picked up an ermine. "This skin was not treated by the same man as were the others. It is different. See? It is much more expertly done, as by someone who loves a nice pelt."

She turned them one by one, checking each one. There was no way out of it now. She saw what he had seen.

She stepped back and turned toward him. She looked at him, coldly, curiously. Then she walked to the door and called out. A moment later the big man appeared in the doorway.

"Stegman, I want to know all this man knows about a former soldier, a Jew named Borowsky. I want to know about these hides." She showed him the hides, turning them rapidly. "I hope he will tell us here so we will not have to take him away."

"He will cooperate," Stegman said. "Comrade Zhikarev and I are old friends." He smiled, showing big white teeth. "How are the feet, comrade?"

Zhikarev was frightened. He stood back against the table. Why had he waited so long? He could have been away. There was all that nice money in Hong Kong, and he knew how to leave the country. Knew exactly how.

"Whatever I can do to help," he said calmly, "I will do. Trappers do not talk of where they trap, or how."

"This batch of skins," Kyra asked. "When did you buy them?"

"It was only yesterday." There was no use lying about that. It could be so easily checked. "Borowsky brought them in. I do not know this, but I believe that when he comes he brings pelts from other hunters as well. The ones you indicate are new to me. I have not seen anything like them in years. The trapper"—he was honest in this—"is extremely expert both in trapping and curing." He gestured toward them. "Look! They were taken with snares. The fur is undamaged. This trapper did not have steel traps."

Kyra Lebedev was excited, but she masked her feelings. This was a fresh lead and a good one. She must move carefully. If she could bring this off, if she could recapture the American—

"The Sinyaya, you say?"

"It is tributary to the Lena. It joins it well this side of Yakutsk."

"I know it." Her tone was sharp. "I know the area very well." Her eyes were cold. "We will look. If we find nothing, we will be back.

"I suggest"—her eyes were hard—"you shake up your memory, comrade. I would suggest you begin to remember everything you know about this man Borowsky and these furs.

"Who else has come in here with him? Exactly how often does he bring furs? Why did you suspect the Sinyaya? I had believed it was trapped out."

She smiled, but attractive as she was, the smile was not nice. "You see, I had an uncle with whom I lived as a child. He was a furrier and a trader in furs."

She started for the door. "Come, Stegman. It will take only a few hours to visit the Sinyaya and return." She smiled again. "I hope we are not wasting our time!"

They left, and Stegman closed the door carefully behind them. For a moment after they had gone, Zhikarev did not move. Had he said anything wrong? Quickly, he reviewed the few minutes of conversation. He had hoped to steer them away, and now he was hoping there actually was some trapping on the Sinyaya and its branches. Formerly, it had been good, and during the interval it could have recovered.

He did not know where Borowsky came from. He had made it a policy not to ask questions. He did not wish to know more than was essential to conduct business, and he knew there were escapees and others who did not wish to be found. Wulff knew it, too.

Those people out there in the taiga, they had to live. They were harmless. They had been there for years, some of them, and had done no harm to anyone. All they wanted was to live quietly in the woods.

Wulff had slowly been getting rich from the furs they brought to him and would not want them disturbed. But what was Wulff to Colonel Zamatev? A word or two from

Zamatev, and Wulff would find himself a mere clerk in some remote outpost. Zhikarev had seen it happen.

So what to do? Wait and see. But meanwhile to prepare. There was little to do. He had had this in mind for so long, determined never again to go through questioning by the KGB or anyone else. He was one of the few in a position to prepare an escape, a procedure carefully developed over the years through his fur trading.

At a remote post along the Amur he had quietly arranged to buy furs from Manchuria. The officer at the guard post allowed the furs to cross and received small favors in return. After more than a year of this, the officer had permitted Zhikarev to cross to pick up the furs. This had become an established procedure, so all Zhikarev now had to do was to cross and not return.

Would his place be watched?

He knew nothing of this stranger, this man who sent furs along with those of Borowsky and others. He might be the American. Evgeny Zhikarev felt an affinity with the stranger because of his handling of the skins. He treated furs with respect. He was not careless. He did not treat them in a slapdash let's-get-it-over-with manner. The stranger was known to Borowsky, and Borowksy was a good man.

Now Borowsky might be in serious trouble. Could he warn him?

Zhikarev might be planning to leave Russia, but he would not betray Russia. He loved his country, even though he did not love some of those who governed it. The local officials, anyway. He knew nothing of those in Moscow. At least, nothing more than anyone knew.

A moment's thought told him he could do nothing for Borowsky. He did not know how to reach him and dared not leave town in any event. Not unless he decided to leave for good.

Then he thought, *If he was not watched—*

If they found nothing on the Sinyaya they would know he had lied. They would be back.

He must escape now, tonight.

FIFTEEN

Joe Mack left the dim trail he had been following and went down a steep hill through the aspens. They grew so close together he had to weave his way, often turning sidewise to get through. Here, on the damp leaves and fallen trees he left almost no mark of his passing. He hesitated several times to look carefully around and to listen.

His hiding place was as secure as any such place could be. He had worked his way around on all sides, and a hunter might walk right over the rock above it and never suspect the presence of the overhang. Yet each time he approached it he tried a different route and each time with increasing care. Confidence could breed carelessness.

He wanted to go to the village. Baronas should be back with Borowsky and Botev. They would have news, and they might have money.

He stopped abruptly. A shadow had moved in the forest. He waited, listening. The sound had been ever so slight, and then there had been a movement. This was not a wild animal. It was a man.

Joe Mack drew an arrow from his quiver and waited, bow in hand.

Again there was movement, a sly, cautious movement. Joe Mack was high among the aspen on the side of the hill. He peered through the forest, waiting. There was no way he could get a clear shot at anything, the trees stood so thick. There were few low branches, and those few were dead, black, and bare. He waited. He was an Indian and he understood patience; he understood wild game, and hunting men.

A movement again, something black, something moving with extreme caution, something stalking.

The shadow moved again, briefly glimpsed among the trees. It was a man. It was Peshkov.

He was searching for Joe Mack's hideout.

They were not within a half mile of it yet, but Peshkov could not know that. He was either looking for the hideout or he was stalking somebody. Not an animal, for in this thick stand of trees there was little chance of finding an animal at this time of day.

Peshkov moved again, crossing in front of Joe Mack but at least a hundred yards away. He was visible only in brief glimpses, as the trees at that distance formed almost a wall, merging one with the other.

Now the man had come into a small clearing. Watching him, Joe Mack decided Peshkov was simply casting about, looking for some indication. He would find nothing where he was, yet had Joe Mack been only a few minutes further along they might have come face to face.

Now he was moving away, and Joe Mack watched him go. At least he knew he was being hunted, and after this he must be doubly careful in going from the village to his hideaway. He remained where he was for several minutes longer, then went down the mountainside, handing himself down from tree to tree.

Returning to the hideaway, he left his furs, then went to the village. Stephan Baronas awaited him with a handful of rubles. "We did well," he said, "but I am afraid there is trouble."

"What sort of trouble?"

"We waited outside of town until dark, and we saw a helicopter land. Two people got out, a man and a woman."

Baronas took up his pipe and methodically stoked it with tobacco. "We do not see helicopters very often. They are used on the big jobs, like building the BAM. Sometimes they drop prospectors off, but as the season grows late we see few of them."

"Did you know the people?"

"No, but the man, and he seemed subordinate, carried himself with a certain air. You know how it is? I would swear he was KGB or something of the sort. Borowsky had the same feeling.

"We had sold our furs earlier, but Borowsky wished to go back. Often there are things we need that we cannot buy ourselves. Zhikarev has often arranged to get them for us. We were going back to see him."

"And—?"

"He was not there. The place was dark and silent. That was unexpected, as he lives on the premises. We were just leaving when a car drove up. It was the same man and woman, the two from the helicopter, but this time Wulff was with them. They tried knocking on Zhikarev's door, but there was no answer. Then the man who looked like KGB forced his way in.

"We watched from some distance off. We could hear nothing, but it was obvious they found nobody inside. They locked up again, got into the car, and raced away."

Baronas was silent, smoking and thinking. "We came away very quickly and returned here by a different route. We have no idea what took place or why Zhikarev left, if he did."

"They look for me."

Baronas shrugged. "Perhaps."

"Peshkov has been looking for me, too."

"You know Peshkov? Oh, yes! I remember! Talya spoke of your meeting with him. Be careful. He is a dangerous and a treacherous man."

Joe Mack stared into the fire. Outside the wind blew cold. Soon he must start back to his own place, being careful he was not followed. Did Peshkov plan to rob him? Kill him?

It was warm and pleasant here. Talya came in from outside. He made a move to rise, but she gestured for him to remain seated. "And stay. I have a ragout. We will eat soon."

Baronas began his instruction in Russian, and Joe Mack listened carefully, repeating the words after him. Soon there was coffee, and the instruction continued while they drank coffee and, later, ate their dinner.

Borowsky came in. "I believe he has gone," he said. "I mean Zhikarev. I think he fled. He told me once he would die before he suffered questioning again, so I believe he simply left everything and ran."

"How can he escape?"

Borowsky shrugged. "Men have done it, and he is a shrewd old man. A trader in furs establishes many strange connections. He knows a lot. After all, he knows where the furs are from, in most cases. Or he can guess pretty close. After all, certain kinds of animals have certain habitats, and from some areas the fur is better than in others."

"I wish him well," Joe Mack said.

"He will need your prayers." Borowsky glanced over at Talya, who had just come back into the room. "I believe I shall disappear for a while."

"At this time of year? Where would you go?"

"I will have been seen entering Zhikarev's. If they look for him, they will look for me, also." He glanced at Baronas. "Be careful, Stephan. They have never found this place, but I do not believe they looked very hard. Wulff has been doing well, but if it is his neck or ours, it will be ours."

When Joe Mack finished eating, he looked up at Natalya who had come back into the room to stand near them. "They will not find my place so easily. You could come there."

"We will be all right, I think."

He got up. "Remember where it is, and come if you can."

"Better find yourself another place, Joe Mack. A place further away. Stock it with firewood and meat. In this weather the meat will keep, but there is frost in the earth. Dig down a few feet and it is better than any of those refrigerators that I hear you have in the States."

"The permafrost?" Joe Mack knew about that. The earth was frozen and remained so, year in and year out. Building became difficult, for anything that brought heat to that frozen ground caused it to thaw and flooded the area around.

They talked long, and he listened, saying little. To talk much was not his way, yet he liked the others to talk, and he learned much.

"Stay the night," Baronas suggested. "The cold is bitter now."

He did not like it, but liked the thought of the cold walk through the woods even less. He stayed, and it was warm and pleasant there. Borowsky left, finally, and they talked among themselves and he asked many questions, but they asked more questions of him. What was it like in America? He told them a little, careful of how much, or they would believe he lied. He got out the map he had stolen and they studied it. Looking at the map, Baronas could tell him much about the country. Some of it he had traveled, of some he had only heard. They spoke in a mixture of English and Russian.

"Do you speak French?" Baronas asked suddenly. "I hear it is taught in the schools in America."

"I speak it."

"In my country there are few who do not speak several languages. We are a small country, and many speak Polish and Russian, but there are some who speak Swedish, too, or French or German. In the old days when I was a boy, there was much travel. My father had been several times to Copenhagen and to Oslo. He had a cousin who went to America.

"When I was young I read some of his letters. Wonderful letters! He lived in Minnesota."

"Some of my people lived there also," Joe Mack said.

"You said you are an Indian? But you have gray eyes."

"My grandfather was a Scotsman, a Highlander. Some of my ancestors fought beside Bonnie Prince Charlie. There were others riding with Crazy Horse when he defeated Custer."

"Ah! I have heard of him!"

"Most people have. He was a great fighting man, and many of my people admired him until they began reading the white man's books about him. We fought him and he fought us. He was a soldier, as I am. He did what he had to do, as I do and have done. A soldier is given a mission to perform, and he does his best to carry it out.

"An Indian is different only in that he chooses his mission. Nobody ever made an Indian hunt scalps. He hunted them for honor, for prestige in his tribe. When I was a small boy, old warriors came to visit us who had known Custer. He was admired by them. They had no use for weak men.

"Later, some warriors claimed to have killed him. The truth was they did not know him. Before that last march he cut his hair, and they were looking for the long hair. Nobody knew who killed him or when. The old men who came to visit us believed he was killed early in the fight."

Joe Mack paused. "So few realize that was not the first fight. Only a few days before, the Sioux fought the great General Crook to a standstill. The Sioux believed they won. Crook thought he did, but Crook's men had to withdraw. Many were wounded; most of their ammunition was gone.

"In that fight the Sioux were better armed, and they outnumbered the soldiers. The Sioux had new Winchester and Remington rifles, repeating weapons far better than the single-shot Springfields the army carried.

"There were Shoshone Indians fighting on the side of the white man, but that was often the case. The Shoshones were old enemies of the Sioux. They did not fear us individually, but they feared us as a people."

"We know so little of your Indian wars, and most of the stories are sensational rather than factual."

Joe Mack agreed. "It is so with us, also. Few take the trouble to understand or to view the American scene with perspective. And we Americans love to find ourselves guilty of something. However, it is never I who am guilty, but those other Americans, the past or present government or the other political party. Americans almost never find other countries guilty. It is always ourselves or our fancied influence in other countries."

The fire crackled. "It is cold," Natalya said. "This night will be the coldest so far."

He glanced at her. "Do you know anything of the country between here and the Bering Strait?"

"You would be foolish to go that way. It is miles upon miles of forest, mountain, and swamp, with many freezing rivers to cross; then there is the tundra. And on the tundra there is no place to hide. Miles upon miles of wide-open country. Your best chance is toward Manchuria."

"Perhaps."

"Talya is right. That way you have no hope. There are few villages and fewer people, except along the seashore. Those you find will be native peoples or government men, those who man the radar installations or the few airfields. As she says, there is no place to hide."

"You may be right."

"You still intend to try?"

"I do, and for all the reasons you suggest. If it does not

make sense to go that way, they will be inclined to believe I went elsewhere."

Joe Mack brought fuel to the fire. The wind was picking up, and it *was* cold. Stepping away from the fire, one felt it at once. A large space could not be heated at all, a small space with ventilation for the carbon monoxide might. He must remember that.

She made a pallet for him near the fire and one for herself across from it. Her father would sleep between the fire and the outer wall, but closer to the fire, with a reindeer hide hung a few inches behind his back to act as a reflector of heat. There could be warmth beside the fire and ice forming on the wall.

They talked, but he was silent, listening. His thoughts were already reaching out to the northeast, toward the Bering Strait and the miles he must cross. When the worst of the cold was over, he would start. He would not wait for spring. With warm weather there would be travel.

He watched her face in the flickering light from the fire. She was beautiful, and she seemed so slender as to be fragile, but she had been strong with Peshkov. She was not afraid.

"You have known nothing but this?"

She looked around. "At first, when I was young, we lived in a town. It was a small town but very nice. I liked it. In the summer we had flowers, and there was a church."

"You went to the church?"

"It was not safe. If one went to church, one was investigated or called in for a scolding. Sometimes a minister would come to our house and talk to us. He was a Lutheran, a man who lived in the village and worked in a mill. I remember him well."

"He was a good man," Baronas said.

"What did you do?" Joe Mack asked Baronas.

"I was a gardener. A farmer in a small way. I raised barley and rhubarb. Rhubarb was very popular as a medicine, as well as food." He looked up from gazing into the fire. "I learned how to raise it, and I learned a little more about gardening. Some things grow very well here, but the season is short. Often the frost comes early and all is lost."

"I have never gardened. In the mountains we raised some corn, and sometimes I helped with that."

The wind was rising.

"There was a sailor I knew once," Baronas said, "and on such a night he would repeat what was said by the wives of deep-sea fishermen and seafaring men. When the winds moaned and the great seas broke against the rock, they would say, 'God have pity on the poor sailors on such a night as this!'"

"Amen," Joe Mack said.

"Ssh!" Natalya lifted a hand. "Someone comes!"

SIXTEEN

Their voices were stilled. Wind moaned around the eaves, and the fire crackled. A stick fell, sparks flew up. Joe Mack smelled the good smell of wood smoke and waited, ears straining for a breath of sound.

It came. A crunch of feet on the gravel outside. One man only. Joe Mack relaxed, watching the door, as they all were. The latch lifted. The new arrival stamped his feet to free them of mud before entering; then the door opened.

It was Yakov.

He carried no weapon. He came closer to the fire and took off his mittens, stretching his hands to the fire. "It is cold," he said, "cold."

His eyes found Joe Mack. "So? It is not easy, what you did. To come here, to find this place."

Nobody spoke, all seemed to be waiting for something. Joe Mack looked over at Baronas. "Should I go? If you have something to discuss—?"

"No. You are one of us now. Please stay."

Yakov looked up at Baronas, rubbing warmth into his hands. "It is no use. He is no longer in Nerchinsk. He was taken from the prison in the night." He poked a small stick into the fire. "We were too late," he spoke almost in a whisper, "too late!"

"But he lives?" Baronas asked.

118

"He lived then," Yakov said, "and when he was taken from the prison he was able to walk. I do not know where they have taken him. We must wait."

He glanced at Joe Mack. "They look for you. The job has been given to Alekhin."

"*Alekhin!*" Baronas exclaimed. "That is bad, bad!"

Yakov shrugged. "He is only a man."

Nobody spoke. Outside the wind whispered. Then Natalya asked, "Yakov? Have you eaten?"

He smiled. "Not today. Yesterday, a little."

"Sit where you are. I shall fix something."

"Meanwhile there is tea," Baronas said. Glancing at him, he said, "You must be tired."

Yakov indicated Joe Mack. "The country is alive because of him. You must be important."

Joe Mack shrugged, accepting a cup of tea for himself. "I have escaped. They do not like that."

Yakov thrust another stick into the fire. "You have not escaped. Siberia is a prison. It has walls of ice. Nobody escapes from Siberia."

"I shall."

"You are a good man in the forest," Yakov admitted. "You left no mark of your passing that I could see, but I am not Alekhin."

"He is good, then?"

"The master. No one is better, no one nearly so good. He is a ghost in the forest, and he can see where nothing is. No one has ever escaped him, no one."

There was talk between them then, but his few words were not enough. When they spoke slowly and directly to him, he could understand if the words were simple. Much he had learned from the miners' children returned to him, and Stephan Baronas was a patient teacher. But when they conversed among themselves, he could catch only a word from time to time. Yet it was warm and comfortable, and he did not wish to move.

The comfort was a danger. He must return to the chill of his own camp, where he would not be so much at his ease as here, where the very cold would serve to keep him alert.

Twenty-nine people, they had told him. He had met no more than half a dozen, and there was little moving about. He knew there was discussion of his presence and argument between those who feared the trouble he would attract and those who valued the meat he could contribute.

Joe Mack got to his feet. "I go," he said, and went out without looking back.

Outside in the dark the wind was raw and cold. The earth was frozen. It was unlikely anyone was watching at this hour and in the cold, but he was wary. When he arrived back at his camp in the rocky hideaway, he built a small fire and prepared his bed. He must make warmer clothing or he would freeze. Yet cold as it was, his health was good, and he lived on the meat he killed. It was a wild life he was living now, but a life to which he was born. He banked his fire and rolled in his bearskin and stared up at the rock overhead. Soon he must be going. He was a danger to them here. A little longer, to learn more of the language, just a little longer.

His eyes had closed, and now they opened again. Was that truly why he was staying on? Or was it that he needed people more than he had believed?

An icy wind whined through the trees, and a branch cracked in the cold. He pulled his bearskin snug about him and tried to hide his head from a trickle of wind from somewhere. He needed to warm the stone before sleeping, to warm it with his fire; this he must do before he slept at night. He reached an arm from the warmth of his bed to push another stick into the coals of his fire. He thought of the rocky cliffs along which he had traveled, of the rivers he must cross and the forests he must travel. And then he thought of Alekhin, the man tracker, of Alekhin who was out there somewhere, out there looking for sign, trying to find him.

He had believed they did not know where he was, but over the past weeks he had seen several parties of soldiers, searching. By chance? Or had he left some clue, some indication of his passing?

Alekhin was good. He must be doubly careful.

For two days he remained away from what he had come to think of as the village, but on the third day he killed a goral and took its meat to share.

He went to the house of Baronas, but there was no one there. Disappointed, he turned to go; then he added some fuel to the fire and left the meat he had brought. He walked away into the forest.

He was deep in the forest, walking on damp leaves among the birch trees and the larch, when he saw her.

She was standing in a natural aisle among the birch and the larch. Her hood was thrown back, and a vagrant shaft of sunlight touched her blond hair. She was, he realized, a beautiful woman. Not that it mattered to him. The days were passing into weeks, and soon he would be leaving.

She came down through the forest to meet him and paused a few feet away. "You have not been to see us."

"I built up your fire, and I left meat."

"Thank you. We found the meat and knew it was you." She paused. "We were not gone long." She hesitated again. "There was a meeting."

He waited, saying nothing. Somewhere, something stirred among the dead leaves.

"The meeting was about you. Peshkov wants you to leave. So does Rusinov. They are important men among us. My father spoke for you, and so did Yakov.

" 'Where would he go?' Yakov asked. 'It is the dead of winter.'

" 'No matter,' Peshkov argued. 'He is a danger to us all.'

" 'And we all eat meat he has killed,' my father said."

"I shall go soon."

"Where will you go? Where can you go?"

"Where I was when I came to you. I shall go back to the forest."

A wind rustled the leaves, a cold, cold wind. "My father says you may stay. It is not Peshkov who speaks for us." A last golden leaf from an aspen fell and lodged in her hair. Joe Mack looked away. She was a woman, this one.

"How are they here? Do they keep hunting even in the cold?"

She shrugged. "Usually, no. For you, maybe. This is Zamatev this time, and it is Alekhin. This has not happened before. I think there will be some hunting but not much. Men could die out there." She paused, considering it. "I think they will go to a few places. They will try to eliminate, to locate you. Then when spring comes, they will move."

She paused. "There was a woman in Aldan. It was she who was directing. I do not know her."

"A woman? What sort of woman?"

"Very attractive, someone said, but we do not know."

She looked at him. "We have ways . . . I mean, sometimes we can find out such things. This woman was in Aldan where the furs were sold. The man with her we know. His name is Stegman. We know him. He is KGB, or he was. He has been assigned to Colonel Zamatev, so the woman no doubt works with him, too. They were using a helicopter."

He remembered the helicopter that had flown over him. The same one? It could be. Whoever was flying it had stopped to investigate that old building.

"At your meeting, what was decided?"

"You may stay, for the time being. Your meat has won you friends. It is very hard here in winter. In the warm times we can all get out and look for food. We plant. We gather in the forest. We do not do badly. In the winter it is very bad sometimes, and you brought us meat."

They walked down the dim path together. There were many deadfalls, often criss-crossed, black with damp. It was treacherous walking. His eyes were busy, watching, seeking. There were few animals in the thick forest. Usually they were found closer to the streams or near clearings or open meadows. The forest was dense and, even at midday, shadowed and dim. But the days were even shorter now, the nights long and bitterly cold.

"You must talk to Yakov. His mother was from the Tungus people. They are keepers of reindeer, great travelers and hunters. They still live much as they wish, and there are many of them northeast of here. You might meet them."

They walked on without talking. Stepping over a deadfall, her foot came down on another and slipped. She caught his arm and was astonished. "You are strong!"

"Where I lived there was much hard work, and then at school—do you know the decathlon? It requires all-around athletic skill. In college I won several meets, but lost out in the Olympic trials. I just wasn't good enough."

"Botev will go to Yakutsk soon. He will take furs."

"I shall have some. Is it not far?"

"We cannot go always to the same place, and Stegman and that woman were seen in Aldan, visiting the place there. It is a danger to return now."

"He will go alone?"

"No. Someone will go with him. They may not have to go all the way. Sometimes they meet with other trappers and trade their furs. We get less for them, but the risk is less, too."

They lingered, neither wishing to end the moment. A cold wind moaned in the larch and spruce. "Come to see us, Joe Mack. I want you to tell me of the cities and the women." She looked up at him. "I have been nowhere since I was a child. We hear so little here. Sometimes, on the Voice of America—"

Surprised, he asked, "You hear it *here*?"

"When we have batteries. There is no power. Yakov has been working on a waterwheel he hopes will generate power for us but it is far from complete."

"I am the wrong person to tell you of the cities." His eyes met hers and he shrugged. "I did not get around very much. Some of my people there drink too much, and I never wished to chance it."

She laughed, but without humor. "It is a problem here, too. We hear of efforts to convince people to drink less, but so far they have not succeeded."

"I know very little of Russia."

"My father says it has not changed. Russia now is the same as under the Tsars. As a nation, Russians have always been suspicious of outsiders. They have always lived outside the community of nations. What is happening now in Afghanistan began long ago. Read Kipling's *Kim* again and especially some of his short stories. Nor have they ever permitted free travel in their country or allowed their people to travel freely outside of Russia. Balzac had to meet his Polish mistress in Switzerland, as travel to France was not permitted for long periods."

"It is a pity. I have seen much beauty here, and I have seen little."

"The Kamchatka Peninsula is magnificent. There are volcanos, snow-covered peaks, waterfalls, and splendid forests. If it was possible, I think your people would come to see it. You are great travelers, I know."

She shivered. "It grows colder. We shall have a bad winter, I believe."

"They have not bothered you here?"

She shrugged. "We are far out of the way, and we do nothing to attract attention to ourselves. Wulff knows we exist, but our furs enrich him. Nevertheless, if we caused

trouble he would have us all in prison or shot." She paused.
"I think he only knows we exist, but does not know where
and does not wish to know. Nor does he know who is here or
how many.

"You see," she looked up at him again, "we are far from
anywhere. No one travels this way. Someday—"

They walked on. "Is it true that everybody in America
has an automobile?"

"Some families have two or three. A car is not considered a luxury, but a necessity. Many people drive many miles
to work, and someone who does not drive a car or own one is
a curiosity."

"And you?"

"I could fly a plane before I drove a car, and I would still
rather fly. In the mountains where I grew up, there were no
roads. Not close by, at least. My grandfather and my father
did not want them, nor did they want visitors. When I left
the mountains to go to school I lived with some Scottish
relatives and rode in a car for the first time."

"Do Indians have cars?"

He chuckled. "The pickup has replaced the pony. I think
every Indian has one, or if he does not own a pickup he soon
will."

They paused again. "The way of life changes very rapidly
in America. When cars became available, Americans began to
travel even more, and at first there were tourist parks where
they could stop at night and camp. Usually there was one
building where there were showers and a place to cook. Then
there were tourist courts where you could rent a room with a
carport attached. That gave way to the motel, and now the
motels are passing. Too many Americans are flying now,
rather than driving. It used to be that there were filling
stations on every corner and almost as many motels. Each
year now there are fewer. I believe that soon there will be
vast stretches in America where nobody travels but local
people. It is faster to go by air."

"But you have railroads!"

"Of course, and for something less than one hundred
years they were very important. They grow less so year by
year."

Joe Mack did not go further. There was a restlessness in
him that he felt was a warning. They parted there at the edge

of the cluster of shelters, and she walked away without looking back. For a long moment he stood looking after her.

It was a grim life that faced her, a truly beautiful young
woman condemned to live her life out in a forest, making do
in a crude shelter, always in fear of discovery and what might
follow. He had never been given to parties or even the
essential affairs an officer was called upon to attend. He had
gone, and he had known the effect he created, but he was
happiest when far out in the woods or when flying alone and
high in the sky. Yet thinking of Natalya he could see her in an
evening gown at some of the balls or dinners he had attended. She was made for that world, not this.

He paused again when well back into the birch forest
and looked carefully around. He must not be followed. And
he must prepare, now, for an escape. Above all he must not
settle down to a day-by-day existence here. True, this was
the best sort of place he could find to ride out the winter, but
he must be prepared to move, and quickly, at any time.

The search was on, and it would be a relentless search.
Remembering Alekhin, he knew the man would be ruthless
as well as persevering. And somewhere down the chain of
days they would meet. Somewhere, somehow, he knew it
would happen.

Man to man, face to face, and death for one or both.

Remembering Alekhin's cold, heavy-lidded eyes, he felt
a chill.

SEVENTEEN

Colonel Arkady Zamatev was coldly furious. He was also frightened.

He had spent the evening at a gathering in the apartments of Comrade Shepilov, where he had been almost immediately surrounded by questioners wanting to know about the American who had escaped.

Who *was* he? What exactly had happened? Where was he now? There were people present who were important. Trust Shepilov to be sure of that. There were also people who would go away wondering and asking questions of each other. The hitherto solid tower he had built was showing signs of wear and tear.

There was but one answer. He must recapture the American without delay. But had he not been trying to do just that? Had he not alerted everyone? Had he not tried everything he could think of? And not a single lead.

Well, not many. There was, of course, Alekhin's feeling and the indications he, Alekhin, believed in.

Zamatev sat down behind his desk and page by page went over the reports he had received from the field.

Negative.

The man had vanished like a ghost. In a vast, only partly explored land, without weapons, without food, without proper clothing, he had disappeared. The man could not speak Russian. He could not possibly know the country well enough to exist. Aside from the one insubstantial story Alekhin had, there were no reports of thefts; yet somehow if alive, the man had to be eating.

Pennington had been brought back and grilled. He had been treated roughly, yet he obviously knew nothing. It was apparent that Pennington was telling the truth. After all, they had had no time together, and their conversation, carefully overheard, had been an exchange of the most obvious kind. As Pennington said, the man would not and could not trust him. Their informant in the prison knew nothing, either.

Zamatev made tea. He liked it strong, and on this night he needed it.

Once more he got out the map and studied it. First, the large map of the Trans-Baikal and the lands to the east. That portion of Siberia east of Lake Baikal, lying between the Amur River border with China and the Arctic Ocean, was a huge piece of territory. He merely glanced at the thick finger of land pointing eastward toward the Bering Strait and Alaska. That was impossible, absolutely impossible. Mountains, rivers, and tundra. Few villages, few people, many small mountain ranges, swamps, and bitter cold.

South toward the Amur; that has to be it. Perhaps eastward, south of Magadan?

He was studying the map when he heard the tap on the door. For a moment he sat starkly still.

The KGB? They usually came in the night. But he, Zamatev, *was* the KGB, or at least he was the GRU, which was almost the same thing.

The knock came again. Too light for that. He walked to the door. "Who is there?" he demanded.

"Kyra."

He opened the door. "Come in! Come in! How are you?" His kiss was brief. Her lips were cold from the night air.

There was no nonsense about her. She walked right to his desk. She placed a typewritten report on the map. "It is there, what I have learned, but let me tell you. I think I have a lead."

He sat down and leaned back in the chair. "Tell me."

"We covered a lot of area and we found nothing, nothing at all. We asked questions, we looked at reports. Nothing.

"In Aldan, however, there is a dealer in furs. A man named Evgeny Zhikarev."

"I know the name."

"Exactly. Stegman had questioned him once."

"What about him?"

"A dealer in furs, as I said, and a small bale of furs had just been received. Obviously he was nervous, and it had something to do with the furs. I went through them, and I know something of pelts. Some of them were very fine skins, and the best of them were treated in a different way from the bulk. Most of the furs were crudely handled, but a number of them showed the skilled hand of a man who both knew about furs and cared about them.

"Zhikarev had obviously noticed it, too, but he disclaimed any knowledge of the man who had done it. I believe him."

"You believe *him*?"

"Yes. The furs come from the forest and are obviously taken and treated by several different trappers. There is no way he could know them all, and this one was new."

"You know that?"

"He swears it and I believe him. I went through many of the furs he has for sale or trade. None of them were handled in the same way."

She took off her fur hat and shook out her hair. "Comrade Wulff wears a beautiful fur coat, and so does his wife, whom I happened to see. That's not unexpected in a section where furs are so common, but I have an idea that the comrade is doing very well by himself. I believe the traders favor him somewhat and that he favors them."

"So?"

"You and I know that happens, and Wulff seems very happy with his position."

"It is a good one, and he has friends." His eyes yielded nothing. "Some of his friends in the higher commands have fine fur coats, too. It is not unusual."

"I do not criticize. I only comment. One comment would be that Wulff knows a good deal about the furs and their origin. No doubt he could provide information if he wished."

"Ah?"

Zamatev was thinking about it. That Wulff was being given furs he did not doubt. That he might overlook a few things as a result was also probable. That he would in any way betray his government Zamatev did not believe. If Wulff knew where the American was, he would arrest him or at least report him. Hence, he did not know. But was he, perhaps, negligent? Did he know of a place where the American might be? Wulff had once been a very good man. He had covered a lot of wild country long ago. Now he was an administrator and content to be so.

"You spoke to him?"

"He was cooperative. He went back to the house of Zhikarev with me, but Zhikarev was gone."

"Gone?"

"Not at home."

"You went inside?"

"We did. Everything looked much the same, except that the bale of furs had been unpacked and placed with other furs of their kind. There were no signs of hurried packing. It looked like he had just stepped out."

"But you do not believe it?"

"I do not. I think Stegman frightened him. I think he is gone. I may be wrong, but I do not believe he will come back. Or, let us say, I do not think he planned to come back."

"But he may?"

"As a precaution I suggested to their commanding officer that the border guards be replaced for a few days. That the guards be given some leave and others put in their places." She smiled. "Just in the event that Zhikarev had made some friends along the border."

"Good! Very, very good! A friend of Zhikarev might also befriend a friend of his. You ordered the arrest of Zhikarev?"

"I did."

Zamatev walked to the window and looked out. The little car was farther down the street tonight. He gave it a glance only. This was a lead, although a slim one, scarcely more than that found by Alekhin.

If the American was an Indian he must also be a trapper. Were they not all hunters and trappers? If so, he might be catching fur to raise money he would need and to pay his way now. In any event, he could not afford to ignore any lead.

"You are tired."

"Not too tired."

He smiled. "Go home and get some rest. It will be busy around here tonight."

"We know nothing," she warned. "It is only the furs."

"And the man Zhikarev, who disappeared. It is only the guilty who flee."

"It is sometimes as dangerous to be merely suspect," she said. "Zhikarev had been questioned before, by Stegman."

"And others."

He paused, thinking about it. "We must find him, but Wulff may know something. He is one who always knows more than he says and uses it for his own benefit. This time he will use it for mine."

"Be careful of him. He has friends."

He got out his maps after she had gone and studied them. Kyra and Stegman had gone to the Sinyaya and found nothing, and so they might be anywhere. They had sold their furs in Aldan.

Because it was nearby? Or because they knew a buyer who would ask no questions? Of course, for the profit that could be made, there might be many such. But supposing they were near Aldan? He drew a mental circle around the area and began studying the streams. It was wild country once one got away from the city itself. The Sinyaya was far from Aldan. It was not even close. It was closer to Yakutsk.

He considered that. A possible buyer in Yakutsk? Of course, in such a large place there was certain to be one or more than one. Stegman would know. He had worked out of Yakutsk at one time and knew them all.

It was three o'clock in the morning before Alekhin arrived. He came quietly, sat down, and listened.

He had only just come from the taiga, and when Zamatev told him of the furs his face revealed nothing, but he was smiling inwardly. Of course! The man was an Indian. He could hunt and trap. If he had found a good place to hide and a way to sell the furs he trapped, he should have made some money before warm weather. With money in his pocket and a change of clothes he would be harder to find. He might even leave the forest.

Zamatev shook his head. Not Makatozi. He would stay in the forest. Besides he did not know the language. How long to learn to speak Russian? Even a little bit?

"You do not believe in the furs?" Zamatev demanded.

"I believe. This man is a good trapper, I think. I think you waste time. Alekhin can catch him. Only Alekhin."

"I want him alive."

Alekhin shrugged. "Always somebody died. Some like to fight me, so I kill. Why not?"

"A man named Borowsky came with the furs. He was not alone. They came to Aldan."

Alekhin considered that. There would be tracks. Borowsky was not the American, who knew so well how to hide a trail. Borowsky would have left something, but finding where he had come into the town would be difficult.

"I will look." Alekhin looked over at Zamatev. "He will fight, this one. If he fights, I kill him."

"I do not want him killed! Do you understand? I want him alive!" He paused. "You are a shrewd man, Alekhin. You have trapped animals, why not a man? Trap him, and bring him to me. When he has told me what I want, you can have him."

Alekhin considered that. To trap him? That would be amusing. He would like to see the American in a trap, helpless.

"I will look." Alekhin got up and, turning, walked out without a backward glance. Zamatev was irritated, but he needed the Yakut. There was no one quite like him, and nobody had escaped once he had started on the trail. The American would not escape, either.

He asked for and received the dossier on Evgeny Zhikarev. Quickly, he leafed through it. There was no harm in the man except it was suspected that he dealt in illicit furs. That was not unusual. Most furs were sold through the proper channels, but some dealers were known to hold back the best furs and sell or trade them on the black market.

Had the man actually fled? He glanced at the dossier again. He had been questioned by Stegman, and Stegman liked to work on the feet. It was unlikely that Zhikarev would be going very far if he had to walk. So they would find him, and they would find where the furs came from.

Kyra—she was like an extension of himself. A shrewd, intelligent woman, but she had been in Shepilov's department. He must not trust her too much, not yet. Not ever.

It was always best to keep one's plans to oneself. Tell no one at all and you were safer.

He walked to the window again, thinking of that vast country out there. Obviously, Alekhin must be right. The man was hunting, somehow. If he had sold furs he had a little money. But how had he sold them? He must have established a connection with somebody who could handle the furs or who had put him in touch with Zhikarev. Find that connection. Kyra had made a start. She had found Zhikarev. Of course, they were surmising too much. The furs might not have been trapped by the American. They were grasping at straws. How had the man disappeared so suddenly, so thoroughly?

Yet he must be wary. Not only within the borders of Yakutia, but all over this part of the country, there had been trouble. There had actually been a move to set up an independent nation, and the army had had to be called in.

Silly fools! How could they hope to exist, situated in the midst of Russian-held territory? Yet there were dissidents still around, and one never knew, in Yakutia, where sympathies lay. The brief revolt, if such it could be called, had been put down quickly and harshly, but the feeling still lurked, hidden in the inmost hearts of many here. A mistake might stir up that feeling again, and they might slow production if nothing else. No doubt there were people in Yakutia who had never surfaced during that aborted nationalistic move who might be willing to help someone escape. Some of their own people were in prison.

He swore bitterly. Why must this happen just when all was proceeding so well? Now his future was on the line. All he had done, his years of work, his careful cultivation of the right people, all could be wasted because of this one man, this American!

He returned to the map. Alekhin would find him. He had never failed, and now for the first time he was officially involved. He had been looking around, asking questions here and there; this Zamatev knew. Now he was involved, and he would discover the American.

Yet he was full of doubt. So many weeks and never even a sighting of the man!

Miles away to the south and east a heavy truck rolled through the night. The road was bad, filled with potholes and unexpected swells or breaks in the surfacing. Permafrost made the building of roads difficult, their maintenance even harder.

It was dark in the cab, only the faint light from the instrument panel picking up highlights on their faces and throwing cheeks and eyes into black shadows.

"I can only take you to Zavitinsk this time," the driver was saying, "and I can pick you up in six days' time when I am on my way back."

"That will be all right," Zhikarev said. "I will pay as usual. Half when you let me off in Zavitinsk and half when you get me back to Aldan."

"Fine! I got the same from Potanin when I took him to Yakutsk."

Zhikarev thought he would faint. His heart seemed to miss a beat, and it was a moment before he caught his breath. "Potanin? You took Lieutenant Potanin to Yakutsk?"

"First leave he's had in two years. He needed rest. That border watch is hard, hard! No telling what those Chinese will do." The driver looked around at him. "Hey! Are you all right?"

"I'm all right." Zhikarev drew a slow, hopeless breath. "Who took his place?"

"Lieutenant Baransky. No nonsense about him! He's a cold fish! Goes by the book!" The driver glanced at Zhikarev. "If you have any idea of dealing across the river, forget it."

Zhikarev leaned back against the seat. His heart beat slowly, heavily. He had come all this way! And back in Aldan—

EIGHTEEN

Huddled over his fire, Joe Mack took out the map he had stolen in the railroad camp. It was far too general for day-to-day use, but enabled him to get the large picture of what he was attempting.

His problem was one that must be faced each morning, and as his grandfather used to say, "sufficient unto the day is the evil thereof." Each day must be approached as a unit; each day must be lived with care; and if this was done, the procession of days would turn out all right.

Tomorrow must be a shadow at the back of his thinking, something of which he must think while living out today.

He must try to get other, more detailed maps. He must try to think out his route while being ready to adapt to any change of plan. He must smoke and dry meat so he could move rapidly once on the way.

Before he left here, he must have a series of goals in mind, each one to be mentally checked off when he reached it. Above all, he must be prepared to move on the instant, from here or from anywhere he stopped. He could not afford to become emotionally involved . . . now why did he think of that?

He shook his head to clear the thought. He was not involved, and it was not likely he would be. Not here, not in Siberia.

He knew they were searching for him, and he knew they were thorough. He knew that at first the search had been quick but haphazard, for in the beginning there had been no doubt he would be recaptured at once. Those first few days had seen them sweeping the area where he should have been. He had not been there because he had traveled too fast and had then taken to the river. Above all, he had stayed in wild country. Now the search would be slow, painstaking and would use every possible angle.

He believed he was now in an area where he would not be expected to be. He did not believe they had any idea where he was and hoped they did not. Yet there was doubt. Suppose they did know? That he must consider.

Each day he hunted; each night he dried meat. He delivered meat to the village and kept them living better than ever before. Constantly, he was told that, and because of that most of them wanted him to stay, at least until spring.

Again and again he went to the house of Stephan Baronas, and each night he learned a little Russian. He could ask simple questions now and was beginning to form sentences. His knowledge was increasing, and it was possible even now that he could get along, for there were many ethnic groups in Siberia, many of whom had little if any Russian. Each had its own tongue, and they spoke Russian, if at all, only as a foreign language.

He now had more than fifty pounds of meat, dried and smoked, and in the intense cold there was no question but that it would keep.

His plan was to follow down the Gonam River to where it met the Uchur, cross that river and head across country to the Maya and then to the Udoma, and follow it upstream and then cross the mountains to the Kolyma. It was but a general plan, and the chances of keeping to it were slight, yet it was that route or something akin to it that he must follow.

The distance he must cover was incredible, but if he was lucky, part of it could be done floating on rivers. That was an outside chance and a risk. There was something else he must consider, yet he shied from it. He might have to spend another winter before he could escape.

No use to worry about that. He must face immediate problems. He needed clothing.

He needed Russian clothing of the kind worn in Siberia.

His present condition would immediately attract attention, something he did not want. Sooner or later a time was sure to come when he would have to mingle with people, and he must look as they did. His dark skin was not unusual here. The Yakuts, the Tungus, the Golds, and the Buriats were all as dark as he and some darker.

Meanwhile he prepared a way in case of flight. Hiking through the dense forest he found a way that was relatively free of obstacles, one he could run over if need be. In his mind he charted every move, every turn, every step he might take. The chance that he might have to escape over this route was slight. No one could guess where he might be when flight became necessary, but if it happened close to the village or at night from his hideout, he would have the route clearly in mind.

Many miles away, near the head of the Ningam River, he prepared an emergency hideout. The region was isolated, and there was much game which he did not hunt. He might need it at a later time. He found a place where several blown-down trees had lodged in the branches of their neighbors. One, a great spruce, had heavy branches that swept the ground. Under it grew a smaller spruce with a skirt of branches that touched the ground also. Other trees had fallen in such a way that any approach was difficult and it looked like just what it was, a tangle of brush and fallen trees.

Under it he prepared a hideout that was perfectly concealed. Here, too, he planned a way in and another way out, if need be. Heavy growth overhead and the recently fallen spruce provided perfect cover. He gathered fuel and stacked it around in sheltered places, but in such a way that it could have fallen where it lay.

If he had to escape suddenly with nothing but what he wore, he could find shelter here. When time came for him to leave on his escape, he could stop the first night in this place.

That night in the Baronas cabin he said, "I must have some clothing. Is there anyone here who can make it?"

"All of us, after a fashion," Baronas said, "but not the things you need. They will have to be purchased."

"You have connections?"

"Of course, but you are larger than any of us but Peshkov, and he is broader in the body than you." He paused, sipping tea. "You must realize that those who are willing to supply us secretly would be immediately alert if they suspected you had come among us. We are considered Russian even if fugitives. You would be an enemy."

"Clothing is not easily obtained. It means standing in line, waiting," Natalya said. "That would be impossible. It is hard enough for any citizens to buy the clothes they need. There is never enough."

She looked at him thoughtfully. "I could make you a shirt."

"It would help," Joe Mack said. "Clothing I can make, but not to pass in a town or city. The clothing I make is for the forest. In a city it would be noticed at once."

"Not so much as you might think," Baronas said. "In Siberia, people wear whatever they have. You dress like some of the Ostyaks. The Ostyaks," he added, "are hunters, too. And along the rivers they are fishermen."

"I will make you a shirt," Natalya repeated. "I have some cloth." She left the room.

Baronas looked up at him, smiling faintly. "Do you realize what that means, my friend? Such material is difficult to obtain."

"She must not do it," Joe Mack said. "I can get along."

"Perhaps. You do not realize how fortunate you have been. You have not been seen. If you were seen, you would be recognized at once for what you are, a stranger and a fugitive. There are spies everywhere, but in your case everyone is a spy.

"To report you or to capture you would put one in a position to ask favors. Your friend Colonel Zamatev, for example, could arrange many benefits for someone who led them to your capture, so it would not only be a duty to turn you in, it could be profitable.

"The shirt," he added, "would help. It would make you look more Russian."

"I must find a way to get clothing," Joe Mack said. "Before spring comes I must have a coat and pants."

Baronas shook his head. "Impossible! And," he added, "even those who look to you for meat would be fiercely jealous if you obtained clothing they cannot get."

"Nevertheless—"

"I know." Baronas shrugged. "We would help you all we can. But we all need clothing. Natalya needs clothing, as do

I. It is hard for anyone, but for us who live in the forest it is almost impossible. Is it so easy, then, to have clothing in America?"

"You have only to buy it. There are many shops and tailors as well. If one has the money it is no problem."

"And the money?"

"Most of us work at something. We have our poor, of course. Our world is changing, as is yours, and new skills are demanded, more training, more education. Trades that once ensured a man of a good living for his family are good no longer.

"When my father was a boy he had a friend who wanted to become a steam engineer. Most of the threshing machines were steam in those days and running them paid well. A few years later, threshing machines were run by gasoline tractors. Now much of that has changed, too.

"Men used to follow the harvest of grain from Texas to Canada, shucking wheat, threshing it. Now combines do it all, and there is no need for all that labor. Once it was not only a way to make a living, but it was an adventure for a young man. All that is gone."

"Are there many who live by trapping, as you do?"

"Trapping? Very few. Some men who live close to wild country, of course, but mostly it is done by boys earning money for school. Trapping is no longer important in America. Once there were many beaver, and beaver hats were in vogue. The style changed to silk hats, and the price for beaver pelts fell drastically. Trappers had to find another way to make a living."

"It is the same everywhere," Baronas commented. "To survive one must adapt."

Natalya returned to the room and knelt by the fire, adding some sticks. She poured tea for them and sat on the edge of the hearth.

Joe Mack listened to the night. If there were footsteps he would hear them. "They will look for me," he warned, "and eventually they will find this place. I would not wish to bring trouble to you."

"We have always known they would find us one day. They have not simply because they have not cared. We have done no harm, we do not wish to do harm."

"What will they do if they find you?"

Baronas shrugged. "Perhaps to a labor camp. If they think we are trouble enough, to one of the extermination camps, working in uranium mines, cleaning the nozzles of atomic submarines. They always know what to do."

"And you?" Natalya asked. "How did you come to be here?"

He glanced at her. "I was a major in the Air Force, but I was flying experimental aircraft. Testing them, if you will. They knew this, of course. They believed I might cooperate and tell what they wished to know. One of the planes I was to test was planned to operate under extreme Arctic conditions, so I was becoming acclimatized. Suddenly, out over the Bering Sea my radio would not work. I was forced down at sea and taken prisoner. Obviously it was neatly planned and carefully orchestrated. The details are not important."

"And if you return to America?"

He shrugged. "I shall leave the Air Force. What I shall have to do they might understand but could not condone. It is better that I am a free agent."

She looked at him thoughtfully. He talked easily enough, and he was friendly, but there was something different about him. Often he was quiet for long periods and he smiled rarely. She was drawn to him and yet a little frightened by him.

"I had friends who migrated to America," Baronas said. "Some went for the greater freedom, some in hopes of becoming wealthy and returning with money. Only one of them ever came back and he only to visit."

"My home was in the mountains," Joe Mack said, "very remote. It was a very large house at the end of a meadow and with a magnificent view, but it was built into the mountain and built of rocks found close by. We had huge fireplaces and we burned down-wood, like in the forest around here. There were many Indian rugs.

"My grandfather, who was a Scotsman, built the house with the help of some men he hired. There was no road to the place, only narrow trails. Anything brought from the outside came on packhorses. Later, I flew home several times in a helicopter.

"It was a wild, lovely country and I loved it. I shall go back there again. From our wide porch we could look into the neighboring state of Washington, and off to the north was Canada."

"It sounds wonderful!" Natalya said. "It would be good to live in a real house again, even one so remote."

"It did not seem remote to us. It was our world, and only the seasons changed. Not far from our house there was a bunkhouse for those who worked for us. They were Indians."

"Sioux?"

"No, that was not Sioux country. It had never been. We had anywhere from four to six Indians working for us, and they were usually Kutenai or Nez Percé. After a while my father hired a couple of Basque sheepherders, and they are still with us, as are the Indians."

"Were there any towns close by? Where there were people?"

"We used to go down to Priest River, sometimes, but often we would ride through the mountains, staying always away from roads and towns until we could visit friends in central Idaho. We didn't care much for towns," he added, "only for shopping."

He stood up. "It grows late, and you will wish to sleep."

"Yours sounds like a wonderful country," Natalya said wistfully. "I wish I could see it."

"Will they let you leave?"

She shook her head. "It would be very hard, I think. Very hard, indeed."

He went out into the night and stood for a moment, standing close to the wall, waiting for his eyes to adjust to the outer darkness.

The wind stirred the dry, unfallen leaves. A branch creaked in the cold. Something moved in the forest and he remained still; then he went along the wall, ducking below the lighted window, and hesitated where the trees began.

All the twigs and sticks had been picked up from the ground to be used in kindling fires, so he moved soundlessly under the trees; then he paused to listen. Something or somebody was out there.

Peshkov? Probably—

He moved on in the darkness under the trees and then went up the hillside under the trees. There he crouched, waiting.

Somebody was coming. Somebody was following him.

Why would anyone follow him at night? To capture or kill him. There could be no other reason.

Unless, perhaps, to enter his hideout and steal his furs and meat.

A footstep crunched on the frozen earth. A huge shadow moved, and he arose from where he crouched and stood behind the man.

"If you start to turn around," he said, "I will kill you."

NINETEEN

Joe Mack held his knife against Peshkov's kidney. "You follow me," he said in Russian. "I do not like it."

"No, no! I go to my own place. I go to sleep!"

"Go, then. But if ever I find you following me or lurking around where I am, I shall hunt you down and kill you."

Peshkov was recovering his nerve, which had been frightened out of him. "Or maybe I kill you!" he blustered.

Joe Mack stepped back, the knife still ready. "Good! Now we understand each other. Go, but do not turn around. The sight of your face might make me change my mind."

He went, hurrying and stumbling. Once, when some distance off, he turned and shouted something, words lost in the wind.

Watching him go, Joe Mack knew it was soon to be time for him to leave. One enemy was all he needed, and an enemy who brought trouble to him would bring it to this small community, and they had befriended him.

Weeks had passed and he had lost count of the days. How long until spring? How long until it would be warm enough to travel? He had no desire to die in the snow, and men froze quickly, almost instantly if somehow they broke through the ice of a stream or became wet.

He went through the trees to his hideout, pausing to listen, to learn if he was followed. It was bitterly cold, and his face was covered to the eyes. He built a small fire when he was safe in his cave, for only a small fire was needed. He would not be warm, only safe from the cold.

Where was Zamatev now, and what was he doing? Cold weather might slow a search but would not stop it, and the Russian colonel was ruthless and relentless. Wherever he was he would be thinking, planning, conniving.

And Alekhin? Where was he?

There had been a woman in Aldan. Women in Russia worked as did men and might be found filling any role. This one must have been someone with rank, perhaps a second to Zamatev himself. Of her he must be especially careful, for women sometimes had flashes of intuition or at least an approach different from that of a man. Her mind, working in another channel, might come up with answers Zamatev and his male cohorts might not consider.

The worst of it was that there might be something he would not consider. As he lay curled in his bear robe he thought of that. Perhaps he should discuss it with Natalya. She might foresee something he was ignoring.

What he must do was simple enough. He must escape from Siberia and return to America.

Their problem was equally simple: to prevent his escape and recapture him. His logical route was toward China, but that way was barred, he was sure, by the careful border watch. Sooner or later they would guess he was going east, and the further he went, the narrower the country through which he must travel and the more confined their search for him.

Even now they would be sitting together, putting their thoughts together with one object only: to capture him.

He awakened rested, and his hunting led him to a fine young moose in good condition. He killed it with one arrow and skinned it rapidly, for fear it would freeze solid before he finished. Yet he managed to save the hide and the best cuts of meat, and he was not fifty yards away before wolves were tearing at the carcass. He took the meat to Baronas to distribute, keeping only enough for himself.

"Good!" Baronas was pleased. "This will quiet some of the talk."

"Talk?"

"Some of them are growing nervous. Botev is back, and

Lermontov has come in from Yakutsk. There are special details there, with helicopters, just waiting for the weather to break. Our people are frightened."

He got up. "I will take the meat to them. They will be so busy eating, they cannot talk."

When he was gone, Joe Mack looked over at Natalya. She was sewing on the shirt she was making, a very handsome shirt. "I will have to go," he said.

She nodded. "I know." She looked up at him, and their eyes met. "It has been good, having you here."

"Yes, good for me, too."

There was a long silence then, and he fed sticks to the hungry fire.

"When you get back to America, will you think of me?"

"How could I forget you?" he said, and was startled at the words. Now why had he said *that*?

"It is very far. Everyone will be against you."

"How could it be otherwise? If our people and your people could sit down together and talk about their families, their farms, and their jobs, I think there would be no trouble.

"It is our governments that are continually fencing for position, each trying to gain some advantage.

"Russia does not trust its own people. They have built a wall to keep them in, and they are not permitted to travel."

"Do your people travel wherever they wish?"

"Of course, and so does most of the world. Each year millions of Americans travel in their own country or go abroad, and many visitors from other countries come to America. They can go anywhere they wish except for a few military establishments that nobody wants to see, anyway. They photograph everything, and we do not mind. It is expected of them. Our people do the same thing when they go to England, France, Japan, wherever.

"The ironic part of it is that the Soviet Union spends millions trying to steal information they could have for the taking if they were friendly."

The fire crackled and a stick fell, sending up a shower of sparks. "It may be," he said, "that I shall have to leave suddenly, with no chance to say good-bye. Do not think me ungrateful."

"Father warned me of that." She held up the shirt to inspect her handiwork. "I cannot imagine how you will live or how you will escape them. They will be searching every-where, and the closer you come to the sea, the more intense the search will be. And how will you escape? How can you cross the sea?"

He shrugged. "That is tomorrow's problem. I think of that always, but meanwhile I deal with today."

"There are few people where you go. If you are seen, they will know it is you."

"I must cultivate the art of invisibility."

"I do not want you to go."

He met her glance and was silent. What was there to say? He must go. To stay was to die. And to stay was to be defeated, and he was a Sioux. He could fight them alone. He had always been alone. It was one of the reasons he had liked flying the aircraft he had flown. He was up there alone, dependent on nothing but himself.

When he had roamed in the forest as a boy, he had been alone. When he went away to school, the only Indian, he had been alone. But he had never minded. He was the stronger because of it.

Thinking about it, he knew he liked people. He enjoyed having them around, enjoyed their voices, their movements, their activities, but he had never had to be a part of it. He was rarely a participant. He was the interested bystander, but when he acted, it was he alone.

He liked being here, now, in this quiet place. He liked having Natalya near him, liked watching her, liked the way her eyelids lifted when she looked at him, liked to watch her fingers move. She was a lovely, graceful, beautiful woman, and here in this place there was no future at all, not for her.

"What are you thinking of?" she asked suddenly.

"You."

"Of me? What of me?"

"Of how lovely you are, how wasted all that beauty is in this lonely place. You should be in America."

"I believe I would like it. I have thought of it; long before you came, I thought of it. It has been a dream."

"I could come back for you."

"*Here*? To Soviet Russia? To Siberia? You are mad."

"I shall come back, anyway." He spoke quietly, and startled, she looked at him. "I have been attacked. I have been taken from my country, brought here a prisoner. I have been threatened, and he who threatened me, he who had me captured, has not faced me alone, man to man."

"But that's absurd! He never will, of course. Things are not done that way."

"He may have no choice."

She looked at him, amazed. Was he mad? "If you are lucky enough to escape, and the odds are a million to one that you will, you had better stay away."

"I do not have your standards. I do not have even those of my country. I am a Sioux. At heart I am a savage." He waved a hand around. "This forest? Do you think it strange to me? The forest is my home. I am a part of it, just as are the tiger, the bear, and the wolf. I belong there and have always known it. I was born out of my time. I should have ridden with Crazy Horse. I should have sat in council with Red Cloud or John Grass, but better still I should have been out there leading war parties against the Crow, the Shoshone, or whoever our enemy was.

"Always, I have known this." He bared his chest. "See these scars? I underwent the trials of the Sun Dance. Rawhide strips were buried in my flesh, and I was hung by them until they tore loose. It was once a custom of my people; it is so no longer, but for me it was necessary.

"Once, long before the Battle of the Little Big Horn, where General Custer was defeated, a warrior named Rain-in-the-Face was arrested by Tom Custer, General Custer's brother. Not only arrested, but physically overpowered by Tom Custer, who was an unusually strong man. Rain-in-the-Face never forgave him. It is said that during the massacre he cut out Tom Custer's heart and ate it."

"How awful!"

"Perhaps. But he never forgot, and I shall not." He was silent for a few minutes, and then added, "Captain Tom Custer was a very brave man. Few have ever been awarded the Medal of Honor, our highest military decoration. Tom Custer won it twice."

"To eat a man's *heart*? It is awful!"

"To our thinking, yes. But to Rain-in-the-Face it was the highest tribute he could pay a brave man. By his thinking he had to count coup upon the body of Tom Custer. Whether Rain-in-the-Face actually killed him we do not know. Some deny the heart-eating episode, but to Rain-in-the-Face it was the greatest honor he could pay him because to eat the heart of a man or animal meant you wished to obtain some of his strength and his courage."

He shrugged. "I do not even know whether I believe it or not. It does not matter. Given the kind of men they were, it *could* have happened. It was what Rain-in-the-Face would have done. In the heat of battle he would have sought out Tom Custer to kill him, and Tom Custer would have been expecting him. Be sure of that.

"Rain-in-the-Face may have hated Tom Custer, but he respected him, too. As for Custer, I doubt if he hated Rain-in-the-Face but he did know him as a fighting man."

"And you call yourself such a savage?"

"Colonel Zamatev sat behind a desk and wrote an order that forced me down at sea and destroyed the plane I was flying, and he had me captured and brought to him. This was not only a blow against my country, but an insult to me, personally."

He smiled, but without humor. "I just want to see if he can do it, man to man, alone in the forest somewhere, or even on a dark street where there are just two of us."

"You are very foolish. If you should escape, stay away and be safe."

"Foolish to you, foolish to me, also, in some ways. But it is the way I feel. The way I am. I have told you I was a primitive and content to be so.

"Oh, I should like to face him across a table at some diplomatic function. Nothing would suit me better. The possibilities of that are slight. So if I escape, I shall come back."

She shook her head in wonderment. "My father will not believe this."

"I think he will. He will not approve, but he will understand. I do not belong in this century, Natalya. I do not even belong in the last. I have always known this.

"I walk in the shoes of the men of today. I fly their planes, I eat their food, but my heart is in the wilderness with feathers in my hair."

"You do not hate the white Americans?"

"Why should I? My people came west from the Minnesota-Wisconsin border, and we conquered or overrode all that got in our path. We moved into the Dakotas, into Montana and Wyoming and Nebraska. The Kiowa had come down from the north and occupied the Black Hills, driving out those who were there before them. Then we drove them out.

"We might have defeated the Army. We fought them and sometimes we won, sometimes we lost. Only at the end did we get together in large enough numbers, like at the Battle of the Rosebud and the Little Big Horn. We might have defeated the armies, but we could not defeat the men with plows. They were too many.

"But that was long ago. The United States is our country, too, and if we do not make the most of it, the fault is ours. Many of us have. Indians are in politics, in the arts, in business, everywhere. Many of them have Anglo names and so are not known to be Indians by those who simply hear of them without knowing them.

"Many Indians like the old life, only now they ride a pickup instead of a pony."

"You are a strange man," Natalya said. "I do not think I understand you at all."

"I am an anachronism. I do not mind. From boyhood I dreamed of the old ways and wished to live the old life. My old grandfather understood, and he often said he would have liked to have lived in Scotland in the days when the clans had power and before the lairds went to living in London and turning their pastures to raising more sheep and fewer clansmen. He was a fierce old man, but a great one."

He went to the shed where fuel was stored and returned with an armful. "Tomorrow I'd better cut wood for you."

They talked quietly then and of many things, mostly inconsequential things. But at the end, Joe Mack added, "If I had a son I'd not raise him as I was raised. The world has changed and is continuing to change, and we must be prepared for it. I can dream of riding a pony over the Dakota prairies, but I fly a plane and have helped to create even more advanced types. One must deal with reality.

"Civilization is simply an organization that man has developed in order that he may live in peace with his neighbors. Laws are the framework of the structure, and if a man adopts a pattern of lawbreaking, he has no place in the organization at all."

He brushed fragments of bark from his sleeves, left by the wood he had brought to the fire. "It will be a bitterly cold night, and I have far to go."

"Father will be home soon."

"It is good, this—sitting by the fire with you."

She lifted her eyes. "Yes, it is."

"I wish it could go on forever."

"I would like that."

"I cannot stay on. They will find I am here." He paused. "I have had trouble with Peshkov," he explained. "He is a bitter, vengeful man, I believe. I must leave."

"It is a pity."

He got to his feet again. "Could you travel a long way in good weather?"

"Yes."

"Do you know the Sikhote Alins?"

"I've heard them spoken of. They are mountains, are they not? Along the Sea of Japan?"

"There is a place there called Plastun Bay. You would like it there. It is warmer than here."

"What are you saying?"

"Get your father to take you there. I'll come for you."

"But that's impossible! That coast is guarded! There is radar! Any plane inside the buffer zone will be shot down."

The outer door opened, letting in a blast of icy air. "Joe Mack! You must go at once!" Baronas was anxious. "Lermontov has just returned, and he came back as swiftly as he could make it. Somehow they believe you are here. They are coming!"

"Thank you." He hesitated at the door. "Remember? It may take a year, even two, but I will come."

She stood up, looking at him. He would remember her as she stood, slim, tall, and blond, standing in the firelight, handing the shirt to him.

"I will be there."

TWENTY

He went swiftly into the night and swiftly through the forest. At his hideout he wasted no time. He took up his pack of meat and placed it at his feet. Then he donned his bearskin coat and shouldered his pack. Taking up his bow and arrows, he took a last look around. Aside from the ashes of his fires, no hint of his presence was left.

He went into the night and ran along the dark way he had learned and prepared. It was not a path, just a choice of openings between trees, but one where he could move swiftly with no fear of falling. It was bitterly cold. His breath crackled, freezing as it left his lips.

How cold? Fifty below, at least. Probably more. He must be careful, moving fast, not to work up a sweat. Sweat could freeze, leaving a layer of ice near the skin.

The earth was frozen hard, and there was ice underfoot. He slowed his pace to step with care, for now he was entering the area over which he had passed but once. He would go to the hideout prepared at the head of the Ningam River.

Moving with care, he was sure he was leaving no tracks. There was no snow. Contrary to what people believed, there was not much snow in many areas of Siberia. The climate is dry. He crossed a stream cautiously, tapping the ice ahead of him to test for weakness.

They need not follow him to find him. They could blan-

150

ket an area with people to hunt him. They could fly over the
country, searching for him. He must avoid abandoned buildings, avoid trails, avoid any place the eye would naturally
seek out.

It was cold. He paused to listen and heard no sound, but
when he moved on it was with extreme caution. From time
to time he cupped a mitten over his nose, although it was
partly shielded by the fur cap he wore.

Here and there he found a drifting of snow, scarcely
more than frost. How far had he come? He hesitated again,
making sure of his directions, and then moving on. What he
must remember was that a great distance for him was only a
short hop for a helicopter, and tracks were easily seen from
the air.

He walked on steadily, avoiding the light snow wherever
possible, keeping to the cover of trees when he could. When
the first feeble rays of sunlight showed themselves, he was
well on his way. He had been traveling for some seven hours,
he believed, but doubted that at any time he had done as
much as three miles in an hour, for the walking was precarious and he had tried to move on rocky, snow-free surfaces
when possible. In another hour he should be close to his
prepared hideout.

The mutter of the distant helicopter had been prodding
at his unconscious for several minutes before it came to his
attention. Quickly, he eased back into the trees, merging
carefully with a tree trunk. He waited, listening. The cold
was intense. He beat his hands together and tried rubbing his
legs to keep the circulation alive. Meanwhile, the sound of
the motor came closer and closer. At this distance and in the
still cold it was audible for some time before he saw it.

When it came within view it was flying very low, and it
just barely cleared the nearest ridge. Such a copter would
probably carry three men.

It came in, flying no more than a hundred to a hundred
and fifty feet off the ground, following the same stream he
had followed. It came on, and when it passed he could see
the faces of the men inside, although he could distinguish no
features. It muttered on by, heading up for the ridge he must
cross to get to his hidden camp.

He waited, stamping his feet against the cold. What if
they landed? The growth was sparse, and they would find

him quickly. His mind was clear. If they landed, he must try to kill the pilot. If there was not a clear shot, he must get the first man who showed in the door of the plane.

He would need three arrows for three fast shots, and then he must try to get away. His camp was at most five miles off and a good place to hide. Of course, if they threw in troops for an all-out search, he was finished.

He waited, his arrows ready, his mind clear.

The helicopter was coming back.

It swung low, a wide, slow circle around the area. Had they seen something? A track? A movement?

Suddenly it began to settle on a bench not forty yards away. There was no underbrush where he hid, only a few low-growing trees and some rocks.

The copter swung lower and settled, its blades beating the air. As it settled down the door opened. He bent his bow. A man with an AK-47 stepped down from the door, and as he started to turn, Joe Mack let go his arrow.

It was an easy shot and took him right through the spine. The man started to fall, and Joe Mack let go with his second arrow.

His target was but dimly seen: a man inside the copter, apparently the man at the controls. Light glinted on a gun barrel, and he hit the ground just as the man in the copter opened fire. Bullets sprayed the trees. Ducking, he came to his feet running, but not away.

The copter would have a radio! When he was almost aft of the copter he let fly another arrow through the wide-open door.

Someone inside the copter was shouting. The man lying on the ground had not stirred.

The propeller started beating faster, and the helicopter started to lift off. He waited, watching. Something was wrong. The pilot was injured or—

It lifted, cleared the ground, started forward, made a wide circle, and then seemed to veer sharply before it crashed head on into a ridge not quite a half mile off. It crashed with a tremendous sound of breaking trees and tearing metal; then there was a puff of flame and a sharp explosion, and the flame was snuffed out.

He ran forward to the dead man, for he was dead, an arrow in his spine. Joe Mack withdrew the arrow, then hurriedly went through the man's pockets. Some matches, a belt knife. He tumbled the body into the draw and scattered brush over it. He did not take the AK-47, for the magazine was empty. He covered that, too, so it would not be quickly seen from the air, and then he started away.

He was running now, running hard.

His hideout at the head of the Ningam was not five miles off. By the time he reached it, night would not be far off. Had the pilot gotten off a call for help?

As he ran he was thinking. They would blanket the area if the pilot had gotten a message through, and he would have no chance. If not, they might think the crash pure accident. The shafts of his arrows would be burned, and unless their investigation was careful they might miss the arrowheads, which might have fallen into the earth when the copter burned.

After a careful look around and intent listening, he crossed the ridge and went down a dry watercourse on the far side. At once he was under cover of the trees, and trotting steadily he headed for his hideout. Night was almost upon him before he was under cover. So far, there had been no sounds of aircraft, although the mountain that now intervened might kill the sound.

He slowed to a walk and began picking his way. The forest was so dense he had a difficult time even finding the marks he had left to lead him back to his hideout.

His heart was pounding as he swung down through the trees and crept into his burrow.

He had been unable to see what happened inside the copter. He had shot his arrows into bodies, he knew. Evidently he had wounded one or both of them—in the crowded confines of the small copter it would not have been unlikely. There would have been small chance of escaping injury.

The pilot, at least, must have been severely injured and must have either died or passed out at the controls.

How much would those who came looking know? Had the pilot gotten off word that they were attacked? He had not seemed to be using a mike, but Joe could not really tell.

Now what to do? To remain where he was and hope he was not found? Or to try to escape and perhaps be seen out in the open?

At Chagda, almost due north, was an airport, a major

flying field, he believed. The search would probably originate there, but his knowledge of the country was too slight. Baronas had mentioned Chagda.

There was a village or town named Algama no more than twenty miles from where he lay. That was to the east, as near as he could remember.

To stay still, to wait, that would be hardest of all; but he was an Indian, and patience had been a part of his training. There was no good hiding place anywhere around, and it would be best to simply sit tight and hope he was not found. Far better than to be traveling when the country was being criss-crossed by planes and helicopters following the crash.

It was bitterly cold, and he chanced a small fire in his well-hidden camp. He prepared some tea, given him by Baronas, and then he slept.

Hours later he was awakened by the drone of a plane flying over.

Huddled in his bearskin coat, he waited. For hours, he heard nothing; then came the drone of a circling plane, not a helicopter. Had they found the wreckage? The explosion and the brief fire could not have left much to see. As near as he could make out from the little he had seen, the wreckage had caught fire and the sudden explosion had put it out. Of course, he could see nothing in the woods where the copter had crashed.

All day long, at intervals, he heard searching planes. For three days, shivering in the bitter cold, he stayed under cover. Finally, when hours had passed with no further sounds of aircraft, he left his hideout, packing all the meat he had, and started toward the river.

The Ningam flowed into the Gonam, and some sixty to seventy miles further the Gonam entered the Uchur. There was a village there. All this he knew from his talks with Baronas and Botev.

He could use the river only as a guide. It would be frozen over now, the chances were, but trusting river ice was no part of his plan. During the night there had been snow, and the river ice would be covered with it. Ice beneath snow often melted, leaving places where one might easily break through.

Joe Mack, running lightly, followed along a dim path close to the river, taking advantage of the easier travel. Hour after hour passed and he saw no one, heard no one. Once, ahead of him and across the river, he heard dogs barking, but he was too far away for them to be barking at him.

The Uchur lay somewhere ahead of him. With luck he would reach it the following night. It was a large river, and crossing it would present a problem.

He slept the night in a small cave warmed by a handful of fire. He slept badly, for the cold kept awakening him. He had been careful to keep his ears and nose covered through the day, knowing they were most liable to frostbite. So far he had been unbelievably lucky.

He was brutally tired, and it began to seem that he had never been warm. There was a mountain ahead of him, and he stumbled along, numb with cold, thinking only of trying to keep to the east of it. Near the base of that mountain the Gonam flowed into the Uchur.

It was after midnight when he came at last to the river's edge. Stumbling, half frozen, he stared at the ice. Was it frozen all the way across? He had no way of knowing. He worked his way along the bank, following a well-worn road. Out upon the ice he could see shelters built by fishermen who fished through holes made in the ice. Some of them showed light.

The road he was following dwindled into a path, and the path led down to the ice. Somebody, several somebodies, had walked out on the ice. Taking up a stick, he started, tapping the ice ahead of him. He followed the tracks, dimly visible in the light layer of snow. A long time later he scrambled up a steep bank, slipping twice and falling before he made the top. Exhausted and half frozen, he stared about, his eyes blinking slowly, trying to see something, anything that might provide shelter.

He started to walk and slipped and fell. It seemed he should just lie there, just give up—

"Get up out of that!" It was a woman's voice, speaking Russian, but a harsh, bitter voice. "Get up I say, or you'll die!"

He got to his knees and then, with an effort, stood up. "Come inside, you fool, before you freeze!"

She shoved him toward the door of a squat, ugly shack in the trees, and he almost fell inside, then straightened up. It was warm inside, almost hot. It was a snug shack with a stove, glowing and red, a table, two chairs, a bunk bed, and a wide bench. There were some shelves against the wall and some clothing hung on pegs.

He turned to face her, and they stared at each other. She was a big young woman with broad shoulders and amazingly blue eyes. "Yes, I'm a woman," she said, "so you can stop staring. I'm a married woman, too, and not looking for a man if that's what you're thinking."

"I'm not," he said simply. "I am just cold and hungry."

"I can see that. Sit down." She came to help him with the pack. "What's in this?"

"Meat," he said.

"You can share some of that with me. It's little enough I have here with my husband gone off and no money."

"Help yourself," he said.

"There's tea on." She delved into his pack. "I'll fix some of this for us."

"Take some for yourself," he said. "I'll be on my way at daybreak. Keep some. If you've no meat, it will help you."

She thanked him and then ignored him, preparing the food. As he grew warmer, he looked carefully around. The place was neat, but everything was shabby. Poverty stared him in the face.

She handed him a thick mug of tea. "Drink that," she ordered. "You're done in."

"Thank you," he said.

She turned to look at him. "What are you?" she said. "Who are you?"

"A traveler," he said, "who wants nothing to do with the authorities. They will not even thank you for feeding me."

"The devil with them!" she said bitterly. "They've taken my man away and left me little enough to do with."

She stared at him. "What are you? You're not Russian?"

"My mother was an Ostyak," he lied.

"They are good folk. I once lived in Baltshara. There were many of them who lived in the forest there. They were all right as long as they were not cooped up." She glanced at him. "You're running from something."

"Not running," he objected mildly. "Just avoiding."

She laughed without humor. Then she dished up the meat. "Eat this. Are you warming up a bit?"

"I am, thank you. You are a good woman."

"Keep that in mind," she said brusquely. "I am and shall be."

They ate in silence. She refilled his cup. "Where do you go?"

He shrugged. "Away."

She looked at the bow and the quiver of arrows. "I've seen nothing like that since I was a child."

"Do you have visitors?"

"Me?" she snorted. "I do not." She indicated the bench. "Sleep there, and when the day comes, be off with you."

"All right," he said. She had taken little of the meat. He took out more. He guessed it was about ten pounds. "Keep this. You're a fine woman, and you have shared with me."

He slept well and quietly, and when dawn came and his eyes opened, she was already at the fire.

"There's tea. Drink it and be gone." She stood up, looking at him. "I have had time to think and I know who you are, although you could pass for an Ostyak with some."

He ate, drank the tea, put on his coat, and shouldered the pack.

"You're a good woman," he said. "I shall pray for you and yours."

"Pray, is it? A long time since I've heard of that. Not since I was a small girl and we had churches where I lived, and priests. Well, pray if you will. I could do with a few prayers. Now be off with you, and if you say you have seen me, I shall say you lied."

"Of course." He smiled suddenly. "But don't forget there's a man walking away who will hold a place for you in his memory."

He went out and walked quickly, taking a forest path. When he looked back she was standing there, watching him go. He lifted a hand, but she turned and went back into her shack, her warm shack.

TWENTY-ONE

Colonel Zamatev spread out the map on his table. "Show me," he suggested.

Kyra Lebedev put her finger on a spot. "In that vicinity. We have a report. He was seen there, in that place. With a woman."

"A *woman*?"

"If we move quickly," Kyra said, "we can take him. Our informant says he does not live with the others but has a place not far from there. Our informant is not sure but believes he is our man."

"And the informant? Is he reliable?"

She shrugged. "When it serves his interest. He has reported to us before, but I think it is only when he has personal animosity toward the people reported."

"There are many such. Nonetheless, if we move quickly, we—"

"You will waste time." Alekhin spoke for the first time. Kyra thought herself important, and he did not like self-important women. In particular he did not like this Lebedev woman.

"What do you mean?" Zamatev demanded.

"If he was ever there, he is not there now. He is gone."

"How can you be sure?" Zamatev demanded irritably.

Alekhin got to his feet and moved to the table. He put a

158

thick finger on a mountainside near the head of the Ningam. "What happened there?"

"Nothing that I know of," Zamatev said. "Oh, yes! One of our search helicopters was lost. It crashed into a mountain or something. I have the report." He gestured toward a box on the table. "What about it?"

Alekhin looked up from under thick brows. "It was I who found it."

"And the bodies of the airmen. So?"

"Of two airmen."

"Two?" He glanced toward the report. "I have not studied it, but there were three men in that helicopter."

"But only *two* bodies. Burned beyond recognition."

"There were three men in the helicopter," Zamatev replied patiently. "Three. They will find the other body when they have searched further."

"I have found him."

"Well, then?"

"I found him on the ground, three miles from the crash site. He had been covered with dirt and brush. He was dead. He had been killed."

Zamatev sat down, staring at Alekhin. Kyra started to speak, but a gesture silenced her. "What are you saying?"

"The American did it. The Indian." He put his finger on the map. "The flying machine landed here. One man got out. He was killed, shot in the back with an arrow."

"An *arrow*?" Zamatev was suddenly impatient. "What are you talking of? Killed with an *arrow*?"

"He was shot in the spine. Very good shot. Then the airmen shot. The Indian ran, shooting another arrow into the open door, I think. The pilot was hurt by this arrow. He took off, and the flying machine ran into the mountain in the forest."

Zamatev stood up, resting his knuckles on the map. "Now let me understand. You are saying this Indian shot one of our helicopters down with a bow and arrow?"

"Men came to the crash site after I found it. They looked around and gathered up burned bones and a few other things. Then they went away.

"I did not go. I stayed three days. I looked to understand. I sifted the burned earth and leaves. I found two arrowheads."

"One of them was seen by those who checked the crash.

It seemed of no importance, just an old arrowhead from ancient times."

"It was not ancient. No arrowhead in Siberia was made like these. I found *two*, not one. I think the Indian shot two arrows into the open door."

Colonel Zamatev sat down again. He was no fool, and if there was one thing Alekhin knew, it was the wilderness evidence left by men and animals. And the third body had been found, he said, some distance from the crash site.

"You are sure about how the third man was killed?"

"I am. There were marks where the flying machine came down. Marks on the ground, in the dirt. There were tracks where the man got out of the machine.

"He stepped backward, with a gun. He had started to turn when the arrow hit him. It was a very good shot. The arrow went through his spine and sank very deep. He is a very strong man, I think.

"Somebody from the machine shot. I found bullet scars on trees, but the Indian was already gone. I tracked him. He ran swiftly to a place further back of the copter, and then he shot two times more. The machine went away, it took off very badly. One runner, or whatever you call it, dragged on the dirt.

"The Indian, he thought maybe the machine had called for help. He covered the body and hurried away."

"And where is he now?"

Alekhin shrugged. "He went far and very fast, I think." He got up. "I will find him."

"Wait! How many men will you need?"

"No men. I will do it. Men walk around all the time, spoil the tracks." He paused. "Maybe you could alert your soldiers between Oymyakon and Magadan."

"Alekhin, do you realize what you are saying? That's an enormous spread of country! It is impossible!"

Alekhin shrugged. "If you want him, you watch. He will go that way; if not now, later. I know him. I feel it here." He touched his heart. "This man does not think of time. He does not think of distance. The forest is his home."

"The man," Zamatev said patiently, "is what the Americans call 'an officer and a gentleman.' He is a graduate, with honors, of a university. He is a highly skilled flyer with a considerable knowledge of mechanics and the science of aerial flight. He is—"

"He is an Indian. I see him clear. All you say is true, but here," Alekhin touched his heart, "he is Indian.

"He has gone to the forest, and his natural home is the forest. Do not look for him in cities. Do not expect him to need what you need. What he must have the forest will give him."

"Out there he will freeze to death," Kyra said.

"He has been there. He lives." Alekhin straightened up. "I will find him. I will kill him."

"You will not kill him! That's an order! I want him back here! I want him in prison. He has information we need, and I shall have it. Cripple him if you will. Blind him if you will, but he must be able to talk."

When the door closed behind him, Zamatev glanced at Kyra. "Can you believe it? A helicopter lost, destroyed by that Indian."

"The report on the crash has been turned in," Kyra spoke carefully. "It has already gone on to the bureau."

Zamatev pursed his lips, then turned to gaze out the window. What was the old saying? Let sleeping dogs lie. Well, why not? It was better than the endless reports, the questions, all that would happen if he amended the report with Alekhin's information. No use to have the loss of a helicopter and three men chalked up against him. He had trouble enough as it was.

"Can you believe it? Oymyakon to Magadan? It is impossible!"

"Alekhin believes he is going north and east."

"That's absurd! It is impossible!" He paused, swearing under his breath. Who would believe that a man could escape from such a prison and vanish? Even now, did they really know?

He glanced at Kyra. "Are you ready for another trip? I want you to take Stegman and whomever you need and find that village. The place where the report says he was. I want you to find the woman, if there is one, and question her. I want to know all there is to know about Major Joseph Makatozi."

"I would be gone for a while."

He glanced at her. "Well, you do not have to leave

tonight. Monday would be soon enough. After all," he suggested, "it will take you some time to get ready."

"Of course. I shall leave Monday, then." She arose and took up her gloves and purse. "The little car? It followed me when I left before."

"Those are Shepilov's people. They watch me always. I do not mind. It keeps them out of mischief."

When she had gone he walked to the window again and watched the little car move off, following Kyra. He chuckled. She could handle that. She was too good for them, too shrewd.

Walking back to the desk, he contemplated the map. Oymyakon to Magadan? It was impossible! He scowled, then put a finger on Nel'kan. Suvarov was there, on other business. Let him make himself useful then.

Nel'kan was closer. There were some good men there, and if they moved down from the north they could, they might, intercept the American.

Alekhin could be right. Perhaps they wasted time searching villages and towns, watching the borders. If the man had reverted to living like an Indian, he would certainly be in the forest. Cold it might be, but the aborigines had lived there for thousands of years. It still might be done.

So? What was the situation? Kyra would find the village where the informant had said there was a woman. Suvarov could move into action from Nel'kan. And Alekhin was on the Indian's trail from the vicinity of the helicopter crash.

But think of it! Three men gone and a helicopter! Kyra was right, as usual; let the report stand. No use to muddy the waters.

Of course, there was Shepilov, but Shepilov be damned!

Evgeny Zhikarev stood alone in the night watching the truck disappear along the bumpy road.

Potanin had taken leave and gone to Yakutsk. A Lieutenant Baransky was now in charge, a stickler for the rules. Standing in the darkness on his crippled feet, he wondered what he should do.

He dared not return to his shop. He would be questioned, and he had been through all that. His escape was cut off for the time being, and to think of all that nice money awaiting him in Hong Kong!

He could not think of that now. To attempt to get past Baransky would be to ruin all he had planned. Baransky would either arrest him or report him if he suggested he had business over the line. He would be arrested, questioned—

No. That was out of the question. So what to do? After all, he was a trader in furs and a few other things as well, and there were others like him, and they knew each other. For the sake of business it was important they know each other. So what to do?

He needed time. Two weeks, perhaps a month, before Potanin was back on the border. He would come back broke, or he was like no soldier Zhikarev had ever known. Broke and ready to do business. So he had only to wait, but where?

Khabarovsk? His cousin was there, doing a little business in furs but holding some government job as well. On the coast, though, was another cousin at a little place on Olga Bay. That might be safer, but was further away, almost twice as far.

Hobbling on his crippled feet and using a cane to good effect, he started down the street to a place he knew. The street was empty. What would he say if a patrol came by?

He heard a confused sound of voices behind him, and he hurriedly drew back into an opening between two buildings.

A gang of hooligans, and if they found him they would certainly rob and beat him. They might even kill him. Such gangs had become common in Russia. Not long ago, one such gang had beaten an engineer to death to rob him of his blue jeans. Fortunately, these had not seen him. They went back in a straggling group, shouting obscenities at each other.

When he reached the place he sought, several trucks were preparing to leave. Known to several of the drivers, he soon found a ride to Khabarovsk.

The driver was talkative. Zhikarev would have preferred to sleep, but he knew there was no better source of information than these drivers, who were continually on the move. What they had not seen themselves they heard from other drivers.

"How are things along the coast?"

"Quiet. Fishing's good, they say." He jerked his head toward the rear. "Back there is trouble. A prisoner has escaped, and he must be a big one. They are asking all sorts of questions. I tell them nothing. Let them find out, if they can.

"Khabarovsk is busy. Filled with soldiers. Builders, too. Always a lot of construction in Khab."

He droned on, talking of this and that, and Zhikarev listened, but with only half his attention. He simply wanted to rest.

"Going on this time. Only stopping in Khab for fuel. Going on to the coast."

Zhikarev's eyes opened. "To the seacoast? I have a cousin at Olga Bay. I have been thinking—"

"Stay with me. I can take you right there."

"I would like that. I would like it very much."

"Cost you," the driver glanced at him, wondering how much the little man was good for. Not much, probably. Might be better just to get him off into the mountains and—

No, no. He had connections. If he did not turn up where he was going, the word would get out. Maybe to the KGB, but more likely to his own people. This one was into furs, and those fur dealers and trappers all worked together.

Try something on one of them and you ended up with your truck in a ditch and your head bashed in. Not for him; he had too many dark and lonely roads to drive.

"Last time I drove to the coast," he said, "I saw a tiger. Big one, too. Right in the middle of the road. Looked as big as a cow. Jumped out of the way.

"Beautiful over there, beyond the Sikhote Alins. Like to live there when I settle down. If I ever do." He swung the heavy truck around a wide curve. There was no traffic on the road. "My girl says no. She likes cities. Wants to live in Khab. Excitement, she says.

"Excitement, huh! She should drive this truck for a while! She'd see excitement!

"Take last night. KGB all over the place. Getting ready to raid some place in the forest. Must have been fifty of them; soldiers, too!"

Zhikarev listened, only half awake. It began to seem that he had decided to move just at the right time. There were furs in his shop, but he had left papers consigning them to Wulff. He chuckled. Let Wulff explain that.

"Where d'you want to go, exactly?" the driver was asking.

"Olga," he said. "My cousin's there."

"Oh, sure! Used to be a tiny place. When I was a

youngster I was there once, only a customs house and a barracks there then. Now it's become quite a place.

"Seafood! Best anywhere around. Fresh caught, right from the bay or the Sea of Japan! Tetyukhe Bay is right along the coast there. Know it well. Plastun Bay, too. Everybody eats well around there! Fish, all kinds, ducks, geese, venison, whatever you want. That girl of mine, she likes the bright lights and the dancing! Me, I like to eat well! I like to fish, myself. Well, I'll just have to talk her into it."

Zhikarev slept, uneasily, bouncing around on the rough road, listening to the drone of the driver's voice. It was warm in the truck's cab and the driver had covered the seat with sheepskin.

Suddenly, a long time later, the truck pulled over into the shadows under some trees. A hand touched Zhikarev's shoulder.

"Go over there under the trees. It will be cold, but you wait there."

Zhikarev gathered himself and buttoned his heavy coat. He took up his cane and got clumsily down from the cab.

"Pick you up on my way out from Khab." The driver hesitated and then said, "I would stay hidden was I you. The word's out to pick up a man with crippled feet. Might be using a cane."

The truck rolled away, pushing an avenue of light before it. How long had he ridden? For days and nights, it seemed.

So they were looking for him? Well, he had expected it. This driver seemed a decent sort. If he could only get to the coast. Nobody knew about his cousin, or he did not believe they did. He could stay there until things quieted down, and then back to the border and after that, Hong Kong.

It was cold, bitterly cold! Using his cane, he hobbled across the road and into the trees.

TWENTY-TWO

Peshkov met them in Aldan. Colonel Zamatev took an instant dislike to the man, but that was the trouble with this business. You encountered many such, and you had to handle them with gloves for they might know something. Yet they were liars as well as traitors, and one had to be careful. Always, there was the chance of an ambush such as had occurred a few months ago, when several KGB officers were led into a trap and murdered. There was so much crime these days. It was never in the newspapers unless there was a trial and the judgment reported.

Peshkov would lead them to the village. Stegman glared at him from cold blue eyes. "If anything goes wrong," he said, "if there is trouble, I will kill you first."

Peshkov swallowed. "There will be no trouble. These people will not fight. Most of them are old people or children."

Hours later they descended on the village. They struck swiftly and from all sides. And they found nothing.

At one shack, there was an old man sitting in the sun, with several grandchildren playing nearby. Inside the crude hut was an old woman with a samovar, making tea.

Every other house was empty.

"I tell you," Peshkov said desperately, "they were here!

The man Stephan Baronas lived there, with his daughter! Day after day I have seen them here!"

Alekhin looked around the cabin. He touched the ashes of the fire with his fingers. "Cold," he said. He knew he could find something, and later he would look. He did not like Peshkov and enjoyed seeing the man sweat.

"They are gone," Peshkov said. "I cannot understand it." He was bewildered. "Where would they go? How would they go?"

"You have led us up a blind alley," Zamatev said coldly. He walked across to the old man sitting in the sun. "Grandfather"—he pointed—"where are the people who lived in that house?"

The old man's eyes were vague. His voice trembled with age. "Salischev? He has gone. I do not . . . I do not remember when. Long ago, I think. Sometimes campers come." He looked up, suddenly angry. "Men come and stay; they kill game; they take food from us. They stay in that place or"—he waved a hand—"in one of these. They steal. Evil men—"

"We are looking for Stephan Baronas and his daughter, or the man Borowsky."

The old man shook his head. "They never say their names. They come and they go. They are strong young men and should be in the army or working on BAM. BAM? Is that the railroad? We had a railroad when I was a boy. It was down by the Amur." He shook his head. "I never liked it. Too close to China! Those yellow bastards, one cannot trust them! I wouldn't trust them!"

"Baronas," Zamatev said patiently. "We were told he lived in that cabin."

"We are alone. Alone! I do not want to be alone! I want to talk! And there are only those strangers. They are hooligans, all of them! Hooligans!"

"Did you know Stephan Baronas?" Zamatev was patient.

"They come and they go. Sometimes they speak, sometimes they do not." He puckered his brow and squinted. "Baronas? Is that a Russian name? I think not."

Zamatev turned angrily. "Peshkov? Do you know this man? Who is he?"

Peshkov was sweating. "I do not know him. He is here. He has always been here. There's been no reason—"

"You brought me here to find the American. You spoke

of this man Baronas. There is no such man here or the daughter. You have lied to us."

"No! No, please! I have not lied! They were here. There were many of them, but they are gone!"

"That place," Zamatev pointed, "has not been lived in, probably, for months!"

Alekhin sat on a fallen log and watched. Of course it had been lived in, but they had not asked him. It had been lived in not long since, and only a clumsy effort made to conceal the fact. He did not care about all this. It was a waste of time. Soon he would be on his way, and he would find this American. He knew where he was going now and knew the farther he went the easier he would be to catch. There was no hurry. He would get him in his own good time. Meanwhile this crazy old man was making a fool of them. And if they tortured him they would get no more from him.

Alekhin was contemptuous of Peshkov, and he was pleased to see him embarrassed.

Obviously the people here had scattered and might return again when things quieted down. What interested him was where the American had lived, certainly not here.

He got up and walked across the small clearing. If he had visited the Baronas family, then he would have left from there. He stood in front of that shelter and looked around. After a bit he walked past the corner of the place and looked up through the trees.

Gathering fuel, they had broken the dead branches from the lower part of the aspen trunks. They had picked up whatever had fallen to the ground, too.

There were old tracks under the trees. Some big square heels he recognized as tracks made by Peshkov. Smaller, older tracks evidently left by the woman. He moved up through the trees. Peshkov's tracks were days old but had not been disturbed. Nothing had been up here since.

Alekhin stopped and studied the ground. Faint smears over Peshkov's tracks here. He studied them thoughtfully, then went on. Peshkov had stopped, flatfooted, his two big feet side by side, the tracks blurred a little as though he had moved. Something had stopped him right about here, stopped him abruptly. There were smudges behind him. He walked about, came back to the tracks, and studied them some more. Somebody had slipped up behind Peshkov and stopped him.

A knife in his back, or a gun. The American probably had no gun and did not even want one. He could have taken the AK-47 from the soldier he had killed at the helicopter, but he had left it.

No ammunition in it, of course, but that was not it. The American wanted to kill silently. A gun was noisy. It attracted too much attention.

Why had he not killed Peshkov? He was weak, this American. He should have killed him and just carried the body off and dumped it. With a man like Peshkov, who would care?

He worked his way up through the trees. The American was wearing something soft on his feet. What they called moccasins. His shoes had worn out, and he had used the skin of an animal to make shoes.

It was not an easy trail to follow and it was many days old, but nobody had been this way before. He lost the trail, found it again, and then found the cave.

A nice place. Oh, a very nice place! Spots of grease from cooking left on the rock, the ashes of his fires. Very small fires of dry wood. Very little smoke, not much light from the fire. Yet this place would have been warm.

Alekhin went outside and stood looking around. He could hear the mutter of voices from what they were calling the village. The American would have wanted a way out, a way to leave here quickly if necessary.

Alekhin took his time. He was learning something about this man he was following. Men and animals form habits. They have certain ways of doing things, and once you have visited a camp or two you always know how that man will camp again. You will know what he looks for, how he builds his fires. And this one was cautious.

Alekhin was pleased with the American. The man used his head. Now what would the next step be? He would have wanted an escape route. He would have wanted a second camp and perhaps a third. If the American had been here long, he would have prepared for escape.

When he came upon the opening in the trees, the hair prickled on the back of his neck. Ah? So! He found a faint smudge here, a piece of a track there, and he turned to look back.

Shrewd! The American had chosen a way of escape he

knew. It was not straight away; it curved back on itself, but always gave a smooth way to go. He had used this way at night; that was why there were any tracks at all.

Slowly Alekhin was building a store of knowledge about the American. If he had planned such an escape route once, he would do so again. It would be something to remember.

Alekhin turned and walked back to the village. The soldiers were assembling.

Zamatev was irritable. He looked up angrily. "Where have you been?"

"I look about. He was here. I must know what he did here."

"That old fool knows nothing! Peshkov has lied, I think, hoping for a reward."

"He did not lie. He is a fool and a traitor, but he did not lie."

"The American was here?"

"He was." He jerked his head. "I found his place. It is a good place." As Zamatev started, Alekhin said, "There is nothing there."

Zamatev stopped. "You looked around?"

"He wears moccasins now. His boots wore out, so he wears moccasins."

"Moccasins? Where could he get them? We must find—"

"He made them," Alekhin interrupted. "He is an Indian. Indians can make soft shoes. He can make clothes to wear. He can live off the country."

"Can you track him?"

"Of course. No need to track from here. I will go to where the helicopter fell. Track him from there."

Together they walked back, passing the soldiers, who fell in behind them. One, a noncommissioned officer, saluted. "Shall we burn the places, sir?"

"Let them be," Zamatev said. "They will come back. Then we will get them."

When they parted, Alekhin took a helicopter and four men to the site of the crash. "Stay behind me," he told them, "and stay awake. Keep your eyes open. Maybe we see him."

"You don't think he's still around?"

Alekhin stared at the soldier from his heavy-lidded eyes until the soldier began to sweat and back up. "We do not know what he is doing. We do not guess. This man is dangerous." He stared at them. "One man died here, and two died up there. He is but one man, but three are dead and a helicopter smashed and burned."

He looked at them with contempt. "Keep your eyes open or you will be dead, too."

He cast about for tracks. The Indian was a tall man with a fairly long stride. If you found one track, you looked the approximate length of that stride for another track. This American did not always choose the easy way. He often stepped on stones. He did not have to try to be careful. He was always careful in the woods. It was his nature.

By nightfall he had learned more about the American's methods of travel.

He did not stop to hunt, so he had a store of food. He had smoked and dried meat back there. Alekhin had not found the rack, but he had found holes where it had been set into the earth. He was carrying a pack. Alekhin could tell that from the increased depth of the tracks since leaving the cave. It was very slight, but it was there.

At the sight of the attack where Joe Mack had killed the soldier, Alekhin had correctly deduced the reason. There was no cover for a man on the ground. When the soldier turned around, he would have been seen.

That night around their fire, Alekhin went over every move in his mind. To follow a trail one had to decide what it was the pursued wanted to do.

To escape? Of course, but to what? To where? It was unlikely the American had friends, so his one object would be to get away, to get out of Siberia, to return to his home. Alekhin had never believed in the border of China. This man was an Indian. He would follow the old migration route, the way the ancient hunters had gone when they followed game into America.

Of course, they had not known they were going to America or even from one continent to another. They had simply gone hunting and followed the game to where they could kill them. And they had continued to follow the game.

The shortest way across the water was at the Bering Strait. He would choose that way. Zamatev had never believed that, but then Zamatev was a city man, a man of the streets and towns.

The American was an Indian. He would go where the

game was because that was how he must live. He dared not go to the towns because he did not know the language.

Zamatev could do it his way. Alekhin had no interest in towns.

Zamatev drew the cork from the bottle and filled two glasses. "I came as quickly as possible," he said.

"I am sorry. When I sent word, I thought they would be there. When we located the village, I did not believe it would be empty."

"Somebody talked," Zamatev surmised.

She lifted her glass. "Perhaps. More likely they just got in a panic and fled. I think the American had already gone."

"Alekhin has his trail. He will get him now."

"Maybe."

"You do not believe it?"

"Who knows? This one is different." She looked across the table at him. "You fly back tomorrow?"

"I must."

"I shall fly to Magadan. Something might be done from there."

He nodded. "Grigory is there. He's a good one."

"I was thinking of him." She paused as if uncertain of what to say next. "Shepilov is there, also."

Zamatev's glass came down hard on the table. "Shepilov is in Magadan? Why?"

She shrugged. "That is why I am going. He knows something or believes he does. You know how it is with him. He does not move if he does not have to. Something important would be needed to take him to Magadan. He does not like the place."

"How do you know that?"

"I worked for him. Don't you remember? It was gossip in the bureau. He did not like Magadan, but he had been posted there once, long ago."

"So he will have friends there?" Zamatev was thoughtful. "Perhaps he has some word from them? Is that what you believe?"

"Grigory will know."

"Yes. Do you think he is loyal to me?"

"Oh, yes. He has told me so, and I know he hates

Shepilov, as much as he can hate anyone. It isn't in him, you know."

"Hate clouds the mind. It is better to have no emotion when it is work. Do what needs to be done, and do it coolly."

After she was gone he took out the map again. The net was drawing tighter now. They knew where he was. Not exactly—that would come later—but they knew where he had been, and Alekhin was following his trail. Kyra would be in Magadan, and Grigory would know what to do. Suvarov was in Nel'kan, even closer.

But what had taken Shepilov to Magadan? Shepilov would not move from his comforts unless he was sure of something. But Makatozi could not be that far along, not unless he had stolen a plane or caught a ride on one.

Of course, Shepilov would dearly love to capture the American. Zamatev could just see the smug satisfaction on his face.

Again Zamatev stared at the map. What a fool he had been not to keep the man in irons. Now all he had done, all he lived for, all he hoped to be, depended on capturing the American.

He stared at the map, stared at the area where he must be. Stared as if his very gaze would make Makatozi emerge from the map in a living presence.

He had to have him. There was no other way. He had to take the American.

There was no time.

Why had Shepilov gone to Magadan?

Why?

TWENTY-THREE

Alekhin was in no hurry. Siberia was a wide land, and the American was walking. To pursue a man effectively, it is best to begin with his thinking.

How did he travel? Where did he sleep? Was he skilled on a trail? What places did he choose when he wished to hide?

What did he eat? If he hunted, how did he hunt? How expert a woodsman was he? How did he cross streams? What did he do to avoid encounters with people? What did he know of the country across which he traveled? What was his eventual destination? Was he liable to alter that destination? What did he plan to do when he arrived there?

These were questions Alekhin asked himself, among many others. Bit by bit, picking up pieces of the trail here and there, he was learning to know Major Joseph Makatozi, and he was enjoying the acquaintance.

In the first place the man was *good*. Alekhin had never trailed an Indian before, although he had tracked down a few of his own people or other Siberians. The trouble was they were becoming too civilized. The Yakuts, Ostyaks, and others were losing their wilderness skills. They were working in factories, becoming soldiers, living in towns where they could see films and go to places where they could dance the new dances. Only a few of the old ones understood the forest anymore.

Alekhin was not given to introspection. He did not examine his own motives. He was given a job to do and he did it. What became of the man after he was caught he had no idea and did not care. He was a member of the Party, but he did not think about it. He knew little of the philosophy of Communism and cared less. Marx and Engels were but names to him. Lenin was one with whom he could identify, Stalin even more so.

These men and their ideas and accomplishments were far from him. He cared about the forest, but only as a place to live. He did not object to the killing of game or the cutting down of trees. He had no knowledge or thought of the future. The possibility of there being a time when there was no more forest was something he could not imagine. It had always been here; it would always be here. The idea that man could not exist on a planet without forests was completely foreign to him. That trees remove carbon dioxide from air and return oxygen to it would have only made him blink or shrug. The idea was something he could not comprehend and with which he was unconcerned. He gathered wood for his fires, he killed animals to eat, and beyond that he gave them no thought.

For all city dwellers he had only contempt. He had no sense of inferiority concerning anybody or anything. There were spirits in the wilderness, in the trees and mountains, he knew that. Occasionally he appeased them in some minor way. He respected them without thinking of them.

He was as elemental as a beast. He had the strength of a gorilla and the movements of a cat. He thought no more of exercise or training than does a grizzly bear or a tiger. His strength had been born into him, and he used it constantly.

When Zamatev said he wanted the American alive, Alekhin was only half listening. Alive or dead did not matter, although it was often less trouble simply to kill them and save himself the trouble of getting them back to a highway or a railroad.

As for taking the American alive, Alekhin had his doubts. The American was revealing himself in his trail. He had also revealed something of himself in the helicopter incident. The only puzzling question to Alekhin was why the American had not killed Peshkov. He'd had him cold.

Alekhin had read the tracks easily enough. The American had had him and let him go, and Peshkov had immediately informed on him. So the American was a bit of a fool.

Not entirely a fool. That would be dangerous thinking, but he had hesitated to kill.

Alekhin wasted no time thinking of motivations. One did what was necessary, and it had been necessary for the American to kill Peshkov.

The American would not be easily taken. Cornered, he would fight, and Alekhin would have to kill him.

He would have no choice.

Those soldiers were as much to protect the prisoner when captured as they were to assist him. So if necessary he might have to kill them, too.

On the third day after Joe Mack's passing, Alekhin and his soldiers came to the shack of the big young woman with the blue eyes. She knew nothing, had seen nothing.

Her manner was brusque, and one of the soldiers did not like it. "I shall come back," he said, "and question you further."

"Bah!" she said contemptuously.

He started back, and Alekhin stopped him with a sharp order. "Do not be a fool! She would take your rifle from you and spank you with it. She cares nothing for you or your uniform."

The soldier grumbled, and Alekhin said, "Look around you. This is where she *lives*. Could you live here? You would starve. You would die in the cold. Women like that you leave alone, or speak to politely, very politely."

The soldier continued to mutter, and Alekhin said, "If we had the time I'd let you go back, just to see the fun. And if you continue to grumble, I'll send you back."

Alekhin found a camp on the slope of Mount Konus. A bed of spruce boughs, the remains of a small fire, a corner of a birchbark dish that had not quite burned, although left in the fire. On the side of the part of the dish that remained, he saw a tea leaf.

So he had tea? Where had he gotten that? Or had he brought it from that so-called village?

The trail away led down into a grim and awful gorge, cluttered with fallen trees, broken boulders, scree, and great slabs of rock, much of it overgrown with thick green moss that was treacherous underfoot. Much of it was easy walking but deceptive, as under some of the moss there was ice formed from moisture that had seeped through to the rock slab beneath and frozen. A misstep and a man's feet shot from under him. A bad fall at any time and death if it happened on the brink of a cliff.

It was slow going, hand work as much as with the feet, and the soldiers were frightened. They were Russians, peasant boys from the flat country, with the exception of one who was from a city.

The American had gone this way and left no sign. Almost none. Alekhin found a place where he had rested his hand in getting past a tight corner of cliff. He found a partial print of an *unty*, a moccasin.

The trail was descending steeply down from the mountain. Every step must be taken with care. A half mile further down, Alekhin found a place where the American had slipped; moss had skidded under his foot, leaving a telltale bare spot where the ice had frozen again.

How far ahead? Alekhin studied the spot and then shrugged. Maybe two days. They were gaining on him.

He was positive now that the American was going north and east. He was planning on trying to cross the Bering Strait.

He would have no chance there. The area was patrolled and covered by radar. Simply no chance at all. Yet the American was no fool, and he was going that way.

Desperate? No other way out? He was a flyer, and yet he had made no move toward an airport where he might steal a plane. The word was that he could fly anything.

Alekhin was irritated by the soldiers. They moved too slowly. Not being woodsmen, they took special care, and it was well they did, for they were clumsy in the forest.

Suvarov was in Nel'kan, which he supposed was less than two hundred miles away to the north and east. He had never been to Nel'kan, but Suvarov was nothing if not thorough. He would have the crossings of the Maya River watched closely.

Now they descended into a burned-over forest. Lightning, no doubt, had started a fire that had burned over several thousand acres. The charred trunks of limbless trees pointed their black fingers at the sky. It was a haunted place, an eerie, lonely place. The soldiers closed in, following Alekhin as if for protection. From time to time their eyes strayed left and right. Once in a while each turned his head to look back to see if they were being followed. The earth was frozen. Snow had fallen in a light film scattered thinly over the charred earth and fallen trees.

There were no animals here nor any birds, only a stark emptiness. It was a place of death. And here the tracks were plain enough. It was as if the Indian had wanted them to see his tracks or had not cared. Did he not know he was followed? The tracks wove a way among the charred logs and blackened trees. Perhaps it was simply that he realized the futility of attempting to hide a trail in such a place.

Oddly, the trail veered west, then east, then north again, and then back to the east. Alekhin stopped, looking angrily around. What was the American trying to do?

Suddenly, he realized and was amused. There were places where the wind or the fire or both had felled great rows of trees, and they were deliberately being led where such trees must be stepped over, climbed over, or crawled under. It was slow, exasperating, and very tiring, and the soldiers were beginning to straggle more and more.

They plodded on. Fearing some ruse, Alekhin stayed to the trail. One of the soldiers, seeing an easier way, instead of climbing over the fallen tree went around the broken-off trunk. Alekhin, glancing back, saw it happen.

The soldier was the last in line, and taking what seemed the easier way, he had just stepped past the base of the broken-off tree when he tripped and fell.

As he fell he gave off a great, choking cry, and the other soldiers started to run toward him.

"No!" Alekhin shouted. "No! No!"

Unheeding, they rushed to their fallen comrade, and suddenly another tripped and fell. He cried out, then scrambled up, bleeding. His comrades had stopped, staring at him.

There was a great, bloody gash in the side of his neck, and he was gripping it with his hands to stop the blood.

"Be careful!" Alekhin warned. "There are traps!"

Stepping with caution, they approached the injured man and began to apply crude first aid.

Alekhin went around him to the soldier who had fallen first. He had tripped over a root tied across the path, and when he fell a sharpened wooden stake had been waiting for him. Hurrying around the trunk of the broken tree, he had tripped, and the stake had gone right through him. The man was gasping his last when Alekhin stopped beside him.

In anticipation that his fall would attract others, another ankle-high root had been tied carefully. The second man had been stabbed in the side of the neck by the sharpened stake. An inch or two further to the side and it would have pierced his throat.

Alekhin was disgusted. Four men had been sent with him. Now one of them was dead and another injured beyond any use, and he must be cared for by a third. Somehow, he must get help. He did not know the full range of the radio he carried, but he attempted a call.

Such a trap was a gamble, of course, yet the American knew he was being followed. Perhaps there had been other traps, further back, which they had avoided simply by accident. Alekhin was angry with himself. He should have been more careful. He knew the sort of man he was pursuing.

Or did he?

His calls were getting no response. "Make a litter," he said. "Get two strong poles and get the coat from the dead man. Your comrade must be carried."

The two soldiers looked at him, staring. "How far?" one asked.

"As far as need be," Alekhin replied. "As far as you would wish to be carried if it were you."

After a minute he said, "There is a village. It is about twenty miles."

"*Twenty* miles!"

"Perhaps further. We've wasted enough time. *Move!*"

Alekhin consulted his map. The village was Mar-Kyuyel, and it was on a road. He looked at the wounded man. He looked bad. He had lost much blood before the bleeding had been eased by cloth pads. Next time he would have a man along who understood first aid.

Next time? His face was somber. He did not care for these soldiers, but he hated to be defeated, to be hampered.

He had a feeling they would lose more men before the American was found and captured.

The worst of it was that it would be Suvarov who got him, and he, Alekhin, wanted to capture this one.

They loaded the man on the crude stretcher and started to walk. Alekhin waited, thinking. Should he go with them or continue the search alone?

They would want a report. They always wanted a report. Everything came second to the paperwork these days. Bureaucratic minds could not comprehend unless it was written out for them or drawn in pictures. Besides, who knew what these soldiers would do if someone did not watch them?

Colonel Zamatev was at his desk when word reached him. Another man dead and one seriously injured.

At least Major Makatozi was not in Magadan. It was a relief to know that somehow Shepilov was not ahead of him.

Yet he still might be. Makatozi might be headed for Magadan and Shepilov might know why. It was on the sea. Suppose the CIA planned to steal him away from there?

Unlikely, but possible. Yet how could it be done? Suppose the American had managed to communicate with his own people?

Just suppose it could have been done? Suppose something had been set up and Shepilov knew of it? If so, Shepilov might capture them all, circumvent him completely, and walk off with all the prizes. Why else would he go to Magadan?

Nobody wanted to go to Magadan. Nobody went there unless they must. Yet Shepilov had gone of his own free will. Surely, he knew something and wanted to be right where he could claim all the credit, personally.

Kyra was there, and Kyra would find out.

Could he trust Kyra?

He sat back in his chair and tried to order his thinking. He liked everything lined up, everything neat and clear.

Fact one: Shepilov never moved unless he had to. He preferred comfort. And Shepilov had gone to Magadan.

Fact two: Makatozi was somewhere north of the Uchur, moving in the general direction of Magadan.

Fact three: headed in that direction, Makatozi would have to escape by sea, and Magadan was a seaport.

Fact four: the Soviet buffer zone was supposed to be

impenetrable, but suppose the Americans used one of their new stealth planes? It would be a test, and if they brought it off, what a coup!

Fact five: if such a thing happened, heads would roll, and his would be one of the first. If Shepilov were in Magadan and the CIA succeeded in getting Makatozi out of the country, Shepilov's head would roll.

But Shepilov never left himself in a vulnerable position. If he was in Magadan, he was there for a reason and he was sure he would succeed.

Kyra would call in, but Kyra's line would certainly be bugged. Shepilov would certainly know she was in the city. In fact, he had probably been informed when she had left town to fly there.

Suvarov. He must be in touch with Suvarov. If they could get the American before he reached Magadan, then they had no further worries.

He got up from his desk and paced the floor. There was no way he could have planes flying back and forth over so many miles of country looking for one man. But what if that man were confined to a much smaller area, like that between where Alekhin's men had been attacked and where Suvarov was?

He opened the door. "Emma. Emma Yavorsky. Get a message to Lieutenant Suvarov. I want some planes out flying." He checked the coordinates and handed them to her. "The planes must fly across that area. A careful search."

Emma Yavorsky's lips tightened in disapproval. "It will cost too much," she said. "They will not allow it." She stared at him. "You are being foolish about this. The man will die out there. Siberia will kill him. Let him alone, let him die."

"Your advice is usually good. But not this time. Many men will die out there; many men can die. But not this man."

TWENTY-FOUR

It was time for a change of direction. Joe Mack rubbed his cold hands, watching his back trail. Something moved back there, probably an animal, but instinct as well as common sense told him he was being followed.

By now they had guessed his intent, and they would prepare for his coming. He had set traps, deliberately chosen difficult ways, done what he could to slow pursuit and discourage those who followed him.

Spring was coming, but it was still some weeks away, and a move toward the coast would put him in somewhat warmer weather. It would also lead to greater risk, for villages were more frequent. To strike back into the interior would increase his distance from his final goal, so he would move toward the coastal mountains.

First, to find a suitable place to make the change. Squatting on his heels he studied the terrain. What he hoped for was a rocky shelf relatively free of snow. As his eyes sought a possible avenue of travel he was alert for any movement. In the vastness of the taiga, there were men as well as animals, and in the wilderness all men went armed. Many of them were bandits, working singly or in company, and robbing any unwary travelers.

Joe Mack carried his bearskin in his pack with the carefully folded shirt Natalya had made for him. Now he wore three lightweight garments, the outer one made from the intestines of reindeer, carefully cleaned and then cut in strips and sewn together with sinew. Such a coat would shed rain and snow as easily as a slicker. He wore the stolen sweatshirt next to his skin and then a loose jacket of wolf hide. Necessarily, Joe Mack had used what could be had, not what he preferred.

Joe Mack came down the mountain in the late afternoon and walked eastward over rock polished smooth by ice. He walked steadily through scattered trees and low brush. It was very cold, but the air was clear. Cold as it was, this part of Siberia had more clear days than any other part of the Soviet empire. Several times he saw deer, and once a moose, a huge old bull who raised his head, staring at him. He had been expecting moose as he had seen their teeth marks on aspen trunks.

Leaving the rock, he climbed up a steep slope, placing his feet with care to disturb none of the smaller rocks, which might mark his passing. He avoided limbs, ducking under them or passing without brushing them where possible. Some had a light coating of snow that could be disturbed, others might be broken or the leaves pushed out of shape, all evidence of his passing if seen by a skilled tracker. When stepping back on a rock surface again, he was careful to knock the earth, sand, and leaves from his moccasins before reaching the rock, so as to leave no traces. These things were done without thinking. They had become habitual.

Crossing the mountain slope, he next went down a gorge filled with a dense growth of spruce, weaving a careful way through them. He did not stop to leave any traps, that would come later, when a follower was apt to be tired and less cautious. He slept that night in a huge hollow tree, the hollow trunk serving as a chimney for his small fire, perfectly shielded by the tree itself. The place was snug, and in a few minutes, with a fire going, it was warm. The opening in the hollow tree had been covered by a crude door made of evergreen boughs woven together.

When morning came he made a stew of some of the dried meat and then made tea, taking his time and resting. It had been weeks since he had slept so well and days since he had enjoyed a warm meal.

The forest was changing. Now there were many cedar

trees, some ash, oak, and walnut. There were more birds, too, and the tracks of deer were everywhere about.

As he moved, his thoughts were busy, not only absorbing the country but trying to guess what Zamatev was doing. They knew about where he was now, not within miles, but certainly within the area. His sudden shift toward the east might delay pursuit for a brief time, but no more. Also, it would have the effect of narrowing still more the area in which they must search. He must at all costs avoid contact with or being seen by people, something that could grow increasingly difficult. Twice on this day he had come upon the remains of old campfires, so hunters did range these woods.

His thoughts kept returning to Natalya. How were they? What had happened after he left? Could she get away to the coast? To the Maritimes? Even so, how could he possibly slip in there and get her out? It was ridiculous to even consider it, yet he *might* get her away from there. The interior? No chance, no chance at all.

He stopped suddenly. He had been following a game trail, and suddenly in the trail before him was the track of a large cat.

A tiger!

As if he had not troubles enough. It was a fresh track, perhaps not an hour old. There were leopards in the area, too, or down in the Sikhote Alins nearer the coast. But this was a bigger track than that made by a leopard, and tigers went further in their hunting than did leopards, and they stood the cold better. This area had long been known for tigers of great size as well as of fierceness, and the Chinese as well as the native Soviet population had suffered from them.

He followed, estimating the size of the beast by its stride and the impression of the tracks, although there was small chance of that because of the frozen earth. But here and there, in a few soft spots, the pugs made a definite impression. The tiger was a large one. Soon the tracks left the dim trail and went off down the mountain to the east.

The months had changed him. He was lean, hard, and even more muscular. More and more he was becoming the Indian, a man of the wilderness. He was no longer a stranger to this country, for he had come to know its ways and had learned to live with it.

As night came on again he moved higher on the slope to find a place where he could catch whatever warm air there was, for it would rise, leaving the slopes often warmer than the valley below.

He found a rockfall where several great slabs had fallen in such a way as to leave a shelter beneath them and a place where he could have a small fire unseen. He was gathering sticks for his fire when he saw the highway.

It was miles away but could be nothing else, for he saw the lights of what appeared to be a convoy moving along toward the east. There were six trucks in the line. Borowsky had told him that trucks often traveled so because of occasional hijackings. The goods they carried were worth so much on the black market that hijackings were not uncommon.

He returned to his well-hidden cave under the slabs and fixed a small meal. He did not make tea. He had enough left for one more brewing, and then he must do without. Coffee was an almost forgotten luxury.

Later, when he emerged to make one last gather of fuel before sleeping, he looked down toward the highway.

There were no lights. He was turning away when he saw one set of lights moving very slowly. He paused, watching.

Something seemed to be wrong. The truck slowed and slid a little to one side, and then the lights were stationary. After a few minutes they started to move once more, barely creeping. Then the truck turned toward him and stopped. The lights went out.

Puzzled, he watched for a few minutes, then returned to his fire and his bed.

It was still dark when he awakened. The first thing he thought of was the truck.

Apparently it had been disabled. Yet that was not necessarily so. Should he go down to it? Almost anything such a truck carried might be useful to him.

Yet he might be seen. He decided not to take the risk and came down off the mountain and started east. The highway, if such it could be called, ran along the river he had crossed a few days ago. That river had taken a bend to the north, and—

He stopped again. Directly before him was a road! A dirt road of simply two parallel tracks, such as many he had seen in his own country. On that road were fresh tire tracks, two

sets of them. Puzzled, he turned left, following along. He
found the tracks of some small animal crossing the fresh
tracks, and there were spots of oil, scarcely stiff from the
cold.

The truck he had seen must have turned off the highway
and come here. The second set of tire prints showed the
truck returning. Wary, but curious, he followed the road but
kept back in the trees.

Something dark and shadowy loomed ahead. He drew
closer. A building, a tailings pile, and a track that ran out on a
dump and ended there.

For a few minutes he watched. The place seemed deserted. An abandoned mine.

Why had the truck turned off the road to come here? It
had not been disabled as he had thought, but simply seeking
the turnoff in the darkness.

No smoke, nothing. He moved down to the nearest
building, where the road ended, and peered inside.

Boxes, crates, and barrels, all neatly stacked!

He had come upon the cache of a black-marketing truck
driver. Not many of the boxes and crates were alike. It was
possible that the driver, either on his own or with the connivance of some others, had been loading extra boxes from a
warehouse, discharging them here to be picked up by others.

Was there somebody around? Someone to guard their
stolen property? Or was it sufficiently far into the wilds
where none was needed?

He had learned to speak a little Russian, but read it he
could not. He doubted if the few words he saw stenciled on
the boxes had anything to do with the contents. Another
quick look from the window showed him nothing, and with a
hammer nearby he opened the nearest box.

Canned goods! He tried a second and a third. Food in
most of them, and then several boxes of clothing.

Running to the windows for another quick look, he made
up a bundle of both clothing and food and carried it into the
forest. What he had hoped to find was a pistol and ammunition, but there was no such luck, and he had already spent
enough time. Bundling the boxes back into shape, he renailed
them, and wiping out what tracks he had left, he slipped
away into the woods.

From first to last, he doubted if he had been in the

building more than twenty minutes. As he was leaving he
heard the distant sound of a truck.

Catching up his bundle he scrambled higher on the
mountain. Looking back, he could see nothing of the building
he had just left or any sign of the road leading to it. A truck
was passing on the highway. Taking his pack, he moved back
deeper into the forest and away from the highway. At dusk he
stopped and building a small fire, ate better than he had for
weeks. When he had eaten and his fire was down to glowing
coals he looked again at the clothes he had taken. There had
been no time to try on what he had found, and he had judged
the coat just by laying it open on its box, but it had looked
large enough. He had taken the pants that went with it, and
now he tried on the coat. It was a passable fit, not good, but
better than he expected. The trousers were too large in the
waist, but that was no problem. A tight belt would handle
that.

He packed the suit in as neat and small a package as
possible and put it with the shirt Natalya had made for him.
If he needed to go into a city, he was now prepared, but for
one thing. He had no shoes or boots. His moccasins would
attract the eyes of any who saw him.

He walked on into the forest. From the ridge where he
had looked at the passing truck he had seen what appeared to
be a large farm in the distance. In Yakutia, he knew, there
were many large farms, and although he had passed out of
that area he was apparently coming into another such.

Steadily, he worked his way east through dense forest,
avoiding roads and signs of cultivation. From time to time he
glimpsed people, mostly dressed in furs as he was, from what
he could make out at the distance. From now on it would be
more and more difficult to hide; nor could he leave traps
here. Joe Mack had no desire to accidentally injure some
unsuspecting person. Those who were trailing him did so at
their own risk, but a trap left for them might be stumbled
upon by a trapper, a hunter, or simply some wanderer in the
forest.

In a thick forest of larch, he found a corner near a huge
fallen tree and bedded down for rest. The hour was early, but
he must travel by night. Yet he was not forgetting the tiger
track he had seen.

With only his bow and quiver of arrows, he had no desire to encounter a tiger.

He was alone, and he was tired. Not physically tired, but tired of running, tired of hiding. The sky was a pale blue, the spruce a dark fringe, almost black against that sky. He stood, looking about him, wondering if it was here, in this far land, where he was to die.

What was he, anyway? Was he an Indian or a white man? And what difference did it make? His blood was Indian blood, but the world in which he lived was that of all men, having nothing to do with race or color. To exist is to adapt, and if one could not adapt, one died and made room for those who could. It was as simple as that. Beating one's fists against the walls did no good. It was an exercise in futility.

The terrorist lives for terror, not for the change he tells himself he wants. He masks his desire to kill and destroy behind the curtain of a cause. It is destruction he wants, not creation.

A political revolution always destroys more than it creates. It had taken the Soviet Union thirty years to rebuild what the revolution had destroyed, and the government that had resulted was no different. Only the names had changed, the names of the people as well as the institutions.

He was a Sioux, and for the Sioux as for most Indians war had been a way of life. More than one Indian had said that without war they could not exist. But it had been the same for the Vikings, whose very name stood for raiding and robbery. It had been no different for the Crusaders, who masked their lust for war under the banner of a holy cause.

When the Sioux had first encountered the white man, the white man was despised. He was a trader for fur. If he was any kind of man, why did he not trap his own fur?

His people had no way of gauging the power behind the westward movement or the white man's drive to own land, to live on the land. Only the first white men to come had been free rovers like the Indian; the rest had been settlers who came and built cabins, who plowed up the grass and planted corn.

Not until too late did the Indian realize what was happening to his country. He and many of the white men, too, bewailed the killing of the vast herds of buffalo, but where millions of buffalo roamed there were now farms that could feed half the world; there were hospitals, universities, and the homes of men.

He was a warrior of the old school. It was the life he had always wanted, the life he knew best, but he could still appreciate the changes that had taken place. Nothing ever remained the same; the one inexorable law was change.

Major Joseph Makatozi, once an athlete and flyer known as Joe Mack, walked down into the forest again, an Indian.

Thinking of what was to be or what should have been did no good now. To exist, to survive, to escape, these must be all his thought, all his wish, his only need.

This was not a war between the United States and the Soviet Union; it was a war between Colonel Arkady Zamatev and himself.

It was also a war with Alekhin, out there somewhere, searching for him and someday, somewhere, finding him.

TWENTY-FIVE

Natalya Baronas stood in the opening of the small, deep valley where they had found a home and looked out over Plastun Bay.

Her father came from the cabin and walked down beside her. "I wonder where he is?" she said.

Baronas shook his head. "Who knows? He is a man of the forest, you know. He does not fight it as we did. He understands it and lives with it."

"They search everywhere. I do not see how he can escape."

"Do you love him?"

She did not answer for several minutes, looking out across the bay, wisps of hair blowing gently in the wind. "How can I know? I do not even know what love is. I only know that I felt good when near him, lost when he went from me. I think he is a strong man. I do not know if he is wise."

"What is wisdom?" Baronas asked. "I have often wondered, and I am not sure. Understanding of life and men, I presume. It goes beyond mere knowledge, as knowledge goes beyond information.

"Your young man has learned how to survive in one world, at least. Colonel Zamatev was unwise in not realizing he had captured something wild that could not stand being imprisoned. He is elemental, your friend. He is basic. His

190

thoughts are simple, direct thoughts, I believe, although I do not know him well enough. I am a little afraid that when Zamatev had him captured he bought more than he bargained for. To Zamatev his action was totally impersonal. He captured a man to squeeze information from him, then to cast him aside. To Makatozi his capture was a deadly, personal insult, I believe. Something to be wiped out in blood."

"He said he would come back. Do you think he could be so foolish?"

"It would not be foolish to him. I think your friend lives by a very simple and ancient code." He paused, watching the gray waters of the bay. "I wonder if anyone has ever understood him? I am sure none of his fellow officers ever did. Probably they took what was on the surface as the man and looked no further. Not many men are given to study of their companions, anyway. They are concerned with themselves, their jobs, their families. Rarely do they question the motivations of their companions unless somehow it affects their own lives."

"I liked him."

"So did I, but I am afraid you cannot hold too long to a dream. He has gone, the odds are a million to one that he will be captured or killed or will die out in the taiga. That he could ever come back for you is almost impossible. Every inch of this coast is covered by radar and patrolled constantly."

Baronas paused. "There is something else, however. *We* might escape."

Surprised, she turned to look at him. "But how?"

"I do not want to raise your hopes, but the American started me thinking of escape. Until then I had only thought of existing and staying away from officials. He started me thinking of what might be done. I have said nothing because I did not want to raise hopes I could not gratify, but escape is contagious, and if your friend did nothing more he started me thinking of what might be done. We are not far from China."

She gestured. "And Japan lies just over there."

He shook his head. "We cannot think of the sea. We have no boat, and I know nothing of the sea or of boats. Also, there is the radar and the patrols. I was thinking of the border."

"It is guarded."

"Of course, but guards are men, and men have failings.

Where men live, there are men who wish to live better. To live better they must have money."

"We do not have enough."

"What is enough? Let us think of that, and let us think of where we are, what the closest border is, and let us make some friends of the soldiers. Sometimes they are allowed to come down here to fish."

"So?"

"We must buy a boat, a small one for fishing on the bay, and we can lend it to soldiers. Soldiers are men and they talk, especially to a pretty girl. From them we will learn how the border is patrolled, and we will listen to their gossip about their comrades and their officers. We will find which ones might be open to persuasion. We might even find a guard who would look the other way for a few minutes."

He smiled at her. "Talya, we need not leave it all to your young man. Why should he risk his life returning for you when we can escape ourselves and meet him?"

"But how could we find him?"

"He is an officer in the Air Force. Once we are in America it can be done, I think."

They walked back to the cabin together. "I did not tell you before, but when we were in Olga to trade our furs I saw Evgeny Zhikarev."

"Zhikarev? *Here?*"

"We talked a little. They came asking questions. Your friend handles his skins in a special way, and it was noticed. So they began asking questions, and Evgeny has been questioned before. He fled.

"I do not know, but I suspect from things he said that he had plans for escaping across the border that did not work out. We are old friends, you know. I guessed that was the case. I also feel that he still has hopes. He is marking time, waiting for something.

"He knows a good deal about China and has friends among the Chinese. Most of the Manchurians do not like the Russians. They live in expectation of border warfare.

"I asked him many questions, and to me he talked readily about China. He has a fixation on Hong Kong, and I believe that is where he intended to go. From there, it would not be hard to get to America if we could arrange it through the American consul. I have friends there who are scholars. They would aid me, I know."

She walked ahead of him and opened the door to the cabin. It was a small place, out of the way and so not preferred. They had rented it for a small sum. It was a cozy, two-room cabin with a fireplace, and a forest crept down the gorge behind it to provide fuel. Each time they walked outside they brought back branches fallen from the trees. Heavier stuff they cut with an axe.

Fishing was easy in the little stream that came down from the mountains, and a walk of a few hundred yards brought them down to the bay.

Living in the little cabin was easy, and the weather was much warmer than at their former home, yet they had no friends here and rarely spoke to anyone except an occasional fisherman or hunter. "What do they think of us?" Talya asked.

He shrugged. "I have let them believe I have been retired because of illness. It will not be long until some official decides to make inquiries. It is you I am worried for."

"Then let us make our plans. Let us approach Evgeny Zhikarev again, and let us buy that boat. I am sure we can find an old one, and we have money from the furs.

"I have set traps," she said. "There are foxes here."

It was warm inside the cabin. She made tea, wondering about him. Where was Joe Mack now? Did he fare well? Was he warm? Was he still free? The trouble was they would never know. Such news did not travel in Russia, although with this one, about whom so much stir had been made, they might learn something. When the hunt ceased they would know he had been captured.

A few days later three soldiers came down to the river's mouth to fish. They were very young, scarcely more than boys, and she showed them the best place to fish. Later they came to the cabin for tea. They were very reserved, even shy.

"We have tea," one of them said. "It is part of our ration."

"Thank you. We have to travel very far to get it. Sometimes there is none."

"In the army we always have it," one boy said proudly.

"But the only fish we get comes from cans," another said. "And where I come from we always caught our own."

They were friendly, and they soon got over their shyness. All three had not been long from home and were lonely. They were stationed at Iman, on the border.

Stephan Baronas talked to them and led them to speak of their families, their hopes. One intended to remain in the army; another planned on returning to civilian life and studying to be an engineer. He had been stationed along the new railroad that was being built and he had watched the work. He was good at mathematics, and one of the engineers had gotten him assigned to him, and he had helped while learning. His application had gone in, and his commanding officer had recommended him. His name was Bocharev, and he spoke of wanting to run the rapids on the Iman River.

"The Captain will not allow it," one of the other boys said.

"We shall see," Bocharev said. "I have run rapids before."

"It is very dangerous. Only the native people do it."

Two weeks later they came again, and this time they brought tea. Bocharev put it on the table. "You have been kind," he said. "We have nobody to talk to."

"Thank you," Natalya said. They were very young, away from home for the first time.

"My father's health is bad. He must live near the sea. He hopes one day to return to teaching."

"My father could help," Bocharev said. "He is an official. He has much to do with appointments. Since I went into the army he has a different job, a more important one. I do not know exactly what it is he does."

"I am content just to rest for a while," Baronas said. "It is very easy here. But we thank you for the tea."

"We will come again," Bocharev said. "You are good people."

Two weeks later, he was dead, drowned in the rapids of the Iman.

The other boys brought them the news and more tea. "He had already gotten this for you." He gave her a sly look. "From the commissary."

"I am sorry," Baronas said. "He was a fine young man."

After they were gone, Stephan Baronas walked out on the slope to his favorite place. It was a large flat rock under some cedar with a fine view of the bay. Natalya walked out to join him.

"I could be content here," he said, "if I could only stay, but sooner or later they will realize we do not belong here and they will send us away."

"Can we not leave before then?"

He shook his head doubtfully. "We must try. I am going down to Olga Bay to see Evgeny again. He is a very shrewd old man and might be able to help us."

"I wonder where he is," Natalya said. "I fear for him."

"He would not wish it. If anyone can survive in the taiga, it is Joe Mack." He paused. "Talya, if we can escape we must get in touch with his unit, with his commanding officer, and tell them what has happened. In that way we will know if they learn anything, and believe me, they have ways of learning, perhaps even of helping him."

Turning, she walked back to the cabin. There was work to do, and she welcomed it. The sea had become gray, and the wind was rising. Angry surf assailed the shore, and the wind whined in the ragged pines. A storm was coming up, and the winter storms could be long and bitter. Her father left his seat on the rock and came to gather wood for the fires they would need.

He walked out under the trees and picked up fallen branches and gathered great strips of bark hanging from deadfalls, bark he would need for kindling. He broke pieces from a pine stump that would be loaded with pitch.

For the time they would be snug and warm, and they had food enough. They had grown accustomed to subsisting on very little.

Her father came in with an armful of wood to dump in the wood box. For a moment then he stood in the door looking out on the bay where the battalions of the sea marched endlessly against the shore, attacking it in ranks of foam. The wind was rising. He closed the door and went to the fire.

"I have something on the fire," Natalya said. "It will be ready soon."

He stared into the flames. "I hunger for books, not food," he said. "I have so few." He gestured toward the door. "So much is happening out there of which I know nothing. Scholars are making discoveries, writing papers, lecturing.

Here, I know nothing of it. Even we in Soviet Russia know so little and miss so much.

"Knowledge is meant to be shared, and much of it is being shared. There is so much to learn, and we have so little time. When I was a young man and lived in Paris for a year . . . how wonderful it was! We paced the floors and walked the streets, arguing, reciting poetry to each other, discussing all the ideas, all the things that were happening. We talked of Tolstoy and Balzac, of Fielding and Cervantes! It was wonderful! We drank gallons of coffee and sometimes wine when we could afford it, and we argued about everything! Those were marvelous times!

"And then when I was older but no longer in Paris, we would meet in our own homes or sometimes in a cafe and talk of books and ideas. Even in the days when we were poor, there were always books. There were libraries, and we read everything. The mind was free to navigate any course; the world of ideas is a vast universe of unexplored worlds, and we were free to go anywhere!

"Those days are past, yet I would like to sit again with men of my kind and hear what they have done and are doing. New avenues are opening with every breath we draw. In America, in England, France, West Germany, people are free to think what they will, to write what they think!

"Russia has so much to give, yet so much to learn. We should be a part of all that instead of being confined as in a prison. I am not a Russian, yet I have lived and thought and worked so much in Russia that I feel like one. But our growth is being stunted by restrictions and rules made by idiots defending themselves against the shadows that are only in their minds!

"So many of our best dancers have fled Russian ballet for Europe or America. It is not that they love Russia less; it is simply that an art must grow. They wish to escape the cocoon of Russia and, like a butterfly, spread their wings in a larger world with greater challenges. An artist needs freedom, he needs innovation, he needs opportunity, he needs to create."

He shook his head, embarrassed. "Talya, I talk too much! But we must escape! We must get out into a larger world where we can breathe deeper, stretch our mental muscles, and see what is happening around us."

Somewhere back in the great forest behind them a tree

crashed, blown down by the wind, a wind that roared overhead with mighty force. Fortunately, their cabin was small,
solidly built, and huddled behind the rocks. Waves crashed
on the shore, and at last she slept.

For three days the storm blew. Rain fell and some snow
at the higher elevations, and when at last the weather cleared
they went out into the morning to pick up the fallen branches
and all the other debris left by the storm.

Down on the shore lay the wreck of a boat, and some
men had gathered about it. The bow was high on the sand;
only the stern post was still in the water. Baronas stood for a
moment watching the boat. It was a good-sized craft, all of
sixty feet long, he guessed, and built for heavy seas. It had
been dismasted, but otherwise, at this distance, did not appear to be damaged very much.

Later, when he had completed the cleanup and had gone
back into the house with more wood for the fire, he dropped
it into the bin and turned to close the door.

A car, a Volga, was creeping up the steep road from the
small village.

There was a driver and in the back seat a big man in a
fur coat.

Stephan Baronas felt his mouth go dry and his chest
constrict. "Talya," he spoke very softly. "I am afraid we're in
trouble."

The car was an official car. A Volga was needed for this
terrain.

"Talya," he said, "come here. We must meet them
together."

TWENTY-SIX

Dark were the forests, dark and still. Now it was snowing again, a thick, heavy snow falling steadily, and there was no other sound but that of falling snow, a whisper, faint yet discernible.

Two days ago he had crossed the Maymakan River and hidden himself deep in the forest. He had found a shelter of sorts built by some hunter and trapper, a crude, hidden place, long unoccupied but snug.

Approaching the Maymakan he had heard a sound in the sky, and for a moment he had stopped under a tree. This was a region of scattered trees and occasional meadows, some of them half swamp, and there were islands of mountain riding above the forest. He listened. Not one but several planes were flying over the forest. This was the most intensive search yet, and he dared not move until the planes had flown over; then he trotted out and headed for a thicker grove of trees. Other planes were coming, and he knew the Maymakan River's banks would be guarded.

He had gone not a half mile when he heard another sound, a sharp command. Close against a tree's trunk, he watched. Below him, not two hundred yards off, a platoon of soldiers was making camp.

He faded back into the forest and went directly away

198

from them for a half mile. When he heard a helicopter, he went under a spruce and crouched in the snow.

They knew where he was. No such search would be permitted unless they were quite sure they were close upon him; otherwise they would not expend the manpower or the fuel. He waited where he was.

Had they seen his tracks in the snow? The copter had been flying low enough.

No matter. As soon as that platoon had eaten, they would spread out in a skirmish line and come through the woods. Undoubtedly, there were other such groups searching also. To move now would be foolish, yet when darkness came—

He had crossed the Maymakan on the ice and had come immediately into these woods and found this place. The falling snow would wipe out his tracks, and if he remained still he would make no more. It was unlikely anybody knew of this place, and he would remain hidden as long as possible.

Now it was the third day, and the search seemed to be moving away from his area. His hideout was situated on a point of a low mountain with a forest-choked valley on either side, a stream in the bottom of each. There was a small spring nearby, for whoever had made this camp had chosen well. Food was no worry, for he had the last of that stolen from the black-market warehouse at the old mine. He sat tight, hoping they would not find him.

Soldiers being soldiers, he doubted that any would choose to climb the steep mountainside to get to where he was. They could look up, and it would seem empty and harmless enough. More and more, Joe Mack wondered about the man who had constructed this place. Obviously he had not wanted it found, for it had been artfully concealed. On the evening of the fourth day, Joe Mack started again.

The earth was white with snow, except for occasional patches blown clear by the wind. During his period of hiding out, he had made moccasins again for the third time, but this time he had also worked on something else. When he had killed the last elk, he had cut off the hoofs and made moccasins from them. They would not be easy to use, nor could he move rapidly in them; so they were made simply to slip on over whatever he was wearing. A skilled tracker would probably understand what had been done within a very short time, but to the average man the tracks would simply appear to be another set of elk tracks.

He moved out now across a snowfield wearing the elk hoofs. When he reached a bare patch he slipped them off.

It was a slow, careful day, ending on the slope of a mountain looking down upon a road and a power line.

For over an hour he watched the road. There was but little traffic. He was, he guessed, no more than sixty miles from the sea, although that was probably but a poor estimate. It was time he moved back inland, for his area of operation was becoming too limited. Soon he would be seen, and the worst of it was he might not even realize it at the time. There was too much movement here, and the odds were against him.

He waited, listening. Then he moved down the mountain, staying under cover, and watched as a truck went by, and a car. Listening, he heard no sound, and the snow fell thick and fast. Emerging from the brush, he walked across the road, under the power line, and into the brush. The snow was very deep, except on the road itself, where traffic had packed it down.

Moving north away from the highway, he went up through woods so dense he could see no more than a few feet in any direction. At daylight he bedded down in the bitter cold in a snow cave he dug out of the side of a drift, packing the sides with his hands and cutting a snow block for a door. With his bow he pushed a ventilation hole through the snow overhead, leaving the bow in place to help keep the hole open.

Slipping out of his snow cave, he found two branches of the right length and brought them back into the cave, stripping the foliage to leave the bare poles. These he warmed over a fire, taking his time and bending them slightly from time to time. When they were sufficiently thawed, he bent each into an oval and tied the ends. Then with rawhide strips he had saved, he made a webbing and thongs to cover his toe and instep.

For two days he stayed in the snow cave, improving his snowshoes and simply waiting. The search continued, and from time to time he heard planes and once a helicopter, flying very low over the treetops. There had been much snow, and whatever tracks he had made had long since been covered. On the third evening he came out of his cave, collapsed it, and started off through the woods with a swing-ing stride, wearing his snowshoes.

Avoiding trails, he kept to the mountainsides, alert for any sound, any search parties. The temperature had fallen, and it was piercingly cold. His body had gradually grown somewhat accustomed to it, although he was careful not to work up a sweat and to avoid falls.

He covered something over twenty miles, as nearly as he could judge, and came to another surfaced road. No tire tracks broke the surface of the snow. For a moment he hesitated. To cross the road meant leaving a trail and the snow was not falling so steadily, yet there was no other way. He crossed the road and went up into the trees.

Despite being well covered, with only slits for his eyes, his face was nevertheless stiff with cold. It had been long since he had been warm, and he was running low on food. He would have to make a kill soon. Meat, and especially fat, was essential.

So far, he had been traveling through thick forest and more often than not at night, yet he had made goggles of bark with narrow slits for vision. These he could tie on to prevent the glare that causes snow blindness.

He was plodding into the forest when he turned to look back. He had heard no sound, but a car had stopped and a man had gotten out to study the tracks. The man looked up and looked right at him. Joe Mack stood within the very edge of the woods, but apparently he was visible, for the man lunged for his car. His intentions were obvious, and Joe Mack whipped an arrow from his quiver. As the man turned, he notched his arrow and let fly. The man's rifle was coming up when the arrow hit him.

He staggered, grasping at his throat, the rifle discharging as it fell into the snow. Joe Mack ran closer and then stopped and bent his bow a second time, for the man was struggling to sit up. The distance was less than twenty yards now, and the arrow went true.

Quickly, he withdrew his arrows, losing the head from one of them but returning the other to his quiver. Inside, the car was warm. There was a pack and, on the seat, a pistol in a holster. There were cartridges also. These he gathered up. There was an emergency kit of food, and that he took. Sud-denly, he stopped.

Stooping, he picked up the dead man and loaded him into the car. Then he put the rifle in the car, too. Its motor was still running. Taking off his snowshoes, he got in behind the wheel and drove off. Somewhere ahead, there would be a village.

He drove steadily. No other cars. The hour was late, and thinking of that, he turned to the dead man beside him and then stopped the car. It needed only a minute to take the wristwatch from the dead man's wrist and the money, little though it was, from his pocket. He would leave the car and the dead man, and perhaps they would believe he had been robbed by hooligans.

The village, when he came to it, after driving nearly thirty miles, was a mere cluster of houses and sheds. It was obviously some sort of a way station, but there was no power line here. Driving the car into the shadows of a shed, he got out of the car and took his snowshoes, the food supply, and his pack. Then he walked away into the night and the swirling snow.

Tomorrow they would find the car. Hopefully, they would not at once think of him. If there were an autopsy, something he doubted, they would find his arrowhead. Leaving the road, he struck off toward the northwest and into the forest.

All was white and still; snowflakes fell steadily and might cover any trail he left. In any event, it had to be chanced. He headed off into the night, moving at a steady pace.

He now had enough food for a day or two, and he had a pistol. He would use it only in dire necessity. The rifle he had not wanted, as the report of a gun might attract undue attention, and he could hunt as well with his bow and arrows.

An hour after daylight he built a snow cave and crawled into it. Almost at once he was asleep.

The man he had killed had known who he was. Furthermore, he had not hesitated to shoot. A bullet could have disabled or killed him. What worried him was that the man had not hesitated, which implied that he knew who he was and was himself probably involved in the chase.

They were closing in. That was the only way to understand what had happened. They were closing in, and they knew he was in the vicinity. The answer to that was to get out of it as fast as possible.

The food he had taken from the car lasted three days,

and at the end of that time he killed a deer. He was in the taiga now, and had seen no sign of human life since abandoning the car. He made camp in a snow cave and broiled a venison steak. As he was now moving away from the coast, his shelters in snow caves would be coming to an end. The snow was not so deep further inland.

As evening came, safely in his snow cave, he built a small fire with a reflector to push heat back into the cave, and he pondered.

Alekhin, being driven in another black Volga, came to Topka late on the same afternoon. Peter Petrovich was awaiting him at the office of the collective.

"I have no idea how long it had been there," he said. "It has been bitter cold, and nobody was stirring around except from the house to the barn. Anyway, the man had been dead for some time."

They walked across to the car. There was no blood on the car seat, and the body was on the passenger's side of the car. His rifle had been fired, but there was no cartridge case in the car. The emergency food his men carried was gone, and so were his pistol, his wristwatch, and his money.

"Thieves," Peter Petrovich said. "They will steal anything they can get their hands on."

Alekhin opened the dead man's clothes to look at the wound. It was round and not too large. It could have been made by a bullet, but something was warning him it had not.

On a table in the house he took off the dead man's coat and shirt. There was a protuberance on the dead man's back. Through a slit made by his knife, Alekhin saw an arrowhead.

Peter Petrovich was astonished. "An arrow! It cannot be! We have no savages here!"

"You have one. You have the American."

"The American? You are laughing at me. How could he exist out in the taiga? It is cold, bitter, bitter cold!"

"He exists. He has been here."

Alekhin thought about it, turning it over in his mind. Evidently, the dead man had seen Makatozi, but had missed his shot.

This had been a good man, one of his best. He had been driving to the coast, heading for Aldoma to interview a man they had taken who might know something.

The man's pistol was gone and the ammunition for it, yet the rifle had been left.

"You mean this American has been here? You believe he did this?"

Alekhin ignored him. The American had a bow and arrow and did not need or want the rifle. He had killed this man with an arrow, then had bundled him into the car and driven him here. It was true, this road went nowhere except to swing in one great circle or to drive back to Nel'kan. And the American was going north again.

Why had he gone east at all? To meet someone? To get into warmer weather for a few weeks? Had he wished to drive to the coast, he could easily have done so, and the chances were he could have driven on into Nel'kan without anyone the wiser.

Kurun-Uryakh? There was a good flying field there, a good base for aircraft. The American was east of the Maya River and living in the forest. The food he had taken would not last long, so he would have to kill for meat.

"We will get him," Alekhin said quietly. "We will get him now."

Suvarov! That fool! Sitting there with all his soldiers, and the American had slipped around them and left them sitting. Alekhin chuckled. Suvarov had failed, but he would get him. He got into the car. "Drive me to the helicopter," he said.

"Is there anything we can do?" Peter asked.

"Stay out of the way," Alekhin replied brusquely. "We do not need you."

The helicopter would fly him to Kurun-Uryakh. There was a gold mine there, he remembered, and they should have communication facilities.

When the helicopter was aloft, Peter Petrovich drove back to Topka. He was a quiet, studious young man who worked quietly at his job and tried to make no waves. He was an able administrator, often impatient with the restraints the bureaucracy placed upon him, but a loyal Soviet citizen. He had read much of America and had often listened to the Voice of America and the BBC, preferring the latter. He did not approve of America. Their government was too confused, too weak. As a Russian he had never known anything but a strong central government. Nor had his parents, grandparents or great-grandparents. Before Lenin and Stalin, there had been the Tsars.

He owned two pairs of blue jeans from America, a few rock and roll records, and even some American books translated into Russian.

He had read everything he could find written by Jack London, and because of that he had strong sympathy for that lone American out there in the taiga. If he had seen him, he would have reported it promptly, but nonetheless, he sympathized with him. Someone had said the man was a Sioux Indian, and Peter Petrovich had read an account of the Battle of the Little Big Horn.

They said the Indian had been a flyer, and he could not imagine that. It seemed impossible. Yet there were Yakut flyers, and one of his favorite writers was a Yakut. He himself was from Kiev. He had volunteered to come to Siberia because the pay was so much greater and the chances for advancement were better.

He drove back to his building and put the car in the garage. He was thinking of a mug of tea with maybe a touch of vodka to take away the chill.

He opened his door and stepped in, closing the door carefully behind him. Now, to relax! To have his tea, the drop of vodka, and to read!

He turned away from the door and looked into the muzzle of a pistol.

The man holding the gun was the American. He was the Indian. And the gun was very steady; the gray, icy eyes held no mercy.

"First," the American said, "we will eat."

TWENTY-SEVEN

Peter Petrovich was surprised, not only by the American's presence but by his reaction to it. He was not afraid. He was not even nervous.

"I am hungry, too," he spoke in English. "You can put down that gun."

"Thank you, but we have an affinity for one another, this gun and I. Be careful, because I do not want to kill you."

"You had less compassion for the man in the car."

"He tried to shoot at me, leaving me small choice. One of us had to die, and I was reluctant, as you can imagine."

"You can't get away, you know. They are following you. Alekhin himself is here."

"Here?"

"He was here. He's flown north now, as he judged you would be going that way. He flew to Kurun-Uryakh, on the Maya."

Peter was heating up some stew. It smelled very good. "Do you prefer tea or coffee?"

"Either is all right. I've been drinking tea here in your country. I prefer coffee."

"So do I." Peter glanced at him. "They tell me you are an Indian?"

"A Sioux. The term Indian is too indefinite. It is like saying European."

206

"But you have gray eyes?"

"One grandfather was a Scot. But it is not unusual. Crazy Horse had gray eyes and sandy hair."

It was warm in the room. The smells of stew and coffee and the warmth were lulling him into comfort. Deliberately, he stood up. "Are you likely to have visitors?"

"No. They know that I read much at night. Unless someone comes looking for you."

"If they do, please stay out of it. I would not want to kill a good cook."

Peter smiled. "I am not a hero. When you are gone I shall report it at once. You understand that?"

"Of course." He tucked the pistol behind his belt. "They were all ready for me up north, so I circled around. I doubted they would expect me to come back here."

They talked quietly, and Joe Mack tried to keep talking. The warmth and the comfort were making him sleepy. To go to sleep would be fatal. He doubted if this young man would attack him, but he would certainly try to capture him. To gain possession of his gun, at least.

When the stew was ready they sat down on opposite sides of the table, with Joe Mack facing the door. The window was thick with frost, and he doubted anyone could see in.

"Don't be ambitious," Joe Mack said, "because I have the gun in my belt. I am very quick."

"I have heard about your cowboys and the fast draw. Is it true, then? Were there really gunfights like in the films?"

"Much more so. Of course, you had them here, too, only you called them duels. Your poet Pushkin was killed in one."

"You know Pushkin?" Peter was surprised.

"Of course. I've read many of your Russian writers."

The stew was good, and for a time they ate in silence. Joe Mack was listening, waiting for a noise from outside and hoping it would not come.

His eyes searched the room. This man read a great deal. There were maps, also. He would have a look at those. He finished the stew and poured coffee for both.

"You do not appear like a savage."

Joe Mack smiled. "Most Indians are not. They are civilized, industrious people." His eyes met those of Peter Petrovich. "I am not like them. I am a savage."

"But—"

He gestured. "All this—the forest, the wilderness—it is my home. With each day I find myself regressing. In here"—he put a hand over his heart—"I am an unreconstructed Indian. I am supposed to be escaping, and to win my own battle, I must escape. Nevertheless, in many ways I'd rather stay here."

"Become a Russian? But I am sure that can be arranged."

"They have already made offers. But you misunderstand. I am tempted not to try to escape but to remain here, in the forest, and wage my own private war against the Soviet Union."

"But that's absurd!"

"Is it? Perhaps. But your people declared war on *me*. They forced my plane down at sea, captured me, and intended to question me. When that was over they would have killed me, I believe." He emptied his cup. "It was demeaning and to me, an insult."

Peter Petrovich refilled both their cups. "You Americans are preparing for war. We have to know how you are preparing."

"Americans do not want war. No sensible person does. Why should we? We have all we need. What we do not have, we can make or buy. We can travel to any place in the world. We have no Berlin Wall to prevent it."

"Many of us travel, too," Peter declared.

"Of course. There are thousands of you in Afghanistan, and many are dying there. Perhaps travel is bad for Russians." He smiled. "But we need get in no discussion; I am sure we'd not agree. But if we talk about books?"

"I am curious about you."

"So was Colonel Zamatev. But to him I was nothing, something to be used and cast aside. This is an offense against my country, but it is also an offense against me, and for this he shall pay."

Peter Petrovich smiled, incredulously. "Pay? How can you make him pay? You cannot even see him. You cannot get to where he is; you cannot reach him in any way. You are simply one prisoner among many."

"I am different. I am the prisoner who escaped."

Peter shrugged. "It will not matter. Here, why don't you

surrender to me? I shall see if I cannot arrange some special treatment."

Joe Mack got to his feet again. He hated the thought of going out again into the cold, of finding a place to sleep in a snowbank, but there was no choice. If he slept here, he would sleep too soundly. Even if he tied Peter Petrovich tightly, he still would not be safe. The man might work himself free.

"Put together a package of food. Move carefully now, and make no mistakes." He pointed at the items he wanted and watched the pack being made up. His eyes strayed, taking in everything. "You have a pistol?"

Peter hesitated. "In the forest it is necessary to be armed. There are wild animals as well as brigands."

"Brigands, in the Soviet Union?"

"They have always been here. It is their life. They rob and they steal, and often they kill."

"All the more reason I should have another weapon or more ammunition for this one."

He gestured with the pistol barrel. "Be quick. I have no more time."

"You will freeze. It is more than forty below out there."

"It has been much colder." He gathered the package and backed to the door. Then he said, "Put your hands behind you."

"Now see here—!"

"Would you rather have me bend my pistol barrel over your skull?"

When he had Peter nicely tied, he picked him up and dropped him on the bed. Then he put fuel on the fire. "Just so you won't freeze. By the time that burns down it will be morning, and someone will come."

He rummaged through the drawers and found what he wanted, a double handful of cartridges for his own pistol, a common enough type. He turned the light down and then gathered his gear and went into the night. Quickly he rounded the house and headed east, picking up his crudely made snowshoes as he went. He walked rapidly and steadily eastward toward the sea.

Hours later he turned north, changed direction several times, and then veered back to the north again. Removing the snowshoes, he slung them on his back over his pack and hit a forest trail in a long, easy run. By daylight, he believed, he was more than twenty miles from the village.

Peter would be free now or would be trying by every means to attract attention. Within the hour, they would be searching for him.

He was going through the thickest of forest now, careful to break no twigs and leave no other sign of his passing. There was almost no snow on the ground, yet the ground was frozen. He stepped lightly, avoiding twigs and leaves.

Finding a large, lightning-struck tree with a hollow trunk, he went inside, built a small fire, and made tea. Then he curled up to sleep. Two hours later, his fire out, he was awakened by the cold, and he started out once more, walking swiftly.

He ran the next twenty miles in almost marathon time, rested briefly, and started again at a much slower pace. By sundown of the following day he had found an overhang in the side of a rocky outcropping where he rested and ate. He had traveled almost seventy-five miles since leaving Peter Petrovich. Building a small, well-hidden fire of dry, smokeless wood, he slept for four solid hours.

The small mountain on which he had camped was bounded by swamp on both the north and east. There was a river on the north also. He could barely make it out beyond the swamp, which extended for miles.

He judged himself to be less than fifty miles east of Kurun-Uryakh and its airport.

In the evening he would start once more, following this river at a safe distance until it flowed into the Maya, as it undoubtedly did.

Three times during the day planes flew over, and once a helicopter working a search pattern went up and down across the country. Once, in the distance and beyond the river, he believed he saw a party of soldiers. Without a field glass he was unable to tell, but they appeared to spread out in a skirmish line, working up through the woods and across the country. From the map taken from Peter Petrovich, he was sure the river was the Nudymi. Shortly before sundown, he watched an elk cross the swamp and the stream and marked the route it took.

Wearing his elk-soled moccasins, he went down and followed it, starting just after sundown when there seemed to

be nobody about. His bow ready, he crossed the swamp and
the river and then followed it downstream. By daylight he
had reached the Maya. Keeping under cover he worked his
way north, seeking a safe place to cross to the other side.

Four days later he hid out in a hastily made shelter near
the headwaters of the Del'ku River.

For two days he had eaten nothing, and the cold was
bitter. To remain alive he must have food. To starve in warm
weather was one thing, in cold it was impossible. Without
food to fuel his body, the heat would quickly disappear and
he would freeze. From the side of the mountain he could
look over a small, sparsely wooded valley. Downstream the
forest became thicker. All day long he had seen no animal
tracks, nor any sign of human habitation. At the same time,
he knew he was not far from some mining camps.

There was less snow now that he was moving away from
the coastal mountains. Much of the earth was frozen hard and
bare of snow, and where it existed it was often no more than
a thin veil. From now on, snow caves would be rare.

He could not remember a time when he had not been
cold, and when morning came he stumbled out on numbed
feet. Long ago he had taken to putting dry grass in his
moccasins as a partial protection. Now he plodded on, hungry, very tired, his faculties dulled by cold.

Forty miles behind him, Alekhin and six men came
down to a small river. One of the men who had scouted on
ahead returned to report. "No tracks," he said. "Nothing but
elk around here."

Alekhin ignored him. He looked around thoughtfully,
then walked toward an opening in the woods. *He's been
running now for months,* he told himself. *He will become
careless.*

He studied the tracks. "You are a fool," he said to the
soldier. "No elk passed here."

"But the tracks! Right there before you."

"They are the tracks of a man wearing elk hoofs. See the
stride? And he has passed by plants where an elk would
browse."

The soldier was unconvinced. "But how could he—?"

Alekhin ignored him. He started on along the trail, but

as they neared a patch of woods he motioned to the soldier. "You go first. You will learn about a trail."

Also, he told himself, if there is a trap you will be caught, not me. And sooner or later there will be a trap.

Yet when it came, even he was surprised. The elk tracks had been replaced by those Alekhin recognized as those of the American. He was hurrying now, running, taking much longer strides, and the river was before them. The soldier began to hurry, led on by the tracks.

The others followed, Alekhin last. Stopping, he turned to look back the way they had come. He was puzzled. The American had held a fairly true course, so why had he suddenly turned now? Glancing through the trees, Alekhin saw the river and a patch of snow-drifted ice. The soldier was headed right for it.

The fool! Didn't he realize it was a death trap? That the ice beneath the snow could never be trusted? Did he not know that snow would act like a quilt or blanket and warm the ice beneath and that the running water would eat away the ice?

Alekhin shouted and then shouted again. The soldier, with his earflaps down, did not hear him. He could see the American's tracks leading down to the riverbank, and he could even see a track in the snow before him. Alekhin shouted again and started to run. The others heard him, and he shouted, gesturing. They did not understand, and the lead soldier knew he was safe. He could see the tracks ahead of him and where—

His boot went through the drifted snow, through the spongy ice, and into the water. He fell forward, screamed, and went into the water.

"Stay back," Alekhin said. "Do not go near him or you will go through."

"But we must save him!"

A soldier started forward, but Alekhin grabbed his arm and jerked back. "You cannot save him. He is dead."

"But I can see! He is alive! I—!" He tried to jerk free.

"It is more than sixty below zero," Alekhin said. "In the water he will last a minute or two. He is soaked now. If you bring him out he will freeze instantly. There is nothing we can do."

The soldier was struggling to get out on the ice. He

fought madly, then rolled out on the ice. The others started forward. "You will go through," Alekhin warned.

They stopped. Their comrade was no longer moving. "He is dead," Alekhin said. "It was a trap."

They huddled closer around him. "A trap? But the American went that way. We saw his tracks."

"A track at the edge of the ice and a smeared place or two ahead of him that looked like tracks. Probably it was done with a long pole or branch to make it appear he had gone that way."

Alekhin turned away, his eyes searching for the real trail. "He knew what he was doing. He knew he could kill one or more of you."

They shivered in the bitter cold and looked at the stiffened body of their mate.

"What about him?"

"He is dead. You can do nothing for him. If you try to reach him, you may break through as well."

They walked away and he said, "If you just get a foot in the water, get it instantly into the snow. Dry snow is the perfect blotter. If you get soaked there is no chance."

It was cold . . . cold.

A soldier turned and looked back. His mate lay, a stiffening gray thing upon the river ice.

Numb and frightened, the soldier followed Alekhin.

TWENTY-EIGHT

Stephan Baronas stood beside his daughter and waited. Fear choked him, but he fought it back. The man who got out of the Volga was a large, strong-looking man, and he strode over to them. For a moment he just stared at them.

"Can we go inside?" he asked them. His tone was mild.

"Please do," Baronas said. "Forgive me. We do not often have visitors."

Inside, the man took off his heavy coat and hat. He looked around him. "Snug," he said, "and warm." He looked from one to the other. "You are comfortable here?"

"Yes." Baronas was surprised at the question. "Thank you."

When he was seated he stretched his hands to the fire. "I am Nicholai Bocharev," he said.

"Oh?" In sudden compassion Talya moved toward him. "It was your son—?"

"Yes. My only son."

"We are sorry," Baronas said. "He was a fine young man. He visited us here."

Bocharev glanced up. "I know. He wrote to me. You were very kind. He said he loved coming here. It was like another home."

He was silent for a moment, and then he added, "We

had so little time together. He was just growing up, you know, coming to think of me as a friend rather than a dominating parent. We had long talks."

"Will you have tea?" Talya held out a cup, which he accepted. "He brought it to us."

"Thank you." He sipped the tea. "My son said you opened your home to him. I am afraid he was very lonely, although he would not admit it."

He looked up. "You gave him the last happiness he had. You welcomed him, treated him as a son and brother."

"He deserved it. It is our loss, too, that he is gone."

"He loved running wild rivers, and he was very skillful," Bocharev said. "Only there was a place where the current swept the boat under a rock. He did not see it in time. He was struck on the head."

"We are sorry. We shall miss him, too."

Bocharev sipped his tea and then looked around. "Is there anything I can do? I am grateful that my son was happy those last days. You have done this for him and for me."

"Nothing," Baronas said. "Nothing at all."

Bocharev's manner changed. He smiled. "Come, come, Baronas. I know you. I have looked at your dossier. You should not have been arrested. It was a precautionary measure at a time when some were fearful of internal trouble. It was a foolish fear."

He held out his cup. "May I?"

When it was refilled and he had had a swallow, he asked again. "You have education, Baronas. There is much you can do here, but—"

"I appreciate that, but there might be others less understanding." Stephan Baronas paused. It was a risk he had to take. "To tell you the truth, sir, I would like to emigrate. I would like to go to Hong Kong. My daughter and I."

Bocharev nodded. "I thought as much. Well, there is nothing in your dossier that indicates that you are an enemy of our people." He paused. "Where would you prefer to go?"

"To Hong Kong. Even to Manchuria."

Bocharev stood up. "We shall see." He put down his empty cup. "My son meant much to me. You see"—he paused—"he was all I had. I am alone now."

Talya put her hand on his sleeve. "Will you not come

back to visit us? As long as we are here, you are as welcome as your son."

He shook his head. "I shall be very busy. There is much to do. I think sometimes we have paid too much attention to what is outside our country and not enough to improving conditions here. Internal strength is of greatest importance."

He turned to the door. "I shall see what can be done. In the meanwhile, if you will permit it, I shall send a few things my son would have wanted you to have. In fact, he spoke to me about it."

They stood in the open door, watching until the Volga was out of sight.

"We must not hope too much," Baronas said, "but this may help us."

Talya did not reply. It might help them. It would not help Joe Mack, who was out there, somewhere. Out there in the bitter cold, alone in the forest, perhaps dying.

She said as much, and her father shook his head. "One thing at a time. If we escape, he will not have to risk his life to return for you. If we get the chance we must go. If they discover that we knew him, were even close to him, we would never be permitted to leave. We might be imprisoned."

"They do know," Talya said.

"No doubt, but one saving grace of officialdom is that one hand rarely knows what the other is doing. We can only hope."

Kyra Lebedev turned her head sidewise to escape the worst of the wind, gasping for breath. The wind blew her breath right back down her throat. The doorway was just ahead, and she ran the last few steps, ducking hastily inside.

Had anyone followed her? She had not taken the time to look. It was improbable, yet Shepilov was somewhere in town, and he missed very little. Pulling the door shut behind her, she waited an instant to catch her breath. The air in the narrow hallway was stale and smelled of unwashed bodies and the heavy odor of old cooking. She started down the hall, and at the third door she stopped and knocked. After a moment a woman's voice said, "What do you want?"

"Katerina? Please! Open the door!"

The door opened a crack, and then with a gasp the girl

inside opened it wider. The girl had on a coat as if to go out.
She was a slender girl with pale reddish hair and wide blue
eyes. "*Kyra!* In Magadan? What has happened?"

"Nothing, yet. I have just arrived. It is business."

"Oh? For a minute I thought you had been shipped
here."

"Is Ostap here? I must speak with him."

"He's asleep, just gone asleep in fact. He worked the
whole night through and he's done in."

"Ostap? I did not think he ever worked."

A young man with tousled hair came in from the other
room, drawing his belt tight. "I work all right, although not
willingly. I thought I recognized your voice, Ky. What are
you doing here?"

"Sit down! No nonsense now. I must talk. You know all
that is happening in Magadan, and I need to know something."

Flattered, he straddled a chair. He needed a shave, and
his eyes looked like he had been drinking too much. "All
right, what is it? If it is for you, it is for free. If it is for the
government, it will need money." He rubbed his fingers
together. "Much money."

"There is a man in town—Shepilov. I need to know
where he is located and what he is doing here."

Ostap lit a cigarette. "Shepilov? Yes, he's been here two
days now. Bigwig, can't miss him. He's had old Kuzmich in,
and Kuzmich means furs. You know the man. He buys from
trappers, knows more about the fur-trapping business than
anybody."

"What else? I mean, what else than trapping?"

Ostap shrugged, expelling a cloud of smoke. "Trapping,
trappers, I expect he knows them all, in this part of the
country. He keeps in touch. His people trap all that country
north and south of the Kolyma."

"How far west? To Oymyakon?"

"Close, I'd say." He drew on the cigarette and brushed
ash onto the floor. "What's going on?"

"It's the American, the one who escaped."

"Oh? I thought they would have had him by now. Ah, I
see it now! Your man Shepilov is trying to reach the trappers
to hunt for him! It's a good idea. They know their country
and are much better than the KGB. I mean, they *know* that

country. They could find anything out there, while the KGB or the army would be just running in circles." He paused. "There's a few here would like to know that old Shepilov's in Magadan. I mean, he doesn't have any friends here. Too many prison gangs in the gold camps here because of him."

"Well, as long as they are in prison—"

"That's just it. Some of them are out and about, only they cannot leave."

"Ostap, you can help me. I want to catch the American first."

"You do? Pretty as you are, I'd think you could get a man without that."

"Don't be silly. It is my job." She paused. "I work with Colonel Zamatev now."

Ostap whistled. "What do you know? He's the one they call the Iron Man. If you're in with him, you are really in. What can I do for you?"

"You know those trappers, too. You sell them vodka. Oh, I know, so don't try to deny it. They all come to you."

"So?"

"If the trappers locate him, I'd like to know it first."

Ostap drew once more on his cigarette, then dropped it to the floor and rubbed it out with his toe. "As I said, there are a lot of people here who do not like Shepilov. I might be able to do something for you." He glanced up, smiling slyly. "We all need something, you know? That includes me. I need a lot of things."

"The Colonel can be grateful. He understands favors."

"Let me get a couple of hours in bed, and I'll get around. There's nobody I could reach, anyway." He paused. "Does Shepilov know you're in town?"

"Not yet, I am sure. He will know, however."

"Don't come back here, then. Where will you be?"

"At Vanya's."

"It is a good place. All right, I will see what I can do."

He got up, hitched up his pants, and went back into the bedroom and closed the door.

"Kyra? Please do not get him into trouble. He takes too many risks. Oh, he does not consider them risks! I know that, but he is always with those people, the black-market people, and all those who live on the edge."

She shrugged. "Katerina, that is Ostap. You know that.

He is such a man. You knew that when you married him. He has always lived on the edge. He thrives on it."

"But Shepilov? He is vindictive, Kyra. You should be careful, yourself."

The street was empty when she reached it, and she stood for a moment looking out. It was a gray, dismal day, and the shabby street made it look no better. It was a long walk to Vanya's, but she knew it had to be done. She avoided Lenin Square and kept to side streets, hoping not to be noticed.

Vanya lived on a back street in a small frame house. He lived simply, and there was no better location if she wished to remain free of observation. Vanya was a writer, working on a history of the opening up of Siberia. Previously, he had written accounts of the animal life of Soviet Russia. He was a cousin whom she had often visited at his dacha near the Black Sea, but he cared little for pomp and preferred the wild country and wild animals. He was now completing research on a book about bears, as well as the much longer work on Siberia.

He greeted her with genuine pleasure. "Oh, this is wonderful! I was beginning to be lonely, and here you are!" He closed the door behind her and helped her off with her coat. "What brings you to Magadan?"

"I work with Colonel Zamatev."

"I see." Vanya knew all about Zamatev, had met him several times, and knew he was a man on the way up. He also knew that one did not ask questions about what he was doing or about to do. "Can you stay for a while, I hope?"

"A few days, I believe, if you can put up with me."

"We're not so crowded here as in Moscow. Most people live in Magadan because they must.

"Some tea? Or would you prefer vodka?"

"Tea." She looked across the table at him. "Vanya, you go often to the forest?"

"I have been writing about bears, and that is where they are. Yes, I have spent months in the forest, but mostly far west or south of here. Some of it is very beautiful. All of it is very wild. Here and there are mines, most of them deserted at this time of year unless they are worked by prisoners."

"Have you heard of the American?"

He shrugged. "Very little. Lieutenant Suvarov is an old friend. He comes here occasionally, and I know that is his mission at the moment. They do not seem to be having much luck."

"We must have him. He is very important to us, and Comrade Shepilov is here also, and for the same reason."

"He must be important, this American. But I thought he had been taken long since. After all, it is bitter cold in the taiga, and how he could survive is beyond me."

"He is an Indian, an American Indian."

Vanya was fascinated. "You don't mean it? An American Indian in Siberia? The story is that they came from Asia and passed over a land bridge across the Bering Strait into America. Supposedly, they were following game, with no idea they were making a migration."

"Apparently that is what he is trying to do, follow that same route."

"Marvelous! He must be an amazing man to escape in the first place and to stay alive so long in the second. But are you sure he is still alive?"

Over tea she explained about the helicopter crash and the dead KGB man found near Topka.

"He is coming this way, then?" He sat back in his chair. "Kyra, do you realize what this man is attempting? To escape through forest, much of it not properly explored even now? I would not be in his shoes for anything, and yet I envy him."

"*Envy?* Are you insane, Vanya?"

"What a man he must be! Alone in all that vast forest! Is he armed, do you know?"

"We believe he is using a bow and arrows. The man found in the car was killed by an arrow."

"Apparently he needs no weapon. Just last night we discovered another soldier has been killed, this one by falling through the ice. But it was a trap."

"Tell me?"

"The soldier thought he was following a trail across a river. The trail seemed to lead through a small snowdrift on the ice. I did not know, but ice underneath a blanket of snow grows soft."

"Nor did I know." He put down his cup. "He's an amazing man, this American of yours. I wish him luck."

"*Vanya!* How can you say such a thing! He is an enemy of the Russian people!"

Vanya shrugged. "One such enemy can do little harm. From all I hear, you would be better off to let him be. If he does not die out there, he can never cross the Strait. Even for such a man it is impossible. When I was doing the book on the walrus hunters I had some experience with the radar. To cross that Strait is—it cannot be done!"

TWENTY-NINE

He stumbled along on feet numb from cold. The snow was thin over the frozen earth, and the trees were scattered, offering only a little shelter from the wind. He was leaving tracks now, but he could not take the time to cover his trail. What he needed now, desperately, was food and shelter.

The icy cold had numbed his mind. He was not thinking clearly. He had to plan, he had to be evasive. He must leave some traps to slow them up. He must frighten them into caution.

If only he could be warm! Just once again!

He heard the wolves snarling and fighting before he saw them. They had pulled down a deer and were tearing at it. He shouted and they looked around at him. He tried to wave them away, but they were hungry, too. There were three of them, big wolves and in no mind to give up their kill.

He shouted again and ran at them. They backed up, snarling. At any other time they would have run off, but meat was scarce in the taiga.

He notched an arrow with stiff, clumsy fingers. He let fly at the largest of the wolves, and the wolf was no more than twenty-five yards off. The arrow took him in the shoulder and he sprang back, biting at it and snarling. The others backed off a little as he closed in. Now he had the pistol out. He did not wish to waste ammunition, but this was a time when he would chance both the sound of the gun and the loss of the cartridge.

The one he had shot with the arrow was dying now. He walked forward a few more steps. He had never fired this pistol, but he had been a dead shot since childhood, when everybody had used guns in the mountains of his birth. As he moved in, they backed off. One made a running charge at him, a bluff only. When he continued to advance, they retreated again.

He retrieved his arrow and then cut meat from the freshly killed deer, backing off, watching them, the meat in one hand, the pistol in the other.

When he had gone a mile or two into the forest, he found a place in the lee of a gigantic fallen tree. Finding some broken stubs of branches and some heavy bark, he put them together on the snow to form a base for his fire. From under a deadfall that lay across the larger tree he took some hanging strings of bark and crumbled them in his hands. From the trunks of trees nearby he broke dead suckers, small branches that had started to grow from the trunks and then died.

With a bow and drill, he started his fire, blowing it gently into flame. Then with other broken pieces of wood lying about, he built up the floor for his fire and, adding bark, coaxed a larger flame into being. He had been tempted to eat the meat raw, but there are often parasites in raw meat that cooking will destroy, so he roasted the meat on sticks over the fire.

When he had eaten, he got up and gathered broken branches for a lean-to shelter. It was hurriedly and clumsily made, but sufficient for the night to come. He paused to warm his hands over the fire and then to hold warm hands over his ears and nose. He tried to remember what month it was and failed. The days had passed into weeks and the weeks into months. Spring was at least a month away, he decided, and perhaps more.

A little warmth and a little food and he felt much better. Man needs so little, he thought, yet he begins wanting so much.

Gathering fuel, he glanced at the mountain ridge opposite. In this area of relatively low mountains it was higher than most, and the side facing him was very steep. Above all, there was snow on the mountaintop, quite a lot of it in fact. A curling lip of snow hung over the edge, and the steep slope below was a litter of fallen trees and boulders. He checked his distance and decided that in the event of an avalanche, he was beyond its reach, but not by very much.

He built up a screen for his fire to reflect heat back into his corner away from the wind. Then he made a bed of spruce boughs and gathered more fuel. It would be a cold night.

Cold it was, even with the fire, bitter cold. He added fuel and thought of Natalya, so far away now, and hoped she was warm and away from the wind.

He shook his head, puzzled at himself and at her. No words of love had been spoken, no promises made, none asked for. Only that he would try to return for her, and she had never questioned his reason. It had just been something between them, an understanding from the beginning. Now, beside the fire, he tried to remember at what point it had come about, and he could not find one. Simply, it had been there, a quiet understanding of something between them.

He had never been in love and, different from most men, had never even thought he was.

Nights came suddenly here and lasted long. It was dark now, and his eyes could no longer reach across the little cove to where the sheer mountain waited with its lips of snow. Huddled against the bole of the fallen tree, he tried to soak up warmth from the fire, but unless he almost hung over it, little heat could reach him.

He gnawed on a bone left from his roast of venison and dozed fitfully. He was tired, so very tired!

Cold was the day when finally it came, a feeble light of pale yellow through the gray. No sun in sight, no warmth, only a greater visibility. A low wind came through the sparse trees, whining among the rocks and across the icy ridges. Joe Mack shivered and fumbled to warm his fingers in their mittens. He peered through the rocks at a small meadow, desperate to see some kind of game. He saw nothing.

He listened, but heard no sound of man or motor. He eased from behind the rocks and went down a slight slope, walking an oblique route of his own choosing. There were no trails here, no sign of men.

Instinct as well as intelligence told him a massive search was on, that every step now must be taken with care. They had found his trail, and men had died. The soldiers who sought him would be all the more ready to kill, and those others, alerted he might be coming, would not be trusting.

Open country now, so he began to trot. Swinging along easily, smoothly. His endurance had grown with survival. The meat had brought back his old strength, but he took no chances, placing his feet carefully, wary of ice on the rocks and of black ice, present but not so visible. For an hour he ran, weaving among rocks, following dim animal paths beside small streams, and finally moving into the forest again.

Here he slowed to a walk and unlimbered his bow. Again, he needed meat. He always needed meat. He still had some of the tea taken from the young engineer or whatever he had been. That night, huddled over a small fire, he forced his cold brain to think.

What would they do now? They had an idea of where he was going, and they knew how he moved, something of what he was prepared to do. They would try to be ready for him in the north. He could expect a more careful search. They would be watching along the Kolyma. Beyond lay the Chersky Mountains.

Baronas had talked much of those mountains, which he had never seen but of which he knew a good deal. They were named for a Lithuanian who had been exiled to Siberia after the Polish uprising of 1863. Chersky had made a study of the region and had later been sent back by the Academy of Sciences to continue his studies. Baronas had read his books and had talked to some younger men who had worked with him. Chersky had died in 1892 somewhere in the Kolyma River region.

One of the things Baronas had told him was of the great canyons in the Chersky region through which the Indigirka and Kolyma rivers flowed, canyons said to be more than six thousand feet deep.

Suppose he fled to those canyons? Lost himself in one of them until the chase was over? Until they had given him up for dead? Or would they ever give up?

Not Zamatev, not Alekhin.

They would come for him there or anywhere; somehow they would find him.

He knew in his heart they would find him one day, and

then it would be just them. They would have to face him somewhere out there in the wilderness, man to man.

He was dreaming. They had armies. They did not depend just upon themselves. They could cover miles with their choppers, studying each mile, looking for tracks. Sooner or later they would catch him in the open. They would hunt him down like a dog.

So far he had survived, at first because they did not believe he could and because he was one man alone in all the vastness that was Siberia.

Now he must make a choice. To go ahead was to go into a trap. By this time they had a general idea of where he was and what he intended, so he must confuse them, do something to throw them off the trail.

The canyons might be it, for they were west as well as north. It would be a change of direction.

Or Magadan . . .

Magadan, a town on the sea, and not too far away. He shook his head. That would be foolish. He would be exposed there. That is, he would know none of the small things residents know, the simple things of everyday living. He would make mistakes and reveal himself.

To even approach Magadan would put him in more populated areas where he must pass in review before more people, and a people inclined to suspicion who knew he was around. Even with his new shirt and the suit he had folded away he would be in danger.

Crouched on a mountainside, his cheeks stiff with cold, he studied the ragged pines along the farther ridge, and the hollow valley that lay between. Death was there and all about him, death from men, yes, and death from cold. If he slipped and broke a leg, he would freeze within minutes.

The icy cold was waiting for the slightest misstep to kill. They were seeking him out, trying to find him, and he must use the land, turn it against them.

He was in the land of the Tungus, the Reindeer People. Yet he had seen none of them as yet. He could come upon them at any time.

He moved along under the pines, looking again across the valley toward the bleak ridges, the massed battalions of the other pines where darkness and shelter might wait or enemies to kill or maim him. Snow crunched under his moccasins, and he came out from under the pines and went down the hill into the icy chill of the hollow. A cold wind stirred, and he felt its added chill.

Each step he chose with care, trusting to nothing. To his left, the end of the cuplike hollow rose up; to his right, it spilled out into another, longer valley. Nothing moved within his sight, and he walked across the hollow and started to climb the ridge and suddenly stopped, brought up short by a crevasse, a deep fracture of the rocky floor that dropped away into some unimaginable depth. A misstep here . . .

One long step would take a man across. There was crusted snow on the far side, crusted snow over rocks. He took the step and then turned around and, with his knife, loosened a rock or two under the snow crust. When he went on he had left a death trap for whoever followed his trail.

A tall man might try to step over, a shorter man might take a small leap. Well, they were hunting him; let them pay the cost.

Lean as a mountain wolf, his face haggard with cold and exhaustion, he climbed the icy slope to the lure of the sheltering pines. He hunted a place to shelter himself, and the sky overhead danced with the weird green and yellow of the northern lights. He crunched through the snow, eyes seeking a place, finding nothing. The trunks of the pines were black against the whiteness of the snow. Wind moaned through the trees, and they bent their tops before the wind. He crouched against the bole of a tree, searching the land before him. His eyes took in everything: the silent avenues among the pines, the blowdown resting, half fallen, suspended by only one slim branch. Soon it would fall and drop across the trail.

It was a moment before he realized what he was seeing. Beyond the edge of the pines lay a long valley and a slope, and coming down that slope in a staggered skirmish line were soldiers.

Not ten, not twenty, but at least a hundred of them, scattered widely out and coming toward him, twenty to thirty yards apart, each carrying a rifle ready for action.

For a moment he did not move, but lay still, watching their advance. It was slow, cautious, but covered a wide front. Behind them, separated by at least one hundred yards from each other, were two officers.

It was that queer half light that often existed at such

latitudes. Fascinated, he watched them come; then, rising, he faded into the forest behind him, careful to step where the snow had been blown from the frozen earth. Now he needed a hiding place or somehow to evade them. He glanced back again. Farther up the valley another skirmish line was emerging from the trees. They were making a careful sweep of the country, and he was directly in its path.

Slowly, he retreated into the forest, looking carefully about him.

Nothing. No place to hide, just the slim dark trunks of trees, with every once in a while a big, older tree. Climb one? The branches were too far apart, too sparse. Bury himself in the snow? In most places the snow cover was too thin to allow it.

He watched the advancing soldiers, still some distance off. Some seemed to be looking carefully about, others simply marched ahead, eyes on what lay before them.

He turned and ran, swiftly and silently, leaping the crevasse when he reached it. Suddenly he was remembering something seen, a slim hope!

Darting into the woods, he looked left and right. The cluster of big old trees! He ran among them, avoiding snow patches. The one he remembered was there, a huge old lightning-struck tree, its top long since fallen. He crawled into the hollow and then stepped on a fallen slab and reached up, grasping for a handhold. It was pitch dark, and somewhere above him was a small circle of lighted sky. He found a hold, tested it, and tugged himself up; then he put his back against one side and his foot and a knee against the other and began inching his way higher. Many times, in mountain climbing, he had climbed rock chimneys by the same means. Now edging higher and higher he came to a place where he could go no further. He felt around for a handhold, found one, and held himself still.

How long could he remain there? His position was relatively secure for the moment. He was, he guessed, some thirty feet above the ground, but it might be further.

No sound. Were they coming? Suddenly he heard a wild cry of fear and a rushing, falling sound, some distance off. Then in the still, cold air a series of commands, angry shouts, and warnings.

Somebody had fallen into his trap.

He waited, finding a better resting place for his foot.

Please, he whispered, let them come soon! Surprisingly, it was warmer here, away from the wind.

Now he heard them. They were, some of them at least, coming through the forest. He heard a sharp command, then a crunch of feet. Somebody was looking into the hollow tree!

Somebody was right below him. He held his breath and prayed no rotting wood would fall into the hollow below him.

He heard a grunt and then a denial, as of someone saying there was nothing there.

Now they would move on. He could get down from his precarious position and escape.

Suddenly came a sharp command and then a sound of breaking wood. Another such sound. They were building a fire! They were going into camp!

For a moment he was choked by sheer horror. He could not remain where he was. He could not remain cramped in that position much longer. He must get down; he must move, or he would freeze.

He could hear them talking among themselves; there were more sounds of breaking wood and then the crackle of a fire.

Slowly, carefully, he began to ease himself back down the inside of the tree.

THIRTY

When his feet were on the ground, he began tensing all his muscles, stretching, working them to get the blood moving again. Group by group he worked on them, listening meanwhile to the movements about the camp. From the sounds, they were all about him.

He could hear them gathering wood for their fires, hear muttering curses and somebody bemoaning the loss of a comrade. Somebody else spoke in threatening tones of the American. "Wait," he was saying, "until we get him! I'll break every bone!"

He dared not stomp his feet to keep warm. He dared make no movement that might be heard. He must remain absolutely still until they bedded down for sleep; then he might dare to escape.

He leaned against the inside of the tree. It was all of four feet wide where he stood, and the hole through which he had ducked was close to the ground, not over three feet high at the opening. A bad place to get out without rubbing the side and being heard.

He was trapped.

He was tired, so very tired. His eyes closed, then opened again. Some warmth from a fire was wafted his way, so very little of it, yet in the piercing cold he could feel it. He heard somebody throw wood on the fire.

One was wishing he was in Khab; another was remembering a girl in Irkutsk.

Joe Mack worked his toes inside the moccasins. He must find more grass to put inside them. He tensed his muscles again and again.

He was cold, cold!

The talk was dying down. They were eating, and some already were getting into sleeping bags for the night.

How many guards would they leave? Certainly one or more. And where would they be stationed? Could he crawl out of the hollow tree without brushing the sides? In the dead silence of night, such a sound could be easily heard and would be recognized instantly as an unnatural sound in the forest.

He heard the voice of the officer again, obviously designating sentries, and then retreating footsteps, wood thrown on the fire, an increased crackle of flames. Through the opening he could see the flickering light.

How long now? How long before the guard became dull with cold and sleep? How long before he himself did?

Again and again he tensed his muscles. He was tired, so very tired! He wanted sleep himself, any kind of rest.

No matter what happened, he was hours from sleep. He felt for his knife, felt for the pistol, to be used only in a dire emergency.

He knelt and peered out. All he could see was firelight flickering on the trunk of the tree opposite.

He waited. Now there was no sound but the fire. If it began to die down the sentry would put on more fuel.

Did he have a stack of it nearby?

Joe Mack waited. He stretched again to get life into his muscles, and then again he dropped to a knee, and this time he thrust his head out far enough to see.

They were bedded down not far from him, with two fires going that he could see and a sentry sitting almost facing him. That was better. He worried more about peripheral vision. His head was in deep shadow and he could watch the sentry. The man was sleepy, and from time to time his eyes closed briefly.

He was a tough-looking, strong young man. His eyes closed again, this time a moment longer than before. Realizing he was growing sleepy the sentry got up and moved around, replenishing the fire. He stood, his back to Joe Mack, staring into the flames.

Dare he try it now? He waited, doubting if he could move fast enough or move without being heard. Finally the sentry sat down again.

The man rubbed his eyes, chuckled at some vagrant thought, and then leaned against the bole of a tree, smiling into the flames.

I hope it's a good thought, damn you, Joe Mack told himself. *Now go to sleep, for God's sake!*

It seemed a long time before the sentry's eyes closed again. He was a good man, this one, Joe Mack thought. He might doze a little, but not for more than a minute or two.

The sentry's head nodded, and with scarcely a whisper of sound Joe Mack eased himself from the hollow tree and stood up. Quickly he stepped around the tree, putting it between himself and the sentry.

He faced more bodies in sleeping bags, and another fire, that one some distance off. There was a sentry there, too. The man was standing up, staring into the fire.

That was a mistake many made. To stare into a fire destroys one's night vision for that important moment when one has to adjust to darkness, looking quickly from the fire toward an enemy out there. A good sentry should sit with his back to a fire, never looking into the flames. Yet it was a temptation and a very natural reaction. One that could cost a man his life.

Joe Mack had been taught that by an old Sioux who was his uncle. The old man had taught him many things, still a warrior at heart, as unreconstructed as Joe Makatozi himself.

He moved suddenly, swiftly, to another tree, melding his shadow into that of the tree.

The sentry went into the darkness to gather fuel, and Joe moved again, further away. The man came back, adding sticks to the fire, his concentration on that, and Joe Mack slipped into the trees and was gone.

Like a ghost, he merged with the forest, moving out, down a slope through the trees, free once more, but for how long?

He had been lucky, so very, very lucky. Such luck could not hold. He must find a way to escape this search, a place to hide.

Some of the soldiers had been raw recruits, young men from cities and towns in Russia. That would not last. He would soon encounter some from the forest, from Siberia or the Urals or from somewhere in the wilderness. He moved off into the darkness, headed west, running steadily along the ghost of a trail.

Westward and north he fled, keeping to the cover of trees whenever possible, using paths only for brief periods and with care. Hunted like a wild animal, he had become as elusive as one. He must, he told himself, be like the mountain lion. In all his years in the mountains, the only lions he had seen had been treed by dogs. They were there; he had seen their droppings and their tracks, occasionally a kill. Of the big cats themselves one rarely caught a glimpse. If they could do it, he could also.

The detachment of troops he had narrowly eluded could not be the only one. At any moment he could encounter more. From each ridge and hilltop he studied the terrain before him, always lying down or crouching in cover, letting his body merge with his surroundings. Only when he was sure nothing awaited him did he advance.

The use of traps had made him wary of them, for Alekhin was somewhere about, and he would understand such things. Scowling, crouched at the base of a tree, he considered that.

Where was Alekhin? Certainly, he would not be idle. His reputation as a manhunter was at stake.

Glimpsing the smoke of a campfire ahead, he turned deeper into the timber, swinging wide around it. On a sparsely forested ridge he looked down and back into the valley of the smoke and saw a cluster of men around two fires.

Soldiers!

He faded into thicker woods and worked his way further west and south before swinging back to the north. He would find the Chersky Mountains somewhere ahead and lose himself in one of the canyons of which he had heard.

Lieutenant Suvarov sat by the fire, studying a map spread out on his knees. As the voice of Colonel Zamatev, he was dealing with officers superior to him in rank, attempting to guide them in a search as Zamatev would want it conducted. He was a tactful young man, and so far had succeeded, although there was at least one officer with whom he dealt who was displeased by Zamatev's assumption of authority.

Colonel Nicolai Rukovsky was an officer of unquestioned ability. He was also well connected and ambitious. His command was one of the best trained in the Soviet Army, and he was constantly striving to improve it in every respect. As a result he welcomed the chance to take his men into the field on something more than a maneuver.

"You can tell Colonel Zamatev that if he is in the area you suggest we will have him."

Leaving the Kolyma River well guarded, he started a line of one thousand men, at thirty-yard intervals, to make a sweep of the forest, meadows, and hollows south of the river.

"Sir," Lieutenant Suvarov suggested, "I believe the interval is too great. This man is like a ghost, sir. He might slip through."

"Nonsense! Not through my men. They will take him."

"He's very elusive, sir."

Studying the map, Suvarov considered the problem. They had been out for three days now and had advanced more than thirty miles and had seen nothing.

Because of the terrain, the line was considerably further south at its eastern end, and here and there, despite the best efforts of the officers, the thirty-yard interval had proved impossible to maintain. Despite that, Suvarov had to admit the sweep had been thorough. Yet there had been no sign of the man they sought.

A Udehe hunter among them had come to Suvarov. "I see tracks," he said.

Suvarov looked up impatiently; then recognizing the man, he asked, "Can you show me?"

The Udehe was a skilled tracker. He pointed out something on the ground that Suvarov failed to see and then led him up a long slope through the trees.

The sound of a motor stopped them. It was Colonel Rukovsky. "What is it, Lieutenant?"

"This man has found some tracks. He is very skilled. He says our man came right through here last night."

"That is impossible," Rukovsky said. "Our men were camped right up there, stationed all along the ridge."

The Udehe had gone on ahead. Such discussions were nothing to him. He found the curve of a heel at the edge of some snow. He showed it to Suvarov. *"Unty,"* he said, "a shoe made of skin. He went up there." He pointed up toward the campsite.

Getting down from his car, Rukovsky followed, watching. He was fascinated. Most of his life had been lived on an axis that included Moscow, Kiev, and the Crimea. Now he was silent, watching the Udehe with interest.

At the hollow tree the Udehe stopped. Bending over, he peered into the opening and then disappeared inside. Some of the rotting wood on the inside of the trunk had been knocked down and lay on the earth inside the hollow. Rukovsky joined him.

"He here," the Udehe said, showing them places where the wood had been brushed or broken off. "Climb up there while people look for him."

Rukovsky swore and turning to Suvarov, he said, "You were right, Lieutenant. This man is elusive."

He ducked out of the opening and straightening up, brushed off bits of bark and wood. "Came right through us, did he? We shall see about that!"

He glanced at the Udehe. "That's a good man. Keep him around. We will need him."

He slapped his thigh with his gloves. "The question is, where did he go? Where is he now?"

"Colonel Zamatev is inclined to think the fugitive is trying to retrace the old route his people may have taken when they migrated over the Bering Strait to America. That would mean he's going northeast."

"It would, indeed." Rukovsky slapped his leg again. "But northeast of here is the Kolyma. A hard river to cross and well guarded. You say this man was a major in the American air force? Then he will be intelligent as well as a good woodsman. I suggest he went west."

"West, sir?"

"West, of course. The Kolyma is well guarded. If he goes further east he restricts his arc of movement. You say he is a man accustomed to the wilderness. Very well, he will go west. He will try to lose himself in the mountains."

"Do you suppose he knows our country that well?"

"We must suppose he does. One thing, Lieutenant, never underestimate an enemy!"

"I shall have to communicate with Colonel Zamatev."

"By all means!" Rukovsky agreed. "Tell him I am prepared to cooperate to the fullest. The man interests me, and I'd like to be present when he is taken."

Suvarov hesitated, and then tentatively he suggested, "There are others in the field, sir. Comrade Shepilov wants him also, wants him first."

"Shepilov?" Rukovsky's face was bland. "Of course! But Colonel Zamatev is GRU is he not? I have every admiration for Comrade Shepilov and wish him success, but we in the military, we must work together, must we not?"

Rukovsky looked toward the soldier; the Udehe was waiting. "Let's get that man seeking out the trail, Suvarov. He seems to be a good man on a trail."

"Yes, sir. Comrade Alekhin is in the field, too, sir."

"Alekhin? And where is he?"

"Nobody knows but Alekhin and perhaps Colonel Zamatev. He reports only to him, but I do know he is very anxious to be the one who takes the American. There is something personal between them."

"How could that be?"

Suvarov explained about the brief meeting shortly after the American was first taken.

At the car Colonel Rukovsky got out his maps. "Suvarov? Let's recall our men and transport them west. Let us make a base of Oymyakon." He folded the map. "He covers country, this American. How does he do it?"

"He is an Indian. Some of them are said to be great runners. The man was an athlete."

"Come, Lieutenant, let's move." He turned and glanced at Suvarov. "Let's make this an army operation, Lieutenant. I've flown over those mountains and know them a little. We will take him ourselves."

"Colonel Zamatev will appreciate your cooperation."

"He shall have it. This American of yours intrigues me. I'd like to take him." He paused, making room for Suvarov to get into the car. "Shepilov, is it? A very capable man, Lieutenant, but never very friendly to the army. Never friendly at all."

On a rocky point under some low-growing, wind-torn spruce, Joe Mack squatted on his heels looking down the valley. At the distance he could see very little, only that the soldiers were being recalled. He had seen the car, even heard it in the cold air.

An officer, probably, a commanding officer taking his men from the field.

Why?

He had eluded them. Had they discovered how? The Russians were good players of chess, and now they contemplated another move. There must be a reason for suddenly leaving the field. They would not be quitting the chase, so they must be changing direction. Had they guessed what he was attempting?

When he got where he was going, would they be there, waiting?

THIRTY-ONE

Now coldly blew the winds, icy blasts from beyond the Arctic Circle. In the small house above Plastun Bay, Stephan Baronas spent much of his time seeking wood in the forest. Here along the Sea of Japan the snow sometimes fell until it was several feet deep.

He came in from the cold, stamping his feet. "It is cold," he said, coming up to the fire. "If this lasts another day I must go to the village for food."

"I will go."

"The snow is deep, Talya."

"I am strong, and much younger than you." She seated herself on the hearth. "I wonder where he is?"

Baronas shook his head. "He is out there; that is all we know except that they do not seem to have caught him. As you know, word gets around. Somebody whispers something and it is passed on, person to person. The trouble is that by the time it reaches us it may be much changed."

"What did you hear?"

"It was just before the storm began. I was down on the shore looking for driftwood. There was a fisherman I know, just down from Magadan, where he sold his catch. The word is they are organizing a search by trappers and hunters, men who know the country."

"Father? Must we wait?"

"Wait? You mean for whatever Bocharev can do? We must. What he can do I do not know, but certainly more than anyone else. Who cares about us? He seems to because of his son. That feeling may pass, and it might be impossible even for him."

"Can we not at least try? That other man? The trader in furs? You suspected he might be arranging to get away over the border? He might take us."

Baronas shook his head. "Zhikarev is a good man but he owes us nothing. Moreover, he will have enough trouble trying to arrange things for himself. My feeling was that he expected to get right away and something went wrong."

"The border is not far, and I am afraid."

"You? You have never been afraid, Talya."

"They might try to use me to capture him." Her eyes were large with worry and fear. "It has come to me in the night. They will do anything to capture him."

"But how would he know? If they took us now, how would they get word to him? It is impossible. You worry needlessly."

"How much longer can we stay here? When spring comes, we can no longer have the house."

He had been thinking of that and shied from the thought. This place, however small and lonely it might be, was snug and warm. It was a refuge, a hiding place from all that crowded about outside. Little as it was, he hated to give up these days of peace. The place was cozy, the view beautiful, and there were no passersby to alert the authorities.

He dreaded another trek across country and the problems of protecting his daughter. So far he had succeeded, but there were bands of young renegades, "hooligans" the law called them, and he was no fighting man. He would soon be seventy and had grown more fragile with the years, although since coming to live in the taiga his health had been better and he was stronger. The north country did not tolerate many germs, and the air was better. They were far from factories and the effects of smokestacks and power lines.

"We must think about it, Talya. I agree we must have an alternative plan if Bocharev forgets or can do nothing. I agree that we must leave, for it is only a matter of time until they descend upon us again.

"We are free now only because they are busy with other things. They have, as the saying is, bigger fish to fry. If they want us, they will have us.

"I think we should make plans now; when this snow is gone, then we can move."

To where? He asked himself this question. The closest point on the Chinese border was beyond Voroshilov. He did not know the towns but must get out his maps and study them. Iman might be better, although farther. There might be fewer people about.

He put on his heavy coat and went out again to gather fuel. It was a never-ending struggle against the cold. Had he been here earlier he would have stacked wood for the winter, but there had been no chance of that.

He walked up into the huge trees in the grove behind the cabin. It was silent there, like walking in a huge cathedral or the temple at Luxor, of which he had seen pictures. It was a good place to think.

Natalya was right, of course. They must not delay. How to get across the border he had no idea. All they could do was get close and study the alternatives. Knowing the thoroughness of the KGB, his only wonder was that they had not already been picked up and interrogated.

Their very presence on this coast was enough to arouse suspicion.

Thoughtfully, he began reviewing all he had learned from the young soldiers during their visits. They had talked a good bit about the borders and their duties, partly to impress Natalya and himself with the importance of what they were doing. This was expected of young men, and their experiences had been interesting as well as informative. Although there were places where troops facing each other verged on outright hostility, there were others where food was exchanged and clothing traded back and forth. At such a point, there might be tolerance unfound elsewhere.

Gathering wood to load the crude sled he had built, he tried to think of every aspect of escape.

To leave here, of course, meant to abandon any help from Bocharev, so all he could do was hope that if such help was to come that it arrive before they fled from here. And the time was terribly short.

It meant crossing the Sikhote Alin Mountains, low but formidable. There were dense forests and man-eating tigers, long feared by the Chinese who lived along the Amur.

There were brigands in those forests now as there had ever been, fierce men who robbed, raped, and terrorized travelers and nearby villages.

Yet if they were to escape, it must be done, and it might be possible to secure transportation. Stephan Baronas was beginning to learn that there were many ways in which to survive and that there existed a clandestine world of which he had never been aware, a half world in which refugees, criminals, and others mingled, aided and robbed each other, and moved across borders without the knowledge of the authorities.

Human nature is such that friendships will develop even among those whose official interests are opposed, and in these days of instant communication such an understanding could possibly avoid a clash that might end in war. Trust is often based on very little more than one's measure of a man.

He loaded his sled with firewood and drew it over the snow to the cabin. By the time he had reached it he knew they must prepare, select several possible avenues of escape and have them ready.

In the village he might establish some contact with a truck driver who would carry them to their destination or at least near to it. Also, he would take a page from Joe Mack's book and scout a trail over the mountains toward the border.

The difficulty was that they must wait to the last minute for what Bocharev might do, while even now their arrest order might lie on a desk somewhere, awaiting implementation.

Fortunately, they had nothing that must be taken, beyond what clothing and food they possessed at the time. Stephan Baronas was beginning to learn that possessions can rob one of freedom just as much as the bars of a cage.

When Stephan Baronas reached the cabin with his sled, he was tired. He paused, waiting outside the door until he had caught his breath, not wanting Natalya to hear how hard it was for him to breathe.

To flee they must cross mountains. How would he manage that? No matter, he would manage it, and the mountains were not so very high.

When he had stopped panting, he opened the door and

took an armful of the wood to its place beside the fire.
Putting down the wood he brushed off his arms.

"Talya?"

There was no answer. Looking around, he saw the note
on the corner of his reading table. There he left the three
books he had succeeded in keeping.

Gone to the village.

He swore, exasperated. She knew he had intended to
go, and he would not have wished her to climb back up that
steep trail. It was a cold walk down to the edge of the bay and
then around by the shore, and that was a rough, hard-drinking
crowd that hung about there.

Adding fuel to the fire, he took off his coat and settled
down. It would be a long wait.

Natalya arranged the few things purchased into her
backpack. She was aware that several of the men who usually
loafed about were watching her and talking in undertones to
each other. She was about to shoulder her pack when the
door opened with a gust of wind from off the bay.

The instant her eyes touched him she knew the man, but
she knew better than to call any such man by name until he
identified himself. It was not impossible that at the moment
he had chosen to use another.

He glanced at her and then went to the keeper of the
store and purchased tobacco.

Taking up her pack, she started for the door. One of the
loafers sauntered over. "Help you with that?" He reached for
the pack.

"I will be all right, thank you."

"Now that isn't friendly," the man said. "Here, I'll take
it." His hand closed on the pack and he jerked it roughly
from her arms, so roughly that she staggered and almost fell.
Somehow she kept a grip on the pack. "I do not want any
help!" she said.

He laughed at her, pushing her away. "Let's see what
you bought," he taunted. "Maybe there's something—"

"Let go of her." Yakov's tone was low, but it carried a
message.

Slowly, still keeping a grip on the pack, the man turned. "Did you speak to me?" he said roughly.

"I told you to let go of the pack and leave the lady alone." Yakov smiled. "I shall not tell you again."

"Ho, ho!" The man sneered, jerking a thumb toward Yakov. "Who does he think he is?"

Yakov was not four feet from him, leaning an elbow on the counter, his pipe in his teeth.

"Move back, Natalya," Yakov said. "When he falls I do not want him to fall on you."

Two of the other men had risen, looking from one to the other, uncertain what course to choose.

"Falls? Who is going to fall?"

Yakov spoke past the pipe. "Let go of the pack," he said, "and step back. The lady is a friend of mine."

"And who are you?"

Yakov's elbow still rested on the counter, his right hand lay flat upon its top. He was smiling.

"I am taking this woman and her pack with me," the man said. He glanced at his companions. "If he gives trouble, take him. I'll share her with you."

Almost negligently, Yakov kicked him on the side of his knee. The crack was loud in the room. The man cried out, staggered, and fell. Yakov faced them. "He now has a broken leg," Yakov said politely. "What do you want broken?"

Astonished, they looked from him to the man on the floor, who gripped his leg and moaned.

The others stared at him, drawing back. Yakov took up Natalya's pack. "We are leaving now, but remember this. I do not want this lady disturbed in any way, do you understand? She is a friend of mine. If I have to come back I will find each of you; alone or together, it does not matter."

He turned to Natalya. "Come," he said. "Enough of this."

They went out, and Yakov closed the door behind them. The man on the floor was alternately moaning and cursing. Now the others were crossing the room to him.

Outside, Yakov said, "Do you live far from here?"

She pointed. "Up there, in the forest. It is several miles."

"Have you room enough for me?" he asked. "I don't want to make any trouble, and I can rig a place in the forest."

"Of course there is room."

They walked on, and after a bit she said, "Yakov? Thank you."

"It was nothing. I have seen many such. They are all mouth and talk very loud when filled with vodka."

He lowered his tone. "It is you and your father? What happened to the others?"

"Scattered. I do not know where."

They were on the shore of the bay. She paused, looking back. Only the few lights were visible.

"Yakov? Have you heard of him? Of Joe Mack?"

He chuckled. "Who has not? He's leading them a dance, I tell you. Has half of official Siberia strung out, looking for him. One part is afraid the others will find him first.

"He's off to the northeast now, and they are mustering men. I would go to help him if I knew how, but he's doing enough by himself."

"Who are you, Yakov?"

"It is better you do not know. Let us say that I love Mother Russia but I do not love her government. I do not like being tied to a certain piece of work. I am a wanderer, a free soul, you might say. As you know I have helped people escape from them. Perhaps I am one of the damned capitalists they talk about, but I've no capital."

"But you're not alone?"

"Oh, no! There are others of us, but we keep out of sight. That little thing just now. I do not like such things because they attract attention."

He looked up the steep path. "You climb this often? With a pack?"

"My father has done it, but I do not wish it any longer. His heart is bad, Yakov, although he believes I do not know it. He stops outside the door to recover his breath before he comes in. If I had not come tonight, he would have come in the morning."

They walked on, and then at the top of the trail and within sight of the cabin she stopped again. "Yakov, we are going to try to leave the country."

Briefly, she explained, adding the story of Bocharev and his son.

"Bocharev?" He was surprised. "He is a good man, Natalya, and a strong man. He can do it if he wishes. He can send you over the border. Not even Zamatev has his power, or Shepilov." He nodded his head. "Yes, it is good that you should go. That is why I am here."

"Why? Why are you here? What do you mean?"

"The order has been issued by Zamatev for your arrest, yours and your father's. You cannot wait. You must go tonight."

THIRTY-TWO

Stephan Baronas got to his feet as they entered. His smile was warm as he greeted Yakov. "Come! Sit by the fire! It is good to see you!"

"I am afraid there is little time for sitting, comrade. You are to be arrested. You must leave this place at once."

"Leave it?"

"You have no choice. Zamatev has ordered your arrest. He is picking up all those who had any contact with the American. You and your daughter are first on the list."

Natalya was gathering their clothing into bundles, collecting what food they had. The packs would be large, but the food would disappear quickly, lightening their load.

She glanced at her father. How would he ever make it? Or would he? Over the mountains in the dead of winter? At least he would not die in prison.

He must not die! He had too much to offer, he was too good a man, and he was her father. He was all she had.

All? She thought of Joe Mack. Was there really anything there? Or was it all a dream? An impossible dream?

What had passed between them? What had been said? What promised? She shook her head, amazed at herself and at him. There had been nothing, really. Nothing one could put a finger on and say this was the moment.

There had been no words of love, no passionate clinging

246

together, only a quiet understanding, something rich and warm and beautiful. Somehow, from the moment they met, there had been no doubt. She had not really considered it; she had not thought about it or dreamed of it. Suddenly he was there and she knew.

Now, packing swiftly, she puzzled over it. What had he said? What had he *done*? How had he aroused this feeling in her? She had always been a cool, sensible sort, but this was a man on the run, a man of an alien people, even of a different race.

He was an Indian, what had been considered a savage people. That, he said, was true no longer of his people, but it was true of him.

Could he be savage? She thought of that and admitted it was more than possible. How else could he exist out there in the wilderness? In the snow? And now, with the terrible winter more than half gone, he was still alive, still out there, still somehow avoiding capture.

She turned on Yakov. "Could it be morning? A few hours' sleep would prepare us for it."

He shrugged. "The further you are away, the better. I can come with you but a little way. I must not be found here, or found at all," he added, somewhat grimly. "I can help you for a few miles, and then I must be away."

"Father? Get some sleep. We all must." She turned to Yakov. "Before daybreak, then?"

He shrugged. "It is a risk."

Yakov built up the fire; then he took an AK-47 from his pack and checked it. The sound of the action opening and closing was ominous in the small cabin.

Her father's weariness was obvious in the quickness with which he slept. She saw Yakov look at him and then shake his head.

She lay down without undressing. There would be no time in the morning. Staring up at the ceiling, she tried to think of what they must do. There was a dim path up through the forest that did not begin until beyond several small clearings. She had walked up that trail no more than a mile, but it led into dense forest. In the summer she would have explored it further, but in this weather, in the winter—

There had been snowshoes in the cabin, and they belonged there. No matter, they must take them. If they escaped, they could send payment for them.

If they escaped—

She lay long awake, staring up into the darkness, lighted only by the flickering flames of the dying fire.

How could they possibly escape? An old man and a young woman, an old man who had never been considered physical.

And even when they reached the border, how could they cross? The river they would reach would not be the Amur but the Ussuri; yet it was a large river, and it would be patrolled.

The opening of the door awakened her, for it let in a cold breath of wind. She sat up quickly. It was Yakov.

"It is time, and we must hurry."

As she moved to stir up the fire, he stopped her. "The fire is out; the ashes are cold. Leave it that way, and they will not know when we left."

She was prepared. Her father dressed quickly, and they took up their bundles and went outside. It was snowing, a soft, gentle snow whispering down, covering all.

She led the way up through the trees where they had gathered wood, across a sort of clearing, and then around the huge tree she remembered and into a trail that was only a mere parting between low-growing shrubs.

Yakov turned to look back. The snow was already obscuring their tracks. "In minutes," he told her, "they will be gone. Let us be moving."

It was cold and crisp. She moved along, purposely holding down the pace because of her father. The trail wound through the trees, and she found her memory of the first mile was good. "I could become an Indian," she told herself. "I could even live in the forest."

The Iodzihe River lay to their right, and the forest through which they were going was cut by a small stream that flowed down to that river. Yakov moved past her. "Let me break trail now," he said. "I did not know where it began."

The snow was deep under the trees. What they could see of the sky was overcast and a dull gray. The trees were stark and black against the whiteness of the snow. Not a breath of wind was stirring now, and the forest was very still.

Once she saw a bird glide off among the trees, following their same path through the forest.

Many massive oak and maple trees mingled with what her father told her were Korean pine and, of course, birch, with which she was familiar. Steadily, by a winding route, they climbed.

Along the streams there were cottonwoods, some of the largest she had ever seen.

The morning was cold, but not too cold, and after they had traveled for what she believed was two miles, they paused to rest. In all this time, except for the one bird, they had seen no living thing. Now, standing close, they talked in low tones.

She looked at her father, and he caught her eyes and smiled. "I am all right, Talya. I will make it."

"We are away now," Yakov said. "We can move slower. Do many know of this path?"

She shook her head. "I doubt it. People from the village did not often come that way. Some knew of the cabin, but the trail was steep and they had no reason to climb it. I think when they went to the forest it was along the river. Most of them are fishermen," she added. "There are hunters who live in the forest. In the old days the Chinese used to come to hunt for ginseng, but with the border patrolled as it is, they rarely come."

Yakov nodded. "I was a ginseng hunter once. The Chinese value it highly. If it were summer I would suggest you find some of it to take with you." He winked. "A valuable bribe, you know! Sometimes they will do things for ginseng they will not do for money."

They moved on at a slower pace. From time to time she paused to look at her father's face. It was composed; he seemed under no strain.

"We'll stop soon," Yakov said, "and make tea."

They walked on until suddenly he stopped. A great tree had fallen, torn up by the roots, and the great root mass, clogged with frozen earth, made a wall. Beside it grew a cedar with outspreading branches, thick and heavy now with snow. "Here," Yakov said, "we stop here."

He led the way off the trail and under the cedar's branches. It was a neat little place, naturally sheltered and with a natural reflector for the fire in the great root mass.

"Always look," Yakov said. "A man in the forest, he watches always and sees many places like this. He remembers, so if he comes that way again he knows where there is a camp."

Soon he had a fire going and tea bubbling in their small pot. From under a fallen tree he ripped a slab of bark for Baronas to sit on, others for her and for himself.

"If you need fire, always carry tinder: an old bird's nest, dry shreds of bark, something to start the fire. There are always dry branches, long dead, on the trunks of trees. Dead-fall trees often do not touch the ground, and the bark on the underside is dry." He looked at her again. "Soon I must go. You will be alone. You must see all and think very much. Always you must camp before dark, so you can see. Build a small fire and get close."

He added sticks to their fire and poured tea for each of them. He grinned at her. "Bears are smart. There is nothing to eat in the winter, so they sleep. There are no berries, roots are deep under the snow, and no small animals run about, so they sleep. Very smart."

"You have to go?"

He nodded. "I must meet four other men far from here. We are helping a man escape from the Sovetskaya Gavan prison." He looked at her. "I cannot be late. They need me. You understand?"

"Of course." She said it and she did understand, but inside she was frightened. To be left alone in all these mountains! What would she *do*? What could she do?

Yet wasn't this where Joe Mack was? Wasn't this where he had been for months and months? What was it Yakov said? Watch and think.

"We will be all right," she said.

He took a map from his case, sheltering it from the few flakes of snow that drifted down into their shelter. "Here we are. You see? You cross a divide here and another divide over here; then you find this river going northwest. It is the Vagou River. It goes to near Iman, on the border.

"I will try to get back. But I do not much know this border south of Iman. Do not look for me. I will find you. But if I am killed, you speak to your friend Bocharev. He is a good man. Maybe he can help. I do not know."

He stood up. "We had better go now. I will find a place for tonight, and then I will go away."

He donned his snowshoes and waited for them to do likewise. Then he led off. When they reached the trail again, they looked back. No tracks remained. Already the trail was white and smooth, as if never touched by the foot of man or beast.

Hours later and a thousand feet higher, he found an overhang partly shielded by cedars. "For tonight," he said, "a good place." He glanced at her again. "In the morning I will be gone. I do not like to leave you, but they are waiting for me. All is timed. The prisoner will be at a certain place for a few minutes. We will help him escape then. If I am late, all will be wasted. I do not know how we could get in touch with him again. Maybe never."

"I understand."

"Of course," Baronas said. "We will be all right."

The camp was a snug one, but it was cold, bitterly cold. They were higher now, nearly four thousand feet above the sea. The Sikhote Alin Mountains were at no place in the southern part of the range higher than five thousand feet, but on the ridges in the middle of winter the cold could be intense.

Talya could see that Yakov was worried. He kept looking from her father to her, and several times he walked out in the snow, muttering to himself.

"Do not worry," she said, over their tea, "we shall be all right."

"But it is winter!" he protested. "It is cold! And where you are going is far, far through the wilderness!"

"It will be all right," she said, and wished she felt she was being honest. She was sick with dread at being left alone, or almost alone, in all that vast forest.

"I had only planned to tell you of the order for your arrest," he explained. "Then I planned to go at once; now I must go very fast or I shall be late."

Long they talked as the night drew on and her father slept. He explained again and again how they must travel, what they had to fear, how they must camp. "Do not think of time," he warned. "Short marches are best for you. Camp early, so you can be snugged in well before dark. In the darkness you can find nothing. Start early, but do not exhaust yourselves. Most people who freeze do so only because they have burned up their stores of energy before stopping to rest and have nothing left to fight the cold. Do not become exhausted.

"I have some dried meat, and I will share with you. I can get more."

He fed sticks into the fire. "It is more than one hundred miles," he said. "A long way."

"We will be all right," she repeated, wishing she believed it.

At daylight he was gone, but he looked back several times and left with reluctance. Natalya stood on the edge of the woods and watched him go off along the trail to the north, as dim a trail as lay before her and her father.

He was sitting by the fire when she returned. "He is gone, then?"

"Yes, Father." She had made up her pack, purposely doing so while he slept, so that he would not realize she was carrying most of the weight. "We must push on, too."

"Yes, yes, of course." He shouldered his pack, and after a long searching look at him, she led off. She was frightened. He did not look at all well this morning. The cold, the rationed food, and the climbing were hard on him.

Shortly before noon they stopped and she made tea. The sun was out briefly, and they felt warm even in its feeble rays. She kindled a small fire and talked of home, of Joe Mack, and of the trail.

"The main ridge of the Sikhote Alin seems to parallel the coast," she said, "but Yakov told me there was another ridge running off to the northwest that reaches almost to Iman. We will reach it soon and follow it until we can descend into the basin of the Vagou."

He made no reply, staring off across the snowy ridges and the treetops, covered with snow. "This is very hard for you, Talya," he said at last. "Somehow I have been a poor father to lead you into this."

"You have been the best of fathers," she replied, "and one day we will look back upon this as only an interlude."

For three days they walked, but on the third day he said, "Talya, I think we should stop early today. I am afraid I need to rest."

The weather was warmer by a few degrees, and the

place they found was nestled among some cedars, a place where a bank had caved away. At its base, shaded by the cedars, they built their fire. They had tea, but the last of the meat Yakov had given them to add to their meager supplies was gone but for three thin strips.

"Save it for yourself," her father said. "I'll drink some tea, but I've no appetite tonight."

Morning came with softly falling snow. She built up the fire and said, "Father?"

When he did not move, she got slowly to her feet and went to where he lay, his blue eyes open to the snow.

"Father?" she pleaded.

Her father was dead, and she was alone.

THIRTY-THREE

On the morning of the day that Bocharev came to the cabin above Plastun Bay, Peshkov returned to the village.

It was a chill, bleak day, and he plodded down the path, finding no footprints in the snow. Nor did smoke arise from any of the chimneys. Hunching his shoulders against the cold, he went first to the Baronas cabin.

He knocked, expecting no answer, and then he opened the door and stepped in. It was cold inside, and the ashes on the hearth were long dead.

He stared around him, angry that they were gone, yet feeling oddly deserted, too. One by one he went to the other dugouts, caves, and shacks.

Nobody. All were gone.

To hell with them! Served them right if they'd all been taken away to prison! Especially that woman, that Natalya.

Leave it to him. He knew how to get even. He hated them all, everyone except Yakov. He was afraid of Yakov.

He had been afraid that night when the American was behind him with a knife. *Damn* him! How had he managed that? Anyway, he'd shown him! He was on the run now with half the army after him. They'd get him, too. He wished he could be there when it happened. He would just like to have the American see him there, smiling at him. Come to think of it, he had never found the place where the American had been hiding.

He walked back to the Baronas cabin, snow crunching under his feet. There was fuel there, and he built a small fire. He would roast some meat over the fire, and then he would go have a look. It irritated him that he had not found it before. Then he could have waited outside and shot him when he emerged. He might have gotten a fat reward for that. They'd given him nothing for telling them where he was hiding.

It was cold and miserable in the long-empty cabin. He stared around angrily. It had always been warm and somehow comfortable when they were here.

He made tea and sipped it, squatting on his heels. Everybody was gone, so there was no sense in staying here. They had never liked him, none of them, but he knew them. That was the thing. He knew them and they knew him. They had always been glad enough to get the meat he brought. He'd made them pay for it, one way or another, until that American came, giving them all the meat he could kill.

Where would he go now? Where could he go? He had thought them a miserable lot, even Baronas and that Natalya. Really thought well of themselves, they did. Well, all that education did them no good. They had been in the same fix he was, but now he had fixed them. And they were gone.

Gone.

The word had an empty sound. He had not liked them, but he had *known* them. Theirs were familiar faces. He had been comfortable around them even though he despised them. Now where could he go?

They had all gone away, scattered like blown snow, but if he sat down he could probably figure out where they had gotten to. Baronas had been no trapper, so he would not be apt to go into the deeper woods. He had heard they were talking of going to some warmer place where the climate would be better for his health.

A warmer place meant the coast of the Sea of Japan. At least, that was the closest place and the only place they could go. They would not dare try to go back into Russia. Anyway, they were not Russians.

Peshkov was a hating man. For the first time in his life he understood that. There had never been anyone he liked.

He had tramped with several men, but just because it was easier that way. He had gone along with them, deserting them when the occasion demanded. He was a trapper and a hunter, but a petty thief as well, taking whatever served his purpose and he could get away with. Larger and stronger than most men, he usually had no trouble. Few men were armed and most of them subject to bluff; the others he learned to avoid.

Stephan Baronas had politely ignored him, and Natalya had quietly been in command at the little settlement, something he had resented from the start. In the first place, that she was only a woman; in the second, that she was Lithuanian. Her father had been looked up to among the refugees, but he was not one to relish command or authority. Little by little it had been Natalya who had responded to the needs of their little community. Peshkov's efforts to take control had simply been ignored by everyone, and he had not known how to cope with that. Several times he had attempted to get her alone, thinking that when he did he would show her who he was and what she was to him. Unfortunately, when he finally succeeded, she proved to have a pistol and a willingness to use it.

Seated beside a fire in what had been the Baronas cabin, he made up his mind. He would find her and show her who was boss. He would wound her if necessary, kill her if he decided it was in his best interests.

To find her would be no great problem. He was a tramp and knew others of his kind. A woman so beautiful would be remembered. He smiled into his empty cup. Then he arose, put out the fire, and stowed away his gear.

First, for his own satisfaction, he would find where the American had been hiding. Then he would hunt down Natalya Baronas.

He was chuckling to himself, thinking of her horror when she would see him again. He would track her down when she was gathering fuel and strike her down. She would be tied up and helpless before she became conscious. He'd show her a thing or two.

It took him a good two hours, during which time he became more and more irritated and impatient. He refused to believe the American could so outwit him, and it was on his third passing that he suddenly decided to explore that crack in the rock. He was a heavy man, and it was a tight squeeze, yet he forced his way through, glimpsing the shelf beyond. Vague sunlight was falling through the trees, and enough was visible so that he was sure he had found it.

Right over there, within a step or two. He could see the place where a fire had been, and—

He pushed himself through the last of the crack and stepped out quickly. After all, he wanted to be away from here before dark. He—

In the instant he took his step he heard the water falling far below, but an instant too late.

He felt himself falling, and wild with panic he dropped his rifle and grabbed out wildly. His fingers caught the edge and held on, and he hung suspended above the void.

He was a strong man, but a heavy man wearing a heavy coat. A moment he hung, choking with fear, and then he tried to pull himself up.

He couldn't do it. His fingers seemed to slip and he cried out, calling for help.

There was no one to hear. The village was deserted.

He fought down the panic. He could get up there; he had to get up there. Using all his strength he pulled himself up and then tried to get an elbow over the edge.

He made it. His elbow rested on the edge, and he pulled himself up further and swung a leg to the ledge.

In one awful instant he felt the rock under his elbow crumble, and then he fell.

He seemed to fall for a long time, and then he struck with a moment of stabbing agony and then brutal, unendurable pain. He lay on the rocks, half in the icy water, and stared up at the feeble light far above and knew his back was broken.

Evgeny Zhikarev had waited and planned too long to accept defeat. Carefully, through his friends among the traders and dealers in furs, he put out feelers. From here and there he received news. An order had gone out for the arrest of Stephan and Natalya Baronas. Zamatev was rounding up all who had had meetings or contact with the American, who was still at large. The village had been deserted, Botev and Borowsky had disappeared, and so had Baronas and his daughter. Evgeny Zhikarev knew his own time was short. Undoubtedly, an order for his arrest was already out.

He was not a man to panic. He did not plan to be taken again. He had gone that route, with crippled feet to show for it, as well as some other scars.

His cousin was growing restless, and he knew that his cousin wished he would go away. It had been a warm, wonderful visit, but as the visit lengthened the cousin's patience grew shorter. No matter, he was going.

He would go suddenly, without warning, for who knew about relatives these days? Which could you trust, if any? The Soviet system was founded upon suspicion and distrust.

He had gone down into the town, taking his time, for he could walk but slowly. It was warm in the sun, and there was no snow in the town, although he could see it on the mountains. He had learned to use his eyes and ears and to pay attention, so within a short time he knew the business and the activities of most people along the street. Trucks and vans came here, unloading goods or loading furs, and he watched for a familiar face.

Suddenly he sighted someone he knew. He started forward and then relaxed. His truck driver friend was involved with the black market, among other things, and might not wish to be seen. However, glancing over, the driver saw him and came over. "Still here? What do you know? I saw Potanin the other day!"

"Potanin?" Zhikarev concealed his excitement. "Where?"

"He's got a post near Iman now." He lowered his voice. "Up to his old tricks, too. If you've got some furs—?"

"Are you going that way?"

"Midnight." He glanced around. "Furs," he said, "Potanin an' me. Trouble is, we've nobody over the river. You know?"

Evgeny Zhikarev forced expression from his face. "There's a man in Hulin, just across the river," he suggested.

"His name?" The driver was excited. "Just the one I need!"

Zhikarev shook his head. "It is not that simple. He is not Chinese, and he had relatives in Yakutia. If it should be discovered that he was involved in anything, they might suffer. He will deal, but only with people whom he knows."

"Could you come? You know Potanin. He trusts you. It is a big deal, and for you there would be something. You could have an edge of the deal."

"Well," he seemed to hesitate. "I am happy here, but—

well, I like to be dealing. This—," he waved a hand, "is a bit tame.

"At midnight, you say? Here?"

"Right here."

"Expect me," he said, and hobbled away along the street.

Iman! It was right on the river! If he could not wangle some way to cross the border to make their deal, he would be surprised. This was it, his great chance. He must be careful not to betray himself to his cousin or his family.

There was always the risk, too, that the truck would be stopped and inspected. There were few roads and they were watched, although carelessly.

When he stepped into the house his cousin was waiting for him, along with his wife and their son, their faces stern.

"Evgeny Ivanovich," his cousin said, "I must ask you to leave this house."

Evgeny Zhikarev tried to look startled. "Leave? Why?"

"We have just heard it. You are to be arrested. The KGB looks for you. We cannot afford—"

"Of course," he said, and waved a hand. "I shall leave at once. I would not wish you to be troubled because of me. I did not know, but—"

They had expected trouble. They had expected argument, pleading. They were both astonished and overjoyed.

"Please. Think no more about it. You are my own cousin. You have a wife, a family! However," he paused, "if you could make up a little bundle? Some food? Anything to keep me alive?"

"Of course! Sonya?"

She bustled about while he gathered his few things. This was easy, almost too easy. So they knew of the order for his arrest? Where were the KGB then? Or was it GRU? He must be careful, and if he could get away, it would be none too soon.

"But how—?" said his cousin.

He put a finger to his lips and looked sly. "I know a fisherman! A good man! He will take me up the coast to Magadan."

At midnight, when the truck drew alongside, he was ready to move from the dark doorway where he waited.

He heard it rumbling over the pavement before it reached him, and he was prepared. Despite his crippled feet, he moved quickly when the door opened. He scrambled in, and the truck roared off before he was fairly seated.

"I am taking a risk, my friend," the driver said. "For anyone else I'd not do it, but we have made a bit together, you and I, and perhaps again, but now they search for you. I'd be arrested if they found you in my truck, so keep low and sit well back. The fewer who see you the better."

"You have heard something?"

"They look for you. Look everywhere." The driver glanced at him. "They must think you important."

"It is the American, the one they search for. Maybe some of the furs I bought were trapped by him. At least, that is what they think. I know nothing! I never saw the man! Some of the furs—well, let us say they were *different*. Let us say I recognized a strange hand. But know? I knew nothing. I know nothing! I do not wish to be questioned, that is all."

"Is Iman good for you, then? I hope so. I can't risk taking you further."

"You say Potanin is there?"

"He is. We did some business. Oh, just a little bit! But he is hungry, that one! He has found a woman, and she makes demands! If you have a proposition, I promise you he will listen."

The truck rumbled on, climbing a steep, winding road. Evgeny Zhikarev leaned back and closed his eyes, praying to an almost forgotten God. "Please, dear God! Just this once! Let me escape them! Let me cross the river into China! I haven't the strength anymore!" He whispered it in his mind, praying, fearful of what lay ahead and of what came from behind.

The dark walls of the forest closed down. Thank God he was not out there, walking that dark forest in the snow!

Where could the American be? How could he escape them? As a boy he had traveled through the dismal forests of fir in the urman, or taiga, in western Siberia. He had been frightened, terribly frightened of the bears, although he had never seen one. And in the eastern forests, he had been afraid of the tigers, and he had seen one take a woman from a field.

There were tigers here, in this forest. He spoke aloud, saying that, and the driver nodded. "Saw one my last trip. Big fellow, standing in the road when my lights caught him.

He wasn't afraid, either! Not afraid of me or the truck. He crouched, and for a moment I thought he was going to jump right over the lights at me. I swerved, almost skidded off the road, but when I got the truck straightened out he was gone!"

They rumbled on into the night and Zhikarev slept, awakened, and slept again.

Once, atop a ridge, they stopped, and the driver awakened him. He had a thermos of tea. "Here! You can share!"

"A thermos?"

The driver gave him a knowing smile. "I do good business and with the right people. I can get anything! Anything at all!" He patted the wheel. "That's what this does for me! I have a truck and I can move! Everybody wants something! Even the leaders! Believe me, if I stopped driving, a lot of people would suffer! They are all on the take! Everyone!"

"Even Zamatev?"

The driver shook his head. "Not him! Nobody can touch him! Offer a bribe and you find yourself in a labor camp! He has plans, that one! I can see it in him! He thinks he will be very big someday and wants nobody hanging to his coattails reminding him he owes them favors!"

He drove on in silence. "Don't ever cross him. Take it from me, he'll have you hunted down and killed! It has happened! When he was on the way up, there was a man who knew him, saw him show cowardice, and spoke of it. That man disappeared.

"Gone! Like that!" He snapped his fingers. "Everybody is afraid of him! He has big ears! If anyone breathes in Magadan, he hears it in Yakutsk!"

The truck slowed. "Look! Somebody walking! And we are fifty miles from a town! Well, of all things! It is a *woman*!"

She turned toward them. "Stop the truck," Zhikarev said. "I know her."

THIRTY-FOUR

Joe Mack lay on a ridge under a wind-wracked cedar, its gnarled and twisted branches almost as thick as the trunk. It was an old, old cedar, over which many cold winds had blown, but now nothing stirred on the ridge, and Joe Mack lay quietly on the cold ground.

Not far away, there was a drift of snow, and it showed a little darkness along its lower, southern edge, where some melting had begun.

Spring was coming, and thus far he had survived the winter. His eyesight, always excellent, seemed to have improved with use. Now he could see, far away, the smoke of a fire. Nothing moved that he could see, for the distance was too great, but men were there, men who were hunting him.

Somewhere out there was Alekhin, and Alekhin was a tracker. A man of his skills could eventually find almost any trail. He was cunning. He had trailed wolves, as well as men, and would know every trick of the wilderness. Yet there were some worth trying. What he needed most of all was a good, safe hideout. Once in such a place he could remain still, and if he made no tracks he would leave none. He could just wait them out.

For that he must have a place with a water supply. He must have meat enough to survive for weeks if need be.

They were coming in force and the search would be

thorough, yet it was Alekhin he feared, Alekhin or the chance discovery of some blundering soldier who just happened upon him.

Down below there where the soldiers would be coming, their walking channeled by the country itself, he had taken the time to prepare some traps. These men would not be the same as those others, so he had used some of the same devices.

At a place where a wide step was needed to cross a small stream, he had left some sharp stakes hidden by leaves and snow. A man taking the long step necessary to step over the stream would drive his foot into the angled stake, placed to receive him.

At other points he had arranged cords made of roots to trip a follower and a sharpened stake to meet him when he fell. He had also arranged some deadfalls of heavy logs. None of these would stop pursuit, but they would arouse caution and slow the soldiers down, make them less eager to try to find him.

At another point, a natural lookout into the canyon, he had undermined a flat rock slab and then propped it in place. A quick step and the slab would fall into the canyon, taking whoever stepped on it.

The canyon he had reached was either that of the Kolyma or the Indigirka, and he suspected the latter, although his map was not clear enough, considering what little he knew of the country. But the canyon was at least a mile deep and probably more. It was wild, lonely, and picturesque. Now to find a place to hide.

Joe Mack was familiar with canyons. He had spent time in both the Snake River and the Salmon River canyons in Idaho, deeper canyons than those of the Colorado. He had spent months wandering their few trails, climbing down their rock walls, taking refuge in caves.

He found himself on a high, wild plateau, swept by icy winds. There were scattered cedars, very little snow, and much broken rock, as well as scattered boulders and uptilted slabs. Careful to step on no fallen sticks, he moved across the flat rock, working his way toward the edge of the canyon itself. Fortunately, he had time.

From a projecting ledge, he studied each side of the canyon, and far down, perhaps a thousand feet from the top,

he saw a small cluster of cedar among a grove of aspen. The
trees seemed to be growing on a level area. A small waterfall
dropped off the side nearby. As the air was very clear, he
knew the place was farther away than it appeared to be. To
the usual eye it was but one of many outcrops where trees
had found a lodging.

He moved slowly ahead, searching for animal tracks.
Soon he found those of a goral and followed them. They
wandered off into the forest, and he looked for others. Finally, he found what he wanted, the tracks of a mountain goat
and later those of a small bear. Their trail followed a narrow,
tree-clad ridge until they suddenly dropped off into a snow-
choked hollow. He followed, and then going around a huge
old cedar, the tracks dropped over the edge of the cliff. He
could see the river, running with white water, a good two
thousand feet lower. The path was narrow, and he edged
along carefully, facing the rock for a dozen yards at a time,
clinging to mere fingerholds. When he could glance down, he
saw fringes of ice in some of the tiny coves, but the river
itself was unfrozen.

Twice he crossed small open areas scattered with trees,
picked up the trail again, and worked his way further along.
Twice he went across acres of scattered rock fallen from the
peaks and cliffs above. Then through a crevasse, along the
bottom of which water trickled. Then ducking under a projec-
tion of rock, he emerged on the cliff face once more. For a
moment he stood there, scanning the rim opposite and the
sky; then he looked back to the vantage point from which he
had chosen his destination.

Nothing. Nobody in sight. He edged out on the trail, but
found he could walk easily. The edge was perilously close,
but he had spent much of his boyhood in such places.

When he came to the area he was seeking, just on the
chance it would provide what he wanted, he found himself
almost cut off by the rushing stream that provided the waterfall he had seen.

Searching, he found a place where he could cross, and
soon he was standing in a small hanging valley, its walls
covered with stone pine and cedar, its basin half choked with
aspen. But there were two little meadows and a small pond,
marshy at the near edge. The marshy part was still frozen and
covered with scattered snow.

The little valley comprised no more than forty acres and seemed to offer no way out that he could see, yet there was nearly always a way, if one had the patience to look and the skill at climbing.

There were many tracks of both deer and mountain goats, most of them fresh. He killed a ptarmigan at the edge of the pond and began searching for a place to camp. They might find him here, but he doubted it.

Alekhin, if he was around? Well, maybe.

Nowhere could he find any evidence of previous visits. He killed a mountain goat and skinned it out, taking what meat he wanted. Most of all, he wanted the hide, for his vest was sadly worn from the rough treatment, and the pelage of the mountain goat is the softest and warmest of any animal in the north country. When he had the meat and the hide, he went to the farthest end of the hanging valley, around a small bend that offered complete concealment. There he built a fire and roasted some of the meat. Sitting by the fire, he studied his surroundings. He must find a place in which to shelter himself, but he must also find an escape route if one existed. Studying the sides of the valley, heavily forested, he decided he might climb through the forest, pulling himself tree by tree up the forbidding cliff.

The hide of the mountain goat he had taken needed work, and he began it as soon as he had eaten, scraping the inside of the hide clean. The hair was pure white, or so it seemed until matched with snow, and then it took on a creamy-white color. With some of the leather remaining from an earlier kill of an elk, he cut out a pair of moccasins to replace the worn ones he wore.

From where he worked he could see the end of the trail down which he had come. It was partly obscured by aspens growing out of the side of the cliff, trees that had been bent down by a weight of snow, now melted or blown away. He had seen several such places on his way along the cliff face.

Huddling over his small fire, he thought out his plan for those trees, knowing what he must do and thinking how best to do it. He had rigged many snares for wild animals, often using spring pole snares. This would be a variation. He had to fight with what he had.

Where now was Natalya? Did they still live in the make-shift village where he had discovered them? Or had they already begun their trek to Plastun Bay or its vicinity? And how could he ever live up to his promise to get them out?

The buffer zone extended all along that coast, and any plane attempting to penetrate it would be shot down. The Soviets had already shown their readiness to shoot down even an innocent passenger plane if it accidentally invaded their airspace. Yet he would find a way. Somehow he would find a way.

A cold wind blew down the raw-backed ridges, and a faint sifting of blown snow came down, icy particles that stung the skin. He went back into the trees and pulled deadfalls together to make a crude shelter, gathering boughs for a bed. The sky above was amazingly clear; the stars seemed to hang like bright lamps just above the canyon's edge. Far below, he could hear the roar of the water, but a distant sound.

If he made no tracks he would leave no tracks. He would, if possible, stay right here for several days, but first he must find an escape route, and he must be prepared for planes or helicopters flying over.

These canyons were wild, almost completely unexplored except by a few passing hunters, and since coming to the area he had seen no signs of man, nothing at all.

At daybreak he went back up the narrow trail down which he had come, scarcely a trail at all, just a route along the cliffs, moving from ledge to ledge. Finding a place where the aspen grew almost horizontally from the bank, he selected one and drew it back, hauling on it until it was bent like a bow. Fastening it there with a trigger to be released by a trip string across the trail, he concealed the trip as much as possible and stepped back to survey it. The young aspen, drawn taut, would be released by the trip string and would swing around like a whip, knocking a man from the trail into the canyon if it did not break his neck or crack his skull.

A mountain goat using the same trail, if it tripped the release, would pass safely beneath it.

Spring came quickly in this northern land and disappeared just as quickly, yet it was weeks away even though here and there ice was melting briefly during the day, only to freeze again at night.

Carefully, foot by foot, he explored the little valley. When he found the escape route he sought, it was wild animals that showed him the way, as he had expected. At the back end of the place where he had built his fire, there was a hollow choked with a thick stand of birch. The animal track skirted it along the rock wall and then dipped down through a mere crack, descending steeply into a rock-walled hollow where he found an overhang with a crude rock parapet of fitted stones, obviously very ancient. Some man or men had taken shelter here in some bygone age. No signs of fire were on the floor of the overhang, these having long since turned to dust. Overhead there were smoke-blackened rocks.

Following the narrow animal trail further, he found that it branched, one branch going up, the other down. This had been, he decided, a trail used by whoever had built the shelter. In places, sections of it had fallen away into the void below; in others, rocks from above had almost blocked the trail, but it led to the top of the plateau. Perceiving this from some distance, he went no nearer, so as to leave no tracks where they might be seen. The trail seemed to emerge in a small grove of birch, several of them having grown up in the trail itself. Retreating, he prepared several traps, which he would remember but which might deal with anyone venturing to explore the area.

For four days then he ate, slept, and searched out the area. It was possible, he discovered, to climb through the forest on the mountainside to a ledge above his hanging valley, and from there a steep path, used by mountain goats, led down into the depths of the canyon.

On the fifth day a plane flew over the mountains, a small plane that could fly very slowly, searching the terrain. Joe Mack remained hidden, watching it, thankful he had been wise enough never to walk the same route twice and so to leave no tracks that could be seen. The search was on now, so no matter how cold, there must be no fires.

The search would be on the ground as well, and undoubtedly they had some kind of a lead to bring them here. It could be mere routine, but he did not believe so.

He worked on making moccasins and preparing a coat from his goatskin.

He doubted they would find how he had come to this place or even realize it existed. Flying over, it was just one more narrow place in the rock walls of the canyon, choked with trees. There would be many such, some reachable, some not. Back in Idaho he had seen old mines and cabins clinging to walls that seemed completely inaccessible. So it must be here. But there was nothing in this place to draw attention.

He would remain quiet for another three or four days, possibly longer. Impatience would be his greatest enemy, although he still had far to go.

Could he make it in the short time of warmth? The ice in the rivers usually broke up in April and by the end of August would be freezing again, or could be. There seemed no way he could cover the vast stretch of country before him in the short time available, especially as the country would be increasingly more open, with much tundra and no cover. At least, there was not much cover until he reached the Anadyr Mountains. Somehow he must cross the Kolyma River and then the Omolon. Beyond that was the limit of the trees.

Crouching under the trees he heard a plane fly over again. Had they found something? Or were they just prowling?

Another long winter? In a still more barren country? He shuddered at the thought. How much could he stand? It seemed sometimes as if he had never been warm and comfortable. Night after night and day after day of piercing, unbelievable cold when he dared not relax, not for one minute, lest he make a mistake and die. It needed but one error, however trivial.

Thinking of another winter, he was close to despair. Could he survive? How? It would be infinitely worse here than further south. By the time another winter came he would be inside the Arctic Circle.

Gloomily, he stared into the coming night. And where was Natalya? Her father? How did they fare? And what had become of Yakov? Of Botev and Borowsky?

So much was happening of which he knew nothing.

Suppose, the idea came to him suddenly, he should try living out the winter in a town? He needed shoes, but he had a suit and one shirt.

Suppose, just suppose, he could do it? Where would he find shelter? How would he obtain food?

Yet it was something to consider, and by now they would be convinced he was only a wilderness man.

And what town? Magadan? It was the closest, but he would be putting himself in the enemy's territory. He was an

Indian, and the wilderness was his. He was a part of it. He belonged here. But in a town?

He shook his head and climbed back to the little ledge he had found. There was shelter there, hidden by trees.

And in the night a great wind blew, trees fell, and rocks tumbled down, crashing into the vast gorge below. Huddled against the cold, he listened, sheltered but awestruck at the storm's fury. A cold, freezing rain fell, turning to ice in the air, making the trails sheets of ice and the trees like crystal forests that clashed and shattered in the night.

Somewhere a great rock fell; he heard it bounding from ledge to ledge down the canyon.

As suddenly as it came it was over, and a vast silence fell upon the mountain, a silence in which at last he slept, worn from travel.

He slept, and out of the storm and the night a man came, a man like a huge bear, feeling his way along the cliffs, then pausing. At last, unable to progress further, he paused. He was near, he told himself, the American was somewhere near.

Tomorrow he would have him.

Tomorrow . . .

THIRTY-FIVE

Ostap stood on the street, a cigarette hanging from his lip. Men were hurrying to work; a few cars passed and a big, clumsy truck. It was early morning, gray and dismal. Across from him was the framework of a huge, rambling structure begun months ago and left standing. In the spring they might finish it and they might not. One never knew in Magadan.

He hunched his shoulders against the cold. Not likely anybody was following him. He was small fry and wanted to stay that way so far as anybody knew. He would get his when the time came, and this affair might be an opening. Ostap was one who lived by the edge.

He had an edge here, an edge there. A piece of this and that. He did not want all of anything. To try to get it all left one vulnerable. But pieces were something else. All he wanted was a percentage.

He had a sort of loyalty to his kind, and his kind did not like Shepilov. He would like to trip Shepilov, do him a dirty one. At the same time, Shepilov was KGB and dangerous. He waited until a big truck passed, and then he crossed the street, started down an alley, and then turned into the incompleted building. In one of the completed rooms on the lower floor, three men were standing around a fire.

It was built on the concrete floor, with broken bits of

lumber for fuel. Lev was there and Kraslov. With them was another man, a stranger.

Noticing his hesitation, Lev said, "This is Botev. He is all right." Lev hunched his shoulders. He was a very young man whose face looked old. His blue eyes were perpetually red-rimmed and he had a slack mouth. Ostap did not like him, but he had connections. He was related somehow to several officials and doted upon by his mother and his aunt. He always knew when there was going to be a shakedown or an investigation, and he always knew who wanted what. He came to Ostap because Ostap knew how to get it.

"Botev is a trapper," he said. "Lives in the forest."

"Shepilov is in Magadan," Ostap advised, reaching his fingers toward the fire.

Lev looked at him from the corners of his eyes. "Now how did you know that? He just arrived."

Ostap shrugged. "I have my ways." Better to let them think he had connections, too. And he did have, a few minor ones.

"Kuzmich is recruiting trappers and hunters to search for the American," Lev said. "Botev has been asked."

Ostap looked at Botev. "Zamatev wants him, too. Zamatev will pay."

Kraslov shrugged. "What do you know of Zamatev?" he sneered.

"He will pay. He wants the American."

Botev spoke up. "He is right. It is Zamatev who needs him most. Shepilov would like to try to get him first. The man escaped from Zamatev." He squatted on his heels, close to the fire. "You cross Zamatev and he will break your back."

Ostap glanced at Botev. "Will you go into the woods after the American?"

Botev smiled. "I will look," he said. Then he added, "He is a Red Indian."

They were fascinated, as he had known they would be. "A Red Indian? Truly? Does he wear feathers in his hair?"

"That was long ago. Some of them are capitalists now. This one was a flyer."

"Think of that! A Red Indian who is a flyer! How did he escape?"

"Who knows? Do they ever tell you?"

Ostap spread his fingers toward the fire. "Zamatev will

pay," he repeated. "Shepilov will clap you on the shoulder and tell you what a great thing you have done for the Soviet."

He glanced over at Botev. "Can you find him? You and the others?"

"What others? I can find him."

Ostap rubbed his fingers together. "I can reach Zamatev," he said. "He will pay well. If you can catch him," he said to Botev, "fine. But speak to the others. Pass the word along. It is Zamatev who will pay." Ostap looked into the fire, then up at them. "I would not wish to be the man who crosses Zamatev." He stood up. "Catch him for Russia, but deliver him to Zamatev."

"You will have no chance," Kraslov said to Botev. "Alekhin is hunting him."

There was silence, and then Botev suggested, "We could get him first."

"Better you do if you want anything from it. If Alekhin gets him, there will only be a body."

They huddled about the fire, and Ostap was thinking of Botev. A tough man, a good man. How did Lev come to know him? Botev was a man he could work with, but dared he trust him? But, after all, who did one trust? Certainly not Lev, and Kraslov least of all.

Ostap was looking at Botev when Kraslov spoke next. "They just took a man up on the road to Semychan, a man named Yakov. They are bringing him in tonight."

Ostap was looking at Botev and he saw the man's expression. Suddenly, he knew. This was why Botev was here. He had been seeking information.

Why? What was Botev's interest in Yakov? He spoke casually, "I never heard of him."

"Who hears of anything?" Kraslov said, impatiently. "What do they tell you? Nothing!"

"They do not have to," Lev said, amused. "Word gets around. Somebody tells his comrade, the comrade tells his girlfriend, and she tells her mother. Soon everybody knows."

Ostap was thinking. Sure, everybody whispered a little, but there were listening posts, such as this one, where one might hear things others did not talk about. How had Botev come to know Lev? Through the black market? Botev was a trapper and Lev dealt in whatever meant money. But why was Botev interested in the prisoner Yakov? And he was. Ostap had seen his expression. He wanted a word with Botev.

Nobody stayed long at the fire but Ostap had seen deals for thousands of rubles consummated here. No prices talked, just casual meetings and a few words dropped as to what was needed and who would pay and occasionally a figure tossed in the air. If there was no reply, it had to be more. Ostap stood up, sure the movement would attract Botev's eye. When their eyes met Ostap gestured with his head to indicate they would meet outside.

"Zamatev will pay," Ostap said again. "He will pay well. If I knew where the American was, I could get us a bit of something very good."

Ostap went outside, glancing up and down the street as he approached it. Bold as he might appear when talking to Katerina or Kyra, he was cautious in all his relationships and in moving about. He watched Kraslov go off up the street, but Lev lingered, seeming to want to speak. When he did he nodded after Kraslov. "I do not trust him."

"Who can you trust?"

"I would trust you, Comrade Ostap." Lev's tone was sincere.

"And I, you." Ostap hesitated, and then he said, "But there are some things best left unshared. Why should either get the other into trouble?"

After Lev disappeared, Botev returned. Where he had been in the meantime Ostap did not know.

Botev approached and then stopped, looking warily about. "You wished to speak to me?"

"Zamatev wants the American. Above all, he does not want Comrade Shepilov to reach him first. You will be out there among them, and I understand there is some feeling among some of them that might work for us." He paused. "We must have the American. He is an enemy of the people."

"Of course," Botev replied, his tone slightly ironic.

"He cannot escape. Where he goes now, there are no hiding places. The country is too open."

"You have been there?"

"No, no, of course not. But I have been told—"

"Do not believe all you are told." He glanced around. "Nonetheless, I shall see what I can do."

Ostap turned down the street, trying to think what else

might be done. He was pleased that Kyra had come to him for help. She was bright, sharp, and hard, nobody to fool around with. Anybody who tried tricking her or playing games would get himself hurt. He had watched her operate from afar and knew what she had done. And now she was associated with Zamatev, of all people. There might come a day when he would need her influence.

He was on the outside of everything, living by his wits in a country that offered little room for it.

If they could just take that American, things would settle down again. He did not like Shepilov being here, nor the fact that because of him everybody was being very sharp and quick. There had been a dozen arrests made that would never have happened had the American not been hunted.

Back in the two rooms he shared with Katerina, he studied the situation in his mind. The American had no chance. No matter how skillfully he had evaded them until now, he was being neatly boxed in. The area in which he could move was narrowing down. There was more tundra, more open country, fewer trees. Further north, there were none until one reached the Anadyr Mountains.

Botev had no intention of helping either Shepilov or Zamatev. He had met the American but twice, but he liked him. He was a true man of the forest, and Botev could not believe whether he escaped or not would matter. Perhaps to Shepilov and Zamatev, but not to Russia. Of course, he knew little of what was at stake, yet what could one man do?

Ostap walked steadily, turned several corners, and then went to the edge of town. He took a lane between two yards filled with rusting machinery and went on into the woods.

Kyra was seated with Katerina when Ostap came in and threw his cap on the bed.

"I have told them," he said. "I told them Zamatev would pay well to have him first."

"I can promise that."

"Good! I believe they will have him. After all, where can he go?"

She got to her feet. It was time she talked to Arkady. She had been too long away and, she reflected, too long in this place. She fastened her coat. "If you hear anything—?"

"Do not worry. You shall hear."

She closed the door behind her and walked swiftly down

the hall. She was about to turn into the street hallway when she saw the car parked in front. Quickly, she turned and ran down the hall to the rear door. There was a man standing there, a bulky man in a gray coat.

Swiftly she turned; nobody was in sight. She went to the end of the hall and opened the small door. It was not for nothing that she had been here before. The small door led to a storage room, where they kept coal to be burned. There was the small door through which the coal was brought in. It opened upon an alley.

She opened it slightly. Nobody was there. Across the alley was an old courtyard that wandered into another and then into a ramshackle building, long abandoned. Magadan was just such a place of empty spaces, structures hurriedly thrown up on somebody's order or some bureaucratic whim.

Stegman was waiting at the helicopter when the taxi let her down. "Now!" she said. "At once!"

He asked no questions until they were in the air. "What is it?"

"Comrade Shepilov is making arrests," she said, "but our work is done."

Would they take Vanya? She hoped not. After all, what had been done? Yet she knew it was not necessary to have done something. It was enough to be suspected.

"Suvarov is with the soldiers," Stegman said. "Somewhere in the north. I have a map if—"

"No. We will go back to Khabarovsk. Is there news of that woman? The Baronas woman?"

"None. When our men reached the cabin they were gone, gone for some time. The fires were out, the ashes cold. They have gone into the forest again, I believe."

He picked up a distant peak and changed course a little. "Comrade Lebedev? There has been trouble."

"Trouble?"

"Yes, it seems Comrade Bocharev has taken an interest in the Baronas question. He has been making inquiries. It was necessary to report this to Colonel Zamatev."

She frowned. Bocharev? What did he have to do with this?

"Our informant, the man Peshkov, has disappeared. Nobody has seen him. The others have scattered. A few arrests have been made, but the man Zhikarev has vanished also."

Suddenly his tone was angry. "I do not know what is happening! There has been much slipshod work! These people should have been arrested at once! At once! And that Zhikarev—!"

If Baronas and his daughter had left Plastun Bay, they had gone down to the sea, or they would try to cross the border into China. The sea was out of the question. Nothing could get past that buffer zone and the strict watch kept over the waters of the Sea of Japan. Hence it had to be the border.

From her briefcase she took a map. A crossing on the Ussuri River would be closest. When they reached Khabarovsk, she would see what could be done. In fact, if it was all right with Arkady she would go herself. She would fly to Iman.

For the first time she began to have doubts. What if Arkady failed?

The thing with Pennington had not gone well. He had protested that his only expertise was in insecticides and assured them he would be glad to help in that area. In fact, he knew a good deal about the infestation of mosquitoes and black flies and would cooperate. He assured them they had taken the wrong man, that he would have enjoyed meeting the Admiral but that they had not come to his section at all. She knew none of the details of the questioning or the methods used, only that they had come up with nothing except that he did know a great deal about insecticides and was willing to help with their problems. As he was valuable in that respect, there might have been hesitation to go further with the questions, but she doubted that, knowing the Colonel.

To have that effort fail, and atop it the escape of a man whom they could not seem to recapture—

It looked bad for Arkady, for Colonel Zamatev.

They would say he was inept. That he was careless. That he had failed.

If he failed, she failed also. He was her ticket to Moscow, her door to the future.

Yet suppose they could recapture the American? Suppose there really had been something between the American and that Baronas woman? If they had her, she might be bait for a trap. She shook her head. No, it would not work. Of course not. The man would not—

But she had heard the Americans were romantic. Was this Red Indian so? Would he come back to try to save his girlfriend? If she could be taken, it was worth an attempt.

Of course, he would not. She told herself that, but she wondered.

Catch her first, and then think about it. Under questioning, she would tell all they needed to know. But how to get word to the American? Ostap would know how; he always knew such things.

But Ostap was a prisoner. Undoubtedly, he had been taken.

Only he had not. Like she herself, Ostap had escaped. He was free, and he had gone into the forest.

THIRTY-SIX

When morning came, Joe Mack stood alone upon the mountain. His hair had grown long, and rather than try to cut it with his knife he had begun wearing it in two braids that hung down over his chest. *All you need now*, he told himself, *is a necklace of bear claws.*

His smile was grim as he studied the country below and about him. Yet his thoughts wandered, and he remembered the story of the Apache, the Indian Massai, who had been deported to Florida after Geronimo's surrender in 1886. He had escaped from the train after they had left St. Louis, and he had worked his way across country, returning to Arizona without being seen except by a friendly Indian to whom he revealed himself. Two thousand miles or more he had traveled, much of it through populated country. Nobody had ever known the whole story, but it had been a tale worth the telling.

In the old days the Apaches would have sung songs of his courage and his skills. Nowadays they did not sing anymore, and too many of the Indians were forgetting the old songs and the old stories. He knew many of them. His grandmother and his mother had told him the stories, and his white grandfather, too, who had known more of them than many of the Indians. He had lived close to the old men, and he knew the value of their songs and their stories. Many he had noted down; others he had simply repeated to Joe Mack when he was a small boy.

Below him was the vast gorge with its roaring river, rimmed with jagged rocks as if born from some surrealistic nightmare, rocks gnawed upon by wind and broken by expanding ice, sheets of rock and slabs of rock and crumbled rock underneath. Below the rim, the wild, wind-torn trees leaned with the prevailing winds and cast their dead branches like skeleton bones along the narrow ledges below.

He knew this land, knew it from his memories of Hell's Canyon, from the Snake and the Salmon rivers of Idaho. This was like them, but wilder, somehow different. More and more he felt himself turning back the leaves of time. Fading into dimness were his days of training as an officer, his years of flying, his neat uniforms, and before them the lessons learned in school. Now he was back to the mountains of his boyhood and his memories of the wild, free mountain life.

He had never been but superficially a civilized man. He knew that, and he knew he could, or thought he could, return to it. Now he did not know. He was a man of the wilderness, living as he had dreamed of living. His life was wild, hard, cold, and dangerous, yet he was ready for it.

"I may be the last Indian," he told himself aloud, "who will live in the old way, think the old thoughts."

He had not chosen his enemies. They had chosen him. They had ripped him away from the life he had been living, to be used, drained, and cast aside. They would have left the pitiful rags of a man, what remained after torture, after repeated, demeaning questionings. This was better. He was not afraid to die. All his life had been a preparation for dying, but dying as a warrior would die. Yet now he would not die, for dying would give them victory. He would live, he would escape, he would flaunt it in their faces. He would show them what a man could do.

They were out there now, seeking him. Very well, let them find him, and find death.

A few had died, he knew that. The pursuit of him had not gone easily for them. How many his traps had killed he did not know, but he knew of three who had died with the helicopter, and there had been others. All right, if they wished to pay the price, he would give them what they wished.

No longer would he simply flee to escape them. Now he would fight back.

Rukovsky was waiting beside the fire when Suvarov drove up. "He's up there somewhere," Rukovsky said. "It is rough, but we will find him." He gestured. "I've a dozen patrols scattered along this valley. When we have eaten, we will start up the mountains. You can tell your Colonel Zamatev that we will have him."

Suvarov nodded, but kept his doubts to himself. "We have pursued him for months. I would like to see him taken."

"Have no fears. My men will take him." He turned his back to the wind that was blowing down from the mountain. It was not a strong wind, but cold, very cold.

"It will be an exercise for them. Get them in shape for the real thing. This could not have come at a better time."

Suvarov looked up at the mountains. Here there was some snow on the ridges and a huge bank of it under one ridge.

"You are from the Ukraine?" Suvarov looked at the mountain again. "Have you traveled mountains in the winter?"

"A little. No matter; my men can handle mountains. They can handle anything."

He looked around. "Personally, I'll be glad to get into the hills. Get away from some of this wind."

Rukovsky glanced at Suvarov. "I've a bottle in the car. How about a nip of vodka?"

"Why not?" Suvarov stood up, nervously. "I thought I smelled smoke?"

"You probably did. My men have fires; they're making tea and having a bite." He glanced at his wristwatch. "They've not much longer."

Suvarov took a swallow from the bottle and passed it to Rukovsky. "I hear Comrade Shepilov has recruited trappers to find the American."

Rukovsky smiled. "No matter. We will get him first."

"That's rough country up there," Suvarov gestured. "I have not seen it myself, but I have heard stories."

He took another swallow from the vodka and reached for his teacup. He filled it and stood up. "I say, that's an awful lot of smoke!"

Rukovsky got to his feet. It was quite a lot. Suddenly he

was angry. "They've let their fire get away from them!" He swore and reached for the radio. He asked a question and then began barking orders.

"Get in. We will see what's going on." They scrambled into the car, and the driver stepped on the starter. It whirred, but nothing happened. The driver stepped on the starter again, and at that moment the smoke billowed up, a cloud of it swept over them, and they saw a wall of flame racing toward them ahead of the wind. The grass in the small valley was dry, and the fire was coming fast. "To hell with the car!" Rukovsky dropped to the ground and started for the rocks. Suvarov and the driver were only a step behind him.

They scrambled up in the rocks where there was very little growth just as the flames swept down the valley. They hit the car and rolled around it, and then the flames got to the gas spilled around the tank. Flames roared, flames leaped up, and then the car exploded. For a moment the flames shot skyward and then roared madly as the remaining gas burned.

Rukovsky swore again. "I will find who is responsible for this, and I'll—!"

The line of flames raced down the little valley, leaving the grass charred and black behind it. Only a few of the soldiers had suffered minor burns, most of them in attempting to save equipment or food.

"Sir?"

Rukovsky glanced around impatiently. Suvarov said, "Before you assign the blame, it would be well to think of the American."

"What do you mean?"

"He could have set the grass afire."

"Nonsense!" Rukovsky spoke and then paused to consider. "Is it likely? Would he attempt such a thing?"

Suvarov repeated the story of the helicopter. Of numerous traps. "It is guerrilla warfare. He's very good at it."

"Come! Let's go see where the fire started."

Soldiers were beginning to climb down from the rocks where they had taken refuge. Most had escaped with their arms; some had escaped with rations. Three vehicles had been destroyed, the last one a truck just beyond the line of the fire.

"This one was set afire after the fire had passed, Colonel. See? It was over this rise, out of sight of most of the command."

"Is anything missing?"

Several cases of rations had been ripped open and both food and ammunition taken. An AK-47 was missing.

Reports came in slowly. Most of the food supplies had been burned and much equipment damaged. The fire had been sudden and unexpected and had moved swiftly ahead of the wind. Most men had saved their weapons; some had rations upon them; some had been hastily gathered among the rocks and out of reach of the flames. Not enough remained to keep the command in the field.

"Did anyone see him?"

Nobody had seen anything, but it was apparent that the flames had come from several points. "Fire arrows," somebody said.

"What?" Rukovsky turned on him.

"In the films, sir. I saw it when I was a boy. The Indians used fire arrows to set wagons afire, and sometimes they shot them over the walls into forts."

Rukovsky swore. "Is there a radio working?" he asked then. "I want a ration drop, and I want supplies brought in. I am going in there after him."

Lieutenant Suvarov said nothing. He was only a liaison officer here, and he wished he was anywhere else. It was cold here, and it would be worse up in those mountains. He was a city man, more at home in the homes of top officials and embassies than here. Why did he not get that assignment to Japan, the one he wanted if he could not have Paris? His father had been an important man with connections. The trouble was, there were others with important fathers who were still alive. And Colonel Zamatev had actually asked for him, which was a great honor, but one he was beginning to question.

The radio was still working, and after a time they picked up a reply. Nothing could be done until tomorrow or the day after.

"No matter," Rukovsky said. "We can equip several squads, and we will send them out. Let's keep moving."

In the shelter of a huge boulder they built a fire, and two soldiers built a shelter for Colonel Rukovsky and Suvarov. It was cold, but spring was not far off. Suvarov said as much, and Rukovsky snorted. "In this country? Is there ever spring?"

He leaned back against the trunk of the tree that formed

the back of their shelter. "Is this man really an Indian, Lieutenant?"

"He is, sir. A very fine flyer, too, by all reports. He had been testing one of their latest fighters, among other things."

"One doesn't think of a Red Indian doing things of that sort, but I know little about them."

"Alekhin's hunting him, sir. Somewhere about here, in fact."

"I wish he'd catch him. Or that somebody would. No; I would like to do it myself. A flyer, you say? An officer?"

"A major, sir."

"Where are the rest of the men?"

"Down the valley, sir. Those who are not out on patrol. There was a more sheltered area for that number. But we've sentries out."

"Sentries? Here?"

"The American is somewhere about, sir. And we do not know just where he is. This is a big country."

It *was* cold, but one of his men had found a ground sheet and some blankets in an incompletely destroyed truck. Colonel Rukovsky found himself liking the campfire and said as much.

Suvarov said, "Yes, sir. It is pleasant." Yet he did not think so at all. How had he ever got into this, anyway? If he could not be in Tokyo or Paris, why not Moscow?

He drank some of the tea the guard had prepared and put the pot back beside the fire. The Colonel was falling asleep, so Suvarov drew his blanket around him and huddled closer to the fire.

He had been asleep for some time, he supposed, when he opened his eyes and saw the man sitting across the fire from him.

"Good morning, Lieutenant. Have you slept long?"

Colonel Rukovsky opened his eyes and sat up. The man across the fire was dressed in furs, goatskins he believed, and he had an AK-47 across his knees. His right hand held the gun. His left a cup of tea.

"I hope you don't mind, Colonel. Your tea is excellent."

The man had two braids of hair falling down on his chest. He had a lean, dark face and startling gray eyes. Perhaps it was only that they looked startling from such a dark face.

"You are the American?"

"Major Joseph Makatozi, at your service." The American smiled. "I have a hard time remembering that. I am afraid I've reverted to what my people once were."

"You will be captured, you know? My men are all about."

"Lying about, you should say, Colonel. I am afraid I had to tie them up. We mustn't leave them too long, or they'll freeze."

"Have you come to give yourself up?"

The American laughed. "When I am in command? Of course not. To be frank, I am just debating what use I might have for you and the lieutenant, but sadly enough I find you'd be more of a trouble than of any value.

"No, I just dropped in for a cup of tea. I shall be leaving soon. To tell you the truth I was getting a bit tired of talking to myself." He glanced over at Suvarov. "What has been happening?"

Suvarov hesitated, and Rukovsky said, "Tell him if you wish. We will have him soon, anyway. By the way, Major, how did you get here?"

"You mean tonight? Why, I just walked in. Your men were so busy talking among themselves—"

He shook his head. "You need Siberians, Colonel. These young men are mostly town boys. I was tempted to gather all their weapons just for the joke of it."

He turned to Suvarov. "You were saying?"

"I do not know what there is that you would like to know. The search for you has been quite general. Comrade Shepilov has gathered a bunch of trappers to come down on you from the north. He is a KGB officer. There have been a few arrests.

"The bodies of the helicopter pilot and his companions have been found. Also the KGB man who was found dead in his car."

Joe Mack finished his tea and came suddenly to his feet. "I would take my men and go home, Colonel, if I were you. They are not suited to the mountains, and they will suffer. You will lose men and equipment, much more than I am worth to you or to the Soviet Union."

The AK-47 was ready in his hands. He took a step back toward the outer darkness. "Along the way," he said, "I have encountered a few civilians. None of them helped me in any way, but I'd not want them hurt because of me. That was the reason for my question."

"I know of nothing of the sort except for that village where it was said you lived for a time among some rascals who had taken to the woods."

"And that village?"

"They were gone when searchers returned. All gone, where we do not know."

At the very edge of the light, Joe Mack dropped to one knee and took up a package of emergency rations. "You will forgive me, of course? The supply system in the mountains is inadequate, to say the least."

One moment he was there, and then he was gone, like a ghost in the night.

Rukovsky came to his feet with a bound, and drawing the pistol he had in his scabbard he fired in the direction the American had gone. Fired, and swore.

"Lieutenant! Find those men and cut them loose! I want an all-out search. *Now!*"

Now, Suvarov thought, when it is too late. Why had he not drawn that pistol when the American was in sight?

For that matter, why hadn't he drawn his?

THIRTY-SEVEN

Rukovsky was furious. The rations taken had been his own, a
packet made up especially for him, at his direction. "Lieutenant! Cut those men loose! I want a search started immediately!"

"Of course, sir, but I am afraid they will not be able to
see much while it is still dark. In another hour—"

"Now!" Rukovsky said. "Before he can get too far away."

He was perfectly aware that in the darkness they would
find nothing. A man who could slip into camp, tie up his
guards, drink tea with him, and then escape would not be
found by the bunch of city boys he commanded, but it would
look good on his report that a search had begun on the
instant.

Secretly, he was amused by the man's daring. Once his
anger at losing his rations had cooled somewhat, he chuckled
to himself. Red Indian or not, the man had a flair. He
glanced at Suvarov. "An interesting man, Lieutenant. Very
interesting. I wish we could have talked longer."

"Men from the lower camp are bringing up some food,
sir. And some tea as well as vodka."

"Good! And it is growing light." He turned to look along
the slope. He could see his men, in a long skirmish line,
advancing up the slope and into the scattered trees. It was,
he told himself again, a good exercise for them. Let them get
a taste of some really rough country.

*   *   *

From high on the slope, Alekhin watched them with contempt. They were not going to find anything or anybody. From the beginning, he had known he would be the one to find the American. Let the others blunder about. They would never catch him. They did not even know the kind of man with whom they dealt. Still, they were near, and he would go down and have tea with them. It would save his doing it for himself. Besides, he knew where the American was and how to get him.

Using the trappers had been a good idea, but not one that would work. He knew them too well. A few might try; others would take what they were paid and do very little. Most of them admired the American and thought of him as one of their own. If they came upon him they might capture or shoot him, but not many of them would try very hard.

Nobody tried very hard to do anything these days. The trappers sold most of their furs on the black market and some of them even into China. Alekhin had done it himself. He knew what was going on better than most of the KGB, although some among them were good, and a few were very good.

By the time he reached the fire, Rukovsky and Suvarov were eating. He moved up and stood on the edge of the camp for several minutes before Rukovsky saw him. The sight of him standing there so near angered Rukovsky, who had had quite enough of people slipping into his camp without warning.

"You!" he demanded. "Who are you?" The sun was in Rukovsky's eyes and he could see nothing.

"I am Alekhin."

"What?" The man was a legend in Siberia. "Come in! Come in! Will you join us?"

He was a big man, Rukovsky noted, who moved like a cat. Alekhin moved up to the fire and sat down cross-legged.

"You look for the American?"

"I know where he is."

"What? Then why don't we take him? If you know—"

"I know. Taking him is not easy. You go with all those people and he is gone, *poof*! I will take him. Me."

"Where is he?"

Alekhin jerked his head to the rear. "Up there. You go

for him, your men will die. They are fools. They do not know how to search for this man."

Rukovsky was inclined to agree, but not to admit it. "He was here this morning, early."

Alekhin's heavy-lidded eyes stared at him. Rukovsky had an idea he had surprised Alekhin.

"He was here; had tea with us. Tied up three of my men. Then he took my packet of rations and was gone."

Alekhin sipped his tea. Inside he was angry, coldly, bitterly angry. The American dared to do this when he was around? He would pay for that.

"I will get him," he repeated. "I will get him soon now."

He looked across the fire at Rukovsky. "If you follow him, men will die. Take your soldiers and go home. It will be better."

Colonel Rukovsky's back stiffened. "Your advice is not needed." His tone was cold. "If you expect to take the American, I would suggest you get on with it."

Deliberately, he turned to Suvarov and began to speak of other things. Inwardly, he was seething. Who was this buffoon that he should tell him what to do?

Alekhin ignored them. He took his time, finishing his small meal and the tea. Then he arose and without a backward glance, walked away. He did not care what they did. If men died, it was of no importance to him. By the time he had reached the forest's edge he had forgotten them. He had not warned Rukovsky because of any humanitarian principles, simply because so many men would tramp out all the tracks, destroy what indications the American might have left.

He had been here this morning? Some sign would be left, then. He cast back and forth. He already knew the length of the American's stride, knew some of his methods of travel. Soon he would know all. Deliberately he had waited, wanting the man to tire himself, wanting him to become overconfident and hence careless, wanting the others to drop the chase.

The American was somewhere near the head of the Indigirka or the Kolyma, and he believed the former. The canyons were excellent places in which to hide, but the man would have to eat, and if he killed for food he would leave a part of the carcass behind. That would attract the carrion eaters.

It was a wild land of broken rock, gray cascades of talus, and a few stunted trees. Alekhin paused to look down a great gash in the mountainside, a gash choked with fir trees. It was a steep descent and a harder climb back up if he found nothing or if it ended, as so many such did, in a vast drop to the canyon floor. Vainly he searched for some evidence of a man's passing. He found nothing but the droppings of a mountain goat and a few patches of snow.

He looked across the canyon at a curling lip of snow below that bank he had observed earlier. Bad country, a slide poised to go with a million tons of snow, rock, and dead trees behind it. Left alone, the snow might melt off gradually, but if someone tried to cross, or if there were some sudden sound, the whole thing would come down.

He shook his heavy head. Rukovsky was a fool! He should go back to country he knew! Such a man was a danger in the mountains, to himself and to others. Alekhin did not care about the others as long as he was not one of them. He did not like Rukovsky. Too smart, too efficient, one of those officer and gentleman types. He liked none of them, but he preferred to work with Zamatev. The man was cruel, ice hard, and ruthless. Alekhin did not like him, either, and it would be only what he deserved if the American turned around and went back to find and kill him.

Zamatev had said he was coming out to take personal charge. The fool! What could he do? Take charge of what?

Yet Alekhin knew that Zamatev had made a sudden flight to Moscow and back. He had returned bursting with confidence. Shepilov was to be called off, told to return to things that concerned him. Zamatev and the GRU would handle the American.

As if they could!

Alekhin paused. A pebble, pressed into mud when it was wet, had been kicked from its socket in the long-dried mud. Something or somebody had passed this way. If it was the American it must have been done at night when he was moving fast. It was unlike him to leave such an indication.

Pausing, Alekhin looked carefully around. A dozen times he had come upon traps left for pursuers, and he had seen several men die from those traps. Others had been crippled, temporarily at least.

Nothing seemed wrong, yet he was wary. With this man you made only one mistake.

He heard the footsteps behind him and muttered angrily. How could he accomplish anything with those fools tramping around over the mountains?

It was Rukovsky again. "We're making a sweep of this slope, Alekhin," he said. "If we find anything we will call you at once."

"You?" Alekhin demanded rudely. "What could you find?"

Colonel Rukovsky controlled himself. "We might find a great deal. A hundred eyes are better than two." He pointed. "I've started a patrol on the other wall of the canyon. We're right here where it begins, so I had them cross to the other side."

Alekhin looked across the canyon. A thin gray line of men walked in single file and then, as he watched, spread up the steep slope in a skirmish line, to cover everything.

Alekhin did not care in the least, but he said, "I hope none of them have families."

"What? What do you mean?"

"They will die," Alekhin said coldly. "You have just condemned them to death."

Rukovsky stared at him. The man was not only arrogant, he was insane!

Alekhin's eyes held contempt. "You! What a fool you are! Whatever you wanted to accomplish is finished. You are finished."

Alekhin turned his back and walked away before he could reply. Rukovsky stared after him. Alekhin was Zamatev's man, and one did not lightly cross Zamatev. Nonetheless—

He glanced around. His men were scattered along the rocky face of the mountain, scattered among the fir and the cedar, their weapons ready, moving forward and upward in an uneven line. There were scattered spruce trees along the slope and several patches of Dahurian larch. Rukovsky paused to take in the wild, barren beauty of the place.

He was a man who read much, who thought much, a man who loved good music and who had been reared in an atmosphere of art and artists. His youngest sister was in the ballet and already accepted as one of the best.

He wished suddenly that she could see this: the vast gray mountain splashed with patches of snow, the dark columns of the spruce, and his soldiers advancing. He turned to look across the canyon. It had widened, and he needed his glasses now to make out the men. They were on bare rock, as here, but were approaching a wide bank of old snow. The snow ran down to the very edge of the canyon, some lopping over the abyss.

Captain Obruchev was in command of that group, a fine officer and a good friend.

Alekhin had disappeared! Irritated, Rukovsky looked around. Where could the man have gotten to?

He was an impudent fool! Yet he had been warned that Alekhin was no respecter of authority. He simply did not care. He wanted nothing they could give him and was afraid of nobody. Zamatev used him, needed him for this sort of thing, and had often said that Alekhin, when he wished, could simply vanish into wild country and lose himself. Just as this American seemed to have done.

He slapped his gloves against his thigh, irritated. He glanced around him, then started forward, his own eyes searching.

What exactly did a man look for, a tracker like Alekhin? Surely, there was nothing Alekhin could see that he could not.

But he could find nothing on this barren, rocky slope. He looked ahead, and along the ridge he saw jagged, serrated rocks with occasional towers, almost like battlements in some places. Directly before him, there was a grove of wild, wind-torn trees looking like a clutch of hags with their wild hair blowing in the wind. Only there wasn't any wind, just those ragged trees.

He stepped carefully, for a misstep on this broken rock could give a man a nasty fall.

What did Alekhin mean that he was finished? That his career was at an end? Hell, if all went well he would be a general before the year was out! He knew he was in line for promotion and knew that the right people had been spoken to and were interested.

He smiled, mildly amused. After all, so little had changed since the time of the Tsars! Only the names had changed, and instead of the old nobility you had the Party members, and in place of the Grand Dukes you had the Politburo. Only, the Grand Dukes had usually had less power.

Gorbachev had more ability than most of the Tsars, and hopefully he would do something to build Russia internally before it came apart at the seams. But it was hard for any man to move against the sheer inertia of entrenched civil servants who did not want change and feared to lose their privileges.

Wild and treacherous as these mountains were, they possessed a rare kind of beauty. He was glad he was momentarily alone. To truly know the mountains, one should go to meet them as one would meet a sweetheart, alone.

Alone as he was now. Colonel Rukovsky looked off across incredible distances behind him. Far below he could see a helicopter setting down. Three trucks were toiling up the very bad road, looking no larger than ants, although he knew the tops of their radiators were as high as his head.

Whatever else the American's escape had done, it had brought him here to this unbelievable beauty, which otherwise he might never have seen.

A cold wind blew along the mountain, and he shivered. There were ghosts riding this wind, strange ghosts born of this strange, almost barren land. Far to the west and against the horizon was the Verkhoyansk Range.

He paused, hearing a bird in the brush near the larch. It was a nutcracker; he remembered them from his boyhood.

What had Alekhin meant, saying he was through? It was absurd, but the words rankled. They stuck like burrs in his thoughts, and he could not rid himself of that dire warning.

He was near the haglike trees he had seen, and close up they looked even wilder. One of the trunks was battered and beaten, struck hard by something until the bark had been shattered into threads. Suddenly he remembered a brother officer, a hunter of big game, who had told him of wild rams battering such trees, butting them again and again in simple exuberance and lust for combat.

He paused again to catch his breath. The altitude was high and the air was thin as well as being crisp and cold.

Far off, he thought he heard a shout. Looking around, he could see nothing.

Then, high up on the mountain, Alekhin appeared, pointing. Rukovsky ran forward, looking across the canyon.

His men were lined out, moving in their skirmish line across that vast field of snow above the canyon's edge.

Then, from somewhere down in the gorge, came a shot.

Colonel Rukovsky saw then a sight he would never forget. His men, twenty-odd of them, were on the field of snow when the shot sounded in the depths of the canyon. An instant of trembling silence when the sound of the shot racketed away along the rocky cliffs, and then horrified, he saw that whole vast field of snow start to move!

There was an instant of frozen stillness as the snow moved, and then his men scattered, some running forward, some running back, a few crouching in place looking for something they could grip. And there was nothing. The whole mountainside seemed to be moving, and then, with a thunderous roar, the snowfield gathered speed and swept toward the rim of the gorge.

Spilling over the lip, it fell like a Niagara of snow into the vast depths below!

One moment he saw his men, swinging arms wildly, fighting to stem the tide; then over they went, and far away as he was he seemed to hear their screams, screams that he would never forget. And one of those who fell was Captain Obruchev, engaged to his sister.

After the roar of the avalanche, silence.

THIRTY-EIGHT

Major Joseph Makatozi crouched beside a giant spruce, looking up the canyon. He was sheltered from the wind, always a major consideration, and his coat made from the hide of a mountain goat was warm. The pelage of the mountain goat is the finest, softest, and undoubtedly the warmest of any animal. Being white, it blended well with the occasional patches of snow. His pants were made of the same material.

From beside the spruce, he had seen the patrol start across the snowfield. This was war, and they were hunting him to kill or capture. And capture meant eventual death.

He watched them move out on the snowfield with exasperation. What could their commander be thinking of? Certainly, he was not a Siberian, but any Russian accustomed to mountain travel should know better than to walk across a slope that was obviously unstable.

He found himself almost hoping they would make it across, but if they did they would be in a position to see into his hanging valley, and they might even see him in his hideout above it. Certainly, a man with a good glass would be able to pick him out. And he was, for the time being, tired of running.

Joe Mack knew that in such cases, with snow poised to start, a sudden shout or a shot might be enough to start it, particularly in the narrow confines of the canyon.

Their movements on the snowfield might be enough to start a slide, but he could not leave it to chance. He lifted the AK-47 and fired.

He did not aim, because he had no plan to hit anything. He did not know the accurate range of the weapon, although all guns carried farther than most people believed, but the men were a good half mile away. He simply fired, and whether it was their movements or the shot he did not know, but the slide started.

At least two of the soldiers at the rear threw themselves back off the snow, while another two or three had not reached it, but for the others there was no chance.

When the roar of the slide ceased and snow puffed up in a thick cloud, he settled back against his tree and waited. He was relatively secure. There was nowhere on this side of the canyon that overlooked his hideout and no way it could be easily reached except above and behind him, and even that was not a simple way.

He guessed that the patrol he had seen was but one of several. No doubt they had planned to work along both sides of the canyon, but only an officer unfamiliar with such mountains would have attempted it. In such canyons there are usually several levels left by the water in cutting its way through the rock and carving out the gorge. A thorough search might be made on one level while leaving unseen hiding places on the next. Of course, many of these were visible from across the canyon, as his would have been had the patrol crossed the snowfield.

The tilted slope opposite him and somewhat higher was now almost bare of snow. He could see several men huddled together, who seemed in shock. He did not blame them. The snowfield had extended several hundred feet above them and back. It must have seemed that the whole side of the mountain was moving. As he watched, the men turned and started back the way they had come, occasionally turning to look back as if in disbelief of what had happened.

Going to the little hollow at the back of the bench, he built a small fire of dry wood that gave off almost no smoke. He made tea and a thick broth of meat scrap and melted snow. Occasionally he peered through the trees, and always he listened. Alekhin was out there somewhere.

The months of living in the snow and cold had built his

resistance to it. It had begun to warm up, and at thirty
degrees below zero he was almost warm. He remembered
long ago reading an account of Byrd's men in Antarctica
shoveling snow, stripped to the waist at ten degrees below
zero. Given a chance, the human body had an amazing capac-
ity for adapting itself to changing conditions.

Undoubtedly a patrol was coming along on his side of the
canyon. Knowing the terrain, he knew that the patrol must
either be well scattered or fail in covering the area. The
nature of the country left only a few possible routes.

His present position was invisible from below. Looking
up, they would see only a forested mountainside much too
steep for travel. From below, as he had seen for himself,
there was no indication of the little bench on which he was
camped.

The only possible way of seeing it was from across the
gorge where the soldiers had been headed who were carried
away by the avalanche. He had meat, and he could afford to
sit tight. Hard as it was to remain still, that was just what he
must do. The risk was great, yet he needed the rest.

The very nature of the traps he had left behind denied
him the chance to know if they had worked. If nothing else,
they would make his pursuers move more slowly and with
greater caution. Yet now he was within a few hundred yards
of at least two such traps.

Here he was sheltered from the wind and from observation except by aircraft, and if he was under the trees they
might see his hideout but not him. However, sighting the
hideout might lead to a search. Was there communication
with the ground forces by radio? He had to believe there
was, although there might not be.

Under the trees he found a viewpoint that permitted
him to see both possible entries into the hanging valley below
him.

Suddenly, on the trail opposite, a soldier appeared. He
was only two or three steps above the flat white stone Joe
Mack had undermined.

The soldier halted, his weapon ready. He was surveying
what he could see of the surprising little valley. He turned
and spoke over his shoulder to someone; then another man
appeared. Joe Mack could not see his insignia, but supposed
him a noncommissioned officer.

There was no way they could see more of the valley without descending into it. As if on command, the soldier started forward; he hit the step above, moving fast, and then he stepped down hard on the flat white stone, as it was somewhat lower than a normal step. Instantly the stone tipped and slid, and the soldier came down hard. The fall was no more than fifteen or sixteen feet, but it was immediately apparent that the fallen soldier had broken his leg.

Others gathered around him while two or three descended into the valley and began a search. An injured man was better than a dead man, for it would take at least two men to carry him back to where he could get attention.

An improvised stretcher was made while two other soldiers attempted to restore the broken step in the path. Joe Mack, resting in his brush hideout, waited and watched.

Only minutes passed before a helicopter appeared. It swung around and surveyed the hanging valley, but appeared to ignore his hideout, which from the air must have seemed no more than a small ledge on the side of the mountain above the valley, a place of no consequence. Unless Alekhin was in that helicopter.

Always, he must remember Alekhin.

The soldiers were laboring back up the path, and he lay quiet, watching them. At last they were gone, and he added spruce boughs to his bed. Taking a chance, he kindled a small fire of dry wood and broiled some meat from the mountain goat. He ate well, drank tea, and extinguished his fire. Again he took a look all about and then returned to his bed.

Lying on his back on the boughs, he stared up into the branches overhead. He had done the right things, made the right moves. Even so he had been lucky, indeed, and such luck could not be expected to last.

He sat up and in the dimming light, studied his maps. Ahead of him lay lower and fewer mountains and many small lakes and tundra. Places to hide would be infrequent, and much of the time he would be traveling in the open.

For three days he remained on the small bench, cold most of the time, having a fire but rarely with which to make tea and boil meat. He saw no more soldiers, although twice planes flew over and once a helicopter. Once, on the far side of the hanging valley, he saw movement in the brush, but nothing appeared. If it was a wild animal, it did not emerge.

He lighted his fire only when the wind was taking the smell of it out over the gorge. He always used dry wood, avoiding smoke.

On the fourth day, he decided to move. Carefully, from a hidden place among the trees, he studied possible routes by which he could keep under cover. He selected a possible destination, although that would vary according to what he found when he arrived. While in camp he doubled his supply of arrows and found two new and better chunks of iron pyrite, which he partly covered with rawhide for a better grip when striking a fire.

He started before dawn on the fifth day, impatient to be off. He went out to the north and stayed under cover of the trees. Now he took special effort to leave no trail. Although he did not like the added weight, he kept the AK-47.

Topping a ridge, he looked over the vast panorama of mountain, forest, and valley toward the east and south. Timbered ridges marched away in endless procession, with hollow basins, ridges of slide rock, patches of snow, and here and there what seemed to be glaciers. Beyond that were great crags and the cone shapes of ancient volcanoes. Avoiding an easy path into the woods, he took a mere goat trail up into the crags and crouched there to study the country. The more he saw of it, the more he was inclined to cut back to the southeast and try to stay clear of regions of small lakes and tundra. It would be much the longer route, but offered better chances of finding cover, as well as wild game.

That night he decided he would turn southeast and try to reach the Kolyma Mountains above Magadan and then follow them to the northeast.

Every few minutes now, he checked his back trail. That somebody was following him he was quite sure, and he began to think of a trap, a very subtle one that might fool even Alekhin.

Dipping down into a narrow opening between two appallingly sheer gray cliffs, he walked along a sandy floor, crawled over boulders, and wended a precarious way through a forest of tumbled rock. Here and there were patches of snow and narrow crevasses into which a man's foot might slip, breaking an ankle. Growth was scarce except for lichens.

Except for his carefully husbanded tea, his food was

almost gone, so he watched for any kind of wild animal that he might kill.

Several times he glimpsed grouse, or ptarmigan, but it was midday before he was able to kill one with his sling. He had just climbed down over a steep wall of black rocks and at their base came on a pile of driftwood stacked up against boulders by the rushing waters of spring runoff in past years. He made a small fire, broiled and ate the grouse, and then carefully covered the feathers and bones.

Looking back up the narrow gorge down which he had come, he was amazed. He must have descended more than a thousand feet, and watching, he could see no signs of movement behind him or on the cliffs above. Finding a break in the canyon wall, he turned into it and climbed steeply up, crossing a wide belt of slide rock that sounded, as he crossed it, like walking on piles of empty bottles. At the top of the slide, he found a few inches next to the cliff where he could walk. The towering boulders at the place he had started his climb now looked like mere pebbles.

Trees choked the great crack up which he was traveling. Mostly spruce and fir, there was a scattering of larch and an occasional dwarfed and gnarled cedar. There was much debris, broken branches and fallen trees, many of them mere bare poles now. He found some long-dead bark and gathered tinder for a fire whenever he might decide to stop.

Looking back down, he judged any follower would have gone on down the canyon, not thinking that a man would choose such a precipitous climb. He turned and kept on, climbing now as if up a steep stairway. Soon the crack became so tight he could touch either side with ease. At the top a raven flew up, flapping its black wings slowly away. He had to use his hands to lift himself out of the crack at the place where it began. First, just enough to look around.

Not fifty feet away was a mountain goat, a big one weighing he would guess not less than three hundred pounds. It was looking right at him, no doubt astonished by the sudden appearance of this weird looking creature in a domain where he no doubt ruled the roost. The animal seemed in no wise frightened or even disturbed.

Carefully, aware that his hands were busy and unable to use a weapon, Joe Mack hoisted himself from the crack and sat on its edge. He needed the meat, but estimating the distance, he did not like the odds.

Cautiously, Joe Mack got to his feet. The goat was amazingly white, his horns jet black and sharp as needles. His build was like others of his kind, stocky and powerful, better for climbing and leaping than running, something he would rarely have a chance to do, living on the heights as he did.

Joe Mack brought his bow around, and then seeing some larch trees not far off, he backed toward them. The goat watched him with interest, once bobbing his head low and giving it a kind of twisting shake.

Having seen goats in action, Joe Mack was perfectly aware of how dangerous they could be. Usually they hooked low and hard, trying to rip the belly of whatever they were attacking. When he reached the trees, Joe Mack retreated into the small grove and began working his way through them. When he emerged, he was upon an almost sheer mountainside, with an enormous panorama of ridges, peaks, and mountains lying before him. He was facing east and a little south and looking at one of the most rugged bits of terrain he had ever seen. It reminded him of the Sawtooth Range in his own Idaho country.

Climbing a promontory, he studied the country behind him. He could see no movement, nothing to indicate pursuit, although he knew it was there. He doubted whether the soldiers would persist, however, but somewhere soon he should be meeting the trappers and hunters Shepilov had sent to find him.

He descended from the rocks and made his way carefully over the bare rock of the mountain's crest. Here and there were loose slabs and patches of snow, some of them extensive.

He was working his way down a steeply sloping dome of granite when he saw them.

Three men, trappers or hunters by their look, far down the slope below him. If they looked up they would see him, unless his goatskin coat and pants appeared to them like snow. These men would be good shots, and all carried rifles.

For a moment he held himself still; then, just a little further down the slope, he saw a big, rounded boulder balanced on the slick rock face.

Carefully, he began edging closer. If that boulder fell—!

They were right beneath it and at least three hundred yards away, but at the base of a steep hillside.

He climbed down, using his hands to ease himself down in a sitting position. The rock was very slick, and at places there was ice. The three men were coming closer.

He reached the boulder, lifted his feet until he could put them high on its side, and then bracing himself against the mountainside, he pushed.

There was a moment when it only crunched slightly, and he pushed again, with all the power in his legs. The boulder teetered, crunched, and slowly began to turn over.

Ponderously, almost majestically, it began to roll over, and then suddenly, seized by the forces of gravity, it turned over and began to tumble down the slope.

It reached a drop, fell, and bounded high, and then as it began to fall, the hunters froze in place, staring up, eyes wide with horror.

THIRTY-NINE

The hunters took that one startled look and then scrambled to escape. All three made it.

The boulder landed within inches of where they had been standing, hitting with terrific impact. Then it rolled back a few feet and lodged against a smaller rock.

Two of the men had fallen. They got to their feet, badly shaken, and looked up at the mountain. They could see nothing.

Hurriedly, they moved back into the nearest trees. There were not many at that point, but they were some shelter.

"That was no accident," one of them said.

For several minutes nobody spoke, and then Hymoff said, "Did you ever think of all you could do to somebody following you into the mountains?"

"Who hasn't?"

"I never liked Shepilov, anyway," Hymoff suggested.

It was a dangerous remark, and they all knew it. If such a comment were repeated, it could mean trouble for the speaker.

"Well, a man could always trap some fur. Doubt if this country has been trapped lately. A man could keep busy," he added.

"How did he come to be a prisoner here, anyway? My

grandfather sold furs to an American trader at Emma's Landing, years ago. Said he was an honest man, as traders go."

"No way he's going to escape, anyway. No way he could cross the Strait."

"The Chukchis crossed it for years, hundreds of years, I guess."

"That was before radar and patrol planes. I crossed it most of the way on the ice, one time. I was with my father, and I was just twelve that year."

From high on the slope, Joe Mack watched them. What reward had been offered for him he did not know, or what other inducement, if any. He had not planned to kill any of them, but that was their problem. If they chose to follow, he would stop them, one way or another.

He arose and went back off the ridge and followed it toward the southeast. It was easy walking here, with few trees, scattered rock, and nothing but sky above. It was clear and blue, like most skies in this part of the country. He did not hurry, but he made good time. Yet at intervals he stopped to study his back trail. Alekhin would be back there somewhere, or perhaps outguessing him and waiting up ahead. That had been one of the reasons he had changed direction so drastically.

Later that day he killed a musk deer and broiled a steak over the fire. He ate hugely, eating as his forebears had eaten when meat could not be saved and another kill might be days away.

When he had eaten he put out his fire, obliterated as much as possible of the sign it left, and hiked on another two miles before finding a place to sleep.

Somewhere far ahead was the Kolyma River and beyond it mountains of the same name. When he reached those mountains he would follow them toward the northeast.

He was tempted to go into Magadan, just for a change of diet, if no more. He had his suit and he had the white shirt Natalya had made for him. At this time of the year, he might even get away with wearing moccasins. He shook his head. Not with a suit. A new suit, at that. It would draw attention he did not want. Nonetheless, it was a temptation.

There was no trail or path where he now walked, and he kept his eyes open to pick up an animal trail. It was easy to get oneself into a cul-de-sac, not knowing the mountains. If

you followed a trail, it was always a way somebody or something had gone before.

It was bitterly cold and getting more so. Before nightfall
he would have to get down off the top of the mountain where
he now walked. Warm air rises, and if he could find a hiding
place on a good slope he would settle in, even if it was early.

He heard the helicopter only a moment before it appeared, and there was nowhere to hide. Hoping they had not
seen him he dropped to the ground among some flat rocks,
hoping they would take him for snow or even a dead animal.
He lay perfectly still, but inside his coat his hand gripped the
AK-47.

The copter swung by, not directly overhead, and started
on; then it around and came back, flying lower.

They had seen something. They were coming back for
him. *All right, Joe Mack*, he whispered to himself. *Get them
the first time*.

He lay still, and they swung by directly over him, not
fifty feet off the ground.

He rolled over as they swung by and let go with a burst
just as they began their turn. They were making a tight turn
not more than fifty yards away, and they believed he had only
a bow and arrows. What they got was totally unexpected.

The copter dipped sharply and then smashed into the
ground, tipping slightly and then righting itself. The rotor
made a few despairing turns and then slowed to a stop.

Lying behind the rocks—a poor cover at best, for they
were very low—Joe Mack watched, ready to fire again.

Nothing happened. Nobody stirred.

He waited a slow count of twenty and still nothing moved.
His gun covering the side of the helicopter, he got to his feet.
Working his way toward the tail, he kept the gun in position
and slowly drew abreast. He heard a low gasping moan, as if
someone had tried to move and had been stopped by sheer
agony. With his left hand he opened the door.

The pilot lay slumped forward, obviously dead. The man
nearest him made a feeble effort to reach for a weapon. "No!"
Joe Mack spoke sharply, the muzzle of his gun against the
Russian's side.

He was a young man with a boyish face, but a tough,
competent-looking man. In Russian he asked him, "How are
you hurt?"

"My legs are broken, I think."

Quickly, efficiently, he searched the man, taking a pistol from him. Then, with infinite care, he lifted him out of the seat to the ground. From the helicopter he recovered the man's heavy coat and several blankets. There was a folded emergency tent, and he took that out and laid it on the ground.

"Not much I can do for you," he said. "I'm no surgeon. Did you get off a call for help?"

"No."

Joe Mack believed him. There had been no time, no chance. "How soon will they start looking for you?"

"When we do not answer."

"All right. I'm going to fix you up as warm as I can, and then I'll leave. Sorry about this, but you shouldn't have been hunting me."

"We were not. That is, until we saw something lying there. We were going to pick up a prisoner. A dissident."

Joe Mack gathered all the coats and blankets from the copter to make the wounded man as warm as possible. As he talked, he built a windbreak of the flat rocks.

"A dissident? I didn't know you had such things." He spoke with a touch of sarcasm in his tone.

"We have our share. This is a bad one. He tried to free another prisoner. Did free him, in fact, but was captured himself."

"Tough."

"Yes, he is a tough one, as you say. Very strong man and not afraid. Too bad he has become a dissident. We need such men in Russia."

"So does every country." A thought came to him suddenly, a wild random thought. Yet why not? "What was his name?"

"Yakov. We do not have a patronymic. He was known to the KGB."

"You are not KGB?"

"I am a soldier," the man said. Then, "How will they find me?"

"I shall build a fire and leave some fuel for you. There is much lying about. And I found a flashlight in the plane." He had found two of them, as a matter of fact. One he intended to keep. He had also found emergency rations, such as every such ship carried in this country, and matches.

He built a small fire and made tea, hot, black, and strong. "Best thing for shock, they tell me."

He drank some tea himself and moved a packet of the emergency rations close to the wounded man.

"I won't be able to stay, you know. In fact, I'd best be off and away."

"I am obliged. You could have killed me."

"You are a soldier. I am a soldier. In combat I might have killed you or been killed, but you are wounded. It is a different thing."

"It is said you are a Red Indian?"

Joe Mack smiled. "I am."

Obviously in pain, the man bit his lip and held himself hard against it. Then he said, "Do not Indians take scalps?"

Joe Mack shrugged. "That was long ago, in another world almost. Yes, it was a way of keeping score. I have never taken one, although in a couple of cases I might be tempted."

He gathered his things, rummaged in the plane for more ammunition, found it, and took what other rations were available. Then he brought more wood for the fire. There was not a shortage of that, except that it needed gathering.

"It will keep a small fire going, and from up there they will see it easily. I must be off now." Yet he lingered. "Yakov, you say? Where were you to pick him up?"

"Near Khonuu. It is not far," he caught himself and was silent for a moment, "if you are flying."

He paused again. "The KGB are holding him at the airfield." He glanced up. "I have feeling for him. They will be rough, I think."

"When were they not? I do not know your country. I did not think there were rebels here."

The flyer shrugged. "There are none, or at least few who speak out. There is corruption, of course, and the black market. Many are discontented but have faith that everything will be put right."

Joe Mack went into the darkness and gathered fuel. There were few trees here and scattered, but there was much debris fallen from them and dead trees, blown down or struck by lightning. He dragged some heavy stuff closer.

"You will not escape, you know," the flyer said. "Alekhin knows where you are. He will find you."

"I shall be expecting him."

"You are not afraid?"

"He is a man. I am a man. We will see."

He added a few sticks to the fire. "Good luck, Russian. Next time, tell your pilot to stay out of matters that do not concern him."

He walked away into the darkness.

Of course, he had delayed too long. When there was no word from the helicopter, a search would begin. Once the helicopter was found, they would know where he was, approximately.

Khonuu? It was a town on the Indigirka, and Yakov was a prisoner there.

Yakov, who had helped him, gone out of his way to guide him. Yakov, who was a free spirit and partly of Tungus blood. Yakov, who refused to be harnessed. Yakov was a prisoner. Yet what could he, Joe Mack, do? He did not know the town or the airfield. The chances were great, however, that Yakov would be held at the airfield awaiting transportation to wherever the KGB wanted him. After interrogation, Yakov would be killed. Of that there could be no question.

Khonuu was not that far out of his way, yet he had avoided populated districts, knowing he would be recognized for who he was almost at once.

When it was light enough to see, he began to run. He ran easily, smoothly, careful of each step. Black, bare trees stretched bare black arms against the lightening sky. He ran into the dawn, an Indian, feeling himself an Indian, and when he found a dim game trail he went along it, finding it led him down the mountain.

The long hard months had left him lean and strong. As a cold sun arose from the far-distant gray clouds, he ran toward it, and then the trail took him north. He was going the way he must. Was it fate? He did not believe in fate, but something seemed to be guiding him as he ran.

He was a warrior, and another warrior, brother to him in spirit, was in trouble. He knew the risk, knew the slight chance he had of even finding where Yakov was held, but he took the chance freely.

Once, long ago, he had seen a young Chinese on the

gallows waiting for the noose. He had said, "Some mans spend nice new money. I spend nice new life."

"If I must, I will," he told himself. "I am alone, and nobody awaits me."

Nobody? What of her? What of Natalya? Did she await him somewhere? Or was he forgotten, something that had drifted across her life like a passing cloud?

What had she promised? Nothing. What had he offered? To come for her, when both knew it was a vain, desperate promise to which no sane person would hold him. Yet in that respect he might not be sane, for he truly expected to return, to take her from the shore at Plastun Bay.

Foolish? Of course, but so many things worth doing may seem foolish to others, may seem impossible.

He ran down the mountain in the morning's gray light and found his way into the shadowed firs, the black guardian firs that clustered along his way. He crossed frozen streams and ran through patches of thin snow where his moccasins barely left a track behind.

When the sun was warm he found a place among the willows and slept, and when the sun was higher still he awakened. For a long time he stood, listening to the wind, hearing what was moving, watching the flight of birds, and they seemed unafraid and undisturbed. He began to run once more, for he had far to go and did not know how much time he had.

He saw no one and heard nothing but, once, far off, the ring of an ax chopping wood.

The morning opened wide before him, and the forest thinned again. In the distance he saw the smoke of cooking fires in the homes of those he did not know, and far off a city against the sky and a river between.

He slowed to a walk. A running man would be seen and would invite questions to which he had no answers. Now he must find the airfield. He was guessing, judging Yakov would be held waiting for the transportation to take him away. Now to scout the field and see where such a man might be held. And after that?

He was a warrior, and for a warrior any day was a good day to die.

Only he expected to live. He needed to live to free

Yakov, to count coup on his enemies, and to meet a golden lady on a distant shore.

He was no longer an officer and a gentleman, no longer a flyer for the American Air Force; he was, for now, an Indian. And he had enemies.

There were scattered houses. One man, carrying an armful of wood, glanced at him, then went inside.

He walked steadily on. He saw a small plane take off and knew where the airfield was. He changed direction, walked among some houses, and crossed a bridge. His heart was pounding, his mouth dry. His AK-47 was hidden under his coat, his bow appeared to be a staff, no more than that.

It was very early and very cold. Nobody went willingly into the cold on such a day.

Two men walked before him, two thick men in thick coats and dark fur hats. They walked steadily and did not look back, but the walk of one was familiar. He unfastened the string that tied his coat and let his hand touch the butt of the AK-47. He was ready, but he took longer strides to move faster without seeming to hurry.

The man turned around, and it was Botev.

FORTY

For a moment Botev stood still. Then he reached out and touched his companion. The other man turned, and it was Borowsky.

Were they to be considered friends or enemies? They were, after all, Russians. Yet they had differences with their government. He walked closer.

"You are still free," Botev said. "It is an achievement."

"Yakov is a prisoner."

"That is why we are here."

"He is at the airfield?"

Botev's eyes swept the area around to see if they were attracting attention. Nobody was in sight.

"He is there. There are four KGB men with him. They are in a small waiting room near the control center, waiting for the plane to come and take them away. It will be a helicopter, I believe."

"You have a plan?"

Botev shrugged. "How can we plan? We know so little. He is there and we wish to free him. If we free him, we can escape into the taiga. We have friends there, scattered friends. We also have friends in Magadan."

"I did not know there were so many of you."

Borowsky shrugged. "We are few, comrade, very few. We are not seeking to overthrow the government, even if

310

that were possible. We only want some freedom for ourselves and to protect our own. Yakov is one of the best. We need him. He has helped all of us from time to time."

"Our choice is limited," Botev said. "The taiga or a prison camp, and for Borowsky and me, they would put us to work that would soon kill us. If they did not torture us to death. We can expect nothing less. Neither can Yakov."

"We had better move on," Borowsky said. "To stand talking in the cold is unreasonable. We will attract attention."

"Four men, you say? There will be others about?"

Borowsky shrugged. "Perhaps. Most of them will not like the KGB, but we cannot tell what they might do."

They walked on in silence along the snow-covered road. They passed a long building like a warehouse and then some smaller buildings. They could see the field now. It had several hangars, a building that was probably an administration building with a tower, and a smaller building nearby with a Volga standing before it.

Joe Mack said, "There's a chopper coming in now. Will that be it?"

"It will. When they start for the chopper, we had better take them."

"No," Joe Mack said. "Let's take the chopper. I can fly it."

"Well—"

"It will get us out of town. There will be planes after us, but we can ditch it and take to the woods."

They paused beside a hangar. "When it lands," Botev said, "they will drive out in the Volga. They will not expect trouble."

They waited, stamping their feet against the cold, shivering and watching. "If we are seen," Borowsky said, "they will wonder why we are standing here in the cold."

"It is a risk we take," Botev said. "Yakov would do it for us."

"He got me out of Kirensk," Borowsky said. "He risked his neck to do it."

"And me from one of the Sol'vychegodsk camps," Botev said.

The chopper was coming in low. It would land on the airfield not far from the hangars.

Joe Mack's hand was on the AK-47. He heard the Volga

start, and from the corner of the hangar they saw two men emerge from the building with a prisoner between them. His hands were shackled behind him.

"There will be two men in the building. Maybe they will be watching."

"No matter." Joe Mack saw the helicopter landing gently on the field and heard the car's motor start. The hatch of the copter opened and a man got down and stood aside. It was a bigger ship than those he had seen before and would carry at least a squad. Inwardly he was praying there was no such force aboard. If there were, nobody would get out of this alive.

"Let's go," he said, and they started to walk, not in a group but scattered out, drifing onto the field with the casual manner of curious country folk.

The Volga swung alongside the chopper, and the driver remained at the wheel. From the Volga, three men got down, and they saw Yakov turn his head slightly, eyes downcast, and glance toward them. Suddenly he fell to his knees. "No! No!" he cried out. "I am afraid to fly! I—!"

Angrily, the KGB men tried to jerk him erect, their attention completely on their prisoner. Even the driver had turned his head to see what was happening. Borowsky stepped alongside the Volga and opened the door on the driver's side. The driver, surprised, turned to look into a pistol. "Get out, very carefully," Borowsky said quietly. "I do not want to kill you."

Botev had rounded the Volga, coming up behind the two men who struggled with Yakov. Yakov was a powerful man, and he had managed, with a lunge, to knock one man off his feet. The other struggled, swearing, to pull Yakov to a standing position. Botev moved in behind him as Joe Mack went to the chopper. He spoke to the pilot.

"Will you step out, please? I am very nervous, and a burst of fire at this distance would empty your guts."

Carefully, the copter pilot began to get out. He was a brave man, but he wished to live, and the AK-47 was very close, and the man who held it was like no one he had ever seen, with the striking gray eyes in a dark hawklike face, his hair in two braids. The pilot moved very carefully. "Be careful with that," he said. "I have two children."

"You are fortunate. Children need a father, so stay alive, comrade, and make no mistakes. I want your chopper."

"You can fly it?"

"I can fly anything." He nudged the pilot with the gun barrel to move him further. "And this seems very like one of our own."

Botev had the two KGB men on their feet against the side of the Volga. From the buildings they were screened. Nevertheless, one of the KGB men had come outside and was looking toward them. "Have you got the key for the handcuffs?" he asked Botev. "If so, disarm them and put them in the copter."

Borowsky was astonished. "You will take them with us?"

"Why not? There is room, and if left behind there's no telling what tales they might tell."

Working swiftly, the four men, the pilot, the driver of the Volga, and the two KGB men were bundled into the helicopter. Yakov, his hands freed, took the guns taken from two of them and climbed in with them. The helicopter was soon airborne.

Joe Mack glanced at his watch. The whole operation had taken just six minutes.

A half hour later he landed on a rugged plateau of the Chersky Mountains. "Yakov? Let them out here. Loosen their bonds so they can free themselves after we are gone. No reason to let them freeze to death."

"To the devil with them," Yakov said. "Let the bastards freeze!"

"The pilot did you no harm," Joe Mack said. "Besides, he's a family man. Let them free themselves and find their way back. However," he added, "I've had some experience with these mountains. I would suggest the first thing you do is build a fire and a windbreak. Then get settled for the night. It is too late to get anywhere today."

He circled once as they took off. The men were on their feet, struggling to free themselves. He turned the helicopter and headed off to the west; then, when some distance away, he circled back to the east.

"Where?" he asked Yakov.

"To the mountains east of Semychan," Yakov suggested. "I've a place there." He took up a map board. "Here, I can show you." He glanced up. "How are we on fuel?"

"No more than an hour's flying time. Perhaps less. I will take you as far as possible."

He kept the helicopter low, barely clearing the treetops, following canyons and low ground wherever possible. By now there would be pursuit, and when sighted they would be shot down without hesitation. But until they picked up the four men left behind, the pursuers would not know who was involved. And the KGB men would not know him, unless the description fitted one they already had. The braids might be a giveaway. Certainly it was unlikely that anybody else would be wearing such a hairstyle. Yet what could he do? There were no barbers in the taiga, and it had been nearly a year since he had had a haircut.

The air was clear, visibility excellent. He had left the Indigirka behind and was flying toward the Kolyma. When he landed the plane, it was in a small clearing among the trees. "We should chance it no further," he said. "They will be searching for us now. Let's camouflage the chopper. It will take them that much longer to find us."

There were, as in all such craft flying in the area, emergency rations. "We will give you half," Yakov said. "We have friends not far off where we can get more. Luck to you, comrade."

"And to you."

Yakov smiled widely. "You know, of course, that if we met in a war I should shoot you. I do not like our government very much, but I am a Russian."

"Of course," Joe Mack replied. "And I am an American. Let us hope it does not come to that. After all," he added, "we want nothing you have. Nothing but free travel and communication. There are millions of Americans who would like to see Lake Baikal and the Kamchatka Peninsula. If Russia would put the KGB to working on farms and doing something productive, tear down the Berlin Wall, and build more good hotels, we Americans would be all over your country spending money, making friends, seeing the beauties of Russia, and making ridiculous all that both countries are spending on munitions.

"If America had had any aggressive intentions against Russia, we could have moved when only America had the atomic bomb. We did not and would not, so don't worry about it, Yakov."

Yakov chuckled. "I like that bit about putting the KGB to work on farms. I doubt if they could raise enough to feed themselves." He lifted a hand. "Good-bye, then!"

He walked away, followed by Botev and Borowsky. Joe Mack waited a while, watching them go, glancing again at the now-camouflaged helicopter. It would be found, but not soon.

He added the additional rations to his pack, arranged his goatskin coat, and started off to the north.

Nothing moved but the wind. The coarse snow stirred along the frozen ground. Spring was coming, but the earth did not yet know it, holding itself back, waiting for some of the frost to go out of the sleeping earth.

Spring was coming and after it, the brief summer. It would be good to be warm again. He had almost forgotten how it would feel.

Where was Natalya now? Would he ever see her again? Ever hold her hands in his and look again into her eyes? Or had she forgotten already? He could not blame her. After all, who was he? A strange young man who came from the forest and disappeared again into that strange forest. A man whose path had crossed hers briefly and who must now seem like a dream. He grinned into the late afternoon. "Or a nightmare," he said aloud.

There was still forest, although the trees were not as tall, the undergrowth less, and there was more moss, lichens, and tundra. Soon he would run out of cover and would have to seek out other ways in which to hide himself.

In the thickest patch he could find, he built a crude shelter, started a fire with his two pieces of iron pyrite, and made a thick broth as well as tea. The helicopter flight had probably given him a little respite. Even Alekhin would have trouble picking up his trail now.

Twice during the day he had seen the tracks of moose and decided it would be good to kill one and save as much meat as possible. In this cold, it was no problem to keep meat. It froze solid almost as soon as it was killed. Tomorrow he would kill a moose. Tomorrow—

Arkady Zamatev looked across his desk at the Yakut. "Why have you not found him?" he demanded. "Has he outwitted you again?"

"I do not have to follow him. I know where he is going. I shall be there."

"Where now?"

"I go to Gizhiga. There I go inland. He will come that way, and I shall take him."

"So you said before."

"And I shall." Alekhin shrugged impatiently. "Those others, they get in the way." He smirked, his sullen eyes showing his contempt. "He made a fool of Colonel Rukovsky. He destroyed him. Ruined him. How does he explain losing so many men, and nothing to show for it? Rukovsky was a fool to get involved. It was not necessary, and I was there. I would have had him then but that they muddied the waters. I knew where he was."

"And you did not tell?"

"To let Rukovsky or Shepilov get credit for capturing him? He cost Rukovsky twenty-nine men, and Rukovsky must explain."

"The American had nothing to do with the slide."

"You say. I say he knew where he hid. He knew how they must search, and he prepared some traps and led them to others. Of course he knew. He planned it that way.

"What of the fire that destroyed so much equipment? The American started that fire. What of the traps along the trail that killed or injured men? He prepared those, too. He is no fool, this American, but I shall have him now."

He looked up slyly from under his brows. "You still want him alive? It would be easier to kill him."

"I must have him alive. I need three to five days alone with him. He will tell me all I wish to know."

"He will tell you nothing. Nothing at all. By now you should know this. You may kill him, but he will tell you nothing. He is not afraid of pain, this one. He knows what he can do."

Zamatev shook his head. "Bring him here. That is all I ask."

"He was one of those who delivered Yakov."

Zamatev sat up sharply. "You know this? Why was I not told?"

"I tell you now."

Zamatev swore. "Then he has Russians helping him! I want them rounded up, brought in, every one of them!"

Alekhin looked at his thick fingers with their broken nails, and then he looked up from under his brows. "Be careful, comrade. He has destroyed Rukovsky, this one. Be sure he does not destroy you."

Zamatev snorted angrily. "Destroy *me*? That is ridiculous!"

Alekhin looked out of the window. "He will destroy you," he said contemptuously, "and then he will return and kill you."

"Bah!" Zamatev said impatiently. "How could he reach me? If he is anxious to kill me, why has he not tried?"

"First," Alekhin said, "he wishes to escape. But to escape is not enough. He escapes to make light of you. Then he wishes to beat you at your own game."

"That's childish! That's nonsense! Why should he care? Anyway, how could you know this?"

"He is Indian. I am Yakut. He is not like you. He is like me. He knows how to hate, this one. He knows how to win. He will make a fool of you, destroy you, and then he will come back."

"Come back to Siberia? You are insane! He cannot escape, but if he should, why would he come back?"

"To kill you," Alekhin repeated. "He has pride, this one. He does not ask reward. He does not care if his government knows. He does not care if Russia knows. It is only important that *he* knows." Alekhin smiled, and it was not a good smile. "And that you know. When he kills you, you will know he is doing it."

FORTY-ONE

Evgeny Zhikarev was frightened. Across the river was China, not a mile from where he stood looking out the dirty, flyspecked window. Now that he was so near, his courage seemed to have drained from him, and for the first time he thought of himself as an old man.

Once he could have swum that river. Once he could have ducked and dodged if necessary to escape them. Now he was no longer agile, and his poor stumps of feet were crippled and broken. To move swiftly or adroitly was impossible.

Worst of all, he had promised a beautiful young woman that he would help her escape from Siberia.

How could he have been so foolish? Was it not enough that he escape himself, without trying to help another? And what did she mean to him, anyway?

She meant nothing. He scarcely knew her. Actually, he did not know her at all. She was the daughter of Stephan Baronas, and he had known, slightly, Stephan Baronas and respected him as a man and as a scholar.

He shivered. Escape was so near, and he so desperately wanted to live his last years in warmth and contentment. He wanted to be away from fear of the authorities, from fear of questioning, of harassment. He just wanted to sit in the sun again, to doze quietly and watch the boats on the bay, any bay at all where he was free.

He wanted to eat well again, to sit in a cafe, order a meal, and talk with people at other tables near him. He wanted to read a book, a newspaper, anything that was simply what it was and not something first approved by the state.

He was an old man, and he was tired.

Yesterday he had ventured into the streets for the first time. He had found his way to a small place where river men went to eat or drink and where fur trappers sometimes came, although free trappers were scarce these days. Soldiers came there sometimes, and he had heard them talking among themselves. Lieutenant Potanin was stationed here, and the men liked him. He was easy on them, demanding little except alertness when superior officers were around, or the KGB.

It was quiet along the border. The Chinese were over there, but they bothered nobody, and a little undercover trade went on across the river. The Chinese had vegetables, fruit, and many other things unavailable across the Ussuri.

What fruit could be found on the Russian side of the river was packaged and sent elsewhere.

He heard the door open behind him and turned. It was Natalya. How lovely she was! She could have been the daughter he had never had, the family he had wanted.

She came over to the window. He gestured. "There is China, and now I am afraid."

"I know." She was silent for a few minutes, and then she said, "We must not be afraid now, no more than we need to be to be careful. I think we will escape, you and I."

The road that ran along in front of the house was hard-packed snow with hoofprints, footprints, and tire tracks.

There were piles of dirty snow along the walks, which were only paths now between the buildings and the drifts. Soot was scattered over the snow, and drifting dust and dirt. Soon the snow would be gone and spring would come. The ice on the river had broken up.

"Potanin is here?"

"He is. I listened to soldiers speak of him and of others. He is here now, and I must find a way to speak to him, but not at his post. It must be here in the town and quietly if possible."

"You do not know where he lives?"

"No, and I cannot ask. I must watch, listen, and hope for

a word or to meet someone I know. That truck driver, the
one who brought us to town, he knows him."

"But he is gone!"

"Of course, but he will return." Evgeny peered into the
street. "I do not like this. Something is *wrong*! Something
feels wrong! I am afraid." He looked at her. "Do not think me
a coward, but we are so close now, and this feeling, this
sense, this foreboding—I do not like it.

"That truck driver? He was kind to give us the ride, but
what is he to us? Nothing! Suppose he is picked up by the
police and just to get them off his back he speaks of us?
Suppose we were seen getting out of the truck? It was night,
I know, but there is always somebody up and about, and
people report on their neighbors, their own families, even!
So what are we? Nobody! He could inform on us with a clear
conscience. It is better to trust nobody."

"What of Potanin?"

"I do not worry about him. Not much. He believes he
will make a little from dealing with me. He will let me go
over, thinking I will come back with a fat piece of whatever it
is for him. He lives well, that one. He eats well, he has a few
things to give to the girls, and he sends a few things to his
family in Irkutsk. Because of him, they live well, too."

A big Kama truck growled past, laboring with its heavy
load on the icy street.

"I must be careful," he grumbled. "On my feet I can
move only slowly, and I think they look for me. I think they
look for a man with crippled feet."

"I can go. I am not afraid."

He hesitated. "It is a risk. If you are stopped—?"

"I will be in trouble," she said, "but nothing is gained
without risk, and how long can we stay here?"

She was right, of course. They had no right to be here.
He knew the owner was a sick man and was far away in
Khabarovsk in a hospital. There had been business between
them, and sometimes furs had been stored here. Nevertheless, if he returned and found them here, he would drive
them out at once. The risk was too great.

"Whatever you do," Zhikarev warned, "do not go to the
post. Do not go nearer the river than you must. They are
very suspicious, and they shoot first and ask questions of the
body.

"Potanin likes to live well, and there is a small place"—
he traced an imaginary diagram with his forefinger—"here.
There is a woman there who makes little pastries and has tea.
Also"—he looked up at her—"she does a bit of business. She
will have a bit of cheese and some sliced meat, and she makes
an excellent borscht.

"Potanin goes there. This our driver told me while you
slept. He goes there each day for a bit of something before
going on duty. He reads a little, that one. He will be a
round-faced one with black hair, and he will have a book."

"A book?"

"He is always with a book. He reads the old ones,
Pushkin, Gogol, Chekhov—"

He paused. "Speak to him of books. You will have his
attention at once. You understand? He is friendly but aloof. I
mean he does not mix. He is not one of your vodka-swilling
young officers who stagger home from duty.

"He will have a drink, of course, but all who approach
him want favors; others are afraid because he is a soldier and
wears that uniform. As for receiving things from across the
border, many of his superiors come to him for a bit of
something now and again. But speak to him of books and you
will not be brushed aside. He will be curious. I know him."

She put on her coat and the fur hat. She was shabby, she
knew. Her clothing was old and much worn. However, there
would be many like her here, and it was well that she would
not attract attention. She must be as unobtrusive as possible.

"You have some rubles?"

"Enough. Say a prayer for me, Father. I shall need it."

She went out and closed the door behind her. *Ah*, he
said to himself, *she called me Father! I wish I were her father.
To have such a child could make a man proud*. Yet he was
frightened. She had been long away from towns and people,
and things in Russia had changed.

She walked steadily, stepping carefully because of the
ice, but not wanting to attract attention by hurrying too
much. As she walked she was alert to all around her.

A Volga went by, slowing a little for slippery places.
Another Kama was parked at the corner. As she passed it, she
felt dwarfed by its size. Few people were on the street. The
Volga had gone on ahead of her and was pulling off to one

side near an official-looking building of concrete, squat and ugly.

She had to pass right by it, but she kept her head down and walked on. Two people were getting out of the Volga, a big man who stamped his feet to warm them and a woman. She was a young woman, dressed very well, but obviously an official.

As she passed the Volga, the woman turned around. She was a sharp-looking, very attractive brunette. Her hair was drawn back, and her eyes were large. For an instant their eyes met, and she saw a puzzled expression come into the woman's face. Natalya walked on, her heart beating heavily.

Had she been recognized? But how could she be? Who knew her? Or cared about her?

Forcing herself not to look back, she continued on, rounded a corner, then went off down another street. Then she came back to the little place of which Evgeny had spoken.

She went in. Several people were present, but no young officer. She ordered tea and a bowl of borscht that turned out to be surprisingly good.

She ate slowly and had another cup of tea. He did not come. At last she arose, paid, and left. At the door she took a moment to straighten her coat and put on her gloves, studying the street. Emerging, she looked again up and down and then deliberately chose a way that would avoid the street along which she had come. Her heart was pounding, and it was all she could do to avoid looking around to see if she was followed.

Several times she changed direction, but the streets were virtually empty in this quarter. She hurried on, returning to the little room in the corner of the old building.

Evgeny Zhikarev was waiting inside. He reached both his hands for hers, drawing her quickly inside, and then closed the door.

"Ah! You do not know how frightened I have been! I have imagined all sorts of things! Please, are you all right?"

"I am all right, but he did not come. Your literary lieutenant did not come. I sat and waited. I drank my tea slowly, but he did not come."

She took off her coat and hat, fluffing her hair a little after the hat's confining. "There was a car, a Volga with two

people in it. The woman looked straight at me. For a minute
I thought—"

"Two people? What was she like, this woman?"

"Dark hair, very striking. A handsome woman, she had
manners like an official. She looked right at me."

Zhikarev could feel his heart beating, and there was a
sick feeling in his stomach. "And the man? A tall, soldierly
man? Very strong?"

"That's the one. Do you know them?"

"I know them." Evgeny Zhikarev sat down suddenly.
"She is Comrade Kyra Lebedev. She works with Colonel
Zamatev, and the man was Stegman." He gestured to his
crippled feet. "He did this to me."

He limped across to the fire and added coal from the
bucket. He straightened up. "We have no time, then. Why
else would they be here but for us?"

"She knows you by sight?"

"Of course. She has been to my shop. We spoke of furs
together. She would recognize me at once."

For a long time they were silent, each thinking, frightened, understanding what impended. "We have no choice,"
she admitted. "I must return to the tearoom. I must meet
Potanin."

He shook his head. "I do not like it. If she looked at you,
by now she knows who you must be. She saw you, and she is
a very astute young woman. I have heard it said that she is
Zamatev's strong right arm. His future depends on capturing
that American, and if they believe you knew him they will try
to discover what you know, or they will hold you to bring him
in."

"How would he know?"

"They would find a way; believe me, they would."
Zhikarev looked at her. "Would he come back for you? Give
himself up for you?"

She shook her head. "I do not know. I hope not. They
lie; they will promise and then do as they wish. I cannot let
that happen. If they catch me I will kill myself."

He shrugged. "It is not easy to do. They will leave you
nothing. Being captured by them is not good. Particularly for
a woman."

"No," he said. "We must escape. We must escape now."

"I will try once more to see Potanin. This afternoon—"

"And I shall be ready to move. It must be today or tonight, no later. No matter what he says, insist."

When Kyra Lebedev realized who she was, would the search begin at once? Or would they try to locate her by other means? Or simply alert their people to watch for her to see with whom she was associated and where she was in hiding?

It was late afternoon before she took to the street again. "If I do not appear by shortly after dark you had best forget about me," she advised. "I will do what I can, but they might arrest me, so I'd be unable to return."

He went to the door with her. "See yonder?" he said. "That grove of birches by the river? If I must leave here, I will go there and wait for you until midnight. We should not try to cross by daylight, anyway."

"What of the Chinese? Will they let us enter?"

He shrugged. "It is a chance we must take. I have the name of a Chinese who might help. One never knows."

The small street was empty. She walked swiftly to the corner, then crossed and went into the street of the cafe, if such it could be called, avoiding the more busy street where she had seen Kyra Lebedev.

Only four tables were occupied when she entered the cafe, and she saw Lieutenant Potanin at once. He was seated near the door, and he was reading while sipping his tea. He looked up as she entered, and she crossed the room to his table. Surprised, he stood up.

She said, "Do you remember Ivan Karamazov, who wanted not millions, but an answer to his questions?"

He smiled. "I have read Dostoevsky," he said, "but do you have questions, too?"

"Several." She seated herself. "But very little time. I bring you greetings from a friend who deals in furs. He does not walk well."

He shook his head, smiling. "Will you have some tea?"

"I also bring you"—she took the book from under her arm—"Balzac's *Le Père Goriot*. It was a book of my father's."

"A gift?" His eyes searched hers. "What is it you wish?"

"My friend has furs awaiting, as usual. We would like to pick them up tonight."

" 'We?' Does it need more than one?"

"It does." She smiled at him. "I do not like being abrupt,

and I know this is not the way such things are done, but I
have no choice."

His eyes searched hers, and the smile disappeared. "I
see." He took up the book she had placed on the table.
"Fortunately, I read French." He spoke very softly then,
keeping his eyes on hers and his face slightly averted from
the room, although nobody seemed to be paying attention.
"At fifteen minutes to midnight, then? No earlier, no later."

"Thank you." She arose. "Until then," she said, and
turned to the door.

The street was dark but for the light from the cafe
windows. Quickly, she crossed the street and stepped into
the shadows of a doorway.

The street was empty, and snow was falling softly. Hesi-
tating a moment, she stepped out into the snow. And then
she heard the car.

It was coming up the street, the headlights pointing a
lighted finger before them. With a step she was back in the
doorway again and out of sight.

The Volga drew up at the cafe. A door opened and a
woman got out. On the other side of the car the driver
stepped out. He was a big, broad-shouldered man. The woman
turned toward him, her face momentarily in the light.

It was Kyra Lebedev.

FORTY-TWO

Joe Mack knew how to wait while the dawn washed color from the sky. He knew how to wait while watching beyond the agonized arms of gnarled trees stretched against the morning. He had killed the moose and skinned it out, eating meat and saving meat against the long days to come.

He knew how to wait and watch for movement. The forest was sparse now, except for occasional tight groves of Mongolian poplar, willow along the streams, and scattered larch. He had found a shadow that suited him, and he waited in the shadow to see what moved in the distance.

Over there, a blue shadow against a paler sky, was another range, and he needed to study it in sunlight and in shadow to learn where the passes might be and where the canyons were.

He had come far, but had far yet to go, and now the land was narrow and the chase would tighten and close in. Alekhin would know that he would avoid the open tundra for its lack of cover and would keep to the mountains along the sea.

Alekhin had been hanging back, listening to what was said, studying his trail, planning for his own move. Joe Mack knew that as well as if Alekhin had told him. Alekhin would be impatient with the blundering efforts made thus far. He would know what to do when his time came, and his time was now.

There had been much blundering. First, Zamatev had not wanted to advertise that a prisoner had escaped him or that he even had prisoners. He had held back, expecting a quick capture.

Bringing soldiers into the field had been a mistake, also. If they had had to bring soldiers, they should have been a detachment of Siberians, not men from the Ukraine. Good men, no doubt, but flatlanders, unaccustomed to Arctic mountains.

The trappers had been a wise move on the face of things, but as Alekhin would know, the trappers were half in sympathy with the American. Not that they were in any sense disloyal, simply that he was one of them, a hunter and a trapper who handled himself as such, and they took pleasure in seeing him outwit the city men who organized the pursuit. The American had used their country as they might have used it, and so when they went into the field they did not look too hard.

Joe Mack studied the distance with care, his eyes sweeping the country bit by bit, missing nothing, remembering everything. He could read terrain as a scholar reads a rare manuscript or a jewelsmith studies a diamond for the cutting. Much of his life had been spent in wild country, and for nearly a year now he had lived in the taiga, learning its moods and its whims. Long ago he had learned that one could not make war against the wilderness. One had to live with it, not against it.

Somewhere out there, before or behind him, was Alekhin, closing in, making ready for the capture or kill. And Alekhin had had time to study him, while he knew little of the Yakut. Now he must learn or die.

Joe Mack knew that every move he made must be calculated, yet he must never establish a pattern of behavior. He must not allow Alekhin to guess where he might be at any given time. He must vary his campsites, be careful of his kills, change direction often.

Above all, he must be prepared for a fight to the death. Alekhin would understand nothing less.

Carefully, from his shadow atop the low ridge, he studied the terrain and plotted his route. There was easy cover ahead and to his right, so he must avoid it. That would be the best way, the likely way, so he must choose another. Yet even that procedure must not become a pattern.

Criminals were almost invariably stupid in this respect. If they escaped from the law, they returned to familiar surroundings to be close to those they knew, people who could help them and conceal them, people with whom they were comfortable. Of course, the law knew this and knew where to look for them and whom to question, and there was always somebody who would talk or who would drink too much and say too much.

Willie Sutton, that skillful escape artist, had rarely made that mistake. He would lose himself in a totally unexpected environment where nobody knew him and nobody would look for him.

So far he had kept to the highlands. Now, for a little while at least, he would take to the low country. Consequently, he must avoid being seen from above.

Seated in his shadow he worked on the moosehide, scraping fragments of flesh from it, allowing the warm sun to reach it. The hide would make excellent moccasins, and he would be needing them.

Nothing moved in the terrain before him. Working on the hide, he took time to watch, ready to catch the slightest movement. He saw nothing but a bird now and again, and just before the sun disappeared he saw three moose come from the willows and amble slowly across the terrain. He stopped his work to watch, for if they were frightened while en route it would reveal a presence there. They walked across the area and disappeared into the trees. Rolling up his moosehide, he added it to his pack, and shouldering it, he left the trees and went down a dry watercourse toward the river.

That night he found an overhang by the river where the rocks had been somewhat warmed by the brief sun. There he bedded down and slept. Before dawn he was moving again.

A narrow stream flowed north through the tundra. There was a film of ice along its banks, no more. Here and there was a patch of thin snow. There were willows in plenty and occasional poplar or larch. He wandered on, pausing at intervals to listen and to watch the flight of birds or the movements of animals. He found no tracks of men, only animals.

It was very still, not a breath of air stirring. He walked

through the day and into the early evening. At night he found a place on a south-facing slope under some larch. There had been a blowdown there some years before and many of the trees stretched out above the bank of a watercourse, forming a roof. Beneath them he found a place for his camp.

Colonel Arkady Zamatev landed in Chersky. Lieutenant Suvarov awaited him as the plane landed. He led the way to a Volga parked near the airfield.

"No question about it, Colonel Zamatev. He has been seen in the forest. He was spotted by a high-flying plane, crossing a clearing."

"You reported this to Alekhin?"

Suvarov's lips tightened. "Comrade Alekhin says it was not him, but who else could it be?"

"Why does he not think it was the American?"

Suvarov shrugged. "He says the American would not cross a clearing at this time. He would go around it. That's absurd! Why go the long way around when he is obviously in a hurry?"

Zamatev said nothing. The Volga was taking them down a bumpy, icy street. Big concrete buildings, most of them five stories high, loomed about him. He looked at them, hating their bleak ugliness. Of course, in such a place as this, what could one expect? It was amazing they had built anything at all in this godforsaken country.

On the desk in the office prepared for him lay a series of reports. He scanned them rapidly. One and all they were, no matter how carefully worded, reports of failure. Not only failure to recapture the American, but losses of men and equipment.

"Any word from Comrade Lebedev?"

"Yes, sir. She is in Iman. The woman Baronas is there also. No sign of her father."

"She has arrested the woman?"

"Not yet, but she is sure she is there, possibly with some intention of crossing into China. She should have her by nightfall."

Zamatev sat down abruptly. He was exasperated. The Baronas woman was not that important. Why was Kyra wasting her time? She should be here, coordinating things, which she could do so very much better than this Suvarov. A nice

young man, but no imagination, too ready to accept the easy
way.

His hurried flight to Moscow had been on orders. He
had been called on the carpet, and his friend on the Politburo
had set it forth in plain, unvarnished terms: get the American
at once or he would be removed from his command.

"You have been a fool, Arkady," his friend had said.
"You began well, and you should have continued with a
series of small fry. Instead you became too ambitious. Taking
this American was a frightful risk. Admitting for the moment
that you carried it off well, you were still taking a chance of
international repercussions. Then you allowed him to escape."

"Nobody could have dreamed a man would attempt such
a thing—"

"Yet he did, and now he is making fools of you all.
Believe me, Arkady, if you do not capture this man and get
something to show for what you have done, you are through.
I can do no more for you. My friends will not accept failure."

"Shepilov—"

"I know about Shepilov. He has been recalled to his
station. There is enough for him to do without being occupied in this nonsense." He had paused. "And what about this
man Stephan Baronas and his daughter? What have they to
do with all this?"

Zamatev was surprised. How did they know about *him*?
But what did they not know? He spoke carefully. "The escaped prisoner was reported to have stopped for a time in a
village where Baronas lived. Baronas and his daughter seem
to have known him there, and we wanted them for questioning."

"How long ago was that?"

"Well, it was several months—"

"You have been wasting time, Arkady. As you say, that
was months ago. Whatever they knew then cannot apply
now. The man has fled hundreds of miles since then. Leave
them alone."

Zamatev hesitated, then said, "But if they aided an
enemy—?"

"We do not know that they did. In any event, the
important thing is to recapture this American." His friend
had turned to Zamatev, and his eyes were not friendly.
"Arkady, you have been a very able man. You have proved
helpful to others as well as myself. We all value that help, but

it is beginning to appear that you have lost your grip. It is a hard world, Arkady. My success depends much on the success of those whom I sponsor, as I have you. Do not fail me."

He took up his pipe from an ashtray. "I wish you to understand something, Arkady. Baronas and his daughter have friends, very important friends. They are to be allowed to leave the country."

"Yes, sir." Zamatev was astonished, but he hoped it did not show on his face.

"Very important friends, and as he is of no value to us, he is being permitted to leave. Do not interfere. Do you understand?"

He understood well enough, but now Kyra was in Iman and about to arrest the Baronas woman. If Natalya Baronas and her father were arrested now, there would be trouble. He, and Kyra as well, might find themselves spending the rest of their lives on duty in some such place as Chersky.

"Suvarov? Can you get a call through to Comrade Lebedev in Iman?"

"I think so, sir."

"Do it then. Tell her Baronas and his daughter are not to be arrested or interfered with in any way. Do you understand? And I want her here, *now*!"

Zamatev walked to the window and looked out over the bleak street and the gray blocks of concrete into the cheerless distance.

Baronas? Who would have believed it? The man was a Lithuanian, if he remembered correctly, some sort of a professor. Well, such men often made friends, powerful friends.

He shrugged. It was no business of his. He shoved his hands down in his pockets. His friend had certainly made it painfully clear. Catch the American and get something out of him, or he was through. All his dreams, his ambitions, for nothing. Once one had a mark like this against him, it was almost impossible to get going again.

He had no doubts about Kyra. She had become a tail to his kite, but if the kite would not fly—?

He walked to the door and looked into the outer office. "Let me know as soon as you have talked to Comrade Lebedev."

"You wish to speak to her?"

"Just convey my message, nothing more."

He walked back to his desk and sat down heavily. He must get into the field himself. He could not simply leave it to Alekhin, although the Yakut seemed confident enough.

On the wall, there was a great map showing the vast stretch of country between Chersky and the Bering Strait, everything from Magadan east. For a long time he stood, hands clasped behind his back, studying that map. Suvarov had placed a pin on the map at the place where the man had been seen. At least, where a man had been seen.

Suppose that man was not the American? Who could it be? And what would he be doing out in that miserable country at this time of year?

He returned to the door of the outer office. "Suvarov? I'll want a helicopter. Didn't I see an MIL-4 out there? I want it and as many men as it will safely carry with their equipment. I want it and the men ready first thing tomorrow. I am going into the field myself. And," he added, "you are going with me."

All right, he would show them what he was made of. He would have that American in his hands within hours.

He turned back to Suvarov. "That man who was seen? I want him, no matter who he is. I want him brought to me. Get some helicopters into the area. Make a thorough search. Alekhin says this is not our man, but I want to see for myself. I want to talk to that man."

Walking back to his desk, he dropped into a chair. He did not like all this running about. There were others to do that, but there was so much wasted effort, so much wasted time! Nobody really cared. That was the trouble.

No, he was wrong about that. Many people did care, and some worked very hard, for one reason or another, but not enough of them. The great problem was inertia.

By now the American was probably somewhere in the Chukchi Region or just over the line into the Koryak. It was wild country, but there were few forests, and the mountains were more icy and barren. The man would be more exposed.

They would get him now. They must get him.

The trouble was, back in Moscow they did not even grasp the sheer size of the country he had been dealing with. To find one man in all that vast area, especially one who wanted to hide and was skilled at it, was nearly impossible.

Suvarov appeared in the doorway. "Sir? I have not been

able to reach Comrade Lebedev. Perhaps if I were to fly
down there—?"

You would like that, wouldn't you? Zamatev said to
himself. "No," he said aloud. "I shall need you with me. Get
in touch with Comrade Yavorsky at my office. Tell her that
the Baronas father and daughter are not to be arrested. They
are to be left strictly alone. Tell her that Comrade Lebedev is
now in Iman for that purpose and must be stopped, stopped
at all costs."

Emma Yavorsky had never liked Kyra Lebedev, but
Kyra had to be reached somehow, and he would be off
searching for the American. It was a pity. Kyra was a lovely
and intelligent woman, but to fly in the face of orders would
be suicidal. Emma Yavorsky would not only stop her in time,
she would take pleasure in it. Maybe he could straighten
matters out later, but for now Kyra must be stopped at all
costs.

Suppose she did arrest them and had Stegman put them
to the question?

FORTY-THREE

Throughout the day, they waited. Several times cars drove by, but usually their street was deserted. It led to nowhere, and easier routes were available to anyone going in either direction. Natalya stood often at the dusty, flyspecked window looking across the river into China and freedom. Or what she hoped would be freedom.

It was cold, and they dared have no fire. The building where they were was supposed to be an old warehouse.

"This woman you saw? You believe it was the Lebedev woman?"

"You described her to me, and the man with her."

"They are searching for us, then. There could be no other reason why she would be here."

She drew her coat more tightly about her, clasping her arms about her body. Across the street, there were other warehouses and some ramshackle buildings along the river. There were old boat landings there and a wharf from which cargo had been loaded on riverboats long ago. Now they were gray, bare, harried by the wind. It was a bleak outlook, and so was hers if Potanin failed them.

Where was Joe Mack? There had been no word of him, but she had been nowhere she would be likely to hear. There was always gossip, but one had to be around, listening, at the places where gossip was repeated.

334

How could he ever escape? She remembered the woods and shivered. There had been brief moments when she had loved them, moments when her father was alive and they had walked out to see the flowers, to hear the birds, to watch for small animals, but the winters were so brutally cold, and it was a fierce struggle to gather fuel, even to keep alive. Often they had starved. There had been weeks on end when they had survived on less food than was needed for a child. Yet somehow they had survived, and then he had come.

Did she truly love him? Or was it that he had brought some strange magic into their colorless, empty lives? He had given them meat, but more than that he had given them hope. If he, pursued by them all, could believe in escape, believe in a future somewhere after this, then it was possible for them to believe also.

What was it that had drawn her to him? Undeniably, he was a striking figure of a man, but it had been something more. When with him, she felt warm, secure, safe. He was not blundering, wishing, complaining, or hopeless. He was going somewhere, and he knew where he was going and how to get there, and suddenly she did, too.

It was he who had given hope to her father. She could see that clearly now. He had become resigned to suffering, resigned to working out a poor existence in the taiga. Or he was becoming resigned.

Now she was here, and across the river was China. If only her father could have lived for this moment! Even if they did not escape, they would at least have tried, and they would have at least seen freedom.

What awaited them in China she did not know, but she knew that somehow they would prevail.

"I am afraid," Evgeny said, coming up beside her. "I have staked everything on this. If I fail now, there will be no further chance for me. I cannot survive another interrogation."

"You will survive. We are going to succeed, Father." She called him so because she could see it pleased him, and how much did he have now that could give him pleasure? "We are going to escape."

Suddenly he spoke. "I think we should leave here. I have a bad feeling about this place."

She had it, too. For several minutes now she had been finding the old building oppressive. "We can go over there," she said, indicating the old wharf. "We can go over there where nobody goes."

"Now," he said. "Let us go now."

She took up her small bundle and they waited, checking the narrow street each way and then giving a quick look around to see if anything had been left. Then they went out of the door and across the street. A cold wind was blowing, and they hurried to get into the lee of the battered old structure across the way. Even as they reached the wharf, they heard a car coming. The wharf was huge and empty, and the wall of the old building fronting it was blank and closed. Suddenly her eyes saw an old path running down beside the wharf.

"Quickly!" she said and almost ran down. Then they ducked under the wharf. It was dark and shadowed there, with only occasional bits of light coming through cracks in the wharf. There was a steep bank of earth sloping down to the rim of ice that bordered the river, and two old boats were tied there, one of them half filled with water filmed with ice. The other boat was empty except for some old nets.

"There!" Evgeny pointed. "Get into the boat and cover up with the nets."

Quickly, they scrambled into the boat and pulled the old nets over them. Then they lay very still.

They could hear the roar of a motor, the screech of brakes, and then a pounding on a door. Natalya lay very still, scarcely breathing, straining her ears to hear.

A door creaked, and there were voices. Then a door closed. The room would have been cold, and they had left no signs of their occupation. The place was as it had been when they had arrived.

She heard the crunch of boots on gravel and then on the wharf overhead. Then the feet retreated. After a moment she heard boots coming down the little path and pausing, and she saw the shadow of a man, apparently peering under the dock. Then she heard retreating footsteps.

After a while came the sound of cars starting and then driving away. She started to move, but Evgeny placed a hand on her shoulder. "Not yet," he said.

They lay still while the time ticked away, and after a long time, what must have been an hour, he sat up. Carefully, they got out of the boat and arranged the nets as they had found them. He sat down on the bank, choosing a piece of plank to keep off the frozen earth. She sat beside him.

"We must wait," he said. "The less movement the better, and it will not be long now."

It was growing dark when they emerged from under the wharf. There were scattered lights across the river. Her feet were almost frozen, and she stamped them on the wharf to get them warm again. Evgeny looked at his watch.

"We will stay here a little longer," he said.

"Lieutenant Potanin said fifteen minutes to midnight," she reminded.

He nodded. "We have a way to go, and we cannot hurry. Along the quiet streets would be better."

"What about the Chinese? What if they will not accept us?"

He shrugged. "We can only try, but they are usually friendly to anyone escaping from the Soviets. This is an old, old border, and there has been much trouble along it for centuries. Once, all this was considered part of China, and it is still shown as such on some of their maps."

Lights stabbed the darkness, reflecting from the open water and from the ice along the edges and the floes. "Now," he said, "we will go."

Coming up from the river, they stopped a minute, looking across at the blank old building that had briefly been a refuge. It looked cold and gray and dismal. Together they started along the street. He used his cane, moving slowly. She thought that surely they would be recognized, for if they were looking for a crippled old man and a young woman—

She said as much. "No," he said, "they will not expect to find you with me. They will expect your father."

"Yes, yes, of course."

Her father? She had buried him herself. Unable to dig a grave in the frozen earth, she had covered him with spruce boughs and then managed to cave part of a bank over him. He had said to her once, long ago, "When I die, remember that what you knew of me is with you always. What is buried is only the shell of what was. Do not regret the shell, but remember the man. Remember the father."

There were lights on the bridge, lights over the guardhouse, a gate across the bridge for wheeled traffic, and a smaller gate for pedestrians. At the far end of the bridge,

they could see another post. It was not until they were on the
approach to the bridge that she saw the Volga. It was standing in the darkness just off the bridge and across from them.
Its motor was running.

"Evgeny . . .?" she whispered.

"Keep walking," he said. "Do not look around."

It was no more than thirty yards to the guardhouse, but
it seemed the longest distance she had ever walked in her
life. Why didn't the watchers in the car stop them? The Volga
merely sat there, engine running, dark and threatening. At
any moment, she expected it to start up, to rush toward
them.

What should she do? Stop and wait? Run back toward
the town? Or run across the bridge? She knew of people who
had been shot trying to flee, but nonetheless, that was what
she would do. She would run, run as she had never run.
Maybe they would let her go, maybe she would be shot, but
she would run.

"Take your time," Evgeny whispered. "We are almost
there. Your lieutenant is standing up, watching us."

"Suppose he isn't on duty?"

"We will try anyway."

Now that they were so close, the old man was strong
again. His fears seemed to have vanished. "I have money,"
he said, "in Hong Kong. You will want for nothing. I shall see
to it."

"I want to go to America," she said.

"We will see to it," he replied confidently. "Now stay
calm. Let me talk."

Lieutenant Potanin stepped from the guardhouse as they
drew near. They could see two soldiers standing inside, warming their hands over a stove.

He looked quickly from one to the other. "This may get
me into trouble," he said, "but I shall do it." He turned
toward the pedestrian gate.

At that moment they heard the sound of a car. It was
some distance away but coming fast. He fumbled with the
lock, and the car wheeled onto the bridge.

Kyra Lebedev stepped quickly from the car. Stegman
got down on the other side. "Dr. Baronas! You are under
arrest!"

Evgeny turned so his face was in the light. "I am not Dr. Baronas," he said. "I am Evgeny Zhikarev."

"Ah? So it is you!" She turned to Natalya. "But you are Natalya Baronas, are you not? Where is your father?"

"He is dead. He died crossing the mountains."

"Ah? Too bad. Come now, both of you. You—"

A boot scraped on gravel, and a low, strong voice said, "Let them alone!"

Angrily, Kyra Lebedev turned. A big man in a heavy overcoat faced her. She stopped, suddenly dry mouthed and frightened.

"I am Bocharev," the big man said.

"But we have an order," Kyra protested, "an order for their arrest. The GRU—"

"I know all about it. The order has been countermanded." His eyes were cold. "You may go," he said. "You are not needed here."

Still, Kyra Lebedev hesitated. "But what shall I tell Colonel Zamatev?"

"He has already been informed, as you will hear." He pointed. "Go now! You are not needed here!"

She hesitated no longer. Stegman was already getting into the car.

From an inside pocket, Bocharev took a sheaf of papers and handed them to Natalya. "Your passport, your visa."

He glanced at Evgeny. "This is not your father?"

She explained, and he nodded. "Do not worry. I shall see his body is found and buried properly." He glanced at Evgeny again. "How about you, comrade?"

"I have papers, comrade." Evgeny's voice was trembling. "I—"

"You have assisted this young lady," Bocharev replied. He turned to Natalya. "Sometime, in a moment, remember my son."

"I shall never forget him," she replied. "Nor you."

"Go now, quickly." Bocharev turned to Lieutenant Potanin. "Pass them, Lieutenant. Their papers are in order."

"Yes, comrade!"

Bocharev stood alone, watching them go, his hands thrust deep in his pockets. Then, at last, he walked back to the Volga.

At the end of the bridge a Chinese officer was awaiting

them. Natalya turned and looked back, lifting a hand in farewell. She saw the lights of the car go on and saw it turn away.

"There are good men everywhere," she said, recalling another.

"Yes," Zhikarev agreed. "I only wish they had louder voices."

Then they crossed a border into an uncertain future. Natalya vowed silently to reach America, where, she dared hope, Joe Mack would somehow be waiting for her, to share the dream he had inspired.

FORTY-FOUR

Within hours after his arrival at Chersky, Colonel Zamatev had motorized patrols driving slowly along the road, if such it could be called, that led from Chersky to Talovka and along that from Talovka to Ust'chaun on the north coast. The two roads cut across the country east of the Omolon River.

Several patrols would work each road continuously until further notice. There were also patrols along the river, and the guards on the few bridges had been alerted.

A very subdued Kyra Lebedev had arrived the following morning, reporting to Zamatev. He listened impatiently, his mind on other things. He waved a hand of dismissal when she completed her report.

"It is well. They will not be needed. Whatever passed between them does not matter. The Baronas woman is unimportant to us. Our man," he touched the map, "is somewhere in this area.

"Patrols will be driving these roads, passing constantly. If he is seen, they will follow and apprehend him.

"I have sent Lieutenant Suvarov to visit personally all the fishing ports and villages along the Bering Sea and the Strait, and somewhere out there is Alekhin. There are few places in which to hide out there, and we shall have him."

He paused. "A man was seen in the Kolyma Mountains

341

north of Magadan. I have sent helicopters to find and bring him in."

"Do you believe him to be the American?"

He shrugged. "Who knows? What would anybody else be doing in that country?"

He walked to the window and stood there, hands clasped behind his back. "We must be alert, Kyra." His voice softened. "This means too much to us both. That prisoner must be apprehended. My career depends upon it." He turned toward her. "As you have surmised, yours does also. You have become too deeply involved in all this, although it was your wish."

Her lips tightened, but she said nothing. It was true. She had insisted on being involved, and now she wished she had never opened her mouth.

"He cannot escape," she said. "If we fail, he cannot get past the Buffer Zone and the radar."

"Do not be too sure. The man is like a ghost. A dozen times we have thought we would take him, and each time he has simply vanished. I am no longer sure of anything where he is concerned. He is not a man but a phantom!"

Kyra waited, apprehensive but determined. "Arkady?" she spoke gently. "I must talk to you. Something terrible has happened."

He turned, surprised by her tone. "What now?"

"My sister has been arrested by Comrade Shepilov. It was in connection with the American's escape." Carefully, she explained. That Zamatev was irritated, she could see. Obviously he wanted no more to do with Shepilov, and to reach him now, to ask a favor, was almost out of the question.

"What does she know?"

"Nothing, except—"

"Except what?"

"Her husband, Ostap. He was always meeting people who were on the fringe of things, black-market people and such. I went to them for you. Ostap always knows so much, so much that is talked about by such people. Much of it is probably nonsense, of course, but he always knows when something is happening. I believed he might help us to find the American. Also, to tell us what Shepilov was doing. He knew all about that."

"He did?" Zamatev was skeptical.

"You must understand, Arkady, that people like that always know what is happening. Very little is secret from them. There is always somebody who talks, you know.

"It was he who told me about Shepilov using the trappers and also that they were not anxious to help. They could, of course, if they wished. They do not like Comrade Shepilov, however."

"Where is this Ostap now?"

"He fled to the forest when Katerina was arrested. I have not heard from him or from her."

He shrugged. "I can do nothing for your Katerina now. Shepilov would simply say he knew nothing about her, and I could do nothing. It is better that we show no interest. He will discover there is nothing there, and he may release her. If she is sent to prison, well, maybe I can do something then."

Suddenly he swore. When she looked at him, surprised, he said, "It is probably this Ostap who is causing us trouble. We are looking now for a man who was seen in the forests near Magadan whom some believed might be the American."

"He could help us. He knows the trappers. He knows what is happening among the dissidents, among the Jews—"

"Do not speak to me of Jews. They are trouble. I want nothing to do with them."

"This man you are looking for? If it is Ostap, I could talk with him? He might know something, and he would tell me whatever he knows."

He shrugged. "Very well. If we catch him."

Joe Mack took his time. Every mile behind him was a victory now, but every mile before him a danger. He overlooked a vast plain now in which there were many small lakes, an area he must avoid. Up here, he could see the lakes easily and the spaces between them. Once down on their level, he would no longer have that advantage and could easily be trapped against one of their shores. The ice, if any, would be treacherous.

His map showed him he was somewhere north of a village or town named Gizhiga. Although there were few roads in the area before him, those few would be patrolled. The area of the search had narrowed, and the search would have grown more intense.

He stood now in a small cluster of larch, carefully examining the country before him, choosing a route to be followed and an alternative if something happened to force him to change.

The air was unbelievably clear, with not a cloud in the sky and no mist in any of the hollows. Far off he occasionally caught a glint of something that might be sunlight on a windscreen. If that was the case, there was an unusual amount of traffic on that road, if such it was.

Nothing moved down below, except near the closest lake, where there were several moose. They seemed to be feeding along the lakeshore.

What he did not know was that Alekhin had landed, only hours before, in Gizhiga. Another thing he did not know was that not two hundred yards away, hidden in the brush, a man was watching him.

Ostap was no woodsman. He had fled Magadan when Shepilov arrested his wife, barely escaping. He had gone to the woods, to a place where trappers sometimes met. None were there when he arrived, but there was food, fuel, and warmer clothing.

He was in serious trouble, and so was Katerina. She knew nothing, but that would not help her and might even work against her. It was always better, Ostap had discovered, to have something to tell.

On this morning he had walked out into the forest and climbed a small knoll. There, in a place sheltered from the wind, he had sat down to study the country. Almost at once he had seen the American, and from the first glimpse he had no doubt who it was on whom he looked.

The man's very caution was a dead giveaway. Frightened as well as intrigued, Ostap had the sense to remain still. Had he moved, his presence would have been revealed. His heart began to beat heavily.

Talk about luck! There he was, the man they all wanted. If he could only capture him—!

But that was foolish. Whatever else he was, Ostap was no fighter. He was a trader, a conniver, a trickster, if you will. To attempt to capture the American was out of the question. Of course, the idea had occurred, but it fled his mind in the same instant.

The point was, he knew where the American was. *He*

knew! That kind of knowledge was worth money. It was worth a trade; it was a chance to save Katerina. For a moment he hesitated: Katerina or the money? No, it had to be Katerina. There was one thing he valued above money, and that was his personal comfort. Katerina took care of him. Above all, she understood him. She accepted his foibles, his trickiness, and his weaknesses and took care of him anyway. He could find other women, he knew. Occasionally, he had, but they were too demanding of him, of money, of his time. Katerina took him as he was, and was therefore priceless. Of course, he told himself, he might get a little money on the side, too.

But whom must he speak to? He was far from Magadan now, completely out of touch with anybody there. Besides, if he went back into that town they would arrest him.

It must be somebody nearer, somebody involved in the search. But if he were to bargain for Katerina, it must be someone in command. Someone who could actually say yes or no. That meant, as far as he was concerned, either Shepilov or Zamatev.

He could not deal with Shepilov. That one would have him up and given the treatment until he told whatever he knew. With Zamatev he might bargain, and with Zamatev he had an in. He had Kyra Lebedev.

He would watch a bit longer and see what direction the American took, and then he would head for Evensk.

He held himself very still, waiting. Would he cross among the lakes? It was a long trek, and there was much swampy country down there, still partly frozen, however.

Joe Mack edged along the woods and started off to the north. Waiting only a few minutes longer, Ostap got to his feet and ran down the dim trail toward the road below. Even as he approached it, he heard the sound of motors and saw four cars coming along the road toward Evensk. The cars slowed and stopped when they saw him, and a man in the lead car motioned for him to approach.

Wary, but unable to avoid the meeting, he went up to the man who had motioned. He had never seen him before, but he knew at once that he faced the legend. This was Alekhin.

"Where are you going?"

"To Evensk. I must speak to Colonel Arkady Zamatev or to Comrade Lebedev."

Alekhin eyed him thoughtfully, his flat, heavy-lidded eyes revealing nothing. "Why must you speak with him?"

Ostap hesitated. If he told Alekhin, he would get nothing, nothing at all. "I have information about the American." Then, firmly, he added, "It is for one of them only. Nobody else."

Alekhin stared at him. This one he could twist in his hands. He could wring him out like a rag, but no one intercepted information meant for Zamatev.

Leaning from his seat, he called to the driver behind him. "Boris! Take this one to Evensk! Call Colonel Zamatev! If you cannot, speak to Comrade Lebedev! Quick now! Then bring him back to me unless the Colonel wishes him."

He looked at Ostap. "You speak to him. Tell him. You better have good information, or I will speak to you after. Go now."

In Evensk, the connection was not a good one, but Boris got Kyra on the phone for him. "What can you tell us, Ostap?" She sounded abrupt, impatient.

"I have seen him," he said, "the American."

"*What?*"

"I want Katerina released," he said, "and a little something for our trouble. You see?"

"You have actually *seen* him?"

"He is not waiting for you," Ostap said, "but if you move now, he cannot have gone more than a few miles."

"Describe him."

Ostap was a good observer. His description was quick, accurate and brief.

"It was one of Alekhin's men who called. How did you meet him?"

"Alekhin has gone north searching for him. I told him nothing. I want Katerina released."

"I know," she replied brusquely, "and a little something for yourself!"

"I could have called Comrade Shepilov," he replied.

"Katerina will be freed. Take Alekhin to where you saw him. I shall be there within the hour. If this is just a story—!"

"It is not."

When he left the office he said to Boris, "Take me to Alekhin. I know where the American is."

"I heard you," Boris replied. "You should have told him on the road."

"Katerina is my wife. Shepilov arrested her. I want her free."

"And a little something for yourself," Boris said. "All the Soviet Union needs is a few more such patriots."

Ostap flushed, but he did not reply. Boris was a very tough, competent-looking man. The less said to such a man the better.

Boris was speaking on the radio. Then they drove off, moving rapidly. Ostap hung on desperately as the car careened around sharp curves and raced over bumpy roads that were hardly more than trails.

Alekhin was waiting beside the road. He reached a hand into the car and jerked Ostap out of his seat. "Tell me! Where?"

Frightened, Ostap led the way to where he had stood and pointed. "Over there, at the edge of the trees."

"Stay back!" Alekhin ordered. Then he walked over. Ostap watched and then said, "By that old tree! To the left!"

Alekhin moved and then stopped and began to look around, very slowly, very carefully. The American left so little sign. He moved a step, looking, then looking again.

Yes, there was a slight indentation in the moss at the foot of the tree. Something or somebody had been there. Slowly, carefully, he began to work out the sign left by the American. As always, there was very little.

He walked back to Boris and indicated what must be done. "There are roads on three sides! I want patrols, very slow patrols! Night and day! He must not escape this area! You understand?"

"I do. It will be done."

"What of him?" Boris jerked a thumb at Ostap.

"Let him stay. We have no time to take him back. Besides, the Colonel wishes to speak to him."

Alekhin paused, thinking about it, and then he added, "If we do not have him by dark, I want cars with headlights on the road. I want him taken. I want him stopped. If you must shoot, shoot at his legs. Break his legs, but do not kill him."

*   *   *

By midday Joe Mack knew he was trapped. Through a gap in the scattered trees he glimpsed several cars on the road below. Moving further north he glimpsed more cars cutting him off in that direction. So they knew he was in here. Somehow they had seen him. Somehow they knew without doubt he was here. Warily he worked his way further north and west into the roughest terrain. They had cornered him in one of the few places around that had roads on three sides, even though they were scarcely more than trails.

At a steady trot, he headed north. They knew where he was, and this time they would not let him get away. He would try, but his chances were slight. They were going to get him, so what could he do?

He could try to escape again, of course, but they would give him no chance this time. They would cripple him or put him so tightly in manacles that he could not escape. Yet, suppose he could?

He would hide his bow and arrows. He would hide his knife. He would hide the little meat he had that was dried and smoked. He would hide his goatskin coat, or better still, the suit and shirt.

Soon they would be making a sweep with helicopters and then ground troops. He could, of course, fight until they killed him, until they had to kill him.

That was one way.

He moved on north into the woods, but when he had gone only a little further he saw from a mountain ridge, saw afar off, the glint of sunlight on the windshields of cars. He could try to run between them, but they would be expecting that, and they would shoot him down.

As he walked, his eyes searched for a place to hide, any place at all where they might not find him.

There was nothing but bare rocks, sparse trees, and occasional clusters of birch. North of here there were, he had heard, no trees at all.

He slowed to a walk. He had the AK-47 and some ammunition. He had the pistol. He would cache the pistol, too. But it must be soon.

Well, Joe Mack, he said, *you gave them something to worry over. Now we will see.* To hold out here, where defensible positions were few, would be wasted effort. He could get a few of them before they got him, but he would not get the ones he wanted.

He walked now, choosing a careful way, ever alert for a place to hide. He found nothing that they would not find within minutes. Some stretches had had many good places for concealment, but this seemed to have none.

Was it all over, then? *Talya*, he said to himself, *you would not like to see this. But we had our dream. We had it for a little while.*

He could not give up. He could not surrender. But these men were not the men he wanted. Zamatev was the one and Alekhin. These others were but tools to be used by them. Good men, some of them, men who did what they were told the best they knew how.

He fought to keep cool. Now he must think, he must plan. Night was coming, and with night there might be a chance.

From a ridge he looked down toward the road. Two cars had stopped, and the soldiers were talking. Others were scattered along the road, the road that was barely a trail.

Crouching at the base of a tree, he tried to think of something he might do, anything he could do.

Nothing. There was nothing. He was trapped.

He could expect some rough treatment. He could expect torture. They would take no more chances with him now. He thought of Pennington's family, never to know their husband and father had not abandoned them.

Never for a moment had he forgotten them or what his message to them would be.

Alekhin! The big Yakut would win after all.

Slowly, carefully, he moved down the slope, keeping from sight. He knew that Alekhin was behind him. He knew his trail was slowly being worked out, and Alekhin would have soldiers with him. There were waiting lines of soldiers and moving cars on three sides now and he was moving down toward the north. Behind him was Alekhin.

He looked at the cars and the men. Could he shoot his way through? There was no chance. There were simply too many, and they were too scattered out.

He crouched by a tree to study a route and saw a long crack in the rock. Suddenly he moved. He laid his bow and arrows in the crack, thrusting the pistol and ammunition into the quiver. When all was hidden, he placed bark over it and then leaves. The earth was too frozen to use.

They had seen him with the AK-47, so he kept it.

He could go down there shooting, but he doubted if they would let their men fire, except at his legs. They wanted him alive, and he did not want to be crippled. If he were crippled, his last chance would be gone. He was going to need his legs.

Zamatev was not down there. Neither was Alekhin.

He walked down the slope and stepped into the open.

"Are you looking for me?" he asked.

FORTY-FIVE

They were wary. Slowly, guns pointed, they moved in around him. One jerked the AK-47 from his hand; another, a man in civilian clothes, struck him viciously in the kidney with a rifle butt. He started to fall, caught himself, and remained erect. His hands were jerked behind him and handcuffs put on.

Several men moved in around him, pushing the soldiers away. These were KGB, and there seemed no good feeling between them and the soldiers, who watched with expressionless faces. Joe Mack stared straight ahead, his mind busy.

What else could he have done? He was surrounded, there were too many of them, they were closing in, and up there he had no place to hide. Not even a good place to make a stand. It was bare rock, a few scattered trees, a few spots of snow.

He knew he would be beaten. He expected to be tortured. He could endure pain. He had been through that before, but what he must do was escape again. If they had shot his legs from under him, he would have had no chance. Now there was still hope.

Long ago, when his people had been captured by other Indians, they had endured torture, and as the poet had said, they 'had not winced or cried aloud.' Indians had known how to endure pain and to laugh at those who tortured them. Often, if they showed bravery, the tortures were stopped and they were adopted into the tribe. Some of the mountain men had survived the same treatment. Joe Mack had taken the greatest gamble of his life, and the chances of escape were a thousand to one against him, yet shot down and crippled he would have no chance at all.

An officer was on a radio, talking. The soldiers stood around, staring curiously. He ignored them, standing tall, looking toward the mountains where he had hoped to be. His heart was pounding heavily and he was asking himself if he was brave enough, if he was the man he wanted to be, the man he had trained himself to be. *Now*, he whispered to himself, *you will find out*. He had been told the story of a great-grandfather who had been captured by the Blackfeet and tortured and finally burned at the stake. Even as the flames rose around him, he had laughed at them. He had sung his death song in a voice that did not quaver, and the Blackfeet had marveled. An old warrior of their tribe had told him the story. Was he that kind of man?

One of the KGB men came to him. "Alekhin comes," he said. "If he leaves anything, we get our chance."

Joe merely looked at the man, and infuriated, the man slapped him across the mouth. Joe Mack's expression did not change. Angered, the man shoved him, then kicked his feet from under him. When he fell the man kicked him brutally in the ribs. Then he stepped closer, drawing back his leg for another kick. Joe Mack rolled over, the kick missed, and the man fell. The soldiers laughed.

Furious, the man lunged to his feet and caught up a heavy club. Frantically, he began beating Joe Mack, striking him on the head, shoulders, and back. Bobbing his head, Joe Mack avoided the worst of the blows, but his scalp was split and blood trickled down over his face.

Suddenly a car wheeled up and stopped. Alekhin stepped down. Joe Mack knew him at once by his size and the small blaze of white where the hair had lost color over an old scar.

Alekhin walked over. "So! We have you. Now we shall see!" He turned to the KGB men and motioned to an old stable that stood nearby. "Take him inside."

A Russian officer started to speak and Alekhin turned his back on him, saying over his shoulder, "You are not needed anymore. Go!"

Ostap got out of the Volga. He stared at the blood on Joe

Mack's face and felt sick inside. He did not know what to do. Nobody had sent him away, and he had no way in which to leave. He must stand and wait for them. He was frightened.

The officer had turned away, angrily. His men were forming up and moving to their trucks. Ostap wanted to go with them, but he had not been dismissed and he feared to displease Alekhin.

It was very cold, and he wished he was back in Magadan. Was Katerina free? Had they lived up to their bargain? Why would they want her, anyway? She knew nothing.

He hunched his shoulders against the wind and shoved his hands deep into his pockets. Several KGB men were standing around, talking among themselves.

Suddenly he heard a loud thump from within the stable, then more. He heard no screams. One of the KGB men came over to him, grinning. "They will teach him! They are artists! They know how to beat a man! You will hear him scream!"

He did not scream. Two men came out after a while, dripping with perspiration, their fists bloody. Two others went in. Ostap turned away, sick to his stomach. He had done this. He had told them where the American was. Many times before, when hearing of such things, he had laughed and shrugged. "Serves them right!" He had said that, said it several times.

He could hear the impact of blows, hear the grunts of the KGB men as they struck.

He walked off a little way, shuddering, wishing he dared leave, that he even had a way to leave. The KGB cars were the only ones left.

Alekhin came out and gave orders. Zamatev was coming. They were to put up a tent for him. He would ask some questions here. Then they would take the American away and fly him back to prison.

Alekhin smiled. "No more beatings!" he said. "We must leave something for the good Colonel!" He looked around, his eyes going from one to the other. "But we've softened him up! We've softened him for the Colonel! Now let's have a drink!"

The tent was rapidly going up, and some folding chairs and a table were taken inside. Alekhin breathed deeply of the mountain air. Suddenly his eyes lighted on Ostap.

"Ah? It is you! Come have a drink with us, and then I'll

send you back to Evensk! I would come, too, but the good Colonel wants to see him before he is moved." He chuckled. "Not that there is much to move."

"I did not hear him cry out," Ostap burst out involuntarily. "I thought—"

Alekhin shrugged. "He did not cry. He is tough, that one." He smiled, looking at Ostap from his flat black eyes. "Zamatev will see to that, and after Zamatev, me again." He clapped Ostap on the shoulder. "It is good! Without your help, we'd not have had him! Maybe for weeks!"

Ostap glanced toward the stable. The door had been closed and an iron pin on a short chain dropped in place to keep the hasp closed.

Two KGB men loitered near the Volga Alekhin had come in. A third man stood near another Volga. "Mikhail," Alekhin said, "I shall give this lad a drink. Then you can drive him back, eh? No need for him to be here, and you won't be needed."

Alekhin took Ostap's arm. "Come! One glass of vodka before the road!" Alekhin pinched his arm. "Maybe two glasses, eh?"

It was an hour before he staggered into the darkness outside the tent. The two KGB men were sitting in Alekhin's Volga, sharing a bottle.

Ostap had to pass by the stable to get to the other Volga, where Mikhail seemed to be asleep, waiting.

What made him do it, he did not know, but he lifted the pin and let it down against the door. He opened the hasp. "Now!" he said, and walked on to the Volga.

Mikhail awoke. "Good!" he said. "I want to get into town." He glanced at Ostap. "I've a friend there, and maybe she has a friend. Do you have any rubles?"

"Some. I'd like to meet your friend."

He hunched down in the seat, trying not to think about anything at all. Why had he done that? The man was helpless, but— He shook his head to drive away the thought. If they found out, *he* would be the one in trouble.

Lying on the filthy floor in the freezing cold, his body heavy with pain, Joe Mack heard the pin drop, heard the low voice and the word *"Now!"*

His brain was fogged with pain. Some vagrant thought

told him he had a concussion. What did it mean, "Now!"? Suddenly through the fog in his brain an arrow of clear light penetrated.

"*Now?*" And the rattle of a chain. He shook his head and almost passed out at the resulting agony.

Now! He rolled to his knees, fighting the agony the movement caused, and brought his handcuffed wrists down over his buttocks. Rolling on his back he drew his knees up to his chest and put his feet through the circle of arms and cuffs, so they were now in front of him. Somebody had lifted the pin! Perhaps the door would open. He forced himself to listen, and he heard nothing but subdued voices and, from somewhere outside, laughter.

He caught hold of one of the posts that supported the stable roof and pulled himself up. Then he leaned there, his brain swimming. He staggered and fell against the next post. He held himself there, forcing himself to listen. His face felt stiff and strange. He lifted his hands and touched it carefully. His face was caked with blood, and his hair. When he moved, pain shot through him. He thought he also had a broken rib.

He fought to clear his fogged brain. He must think. He must act. Somebody was outside. Somebody would be on guard. They believed they had beaten him into helplessness. Maybe they had. He could only try. He took a careful, trembling step to the door. Gently, he touched it with his fingers. A crack of light showed.

Ever so carefully, he widened the crack. There was a pyramidal tent opposite with a light inside and several men sitting. He could see their shadows against the light. He saw a Volga with two men sitting in it, their backs to him, talking. One man's hand hung outside, holding a bottle. Beyond, close together, stood three trucks.

His head was heavy with pain, and he had trouble bringing his eyes into focus. Inside him, something was pushing, driving, something that said, *Now! Now!* And something else that warned him there was no other time than now.

He took a step, staggered and almost fell, caught himself, and moved closer to the Volga. The door of the car was open, and the hand holding the bottle was outside. He could hear the man mumbling, and he heard a snore. The other man was asleep!

A step closer. Another step. His forearm slid across the

man's throat, and the other hand slipped into place. The KGB man reared up, struggled briefly, then subsided. Lifting him from the car, Joe Mack frisked him quickly, expertly. He took the man's pistol and ammunition. Walking around the car, Joe jerked the drunken man from his seat behind the wheel and threw him to the ground. As the man started to rise, he kicked him.

For a moment then, Joe Mack stood still. His head was spinning and his eyes still would not focus properly. He steadied himself, and then kneeling, he searched the man he had kicked, recovering another pistol and ammunition.

At the car, he felt for the keys. They were in the ignition. He was in a fog, almost as if he were drunk himself, but some inner drive was pushing him. On the back seat of the car was a gun, different from but similar to an AK-47. He picked it up and turned toward the tent. At that moment the flap was thrown back and a man emerged. His brain buzzing, Joe Mack turned the gun toward the tent and let go with a long, continuous burst. Then, turning, he sprayed the trucks with gunfire. He shot into the nearest gas tank and saw flames leap up and the wind catch them.

Getting into the Volga, he turned the car into the road and drove away. Behind him he heard a dull boom as a gas tank exploded.

A dim road took off toward the north and he accepted it. His eyes, almost swollen shut from the beating, offered only slits from which to see. With his fingers he tried to push the swollen openings wider, without much luck. His head throbbing, his body in agony with every move, he drove north. Then, like a drunken man, he began to sing "The Frozen Logger."

The road was winding and bumpy, a mere trail most of the time, but he drove steadily, and after driving for a time he switched off the lights. The moon was up, and he could see enough to drive.

His thoughts fought for acknowledgment, but his brain was foggy. Where was he? In Siberia. He was in a Volga, on a road going—? He did not know where. Worry intruded itself. There was something he had to do, something which he must acknowledge. It was—

He had to leave this car. It was such an easy way to

travel, but it held him to a road and they would be looking along roads. They would be looking soon.

They had not taken his watch. They had searched him for a gun. The rest was left for Alekhin.

And Alekhin was probably dead.

No, he did not know Alekhin was dead. He had fired a burst or two into the tent. The light had gone out, and he had heard some scrambling, and the tent had caught fire. Several of them might have escaped.

How long had he been driving? He did not know. Too long, probably. They would have helicopters looking for him again. Miles unrolled beneath him. He was not going fast; one could not over this road.

There was a river ahead. He could see moonlight on the ice. Stopping the car, he got out and went through it carefully. Emergency rations for two, two bottles of unopened vodka, and some further ammunition. He loaded his pockets, turned the car toward the river, and drove it under some overhanging willows. There he left it and turned eastward into the mountains.

He had to have rest. His legs, body, and head were badly bruised and beaten. Every step was sheer agony, but he pushed on. Snow was almost entirely absent, but the earth was frozen and rough. There were few trees. He was going to have trouble finding cover. He plodded on, stupid with pain and whatever had happened to his brain. A concussion, he told himself. He hoped that was all it was.

He should have taken a coat from one of the KGB men. It was cold, and all he had was a fur robe taken from the Volga. He drew it tight around him and hobbled on. Twice he fell, and each time it was a struggle to rise.

He was no longer thinking well. He was aware enough to realize that. He kept thinking of Talya, expecting to see her. But how could he see her here?

He no longer had a map. What river was that where he had left the Volga? It was a large river. It could have been the Omolon.

He fell, catching himself with his hands and lacerating the palms on the rough, frozen earth. He got up. He could go no further. He looked at the cuffs. He had to get rid of them.

He stared around, blinking slowly. He did not know

where he was. He knew what to do about the cuffs. He had a shim, a bit of wire.

East, he had to go east. He must go east. That was the way his ancestors had gone, the ancient ones who had followed the game to America in the years before there was a Bering Strait.

Bering Strait? What was that? Something to be needed, to be sought for. He stumbled on, then went down into a creek bed and found a place where a bank offered shelter from the wind.

He would build a fire. He needed a fire. He did not want to freeze. But a fire would attract attention. No, not if there was no smoke.

Dry wood. He needed dry wood. Fumbling, he got the wood together. He found some dry moss, gathered some dry brown grass and bundled it together. He built a cone of thin sticks over it and struck a match. Huddling close to the fire, he got out the thin strip of metal and went to work on the cuffs. They were old-fashioned cuffs, but his hands were bruised and clumsy. When he had them off, he put vodka on the cuts. He wiped it dry with a handkerchief and the fur of his robe. He capped the bottle and huddled under the bank and tried to sleep.

FORTY-SIX

Three weeks later Joe Mack huddled in a cave above one of the minor tributaries of the Oklan River. The terrible beating he had taken had not sapped his courage, but something had. He was not even sure of what it was, except that he was very ill.

Day after day he had slogged along through storm and sun, working his way, mostly by night when there was any night, toward the east. He had camped in the cold, slept on boughs over icy ground. His feet were in terrible shape, and desperately he needed moccasins.

When the emergency rations taken from the Volga had given out, he had subsisted on marmots, even voles, and occasionally a ptarmigan.

Shortly after he abandoned the Volga, the country had been crisscrossed by helicopters and planes, and during most of that time he had huddled in a niche in a clay bank behind some dead poplars and a few straggling willows, a place planes flew over time and again, the searchers never imagining that even a marmot might conceal itself there. For three days he had had nothing to eat; then he caught some fish in a trap he had woven from plant fibers.

Spring was here, and the tundra was aglow with wild-flowers. They were flowers found above timberline in his own country.

He made a new bow and arrows, as well as a sling, but it was the sling that served him best. He had found the cave by accident, while kneeling on an icy rock near a small stream. As he had started to rise he had seen the opening. It was not three feet wide and scarcely that in height. It was masked by some dwarfed stone pine, and when he examined it he found a spacious cave with a sandy floor.

He was not the first to use the cave. Someone else, long ago, had built fires here. He found the crack used for a chimney and gathered driftwood along the stream and broken branches from under the stone pine.

For the first time in days he was able to be warm, and in another gorge a half mile away he found some birch. He gathered bark to make a crude raincoat for himself and used some of the leaves to mix with vodka as a rubdown for his bruised legs.

Despite the fact that spring had come, the nights were piercingly cold, the skies very clear, and the stars unbelievably bright. He was always cold, huddling above his fire like some Stone Age creature. He made moccasins of the skins of marmots, but they wore through quickly, and he could find no larger animals. Occasionally he came upon the droppings of mountain goats, but saw none of them. Once he came on the sign of a very large bear, a huge beast, judging by the size of the tracks. He comforted himself with the thought that no bear of that size could get into this cave now, although once the opening had been considerably larger. Floods had piled up sand and rocks until much of the original opening had become covered.

He existed like an animal, and a poor creature at that, with little food and never enough of a fire to really become warm. Fuel was scarce, and soon he must move on.

Here and there on the smooth rocks he had seen scratches left by glaciers in the remote past, but there was no evidence of them in the low country. They seemed only to have affected the higher rock formations.

He must move on. He told himself this as he huddled, shivering over his small fire. He must move on, find another place, try to find some large animals that he might eat. How long since he had not starved? How long since he had anything but the most meager meal?

Yet it had been days now since he had seen a plane, days

without seeing a helicopter. No doubt he had been given up for dead, and well he might be. He had been kicked and pounded, struck with clubs and doubled belts, but he knew that was nothing to what awaited him if he were recaptured. Such beatings were sheer brutality, not the refinements of torture that he could expect from Zamatev.

He dreaded the thought of moving. He dreaded the cold, the wind, the nights without a fire, the cold, icy rains.

It would be easier, far easier to just lie down here and die.

Why fight a losing battle? Even if he got to the coast, how could he ever get across the Bering Strait or the Chukchi Sea?

Yet when morning came he took up his bow and arrows and started once more. He had never gone back for the things he had cached. He had feared to lose the time, so he had driven the Volga until the gas was almost gone.

Had they found the car? No doubt, although he had left it hidden under the willows and standing on ice that by this time had melted.

He no longer thought of Alekhin or Zamatev. Nor did he even think of Natalya. All that was far away and in another world, a world of much meat and of at least a little warmth. For weeks now, he had been merely surviving, and for what? If found now he was in no shape to resist or even to try to escape.

He walked slowly up a shallow draw toward the crest of a low hill. He picked his way over bare rocks. Ice still lingered in shady places, and a small trickle of a stream found its way down a deep crack. From long habit, he approached the crest with infinite care and then peered over.

He had expected more of the same terrain. Instead he looked across a tremendous valley, many miles wide and through the center of which there was obviously a river. He could not see it, but he could see where one had to be, and many small lakes. Below him, there was a road or trail, and some six or seven miles away, a town and an airfield. Between himself and the town there was tundra, with no cover except along some of the smaller streams where there were clumps of Manchurian poplar and tight thickets of willow. There was simply no way he could cross without being seen. Wearily, he turned back and went down the mountain and began working his way through the low hills toward the north.

Now he must be doubly careful, for he was within the vicinity of people, and planes would occasionally be flying to or taking off from that airfield.

Remembering the map, he thought the river was the Penzhina, and if so, it flowed down from the mountains before him and he would have it to cross.

That night, descending the mountain, he came upon three goats lying among the rocks. They were accustomed to enemies coming up from below, and because the wind was from them and toward him, he was unnoticed.

His first arrow was a kill. One of the goats ran off, but the old ram stood up, head down as if to attack. He was a big fellow and surly, yet when Joe Mack began to approach, he backed off. Then with many a backward look, he went away.

He skinned out the goat to save the hide, then cut out what meat he needed. Descending into a hollow, he found a secluded nook and built a fire, roasting his meat. It was his first good meal in weeks. He packed the rest of the meat and spent some time working on the hide before rolling it up. He doubted the small smoke had drawn attention, but wished to get away from the vicinity in the event it had been noticed.

Joe Mack was alone upon the mountains, and he idled his way across vast slabs of tilted rock, edging ever north, avoiding the few villages and the fewer houses. He ate good meat again and gained in strength. In a stream where a warm spring flowed, he bathed, enjoying the warm water. That evening before sundown, he killed a deer and renewed his meat supply.

He kept to low ground when possible and walked through the larch forests when he crossed the Mayn. He was nearing the sea again. Sometimes in the morning he could almost taste the salt wind. For days he had seen nothing human, nor had he seen a plane. Yet he knew they would not have given up. They would be seeking him even more seriously.

His wounds were healed. His jaw was back to normal. His eyes could focus again, and the ache in his skull seemed to have gone away. Sometimes he would stop to lift rocks, building back the muscle he had lost.

He made pants of buckskin and a coat from the skin of the mountain goat. He made a belt to carry his pistols and a quiver for his arrows. He carried the bow in his hand, and he walked with an easier step.

How long since his escape? Spring had come, summer and now fall, and another winter lay over the edge of the world, waiting to kill him.

"Not this time, old friend," he said aloud. "I shall be gone, or killed by others."

Twice during the day he saw birds of the sea. Once he saw some gulls, and another time what he believed was a tern. He walked upon a mountain and saw the sea's reflection in the sky. He was close, and over there, across the horizon, was Alaska, was America, his country, from which he had been too long away.

This was the way by which his people had come. He only knew what the scholars said, for his people had no written language, and tales told by a campfire have a way of changing and growing or even lessening in the passage of time. In any event, that over yonder was his land, his home. There lay the mountains of his birth and the soil to which his people had given their blood and their flesh. They had fought well in their time, they had won many battles and lost a few, but they had died well when their time came.

"Do you be the same," he said. "It is the measure of a man to die well."

He was walking on the mountain, through the forest, when he saw them. "You have followed me too far," he said. "I will not be taken again."

He was within sixty feet of the soldier when he turned and saw him. The soldier did not speak, but with a kind of triumph he lifted his rifle, and he must only have seen the arrow flash in reflected sunlight before it transfixed his throat. He was the last man in line, and he fell, his hands grasping the arrow, his eyes glazing.

At the edge of the woods, Joe Makatozi ran softly on the moss. He ran and then waited, and as the next soldier appeared between the trees, he let go his arrow. The soldier cried out and fell.

The man ahead of him in the single file turned impatiently, then stared in horror at the arrow and died beside him.

There were six men in the patrol and a huge, bearlike man who led them. Joe Mack ran on, and when they stopped at a small stream, he let go another arrow. The target turned and took the arrow in the shoulder instead of the throat.

He cried out and the others turned. Joe Mack dropped his bow and drew a pistol.

He fired once, caught up his bow, and vanished into the trees, not waiting to see the effect of his shot.

It was growing dusk, as dusk as it ever became at this latitude, and he faded back among the trees.

On the soft moss, his moccasins made no sound. He moved among the trees, listening. There was no sound but a subdued murmur from a stream.

Alekhin had survived, then? He was here. "Now, my friend," Joe Mack said aloud, "we shall meet, you and I, and I am ready for you."

He circled the camp, but there was no camp, and they had no fire. They waited for him somewhere in the woods.

He crept close and lay still in the brush. How many were Siberians, he wondered, aside from Alekhin? He waited, and feeling about he found a rock and threw it, arching it high. It fell into the brush and he lay still. They would be waiting, and they would be fearful, for three or perhaps four of their mates had died.

Where was he? They did not know.

Did it mean he was there? Or somewhere near? He threw another stone and heard it land.

No sound, and he expected none. Would they remain where they were until morning? Or would one or more of them try to slip away to some further spot? He believed they would think of going but would stay.

He waited, resting easily on the moss, ears tuned to the slightest sound. Then he threw another stone. This time there was a subdued gasp, not too far from where the stone landed. There was vague light, and something stirred in the shadows; something moved. He let go an arrow and heard the thud of its strike and then a rustling in the brush. He let go another arrow. It was a miss, he believed, but a close one.

Gently, ever so gently, he eased back, went down into the hollow behind, and crossed a stream. He climbed into the rocks to a place he had seen earlier. Then he settled down to rest.

When the dawn was yet an hour away, he prepared several traps, and when he went back he left several slight tracks. Not enough to make them suspicious, but several. Then he went down the mountain toward the shore.

Major Joseph Makatozi walked along the shore in the gray morning and looked at the gray seas rolling in to beat against the rocky shore. He looked at the piled roots of great trees and at the little cove where a man worked upon some nets. He walked down to him and stood for a moment, watching. "I have come far," he said at last, trying his English, "to see the place where once Olaf Swenson traded. He was an American, I think."

"And an honest man," replied the old Chukchi. "I knew him when I was a boy, but he traded with my father and my grandfather."

"My grandfather was a Scot. Once long ago he sailed to these shores and traded here with Swenson."

"That was long ago. Nobody remembers Olaf Swenson anymore. They do not remember the good days of trade, nor do they remember that we Chukchis crossed the narrow seas to Alaska each year, sometimes more than once in the year."

"You caught salmon there?"

"No more. All that is gone. They will not let us go anymore, but sometimes—

"Sometimes I wish I could go again, but I am old, old."

"I would go," Joe Mack said, "if I had a kayak."

The old man looked up. His brown face was deeply lined under the mane of white hair. He looked at Joe Mack and at his braids. He looked at his face again.

"It would need a man who knew the kayak to do it. Such a trip is not easy."

"But with a kayak, they might not know he was going. It is a small thing, made of hide only."

"It might be done. I am an old man and have not tried."

"But I am a young man, and my home is over there. I want to go home, Grandfather."

"I have a kayak, a very good one. For the grandson of a man who sailed with Olaf Swenson—I do not know. Perhaps."

"I have some rubles. A kayak is not a small thing. It is made with craft not many possess. I would pay."

"What are rubles to an old man? The sea gives me my living, and I give it my blessing."

"Once long ago, Grandfather, it is said my people came

this way, crossing when there was no water here. I follow in their footsteps."

"I have heard of this, and I have found arrowheads and bones. Yes, I believe it is true." The old man looked up from the net. "Those who watch have eyes to look where we cannot see. They have wings to fly over."

"I shall go at night, Grandfather."

"Ah? It has been done by day, and long, long ago. One must understand the kayak."

"We are not strangers. I have used them at sea, and upon rough rivers."

"When?"

"Tonight, if I live."

The old man looked at him again. "I have heard some shots fired upon the mountain."

"Yes, and today I shall go back to find one who looks for me. I do not wish him disappointed."

"There will be shooting?"

"I hope not. I wish to do it with these." Joe Mack held up his hands. "My people were warriors once. Am I to be less than they?"

"If you come in the evening when the sun is low, the kayak will be lying by those roots. What you do is your affair."

"Speak to the spirits of the sea, Grandfather. My voice is lonely in the night."

FORTY-SEVEN

He smelled the smoke before he saw the fire, and when Joe Mack walked through the scattered rocks, Alekhin was waiting.

Joe Mack's eyes swept the little hollow, but the Yakut said, "They have gone to recover the bodies you left."

"I came for you."

"I am here."

Colonel Arkady Zamatev took up the package the soldier had placed on his desk. Slowly, with careful fingers, he began to undo the knots.

The package was very light, and it was wrapped in the skin of some small animal, but there was something inside, part of which felt like bark from a tree.

The last knot came loose, and the package opened. Colonel Arkady Zamatev sat very still, his mouth dry, his heart beating heavily. What lay on the table before him was obviously a human scalp with a small, distinctive blaze of white on one side, white hair growing where an old scar had been.

With it was a narrow strip of birchbark, and on it, printed in neat lettering:

THIS WAS ONCE A CUSTOM OF MY PEOPLE.

IN MY LIFETIME I SHALL TAKE TWO. THIS IS THE FIRST.

ABOUT LOUIS L'AMOUR

"I think of myself in the oral tradition—as a troubadour, a village taleteller, the man in the shadows of the campfire. That's the way I'd like to be remembered—as a storyteller. A good storyteller."

It is doubtful that any author could be as at home in the world re-created in his novels as Louis Dearborn L'Amour. Not only could he physically fill the boots of the rugged characters he writes about, but he has literally "walked the land my characters walk." His personal experiences as well as his lifelong devotion to historical research have combined to give Mr. L'Amour the unique knowledge and understanding of people, events, and the challenge of the American frontier that have become the hallmarks of his popularity.

Of French-Irish descent, Mr. L'Amour can trace his own family in North America back to the early 1600s and follow their steady progression westward, "always on the frontier." As a boy growing up in Jamestown, North Dakota, he absorbed all he could about his family's frontier heritage, including the story of his great-grandfather who was scalped by Sioux warriors.

Spurred by an eager curiosity and desire to broaden his horizons, Mr. L'Amour left home at the age of fifteen and enjoyed a wide variety of jobs including seaman, lumberjack, elephant handler, skinner of dead cattle, assessment miner, and officer on tank destroyers during World War II. During his "yondering" days he also circled the world on a freighter, sailed a dhow on the Red Sea, was shipwrecked in the West Indies and stranded in the Mojave Desert. He has won fifty-one of fifty-nine fights as a professional boxer and worked as a journalist and lecturer. A voracious reader and collector of rare books, Mr. L'Amour's personal library of some 10,000 volumes covers a broad range of scholarly disciplines including many personal papers, maps, and diaries of the pioneers.

Mr. L'Amour "wanted to write almost from the time I could walk." After developing a widespread following for his many adventure stories written for the fiction magazines, Mr. L'Amour published his first full-length novel, *Hondo*, in 1953. Mr. L'Amour is now one of the four bestselling living novelists in the world. Every one of his more than 95 books are still in print and every one has sold more than one million copies. He has more million-copy bestsellers than any other living author. His books have been translated into more than a dozen languages, and more than thirty of his novels and stories have been made into feature films and television movies.

His hardcover bestsellers include *The Lonesome Gods, The Walking Drum*, his twelfth-century historical novel, *Jubal Sackett*, and *Last of the Breed*.

The recipient of many great honors and awards, in 1983 Mr. L'Amour became the first novelist ever to be awarded a Special National Gold Medal by the United States Congress in honor of his life's work. In 1984 he was also awarded the Medal of Freedom by President Ronald Reagan.

Mr. L'Amour lives in Los Angeles with his wife, Kathy, and their two children, Beau and Angelique.

SPECTACULAR ENTERTAINMENT ALL SUMMER LONG!
SUMMER SPECTACULAR FREQUENT READERS SWEEPSTAKES
WIN *A 1988 Cadillac Cimarron* Automobile or
12 other Fabulous Prizes

IT'S EASY TO ENTER. HERE'S HOW IT WORKS:

1. Enter *one* individual book sweepstakes, by completing and submitting the Official Entry form found in the back of that Summer Spectacular book, and you qualify for that book's prize drawing.

2. Enter *two* individual book sweepstakes, by completing and submitting two Official Entry Forms found in the back of those two Summer Spectacular books, and you qualify for the prize drawings for those two individual books.

3. Enter *three or more* individual book sweepstakes, by completing and submitting—in one envelope—three or more Official Entry forms found in the back of three or more individual Summer Spectacular books, and you qualify not only for those three or more individual books but also for THE BONUS PRIZE of a brand new Cadillac Cimarron Automobile!

Be sure to fill in the Bantam bookseller where you learned about this Sweepstakes . . . because if you win one of the twelve Sweepstakes prizes . . . your bookseller wins too!

SEE OFFICIAL RULES BELOW FOR DETAILS including alternate means of entry.

No Purchase Necessary.

Here are the Summer Spectacular Sweepstakes Books and Prizes!

BOOK TITLE	*PRIZE*
On Sale May 20, 1987	
ACT OF WILL	A luxurious weekend for two (3 days/2 nights) at first class hotel, MAP meals—(transportation not included) Approximate value: $750.00
MEN WHO HATE WOMEN & THE WOMEN WHO LOVE THEM	Gourmet food of the month for 6 months N.Y. Gourmet Co. Approximate value: $750.00
VENDETTA	Schrade Collector's Knife set Approximate value: $750.00
On Sale June 17, 1987	
LAST OF THE BREED	Sharp Video Camera and VCR Approximate value: $1,600.00

| WHITE DOVE (available in US only) | Lenox China white coffee service |
| THE MOTH (available in Canada only) | Approximate value: $750.00 |

| THE BE (HAPPY) ATTITUDES | Set of DP workout equipment
Approximate value: $1,000.00 |

On Sale July 15, 1987

| THE UNWANTED | Bug Zapper and Samsonite Chairs—
Table—Umbrella—Outdoor Furniture
Approximate value: $1,300.00 |

| A GRAND PASSION | Cake of the month plan
Approximate value: $800.00 |

| 110 SHANGHAI ROAD | $1,000 American Express Gift
Certificates
Value: $1,000.00 |

On Sale August 12, 1987

| HIS WAY | Disc Player with library of
Sinatra discs
Approximate value: $1,000.00 |

| SUSPECTS | Home Security System
Approximate value: $1,000.00 |

| PORTRAIT OF A MARRIED WOMAN | Minolta Auto-Focus Camera Kit
Approximate value: $750.00 |

OFFICIAL RULES

1. There are twelve individual sweepstakes, each with its own prize award. There will be twelve separate sweepstakes drawings. You will be entered into the drawing for the prize corresponding to the book(s) from which you have obtained your entry blank, any one or up to all twelve. Submit your completed entry on the Official Entry Form found in this book and any of the other participating books ... mail one or up to all twelve completed sweepstakes entries *in one envelope* to:

   Frequent Readers Sweepstakes
   PO Box 43 New York, New York 10046

2. NO PURCHASE NECESSARY TO ENTER OR WIN A PRIZE: Residents of Ohio and those wishing to obtain an Official Entry Form (covering all 12 sweepstakes) and the Official Rules send a self-addressed stamped envelope to: Frequent Reader Sweepstakes, P.O. Box 549, Sayreville, NJ 08872. One Official Entry Form per request. Requests must be received by August 14, 1987. Residents of Washington and Vermont need not include return postage.

3. Winners for each of the 12 sweepstakes will be selected in a random drawing to be conducted on or about October 19, 1987, from all completed entries received, under the supervision of Marden-Kane, Inc. an independent judging organization. If any of the 12 consumer winners selected have included completed Official Entry Forms from three or more books, or have included completed Official Entry Forms from three or more books, or have entered 3 or more sweepstakes on the Alternate Mail-In Official Entry Form (See Rule #2) they are qualified to participate in a separate BONUS DRAWING to be conducted on or about Oct. 19, 1987 for a 1988 Cadillac Cimarron. In the event that none of the twelve individual sweepstake prize winners qualify for the BONUS PRIZE, the bonus prize will be selected from all completed sweepstakes entries received. No mechanically reproduced entries accepted. All entries must be received by September 30, 1987 to be eligible. Not responsible for late, lost or misdirected mail or printing errors.

4. By entering this Sweepstakes, each entrant accepts and agrees to be bound by these rules and the decision of the judges which shall be final. Winners will be notified by mail and may be required to execute an Affidavit of Eligibility and Release which must be returned within 14 days of receipt. In the event of non-compliance within this time period, alternate winners will be selected. Winner(s) consent to the use of his/her name and/or photograph for advertising and publicity purposes without additional compensation. No substitution or transfer of prizes allowed (vacation prize subject to availability, and must be taken within one year of notification). Taxes, License and Title Fees are the sole responsibility of the prize winners. One prize (except for Bonus Prize) per family or household. Retailer named on winning twelve blanks will win duplicate sweepstakes prize. (Retailers are not eligible for bonus prize.)

5. Sweepstakes open to residents of the United States and Canada except employees and their families of Bantam Books, its affiliates and subsidiaries, advertising and production agencies and Marden-Kane, Inc. Void in the Province of Quebec and wherever else prohibited or restricted by law. Canadian residents will be required to answer a skill testing question in order to be eligible to receive a prize. All federal, state and local laws apply. Odds of winning a prize in each sweepstake depend upon the total number of completed entries received for that sweepstake. (All prizes will be awarded)

6. For a list of major prize winners, send a stamped, self-addressed envelope to: Frequent Readers Sweepstakes, c/o Marden-Kane, Inc., P.O. Box 711, Sayreville, NJ 08872.

LAST OF THE BREED
OFFICIAL ENTRY FORM

Please complete by entering all the information requested and
Mail to: Frequent Readers Sweepstakes
P.O. Box 43
New York, N.Y. 10046

NAME _____

ADDRESS _____

CITY _____ STATE _____ ZIP _____

BANTAM BOOK RETAILER WHERE YOU LEARNED ABOUT THIS SWEEPSTAKES

NAME _____

ADDRESS _____

CITY _____ STATE _____ ZIP _____

Completed entries must be received by September 30, 1987 in order to be eligible.

ISBN-0553-26499-0

LOUIS L'AMOUR
BANTAM BOOKS
SHORT STORY CHECKLIST
Be Careful.

The only authorized Louis L'Amour short story collections are published by Bantam Books. All Bantam paperbacks have a rooster trademark on their upper or lower left corners and on their spines. If a L'Amour short story book does not carry the rooster logo it is unauthorized and may contain stories you already own in Bantam editions.

For your protection, you may want to detach and save this L'Amour short story list, checking off the box as you read each story.

1. ☐ WAR PARTY
☐ Trap of Gold ☐ One for the Pot ☐ War Party ☐ Get Out of Town ☐ Booty for a Badman ☐ The Gift of Cochise ☐ A Mule for Santa Fe ☐ Alkali Basin ☐ Men to Match the Hills ☐ The Defense of Sentinel

2. ☐ THE STRONG SHALL LIVE
☐ The Strong Shall Live ☐ One Night Stand ☐ Trail to Squaw Springs ☐ Merrano of the Dry Country ☐ The Romance of Piute Bill ☐ Hattan's Castle ☐ Duffy's Man ☐ Big Man ☐ The Marshal of Sentinel ☐ Bluff Creek Station

3. ☐ YONDERING
☐ Where There's Fighting ☐ The Dancing Kate ☐ Glorious! ☐ Dead-End Drift ☐ Old Doc Yak ☐ Survival ☐ Thicker Than Blood ☐ The Admiral ☐ Shanghai Not Without Gestures ☐ The Man Who Stole Shakespeare ☐ A Friend of the General ☐ Author's Tea ☐ A Man of the Trees Broken By Snow

4. ☐ BUCKSKIN RUN
☐ The Ghosts of Buckskin Run ☐ No Trouble for the Cactus Kid ☐ Horse Heaven ☐ Squatters on the Lonetree ☐ Jackson of Horntown ☐ There's Always a Trail ☐ Down the Pogonip Trail ☐ What Gold Does to a Man

5. ☐ BOWDRIE
☐ Bowdrie Rides a Coyote Trail ☐ A Job for a Ranger ☐ Bowdrie Passes Through ☐ A Trail to the West ☐ More Brains Than Bullets ☐ Too Tough to Brand ☐ The Thriller From the Pecos

6. ☐ THE HILLS OF HOMICIDE
☐ The Hills of Homicide ☐ Unguarded Moment ☐ Dead Man's Trail ☐ With Death in His Corner ☐ The Street of Lost Corpses ☐ Stay Out of My Nightmare ☐ Collect From a Corpse ☐ I Hate to Tell His Widow

7. ☐ BOWDRIE'S LAW
☐ McNelly Knows a Ranger ☐ Where Buzzards Fly ☐ Case Closed—No Prisoners ☐ Down Sonora Way ☐ The Road to Casa Piedras ☐ A Ranger Rides to Town ☐ South of Deadwood ☐ The Outlaws of Poplar Creek ☐ Rain on the Mountain Fork ☐ Strange Pursuit

8. ☐ LAW OF THE DESERT BORN
☐ Law of the Desert Born ☐ Riding On ☐ The Black Rock Coffin Makers ☐ Desert Death Songs ☐ Ride, You Tonto Raiders! ☐ One Last Gun Notch ☐ Death Song of the Sombrero ☐ The Guns Talk Loud ☐ Grub Line Rider ☐ The Marshal of Painted Rock ☐ Trap of Gold

9. ☐ RIDING FOR THE BRAND
☐ Riding for the Brand ☐ Four-Card Draw ☐ His Brother's Debt ☐ A Strong Land Growing ☐ The Turkeyfeather Riders ☐ Lit a Shuck for Texas ☐ The Nester and the Piute ☐ Barney Takes a Hand ☐ Man Riding West ☐ Fork Your Own Broncs ☐ Home in the Valley ☐ West is Where the Heart Is

10. ☐ DUTCHMAN'S FLAT
☐ Dutchman's Flat ☐ Keep Travelin' Rider ☐ Trail to Pie Town ☐ Mistakes Can Kill You ☐ Big Medicine ☐ Man From Battle Flat ☐ West of the Tularosas ☐ McQueen of the Tumbling K ☐ The One for the Mohave Kid ☐ The Lion Hunter and the Lady ☐ A Gun for Kilkenny

11. ☐ THE RIDER OF THE RUBY HILLS
☐ The Rider of the Ruby Hills ☐ Showdown Trail ☐ A Man Called Trent ☐ The Trail to Peach Meadow Canyon

12. ☐ THE TRAIL TO CRAZY MAN
☐ The Trail to Crazy Man ☐ Riders of the Dawn ☐ Showdown on the Hogback

13. ☐ NIGHT OVER THE SOLOMONS
☐ Night Over the Solomons ☐ Mission to Siberut ☐ Pirates with Wings ☐ Tailwind to Tibet ☐ The Goose Flies South ☐ Wings Over Khabarovsk

14. ☐ WEST FROM SINGAPORE
☐ East of Gorontalo ☐ On the Road to Amurang ☐ From Here to Banggai ☐ The House of Qasavara ☐ Well of the Unholy Light ☐ West From Singapore ☐ South of Suez